It All Began in Monte Carlo

Also by Elizabeth Adler

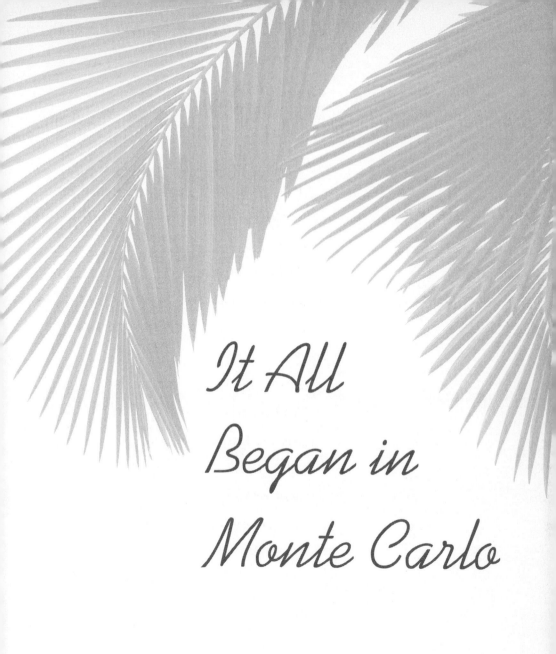

It All
Began in
Monte Carlo

elizabeth adler

St. Martin's Press  New York

This is a work of fiction. Names, characters, places, and incidents either are the product of the author's imagination or are used fictitiously, and any resemblance to actual persons, living or dead, businesses, companies, events, or locales is entirely coincidental.

www.stmartins.com

Design by Patrice Sheridan

LIBRARY OF CONGRESS CATALOGING-IN-PUBLICATION DATA

Adler, Elizabeth (Elizabeth A.)
  It all began in Monte Carlo / Elizabeth Adler. — 1st ed.
      p. cm.
  ISBN 978-0-312-38515-6
  1. Americans—France—Fiction.   2. France, Southern—Fiction.   3. Monte Carlo (Monaco)—Fiction.   4. Jewelry theft—Fiction.   5. Extortion—Fiction.   I. Title.
  PR6051.D56I7 2010
  823'.914—dc22

                                                                            2010013031

First Edition: July 2010

10 9 8 7 6 5 4 3 2 1

To Richard

acknowledgments

Thanks, as always, to my dedicated St. Martin's team, especially Sally Richardson and, of course, my editor, Jen Enderlin—simply the best. And to my lovely agent, Anne Sibbald, and the wonderful team at Janklow & Nesbit Associates. And, of course, to those girlfriends who are always there when I need them—and always make me laugh. In strictly alphabetical order: Lynn Blackwell, Francesca Bowyer, Sandi Phillips, and Priscilla Rendino. Is there some reason we are all blondes!

It All Began in Monte Carlo

Trust is often a misplaced emotion.
Like love.

—Maha Mondragon

prologue

Paris. December 24. A cold Christmas Eve. Lights sparkle in the leafless trees, the windows of expensive boutiques glow with treasures. It's almost closing time when the black Bentley pulls up outside the fashionable jeweler, La Fontaine. Three women step out, wrapped in furs, high boots, long blond hair flowing, dark glasses despite the fact that it's already gray dusk; Hermès totes, exclusive shopping bags.

Watching them walking across the sidewalk toward him the uniformed guard notes that the Bentley is already stuffed with more shopping bags. The women are laughing, heads together, faces hidden as they approach. He smiles as he opens the door for them.

A shiny steel gun with a silencer is jammed in his back. A woman's voice tells him to get inside, not to put up his hands. Swiftly the others remove weapons from inside their fur coats. The gun jams against his spine once more. "Walk normally," the woman says. The guard does as he is told.

Inside the store the last three assistants are tidying up, checking the display cases, rainbows of lights sparking off the diamonds. They raise their heads as the guard comes in followed by the three women. They sigh, it's getting late, it's Christmas Eve and they want to be home with their families. But a sale is a sale and with women like this, expensive, fur-wrapped women, it could be a big one. Women as rich as these buy on impulse. And after all, it *is* Christmas.

The manager raises his head, smiles. The assistants call a greeting, *"Bonsoir, mesdames. Bon Noël."*

Walking behind the guard, the other two women raise their guns. They swing back their long blond hair and expose bizarre Marilyn Monroe masks, red lips stretched in her famous smile. One shoots out the video security camera, another stands guard. The first instructs the manager, harshly, to open the display cases and the safe. And fast.

He hovers uncertainly. The woman's laugh is muffled by the mask. "Don't even think of the alarm, *monsieur*. You would be dead before a cop could even get here. And I'm sure you still want to see your children this Christmas Eve. After all, Santa has to bring presents for everyone, including us."

The manager hurries to open the shop's display cases as well as the ones in the window. The first robber covers him with the gun while the two terrified female assistants hover behind, ghostlike, trembling. One's lips move in a prayer. The younger one buries her head in her hands, unable to look.

The second robber plucks the jewels from the window display, sweeping her hand through the case, shunting rings, earrings, bracelets, dazzling necklaces into a large Hermès tote. The third guides the manager, with her gun, to the safe. He opens it. She takes out the jewels, many unset diamonds of large carats. La Fontaine is famous for the quality of its diamonds.

Now all the jewels are in the Hermès tote or scooped into a Dior carrier, an Eres shopping bag.

The masked robbers line up the staff plus the guard behind a counter. Two walk backward to the door, guns drawn. The other woman, the one in charge, walks closer to the terrified staff. She points the gun at each one in turn. "Give me the store keys and your cell phones." They comply. She pauses in front of the youngest of the sales assistants. The masked robber stares at her for a long moment. The girl lifts her head, meets the eyes behind the mask. Swiftly, the woman raises the gun, brings it down with a crack of breaking bone on the assistant's cheek.

"Bitch," she says as she walks away.

The three robbers, expensive in their furs and with their designer bags loaded with loot, walk out. The first woman locks the door behind them. The staff remain frozen, expecting their end to come.

There is no Bentley waiting outside. Instead, a gray van. The door slides open, the women climb in and the van speeds off into the Christmas Eve traffic.

The heist has taken maybe five minutes. The loot is worth many millions of dollars. It's the second time they've struck this month.

chapter 1

Los Angeles. Christmas Eve.

Sunny Alvarez boarded the Air France flight to Paris. It had taken all her precious air miles and a great deal of money but if she was going to be unhappy she was going to do it first class. In style. And alone.

She wore no makeup, not even her trademark brave red lipstick. Tinted frameless glasses helped disguise her eyes, swollen from crying. Tall, slender with a fall of dark hair that swung over her face, she looked younger than her thirty-six years and somehow vulnerable. She wore narrow jeans stuffed into tall black sheepskin UGGs, a black cashmere turtleneck, a black peacoat that she now flung off and handed to the waiting steward, before flinging herself into the comfortable leather seat that could be made to recline, so that later she might sleep stretched out full length. If she could ever find "sleep" again. The flight was a long one. Eleven hours.

Eleven hours without Mac Reilly.

Her fiancé was TV's famous detective with his own program, *Mac Reilly's Malibu Mysteries,* handsome in his own slightly worn, casual, confident, way. . . . *No* dammit! Mac was more than that. He was sexy, good looking, blue eyes that looked into hers with passion when he made love to her—*No!* Change that to when they made love *together.* Because making love with Mac Reilly, the feel of his hands on her body, the way his skin smoothed under her own hands, the way her own skin seemed to melt under his, the electric shock his lips on hers always gave her, hot-wiring her, sending tremors through her until all she could think about was sex, sex with him . . .

She had met Mac at a press party for his TV show. He'd told her he'd noticed her across the room. "How could I miss you, in that outfit?" was what he had actually said.

She had on a black turtleneck and a tiny white miniskirt and her tough-girl motorcycle boots because she'd ridden there on her Harley. Mac tapped her on her shoulder and she found herself looking at this rugged guy in jeans and a T-shirt, whose deep blue eyes were taking her in like she was the best thing he had seen all night.

He asked her name, she'd said she knew his. Neither was drinking because they were driving, but both had that elated feeling of being on another planet where even the noise of the party seemed suddenly muted. Later Mac told her he noticed her clunky boots first, and she told him she'd noticed his muscular arms and had wanted to be wrapped in them right there and then, she didn't care who saw.

Of course they were total opposites: Mac, dragged up by his bootstraps from the streets of Boston and the Miami crime scene to the Private Eye and TV personality he now was. And she, the half-Latina wild child brought up on a ranch, beautiful and brainy and ditzy, but with a business degree from Wharton and the determination to be her own woman.

It had been, as they'd told each other so often since, love at first sight. Eyes across the room—or maybe a bit closer.

And that was the way it was. And had been. Until now.

Stop it! Sunny sat up straight in her airline chair, pushed back her long dark hair, skewered it in a ponytail and accepted the glass of champagne the steward was offering her.

She stared at the glass in her hand, not really seeing it. She was Mac's fiancée no longer. They had been together four years and were to have been married next month but he'd changed his plans yet again. Mac had also agreed they would get married last year, and a couple of times preceding that. Every time it got close something else came up. Another mystery he simply had to take on. He couldn't say no. Except, it seemed, to Sunny.

This time was the last straw, she had even bought the dress—cream—white didn't look so good in winter. And lace, although she was not usually a lace girl. Sleek, fitted to her rather good body, because even though she said it herself, it *was* a good body. A *great* body, Mac had always said that.

Sunny stuck out her long legs in the comfy sheepskin knee-high UGG boots, staring at them, but again not seeing them. She was seeing the heart-shaped pink diamond engagement ring she had left on Mac's pillow, with a little note telling him goodbye. *I'm leaving your life,* she had written. *There is no room for me, only for your work. Good luck.* She had signed it simply with the initial *S*.

A whine came from the Vuitton dog carrier. She looked at the small Chihuahua, peering mournfully out. Tesoro weighed all of three pounds. "A fiend on four paws," Mac called her, and he was right, the Chihuahua had sunk her teeth, and her claws, into Mac many a time, as well as intimidating Mac's own dog, the one-eyed, three-legged ragamuffin he adored and whose life Mac had saved, and who went by the name of Pirate. It was Tesoro's feud with Pirate that had kept Mac and Sunny from living together, though now Sunny thought maybe that wasn't such a bad thing. Leaving a home they had shared, Mac's funky little cottage on the shore in Malibu, would have been twice as hard.

They braced for takeoff. She strapped Tesoro in her carrier into an adjacent seat, leaned back, felt the thrust as the plane lifted off. It was over. She was gone.

A tear trickled down her cheek. She was on her way to Paris. *Alone.*

chapter 2

"Merry Christmas."

The man on her left was raising his glass to her.

"It *is* Christmas Eve you know," he said. "Even with the nine hours' time difference it's still Christmas Eve in Paris."

Sunny nodded distantly. She definitely did not want to talk. She couldn't even talk to a friend right now let alone a stranger. She had walked out on impulse, bought her plane ticket online, thrust a few things into a bag, packed up Tesoro, left the note for Mac, taken a cab to the airport. She had no idea where she would go when she arrived in Paris.

Panic set in. She wanted to get off the plane, go back to Mac. *She didn't know how to be "Alone."*

She pulled herself together. The man was still looking at her, a quizzical smile in his eyes. She managed to say, "Thank you. And Merry Christmas to you," but her lips felt stiff, as though she were unused to speaking. She took a sip of the champagne in an effort to unglue them.

"You're spending Christmas in Paris?"

This guy didn't give up. Couldn't he see she didn't want to talk?

"No," she lied.

"Me neither," he said, smiling and stretching out his long legs.

He looked so at ease, so comfortable with himself and with his life, Sunny suddenly hated him. She inspected him from the corner of her eye, behind her amber-tinted frameless Silhouette glasses. He was attractive. Tall, angular body, dark blond hair that flopped silkily over dark eyes. Were they blue or brown? Hazel, maybe? She couldn't tell because of the shadow that fell over them. Strong nose, full mouth—a sexy mouth—she wasn't so far gone in her woe that she couldn't notice that. And where did he get that tan? Not in California this winter, that was for sure. The weather had been cold and damp.

"Too cold for Paris," he said. "They're forecasting snow."

"Snow?" Sunny repeated, astonished. She had thought "cold" maybe, but not "snow."

"You're okay, though, you're dressed for the role."

He was smiling, looking at her boots. Sunny loved those UGGs. They felt like the warmest coziest of slippers, the sheepskin curled round her numb toes so gently, so tenderly. Godamit she would never wear anything else but these boots. Not even the gorgeous new ones she had bought just last week, anticipating a round of Christmas parties, jollity and holly; a tree; a log fire; perhaps even a kiss under the mistletoe.

She hadn't considered what to do once she got to Paris. She hadn't even booked a hotel, not given it a thought. Getting on the plane was about all she had been able to manage. Well, now she had about another ten hours to figure it out.

The stranger accepted a second glass of champagne from the steward, along with a small tray of hors d'oeuvres. Sunny did the same.

A large gulp of champagne did not make her feel any better. From the corner of her eye again she saw the man was looking at her, the amused smile now lifting the corners of his mouth. The *sexy* mouth, she thought bitterly. Why did he have to have a sexy mouth that reminded her of Mac? Why couldn't he have been some ordinary businessman with his nose buried deep in important business papers that he was to read to a conference in Paris tomorrow? Oh. She forgot. Tomorrow was Christmas Day. The "businessmen" were already home with their families. So why wasn't *he*?

"I see you like champagne." He took a sip out of his own nearly full glass. Hers was already half-gone.

"Sometimes," she replied, shortly.

He sighed, but his smile broadened. "It's meant to be a celebratory drink. Perhaps we can celebrate Christmas together?" She did not reply and he shrugged, glancing round. There were only two others in first class; a couple, heads together, several seats away. Sunny could hear their low laughter from here. She tried to close her ears to it. It wasn't fair that they were happy and she was dying inside.

"I suppose you're on your way home to see your family," she said, gulping down the other half of the glass of champagne. She immediately wished she had not asked something so personal. But she had. What difference did it make, anyway?

"No. I'm alone for the holidays."

She looked at him, full on, for the first time. He looked gravely back at her. "So am I," she said.

Sunny sensed that like her, this man had a backstory but he was not going to tell her. And nor was she. They were on an eleven-hour flight to Paris; temporarily, the rest of the world did not exist. For the moment, she was no longer "Alone."

Tesoro whined in her carrying case and Sunny took her out. She held the tiny chestnut-colored dog close, kissed her tenderly, smiling for the first time as she said, "This is Tesoro and she's quite fierce."

"I'll bet she is." The man held out his hands and Sunny put the little dog into them, heart in her mouth, knowing Tesoro's penchant for a fast nip. He held the small dog up to his face, eyeball to eyeball. Tesoro did not even wriggle. She didn't whine. She didn't yap. He put her onto his lap where she curled up, tail snugged over one small flank, eyeing Sunny as if to say, well what did you expect? You left me in that stupid carrying case for an hour, and now this man is showering me with attention.

Maybe she should learn something from the dog, Sunny thought, looking at the man with new respect.

"Are we going to tell who we are?" she asked, still looking at him.

He smiled. "Just call me your Prince Charming."

Sunny found herself smiling too. A watery smile, but still a smile. "In that case I must be the Princess," she said.

She hadn't thought of Mac in at least three minutes.

chapter 3

Malibu. Christmas Eve day.

Mac Reilly was still at the big, hangarlike TV studio in Santa
Monica, California. He knew the shops closed early on Christmas
Eve and he still had not gotten Sunny a gift. Or half-a-dozen gifts,
which was his usual style. He loved to pamper her with the unexpected. He couldn't recall exactly what he had bought last Christmas,
but he did remember being sorely tempted by a beautiful Siamese
kitten, offered by a well-known breeder. The online picture had
shown a cream and chocolate skinny little beauty with enormous
eyes of such a bright glistening blue, that he, a dog-lover, had fallen
in love. In the end though, he had been forced to be practical. His
dog, Pirate, would no doubt also have fallen in love with the kitten,
but as for the Chihuahua—forget it. Tesoro would have stood her
ground against a grizzly if it came anywhere near Sunny. A bit like
Mac himself. Eventually, he had bought her diamond drop earrings, as small and delicate as her beautiful ears.

Later this afternoon, the gift choosing and purchasing hopefully having been quickly completed, he and Sunny would rush to
the Malibu lot where they sold Christmas trees and where no doubt
she would, as she always did, choose a tree so tall he swore would
never fit into his cottage. And as always, he would be correct and
would end up sawing off the top, which Sunny would then tie onto

the deck rails overlooking the beach, and fashion into a minitree with twinkling lights of many colors, none of this prissy all-white for his girl, and always with a star on top improvised from tinfoil. They'd hit the supermarket and pick up a turkey and all the fixings; he would haul a batch of logs into the car, and at the liquor store pick up a bottle of port for after dinner because somehow that always seemed very Christmassy to him.

Later, huddled under blankets out on the deck with the dogs, hopefully content and picking at the bones Sunny had begged from the butcher, they would share a bottle of champagne. They would hang their stockings over the fireplace, the dogs' stockings too. And, as the clock struck twelve signaling the beginning of Christmas Day, they would kiss. A deep loving kiss because God knows he loved her and he knew she loved him. They would go to the bedroom and snuggle deep under the down coverlet that always left her too cold and made him sweat and they would either make love or fall asleep in each other's arms. Or hopefully both.

A smile lit Mac's face as he thought about the pleasures to come. Once they had gotten these last few shots. Lord knows why they couldn't have finished yesterday, but somehow it always seemed to happen this way.

He checked the set but things were still being shifted around and the director was deep in consultation with the lighting guy, all longtime friends of Mac, and all, he knew, as eager to get out of here as he was. Bored, he checked for e-mail. Nothing important, which meant nothing from Sunny.

Mac understood how upset Sunny was at putting off the wedding—"one more time" as she had said in a tone half-disbelieving, half-saddened, in a way that had stabbed at his own heart, even while he was trying to get her to understand that he had commitments with all these people relying on him for their own jobs, as well as those with unsolved murders or disappearances of loved ones who needed him for their peace of mind. Except this time Sunny had not cared for anybody else's peace of mind, and in his heart Mac knew what she had said was true. He could just never say No to someone in need of his help.

The name *Paris* caught his eye on the news headline. *Paris*. A place that only last year had delighted both him and Sunny. He remembered the room at the Ritz she had talked the manager into giving them when all of Paris was full; the gorgeous bed, the bath for two, her beautiful body, her luxuriant long dark hair soaked from the shower where they had made love . . . But this news flash was not about *their* Paris. This was about a daring heist at a fashionable jeweler's, three masked blondes and a sadistic act of violence that had left a young woman assistant with a broken face.

His own assistant called him back to the set. "Another half hour and we're finished, buddy," he said with a thankful grin, and forgetting Paris and the robbery, Mac headed back. Half an hour and he would be free to do his shopping, free to be with Sunny for Christmas. Maybe tonight, after dinner, they would even watch reruns of *White Christmas* on TV. Or was it *Holiday Inn*? Anyway, the one where Bing Crosby says something like, "Okay kids, let's put on a show," and saves the old inn from bankruptcy. It was one of his and Sunny's favorites, they almost knew the dialogue by heart. They watched it together every Christmas and he knew this year would be no exception.

chapter 4

Christmas Eve

The low drone of the plane's engines was drowned out by the voice of Leonard Cohen on Sunny's iPod earplugs, half-singing, half-talking his story of love lost; love remembered; love never to be regained. Sunny silently sang along with him. She knew every word of every one of his songs from back in her college days when he had been the soulmate of every girl she knew. They had all felt what he felt, been heartsick like him, emerged from the despair of love into the joy of love. He was, next to Van Morrison and, for those doing French studies, Serge Gainsbourg, their favorite. He knew them. He understood them. Why, they'd all wondered, did they never meet a man like Leonard Cohen?

The song was "Dance Me to the End of Love." When it finished, quietly drifting into "Chelsea Hotel No. 2," Sunny opened her eyes, shocked to suddenly meet those of her attractive neighbor, Prince Charming.

"Leonard Cohen is wonderful," he said. "Somehow when he sings he feels like an old friend."

"You feel that too?" Sunny was astonished. Then she realized if he could hear it the iPod must have been too loud. He waved a dismissive hand.

"No problem," he said with that easy smile. "I only caught a hint of it, and anyhow, I liked it."

The steward fixed small tables in front of them, then covered them in pale gray-blue linen cloths. A young flight attendant, smart in her gray-blue blouse and navy pencil skirt, a small patterned scarf tied jauntily at her neck, offered more champagne, which Sunny had the sense to refuse. She studied the wine list instead. They had already been offered the menu and made their choices. She thanked the Lord she wasn't flying Delta because she knew she would have been unable to say no to their ice cream sundae. The ice cream, with sprinkles and chocolate sauce plus nuts and cream and anything else they cared to pour over it might have taken some of the ache away, at least for the five minutes it would have taken for her to devour it. Instead, she tasted the white Burgundy she had chosen. It was astonishingly good, and unbidden, her mind went to Mac, a man who enjoyed fine wine.

"This drinking thing is quickly getting to be a habit," she told Prince Charming, who was sipping a deep red Bordeaux that must surely have been distilled from very old and very precious rubies. "I'm likely to stagger off this plane."

His laugh lit his whole face. She wondered again where he had gotten that tan. "Don't worry," he said, "I'll hold you up." He threw her a teasing glance. "It might suit you, being a bit tipsy," he added. "For a day anyway. Because that's all this is, isn't it?"

Sunny wondered exactly what he meant. "I guess so." She was cautious. "I'm not really a drinker, you know. A drinker-kind-of-drinker, I mean," she added, sitting primly a bit straighter, wanting him to know that she didn't always act this way.

"Hey, a couple of glasses of champagne, a couple of glasses of wine, eleven hours . . ."

"Three," she corrected him. "Three glasses of champagne. I had one in the lounge."

He grinned. "Okay, you're the one who's counting."

She took another slug of the white Burgundy, telling herself it was too good to take slugs of, but what the hell Prince Charming was right. *Eleven hours was a long time. Eleven hours without Mac. Eleven hours alone . . . oh God . . .*

"Where did you get that tan?" Once again the words flew right out of her mouth. She should not have asked such a personal question; he was a stranger and obviously meant to keep it that way.

He held out his glass, touched it to hers in a silent toast; took a sip. "Actually, Tahiti. A week on a beach."

"Alone?" Shit, she'd done it again. But his words had brought to mind the image of a long white sugar-sand beach, a tranquil blue bay, the small thud of tiny waves, the gentle heat of the sun, the smoothness of bodies glistening with lotion and the sweet smell of sweat and sex. It had just jumped into her overstressed mind.

"Princess," he said, "I will confess to you. Yes, I was alone."

For the first time Sunny realized that Prince Charming had a slight accent. He was definitely not American. "By choice?" she asked, bolder now.

"Definitely by choice."

Sunny was silent while the steward served their first course. "The red won't go with the smoked salmon," she said, eyeing his plate.

"Then I'll have to taste your white."

He was looking into her eyes, his glance intimate. And she was staring straight back. Jesus! Was she crazy? What was she doing!

He smiled. "I won't put you to that test," he said, calling the steward over and ordering the white wine.

"How do you know you'll like it?'

"If you approve, then so will I."

Sunny's smile finally emerged. "You know something?" She leaned over, touched her hand on his shirtsleeve, a blue fine-cotton shirtsleeve, rolled to show a tanned forearm with a dusting of golden hair. "I like you," she said. And they both laughed.

Prince Charming said, "Actually, I'll confess something else."

Uh-uh, now he was going to spill the beans, tell her everything; he was just a flirt after all, coming on to her. Sunny cut a small piece of the smoked salmon, chewed it slowly, then forced herself to swallow. She *had* to ask him though. "What?"

"What, what?"

"What are you going to confess now? That you are an ax murderer? A movie star? A rock legend I'm too young to have heard of?"

His laugh boomed out causing the couple in front to turn their heads. "Actually, I was going to confess that I'm in love."

Sunny looked down at her unwanted food. What did it matter to her if he was in love? He was simply a fellow traveler, trapped next to her on an eleven-hour flight. She said, "Who with?"

"You mean 'with whom'?" Prince Charming finished his salmon. He put his knife and fork carefully on his plate at the correct angle, then took a sip of the white Burgundy. He pushed back his dead-straight, slightly too-long dark blond hair and leveled his eyes at her again.

Sunny lifted a shoulder in an exaggeratedly indifferent shrug. "So okay, with *whom*?"

"Actually, I'm in love with Paris."

"You are?"

"Definitely."

"*Actually,* definitely."

"What?"

"It's just that you say *actually* a lot."

He nodded. "*Actually,* I'm sure I do. It's a habit, but this time it seemed to fit the occasion."

The steward cleared their dishes, poured a little more wine, brought extra bottles of Evian, smiled at them, asked if they had everything they needed, were they comfortable.

After he'd gone, Sunny, with a strange flutter of relief, asked Prince Charming, *why* Paris?

"Because it's simply the most beautiful city in the world. Especially at Christmastime, sparkling in the dark and the cold, like a woman wrapped in sables, and glimmering with diamonds."

"So you're a romantic."

"Certainly."

She said, "I've always thought it's hard to beat New York at Christmas, but then I've never tried Paris." She picked at the salad in front of her, sipped the wine that was flowing down like nectar. Who knew an airline served such excellent wine? "I lived in Paris for a couple of months when I was very young," she added. "A sabbatical from college. But then I had to get a grip on reality and go to work."

"I'm not permitted to ask what you do?" He did not touch his salad, watching her.

"No, but anyhow I'll tell you. I work in PR. Selling people to the public, if you want to look at it that way. Or at least selling what they do, or make. Actors, artists, anyone in need of an image, a public boost of their confidence. *Actually,*" she gave him a little wine-induced smirk, "I was in Paris last summer. I think it's the most beautiful city too." She paused, thinking about it, then added sadly, "When you are with someone you love."

Prince Charming's face was grave with understanding, but he said nothing.

"This trip was spur of the moment." Sunny covered her sadness quickly. "I just decided I needed to see Paris . . . I threw a few things into a case, packed the dog, bought a ticket online and went straight to the airport."

"Without even stopping to think?"

"Without even stopping to think."

"Sometimes it's better that way. And do you know where you'll be staying, in Paris?"

The salads were replaced with a wild mushroom risotto. "Please don't think I'm asking you to tell me where, Princess," he added quickly. "Your privacy is complete."

Sudden tears welled in Sunny's eyes as she remembered Mac and the Ritz and the golden view of summer Paris rooftops from their window, and the big bed, and the story of the strange art collector they were investigating together, and the delightful little restaurant later, with the great food, then the walk back to the hotel through the narrow streets and tree-lined boulevards, and oh God all the magic that was Paris and love. And now she was Alone and she didn't know how to handle *Alone.*

Prince Charming reached for her hand. He didn't attempt to staunch her tears, he didn't fuss or say don't worry everything will be all right. He simply waited.

After a while Sunny mopped her face with her napkin. "Sorry," she said.

"I understand. But Princess, let me ask you something. Do you think Paris is the right place for you now? It's cold, it's going to snow, the entire city will grind to a halt. You'll be trapped in some hotel, your favorite bistros will be closed, nothing happening anywhere, everyone with their families."

"Oh God." It sounded so depressing. Sunny gave him a watery smile.

"There's always Monte Carlo," he said, squeezing her hand. He wasn't coming on to her, though, it was more of a comfort thing. Sunny gave him a sudden suspicious glare. *Why* wasn't he coming on to her? Did she look so terrible he didn't even fancy her a little bit?

"Monte Carlo?" she said.

"Actually, it is warmer on the Riviera, there's even a strong possibility that the sun will shine. The hotels are good, the food is wonderful and you'll very likely find good company, people like yourself, escaping for a while."

"Monte Carlo," Sunny said again, remembering the South of France, how wonderful it had been just last year with Mac and of course with the group of international misfits who had somehow become their friends. She and Mac had almost gotten married there. Story of her life, right! Hadn't *she* turned him down that time though? Still, perhaps Prince Charming was right, Paris would be cold and deserted. Exactly like herself. Monte Carlo would be alive, bustling with people and distractions that might even take a woman's mind off her troubles.

"Okay, so I'll think about it," she said cautiously.

"Then allow me to help you with a hotel reservation at a place I know." Prince Charming plugged in his laptop. "Just one thing," he said, "I need to know your name."

So Sunny told him, but she did not ask for his. She wanted him to remain, quite simply, "Prince Charming."

What with all the wine and the distress and her broken heart, in the darkened plane, Sunny found her eyes closing. Soon she was asleep. All she wanted was to forget.

chapter 5

Malibu. Christmas Eve.

It was still only lunchtime and Mac Reilly was alone. The good-bye note from Sunny was crumpled in his pocket, his phone was switched permanently onto her number, his urgent voice mails had gone unanswered. He had not seen Sunny since they'd had the row yesterday about putting off the wedding . . . *"one more time"* as Sunny had said bitterly. And Mac knew she was right. It wasn't that he didn't love her, it was simply that he had work that must be done. He had people, sometimes desperate people, depending on him. How could he put *that* off?

Anyhow, he'd always believed he and Sunny were good as they were. They were right for each other. They loved each other passionately, completely, wonderfully. There was only one woman for him, and that was Sunny Alvarez.

He took the crumpled note from his pocket, read it again, thought about the pink heart-shaped diamond she had chosen with such delight when they became engaged. Had he actually *asked* her to marry him then? Or was it meant always to be just an "engagement," the sort many people "committed" to each other had and whose lives went smoothly on without all these complications. God, I mean he *Loved* Sunny.

She would come round, he told himself, while searching for a parking spot at the Cross Creek shopping center. He would buy her something she really liked for Christmas. Then he would go to her place and apologize. They would make up, she would come and cook turkey at his cottage—they would have drinks on his deck overlooking the Pacific, warmly wrapped in sweaters—always his old cashmere, because Sunny said she liked the way it smelled of him, arms round each other, if Tesoro would allow them, that is, without biting at Mac's heels, or other more intimate parts. Still, he would even put up with the Chihuahua's bites if it meant having Sunny back in his arms.

After he had done Christmas shopping for her, he would go round to her place; she would open the door and see him standing there, gifts piled in his arms and love in his eyes. His Sunny would never leave him.

He swung speedily into a parking spot, barely giving the departing car time to leave and beating out an irate SUV driver. It was every man for himself in parking lots at Christmastime.

Mac's scruffy dog, Pirate, was on the front seat of the red Prius hybrid, already up and waiting, head sticking out the window, eager to be freed. The dog loved Mac, and Mac loved that dog. He had found Pirate one dark night, a couple of years ago, when he'd been driving over Malibu Canyon, a bloody, battered shape in the middle of the road. Mac had scooped him up, thinking he was dead, but then the dog opened one eye and looked gratefully at him. Of course, then Mac was sunk. He'd taken off his shirt, wrapped the dog in it and driven all the way to the emergency vet clinic in Santa Monica with the almost-dead dog on his knee. The vet amputated one leg, rescued one of his eyes and saved the dog's life. And Pirate had been Mac's best buddy ever since.

Mac opened the door and the dog jumped out, wobbling because of his missing back leg and shaking his rough gray-brown fur. His single bright brown eye blinked pleasure as he limped happily alongside Mac, who was checking shopwindows for he knew not what. Surely there would be something here Sunny would adore.

He stopped to look at a dress displayed at Madison. Red. Silky-looking. A deep décolleté, smooth, sleek—and very Sunny. A pair of high boots stood next to it, the softest leather, spiky heels, black. He could just imagine Sunny in that outfit. It was exactly her.

The salesgirl smiled as he entered. She recognized him and besides Sunny often shopped there. "Sorry," she said when he asked. "You're too late. Sunny was in here last week. She already bought that dress. *And* the boots."

Mac's heart sank. He'd thought he had found the perfect gift, something that would really please his woman, and God knows he wanted to please her. The salesgirl showed him other dresses, sweaters, jackets, but nothing was right.

He headed out to Tiffany, the safety valve for a man in search of a gift for a woman. Tiffany would always come through with something in that pretty robin's-egg blue box tied with white ribbon.

chapter 6

Monte Carlo. Christmas Day.

It was seven o'clock in the evening and Sunny was in the bar of the luxury hotel where via e-mail Prince Charming had booked her a room. Happy to do her a favor, he'd said politely, as they stood, saying goodbye in Paris's Charles de Gaulle airport.

"Paris is no place for a woman alone at Christmastime," he added. His hands gripped her shoulders as they gazed at each other. "Your flight leaves in an hour. Good luck, Princess." And he'd kissed her lightly, two kisses, one on each cheek, then an extra one because, he told her, it was always three for "special" friends.

Sunny had watched him stride off into the crowd, taller than most, handsome in his black overcoat. Tesoro gave a mournful whine that Prince Charming must have heard because he'd turned his head, smiled, waved his hand and was gone. And Sunny was alone. Again.

She had not even known his name, who her savior was. *Savior* was not quite the correct word. *Mentor*, perhaps? And now, watching him leave, she never would. Pushing her carry-on and with Tesoro still whining she galloped through the immense airport, only just making it to the gate in time.

The flight to Nice was short but snow was falling as they left Paris and they were buffeted by strong winds that terrified the dog, and also terrified Sunny. She'd asked herself why she had done this. She should simply have stayed in Paris, gone to a hotel, climbed into bed and hidden under the covers.

She fed Tesoro some dried food that the dog promptly threw up. Sunny sensed they were not popular with the flight attendants and certainly not with their fellow passengers. She was relieved when they finally landed in Nice and were in a taxi on their way to the Grand Hotel in Monte Carlo. The thought of a bed, snuggling under the covers, giving Tesoro some proper food, made the endless journey almost worthwhile. And besides the sun was shining, or almost anyway; fragile beams of sparkle, not quite yellow enough for sunshine, not quite transparent enough for fairy dust. And at that moment Sunny was wishing with all her might for a little fairy dust.

What she got was a beautiful hotel: an enormous Christmas tree smelling of pine in the hall, soaring arched ceilings, soft lighting, elegant décor, deep gray suede sofas and chairs, huge bouquets of flowers and a pretty room, not too big but certainly enough space for the "one" that she now was. Gold silk curtains, a downy mint-green Empire-style bed, one of those dark gray suede sofas, a coffee table, a desk, a flat-screen TV showing a French re-run of Christmas Eve's midnight mass in Rome, a pale marble bathroom to die for, and room service for dogs. Sunny herself was not hungry.

At seven that evening, after a restless nap, she made for the hotel's luxurious bar which was swagged with Christmas pine garlands and twinkling fairy lights. She perched on a tall chair with the little dog on her knee. A silver-haired barman who seemed to go with the muted gray decor, was shaking a martini. *Oh God, how she hated Christmas!*

She had put on her best look, even though with a combination of stress and fatigue, it was tough to maintain. She was wearing her new red dress but had drawn the line at the tall leather boots, and instead pushed her bare feet into those flat clumsy comfy UGGs. Of course she no longer had her engagement pink diamond and wore no jewelry. Her long black hair swung over her face, hiding her from prying eyes, or hiding her from herself, she was not sure which. Anyhow, she needn't have bothered since there was no one else in the bar. Well, only one person. Another woman, also alone.

"Where is everyone?" she asked the barman as he served her martini.

"*Madame,* it's Christmas Day. Everyone is home with their families."

Of course they were. Everyone, that is, except her. And the woman tucked into the corner, a woman so ordinary that, apart from her bright red hair, she was all but invisible. Sunny took a quick look at her over the rim of her martini glass.

The woman's hair was that too-vivid red that gave away its origins in the supermarket do-it-yourself aisle, and she was wearing a blue shirtdress with the bottom three buttons undone, exposing quite a few inches of plump thigh to the gaze of anyone passing. Of course no one was passing so Sunny guessed it didn't really matter. The woman wore black stilettos with a classic black quilted Chanel bag prominently on her lap. Her dangling earrings spelled DIOR in white. She had the look of a bourgeois woman trying too hard to rise from suburban obscurity.

Sunny told herself she was a bitch for thinking that. Still, she took another peek at her. A fringe disguised a prominent forehead beneath which small predatory blue eyes were now gazing back at Sunny. There was a boldness about her that made Sunny nervous, and besides, she had a sort of "come-on" look, with the unbuttoned-up dress and the stilettos.

Then, before her eyes, the woman seemed to change. Her glance became gentle, intimate, as though she and Sunny were sharing their aloneness. She raised her glass and quietly wished Sunny a Happy Christmas. She spoke English, but with an accent that Sunny thought was probably Slavic or Russian.

chapter 7

The redhead's name was Kitty Ratte and she was in the bar looking for "company." Unfortunately, it was Christmas and any "company" she might have found was at home with their families. Not that Kitty was a high-end call girl; she was too old and ordinary for that. The only thing that drew the eye to Kitty was her flaming red hair. She'd had a few years as a blonde but had recently decided red was her color, and men—her "company"—seemed to like it. Of course the red hair was only on her head. There was not a hair anywhere else on Kitty's body; she took care of that herself with hot wax strips that hurt like hell but did the trick and solved the problem of not matching all over. Kitty was a practical woman.

She was alone in the bar when Sunny walked in. Of course Kitty did not know her name, had no idea who she was, but the fact that she was alone in a hotel bar on Christmas Day evening, to a professional like Kitty spelled trouble. And there was nothing Kitty liked more than trouble.

She noticed the new woman was wearing an expensive dress but oddly with old fur boots. There were no rings though Kitty's eagle eye caught the slender lighter circle around that telltale left hand third finger. Husband dumped her? Boyfriend found someone else? Kitty drained the Red Bull that gave her a permanent caffeine high, ordered another and poured a third glass of red wine.

The new woman looked expensive, an air that Kitty longed to acquire. So far she'd only managed to buy a secondhand Chanel bag on eBay and a pair of Louboutin stilettos at an outlet sale. Kitty did not own a diamond ring, not even a small one; not even the diamond ear studs that were a simple symbol of a woman's success; and certainly not that pricy gold Rolex. Kitty did not even own her own apartment. Age was creeping up on her and with it had come a desperate need for money and a new career.

Kitty Ratte was a predator. Seduction was her game, man or woman. And she was good at it, always playing the subservient friend, the wannabe lover who promises to give you everything you ever wanted sexually, and then more, who could flatter a man into feeling twenty years old again.

Kitty was admitting to forty-nine, at least that's what she told her current lover, Jimmy, the failed English accountant and used-car salesman, married and living in suburban Surrey, England, where, of course, he was at this moment. In fact the true number was twelve years higher, and now her body was starting to reflect that lie. No towering stilettos could disguise the cellulite thighs, and no padded bra could give her breasts the lovely upward thrust of youth, nor take away the creases between them that were becoming daily more apparent. Faking it was becoming more and more difficult. Time was running out.

Kitty had almost had her chance for the brass ring once. Not so long ago. He was married of course. Weren't they all? And old. In his seventies. But he was rich. After all, why else would a woman fuck an old man but for his money?

She'd seduced him, parading in front of him in leopard bikini pants and stilettos. She told him she loved him and the poor old idiot believed her. He was wonderful, she said. He was so attractive, and so sexy. How could his wife *not* want him? Ooh, how he'd loved it. She had him entranced. Of course she made him promise never to betray her, never to tell the wife, or anyone her name, because she didn't want to be named in the divorce. She threatened him with silence, if he did tell her name, she said her "real" lover would make sure the man and his wife would suffer in ways he couldn't even begin to dream of. I'll never name you, never betray you he promised eagerly.

Let's run away together, she said to him. To Paris, St. Tropez. Just you and me. How wonderful it will be. I love you so much.

He said he would give up everything for her. But first he had to go back, work out the financial situation. What financial situation? Kitty wondered.

Still, she'd won. He left the wife, the family, the home, even the three dogs. He had nothing.

Turned out that was the truth. He had nothing. The wife was the one with all the money.

What do I want with an old man like you, with no money? she'd asked, when he tried to take her in his arms and tell her everything would be all right, they loved each other and he would be divorced and they would be together and that was all that mattered. Go back to your wife, she said contemptuously. She'll take you back. They always do. And she was right. The wife did. And that was that.

At least, sort of. He still promised he would get his hands on the money. Half of it was his, he said. So Kitty kept up the torture just in case. Besides she wanted to hurt him for deceiving her about his finances.

Just wait, he begged.

So Kitty waited. Screw the wife. Now Kitty wanted *the wife's* life; she wanted to *be* the woman his wife was; she wanted the respect and the money that came along with it. She wanted to be *her*.

She left a message for him on their private phone, the prepaid one where only she and he had the number. She told him she was coming back. She needed him, she wanted him, only him. She would give up her lover for him. They had to be together.

He was away on a vacation but he called her when he got her message and they arranged to meet.

He took a room at their usual hotel and she met him there. She told him she still loved him, but they could not be together without the money. He had to get it. She was expensive; only five-star hotels for her. She pushed it to the hilt.

I'll get it, he said, desperate. We'll be together. I'll never betray you. I'll always love you.

And the poor bastard probably would always have loved her, if his wife, grief-stricken over the demise of her long and loving marriage, had not shot him dead, and then turned the gun on herself. First, though, she killed their three dogs.

Kitty thought it was a pity about the dogs. But then Kitty was a psychopath, she cared for no one but herself. Her needs came first.

The whole event left her in a financial dilemma. Age was not making it any easier in her work as an escort. She wasn't being chosen from her Craigslist and Eros.com ads, or picked up in the bars and clubs. There were younger and certainly sexier women than the "mature Russian redhead" she claimed to be in her ads, and the truth of the matter was that Kitty was not a sexy woman. She did not even like sex, only the control she felt. And of course the money. Now, money was at the heart of her problems.

She and her English lover, Jimmy, had devised a new plan. Blackmail. They had successfully tried it out several times, using Ecstasy pills and the date-rape drug on small-time businessmen, in town for a convention, but had only made small amounts. And the expenses were terrific, especially the cost of the video camera, so precise it could capture every expression, and so tiny, the size of a nail head, it was easily hidden in a corner of her ceiling, in the AC duct. The payoff wasn't enough and now Kitty was desperate. She owed three months' rent. She had to do something. Something big.

* * *

Eyeing the dark-haired American woman sitting alone at the bar, Kitty recognized her vulnerability. She was troubled and Kitty would bet it was about a man. Plus she looked like money. That dress was expensive. Kitty pulled down her skirt and tucked her old Louboutins under her chair, red soles flashing. She'd bet this woman didn't have to buy good accessories secondhand. Plus, despite the fact that she wasn't wearing a ring, she would also bet she had a rich husband. Whatever, there might be an opportunity there. And besides, Kitty was bored, alone in the hotel bar on Christmas Day.

Calling over the waiter she ordered another Red Bull, her third—she adored the caffeine high—and another bottle of red wine. Jimmy said she drank too much, but so what? What had she got to lose?

chapter 8

Just then, another woman swept into the bar, Indian, exotic in a pale gold sari that sparkled as she walked confidently to a table and ordered a bottle of good champagne.

Beautiful: sleek black hair pulled so severely back it left the pure profile of a goddess exposed; aquiline nose, short upper lip, full mouth, immense dark eyes fringed with thick black lashes—real ones. There was no artifice about this woman. Unlike the redhead, she didn't even have to try.

The Indian woman's quick glance took in Sunny then Kitty. She did not acknowledge them. The waiter brought her the bottle of La Grande Dame she had ordered, in a silver bucket misted with icy drops. She asked for a bowl of nuts. "Pistachios," she said in a light clear singsong voice. "And two ounces of Beluga caviar." She sat back in her gray suede club chair while the waiter poured champagne into a delicate crystal glass. It had taken only that one quick assessing glance for her to understand exactly where the two other women were at.

Though she could have played the role of the aristocrat in a Bollywood musical, Maha Mondragon had been raised in terrible poverty, without any family, on the meanest, cruelest and most squalid streets of Mumbai. By the time she was seven, there was nothing Maha did not know about "real" life, and her one desire was to escape that reality, where violence was an everyday event, along with brutality and murder. Honed by those mean streets, Maha could smell evil like a second sense. She knew corruption firsthand. And she sensed it now, in the red-haired Kitty Ratte whose serpent's eyes met hers across the room.

Turning away Maha sipped her champagne, and checked out the beautiful woman sitting up at the bar, the one Kitty now had those hard eyes on. The intensity of the redhead's gaze was like an electrical current across the room, and looking at Sunny, Maha saw her innocence, and her vulnerability. She also sensed that she was troubled. A victim, if ever she saw one.

Maha's emerald-and-ruby-studded gold bangles jangled as she picked up her glass. She felt Kitty's eyes on her again, knew the woman was examining her expensive gold necklace, studded with cabochon emeralds. She refused to meet Kitty's eyes. She wanted nothing to do with her.

Maha was known for her particular type of jewelry made in Rajasthan by artisans who had perfected their craft over centuries, the necklaces of thick gold swirled around the emeralds for which the area was famous, as well as rubies, sapphires and lesser gemstones like topazes and tourmalines. They were a wonder of workmanship and artistry. She sold them to specialty boutiques and stores in Europe, and soon was to branch out in America. Maha was on the upward move, and would let nothing stand in her way.

She had come a long way from the poverty-stricken terrified seven-year-old, alone on Mumbai's sordid and most dangerous streets. But she never forgot her background, and the lessons she had learned.

* * *

Curious, Sunny tried not to stare at Maha. Now she wished she had ordered champagne. No point in ordering a bottle just for one, though.

Sudden anguish at being alone, of missing Mac, ripped through her. Desperate, she caught the barman's eye, asked for a bottle of champagne anyway. No caviar though. That used to be her and Mac's New Year's Eve treat: caviar and smoked salmon flown in from Harrods in London and lobster from Maine; more often than not eaten in bed with both dogs curled up on the blanket eagerly watching out for scraps. They never waited up for that ball to drop in Times Square though. They were too hot for each other to care about the rest of the world.

Oh God, her heart was breaking all over again. She should not be thinking of Mac. Her head suddenly felt empty as an air balloon, and she was the panicked balloonist. What was Mac doing right now? He must have found her note, perhaps he'd be searching for her, maybe he'd bought her a Christmas gift, something extravagant enough to bring her back into his arms . . . into those strong, welcoming arms that made her feel so safe, so loved when they enfolded her . . .

She kept back the tears with a huge effort. Tears were like rain, she thought. And it always seemed to rain in Malibu, at Christmas.

Rain fell on Mac's head, large drops, coming down in sharp gusty spatters. Pirate looked pathetically up at him. Pirate did not like to get wet and Mac picked him up; he was not a big dog but he hefted in at more than one might expect. Still he was so happy, cuddled under the jacket, Mac didn't mind.

Though it was evening in Monte Carlo, it was still Christmas Day morning in Malibu and he was walking the beach in the rain, thinking about Sunny, wondering where she was, who she was with; if she was wearing the beautiful red dress and the sexy boots. He was going crazy without her. He'd called everyone, tried everywhere.

Nobody knew anything, or if they did, they were not telling. And anyhow, shouldn't he, the famous Private Detective, be able to find the woman who'd run away from him?

Rain. If Sunny were here they would have thrown another log on the fire, had a festive drink, the delicious smell of turkey would be coming from the oven. Now, though, that turkey was still in the market, and there was no great smell of cooking, no blazing fire to lounge in front of, no festive drinks. Life, as Mac Reilly knew it, was over.

With Pirate cradled in his arms he walked back to his cottage, a thirties wooden shack tacked oddly onto the very end of the row of smart Malibu beach houses. He climbed the wooden steps to the deck, stood for a long moment staring out to sea.

Finally, he turned and went inside. He fed Pirate, poured himself a bourbon on the rocks and took a seat on the dog-hairy blanket on the old sofa that was the most comfortable piece of furniture he'd ever owned, and that, despite Sunny's complaints, he refused to get rid of.

Pirate went to sit next to him. The dog gave an anxious whine and automatically Mac reached out and rubbed a hand through his rough fur. He stared straight ahead at the empty fireplace. At his suddenly empty life.

chapter 9

*Monte Carlo, the hotel bar.
Still Christmas Day evening.*

A man in a white dinner jacket was playing cocktail piano, nothing "festive" thank God, Sunny thought, just good old Cole Porter and Jerome Kern, with a bit of Brazilian bossa nova. The music drifted softly into the silence. In the red dress and furry boots Sunny had never felt less like The Girl from Ipanema. Maybe she should have gotten on a plane to Rio instead of Paris. Wasn't it hot there at this time of year? Here in the South of France, a cold wind was fluttering the palm trees along the seafront, lifting women's skirts, ruffling their hair.

The barman poured her champagne so perfectly there was barely a froth to rim the flute, only those precious bubbles that usually so delighted her. Gloomily, she regretted ordering it. She wondered if a broken heart could turn a woman into an alcoholic.

A waiter arrived with a platter of *amuse-bouche,* small bites to take the edge off hunger and ease down the champagne. Was she hungry? Would she care if she ever ate again?

She noticed that the redhead in the corner, skirt sliding up over her plump thighs, her cheeks clashing pink with her metallic red hair, seemed to be hefting the drink back too. *And* she was alone. She had called the waiter, flicking her skirt carelessly over bare knees and ordered a bottle of wine and also a Red Bull. Sunny wondered what her story was. Because, as Mac always said, everybody had a story.

She switched her gaze to the beautiful Indian woman. The three of them were still the only customers in the bar on this Christmas Day night.

The Indian woman's heavy gold necklace was set with large cabochon emeralds, plus she wore a dozen or more jangling gold and bejeweled bracelets. Sunny would bet they were real. She watched her spoon the gray-black beads of expensive caviar onto tiny blinis, saw her eyes close with pleasure as she tasted.

The piano player switched to "Smoke Gets in Your Eyes," singing of love lost and of tears disguised behind the excuse of cigarette smoke.

Quite suddenly the air seemed to tremble as another young woman stormed into the bar. She was wearing a wedding dress, a short satin sheath, a shimmer of crystals. No veil, a bouquet of lily of the valley, a droop of jasmine pinned behind one ear with a diamond star. Anger vibrated from her. Tears slid down her pretty, uncaring face. Sunny could smell the lilies and the jasmine from where she sat.

The three women and the waiters watched, alarmed.

The bride hitched herself onto a barstool, slammed the lilies on the counter. "Martini. On the rocks," she snarled. Then added, humbly, *"S'il vous plaît, monsieur."* Tears fell off the cliff of her cheekbones. She sat, staring straight ahead while the barman shook the martini.

Uncomfortable, Sunny glanced away. She caught the eye of the Indian woman, who raised a shoulder and sighed.

The bride downed her martini in two gulps, grabbed her posy, slid from the barstool, smoothed her silk-satin shift and stalked, head up, chin determinedly jutted, from the bar.

Their eyes followed her.

"Poor girl."

The comment came, unexpectedly, from Kitty Ratte. "It's sad to be so deeply involved with a man who makes your life such hell."

Maha's large dark eyes took her in first, then Sunny. "That girl has probably found out the truth about her fiancé, but it's too late to back out. She has to go through with the marriage. She is looking at a lifetime of misery."

"Or a quick divorce," Sunny said, not wanting to think about erring fiancés.

"She could always take a lover." Kitty's prominent buckteeth stuck out as her jaw dropped in a giggle. She flicked her hand to summon the waiter again. "You know, to lighten her burden." She ordered another Red Bull, downed it quickly, then returned to the bottle of red wine.

Sunny watched her glug the Red Bull. Perhaps she was drowning her sorrows too. Somehow though, the redhead didn't look the type to be indulging in sorrow.

Maha sat back in her elegant gray suede club chair, looking at Kitty. "I'm assuming you speak from experience?"

Kitty lowered her chin, glancing demurely up from under her lashes. "Oh . . . not really . . . I mean I've heard it's the best thing to do, the best way to catch a man." Her small blue eyes disappeared in her cheeks as she laughed and said to Sunny, "Anyhow, it doesn't leave me looking as sad as you do."

Shocked, Sunny sat up straighter. She was damned if she was going to show the world—well anyway, these women—that she was devastated. Her attention shifted as three more people came into the bar, two men and a tall woman with cropped dark hair, and winging brows over eyes so green Sunny noticed their color from across the room. She wore a simple black suit with a skirt just at the knee, obviously designer, and her only jewelry was a pair of large diamond studs.

The two men with her were also very well dressed and to Sunny, used to "casually chic" California, very European in their pin-striped business suits, obviously custom-tailored.

Sunny had been known to be a bit of a clotheshorse herself, when the mood struck, and she knew good shoes. The woman's were Jimmy Choos, black satin laced around the ankle. Sunny had tried them on herself at Neiman's. She also knew the men's were hand-made and, she would bet, Berluti. Standing at the entrance to the bar, the three emanated an air of money-no-object expensiveness. Confident. Cool. And kind of attractive in that very European way.

They waved at the Indian woman, walked over and took seats at her table. Maha signaled the waiter for more champagne, more caviar. It came quickly and they raised their glasses in a toast. She glanced over at Sunny. "*Bon Noël,* Happy Christmas," she said, smiling.

"The happiest," the woman with the beautiful green eyes replied, in English. "For all of us."

Sunny couldn't stand it any longer, being here in a bar. Alone. It came to her in a flash. Her friend Allie Ray Perrin lived here in France. Miles away from the south, but still, she was here. In fact she and her husband Ron were good friends of both Sunny and Mac; they had been through a lot together, too much ever to forget.

She dialed Allie's number on her global BlackBerry and heard the odd beeping sound that was the French telephone "ring." It beeped on and on. Could they have gone away for Christmas, perhaps to the mountains? Allie was an avid skier. She couldn't bear it if she couldn't talk to her.

At last the ringing stopped and Allie's familiar voice said they were unable to answer the phone right now but please leave a message and they would get right back.

Sunny spoke quietly so no one would hear. "Allie, it's Sunny. I'm desperate. I've left Mac. It's over, there will never be a wedding. Oh,

Allie, I'm dying inside. Where *are* you? I need to talk to you, my beautiful friend. I'm in Monte Carlo. Mac doesn't know where I am and please, *please,* if he should call looking for me, do not tell him. *Please,* Allie, it's important. You have my cell phone number. I love you."

She closed the cell, lifted her head and looked straight into Kitty Ratte's eyes. She was on the barstool next to her. Tesoro, who had been sleeping, bared her teeth in a snarl and Sunny quickly apologized.

"Oh, but I adore all animals," Kitty said. And her face shining with sympathy, she reached out and patted Sunny's hand. "I get the feeling you need to talk," she said gently. "My name is Kitty Ratte and I live here."

"You live here alone?" Sunny shouldn't have asked such a question but alone was the first thing on her mind and it just came out. Still, the woman didn't seem to mind, and after all it was *she* who had come over to Sunny and started up this conversation on a very personal basis.

"Mostly, I am alone," Kitty said. "I live with someone, part of the time." She shrugged in a "who-doesn't" kind of way. "But he travels a lot and I am very much my own woman. When he is here, there are many things we enjoy together." Then she added with a mysterious smile, "And there are many things I like to do on my own. But for you, I can tell it's all fresh, all new, this 'alone' business." She shook her head, giving Sunny a knowing smile. The clumsy veneers on her two front teeth gleamed white. Then she leaned forward and patted Sunny's hand again.

"Trust me, *chérie,*" Kitty Ratte said oozing feminine sympathy. "I've been there."

chapter 10

Christmas Day evening

Allie Ray Perrin, better known simply as Allie Ray, one of the world's foremost movie stars and America's blond girl next door, with eyes of turquoise blue, so tender they melted your heart, and blond hair that fell straight as a die past her slender shoulders, long-legged, and complete with all the assets any seriously successful movie star required, was walking through her French vineyard, somewhere between Bordeaux and Bergerac, wearing old gray sweatpants, a bulky navy sweater and sneakers. She was holding the hand of her friend Prudence Hilson, who happened to be crying. Prudence had been crying since she had arrived first thing this morning.

Allie could see the silver glint of Pru's tears in the sudden shaft of moonlight peeking from behind the storm-dark clouds. She thought it was a wonder they didn't freeze on Pru's face the night was so friggin' cold. She shivered, clutching Pru's hand tighter, as though to lend her friend strength. In the dark in front of them she could hear her dog, Lovely, a black Lab who was poor Dearie's replacement, though no dog could ever truly replace Dearie, the stray she had picked up beside the French autoroute and who had been her "dearest" friend. Not even Frankie, the pup Mac had given her but who somehow never got the hang of French country life.

Pru let go of Allie's hand and bent to pat Lovely who'd come ripping through the long row of vines like a rocket heading into space, regardless of the two women standing in her way. Allie knew Labs were like that; you either got out of their way or you got mowed down. Staggering as Lovely smacked into her legs, Allie laughed and, to her surprise, so did Pru.

"There, you see," Allie said, filled with sudden triumph that her desolated friend had actually been made to laugh for the first time since she had arrived. "Everything's okay. Life goes on. You can be 'You' again, Pru. All you have to do is try."

Pru's sniff echoed through the silent vineyard, row upon row of naked branches months away from the fresh pale leaves of spring, and even longer to the heavy bunches of fat grapes that Allie was hoping one of these years might bring her own *Appellation d'Origine Contrôllée,* giving her brand-new wines a leg up in the very competitive wine market.

"'Silent Night,'" Pru said sadly.

"That was last night. Christmas Eve." Allie inspected a mangy-looking rosebush at the end of a row of vines, planted there to catch the first bugs so she might spot any pests early, before they could get as far as the grapes.

"Oh my God, I forgot, it's still Christmas Day." Pru began to cry again, a loud tearing sound that made Allie shudder and brought the dog running anxiously back, climbing up on Pru and licking her face.

"Labs are like worried mothers," Allie told her. "Always there to comfort you when you fall down. And you have fallen, Pru, but it's not the end of the world."

"Oh yes it is." Pru stopped and peered shortsightedly at Allie. "And it's my own fault."

"Well, not totally," Allie said cautiously, though she had to admit Pru looked like hell: overweight, dowdy, unmade-up and miserable. For a guilty minute she couldn't blame the husband for trading Pru in for someone who in fact, Pru herself said, looked the way she had looked not so many years ago.

"It was my fault," Pru wailed again. "He was away so much, I was so lonely, no children, not even a dog like Lovely."

"You had friends," Allie insisted.

"*His* friends. Come the divorce guess where all of them will be."

Allie knew what she was talking about.

"So he fucked her, and I ate to get over it," Pru said in a flat kind of voice that admitted her problem and that there was no solution. "I ate myself out of my clothes, then I bought new ones, then bigger. It got so I couldn't even get into normal underwear and had to go to a special store to buy the big ones, you know the granny pants we always laughed about when we were girls."

"But you were always *pretty*," Allie said loyally. Pru had been her friend since high school—and that was an era Allie no longer wanted to think about. She'd had her own battles to get where she was, to leave Mary Alison Raycheck, the poor kid from Texas, behind and turn herself into Allie Ray, the movie star, and then to have the strength to give it all up, all that fame, all that success, all that money. Everything comes with a price and Allie had paid hers. But now she had found that girl again, found her husband again, found love and peace and the quiet life that suited her. Glancing at Pru, still staring vacantly into the Christmas night, Allie knew she had to help her. It was a given. Allie was a good friend.

"Listen," she said, putting an arm round Pru's ample shoulders, and turning her around in the direction of the crumbling cottage she and Ron had invested with new life, as well as with a great deal of money and their sometimes acrimonious fights, but now, always, with love. "Listen Pru Hilson, you are going to get *yourself* back and that's that. No more stuffing yourself to hide the pain, no more pretending the husband is faithful, no more being lonely. *You* are in charge of your destiny, not him. I'm telling you, Pru, together we can do this."

The eaves of the cottage were picked out in bright Christmas lights and the pine tree in front sparkled with yesterday's frozen snowflakes, mirror balls and fake candles. The smell of that after-noon's turkey lingered in the doorway and Lovely bounded past, hurling herself this time at a short, wide-shouldered man who obviously kept himself in good shape. His hair was thick and dark with a slight wave, his eyebrows met over his sharp nose and his mouth was full and sensual. He was attractive in an offbeat way that had attracted the beautiful young Allie to him, years ago, yearning for his underlying strength, even though he had often behaved like the bad guy—*and* had done time for it. Jail time or no, Ron was her love and always would be. And she knew without any doubt that Ron Perrin loved her.

"Hey," Ron said, leaning back against the stainless-steel fridge, arms crossed, one leg folded over the other, as he inspected the two of them. Pru Hilson looked about as bad as any woman he had ever seen, but he did not allow her to see that from his face. His expression did not change. Soft flesh rippled around her neck, covered her breasts, imploded over stomach and thighs. She was wearing a caftan-like garment in some horrible shade of red, as though in tribute to the fact that it was Christmas Day. Her brown hair hung lank and uncurled to her shoulders, and her face was a pink full moon.

Jesus, Ron thought, but he didn't say that. Instead he said, "How about a glass of brandy, girls. Looks like we all could use one about now."

Pru lifted her head, covertly inspecting the remains of the tur-key, still on the chopping block. "And maybe a turkey sandwich?" she suggested, sniffing the way Lovely was, at the edges of the meat.

Ron's eyes met Allie's. She nodded permission. "Okay," he said. "Allie will get the brandy, I'll fix you a sandwich."

"Thank you." Pru took a seat at the kitchen table, simple with its blue-and-white-check oilcloth cover (easy to wipe up, Allie had told her, we're a bit messy, Ron and I). She shifted the poinsettia in its terra-cotta pot to one side, so she could watch Ron.

"With mayo please, and a bit of gravy. If there's any left, of course."

"Of course."

Ron busied himself slicing turkey breast. He didn't know what to make of this friend of Allie's, a woman from her murky, hated childhood, and a woman she obviously felt something for. Or had in the past, anyway. When Pru had called the day before Christmas Eve and said could she come see Allie, Ron objected. He wanted them to spend Christmas alone. It was the quiet time in the vineyard, no work to be done till spring. They were even thinking of going on a vacation, though he doubted they would make it, they were too content here, the two of them. Who would have thought a couple of years ago it would turn out like this? God had been in his heaven for them, and now Ron thought Allie felt the need to give back and help this woman from her past.

"I'm sorry," Pru said.

Ron glanced up from the turkey.

"For invading your Christmas. I shouldn't have done it. I'll be on my way tomorrow, leave you in peace."

Ron said nothing, went back to slicing the turkey, cutting a couple of slabs of good bread, spreading mayo thickly, he guessed that's the way she would like it; layering the turkey, drizzling a little gravy, topping it with the other slice, pressing it flat with the palm of his hand, then cutting it crossways in bulky triangles. Just like a goddamn professional, he thought, remembering the time all those years ago, before he became the big shot he used to be; the time when he was a young boy and life was tough and he'd worked his way through a few delis, a few summer hotels, a few beach clubs— until here he was fixing a sandwich for a woman who most certainly did not need the food. What she needed was food for her soul.

Allie returned with a tray of glasses and the brandy bottle and a Diet Coke for herself. She set it on the blue-and-white oilskin cloth and Ron came over and put the plate with the sandwich in front of Pru. In a flash, Lovely bounced over Pru's knee, grabbed a triangle of sandwich, gulped it down, grabbed another, fleeing as Ron hollered and Allie broke into helpless laughter, while Pru stared, dismayed at the remains of her snack.

"Jesus," Pru said, impressed, "that's some fast dog."

"She just did you a favor and ate half that sandwich. Remember that," Allie said. "Because tomorrow you and I are working out a whole new regime for you."

"But I'm leaving tomorrow, I can't stay and be a burden to you, or to anyone. I have to work out my life myself."

"Oh, stop it." Allie stared exasperated at her.

Then Ron said, "By the way Allie, the phone rang when you were out. I only caught the end of the message. I didn't check it, but I know it was Sunny Alvarez. And it sounded to me as if she was in trouble."

chapter 11

Monte Carlo. Christmas Day evening.

The hotel bar was quiet, just the Indian woman with her elegant friends, and Sunny and her would-be new friend whose bright red hair fell in fluffy bangs over her small secretive blue eyes.

Kitty put her hand over Sunny's. "I've been down that road myself, a few times," she said, with that demure chin-down bucktoothed smile and upward glance that, Sunny thought, seemed to be her trademark. She wasn't sure she liked Kitty Ratte, wasn't sure she wanted to be consoled by her, wasn't sure she wanted to be anybody's "friend" simply because she was lonely and desperate about Mac and feeling like hell and really, truly, thought she might die.

Still she found herself saying, "Hi, I'm Sunny Alvarez," through a large gulp of good champagne, glad after all, just to be talking to *someone*. Allie wasn't at the end of the phone; Prince Charming had disappeared in Paris, and Mac . . . well Mac was probably in Malibu, gazing out at the Pacific Ocean and wondering where she was and why on earth she had left him, when he'd just told her he couldn't marry her that's all.

"He told me he couldn't marry me," she said flatly.

Kitty Ratte looked interested and sympathetic at the same time. The barman refilled Sunny's glass and she indicated she needed a second glass for her friend. The barman did not look at Kitty as he put a glass in front of her, filled it, placed the bottle back in the silver ice bucket.

Sunny noticed his attitude. "Does the barman know you?"

"Ooh, I come here occasionally. It's convenient, a pleasant place for a woman alone. A woman can simply be herself here, drink what she wants, think what she wants."

"And what exactly is that?"

Kitty's small blue eyes crinkled into pinpoints when she laughed. "What do I think? Or what do I want?"

"Both." Sunny sipped the champagne, suddenly very interested in what Kitty Ratte had to say. For an insignificant woman she seemed pretty full of herself.

"Well," Kitty said slowly, as though she were thinking hard about Sunny's questions. "I like to be free. I'm successful in the modeling business. I have an apartment in Cannes. I have a lot of friends. I enjoy myself."

"You work?" Practical Sunny wondered where the money was coming from to finance an apartment in Cannes and a life alone.

Kitty shrugged, leaning closer to Sunny. The V of her dress fell away, revealing a heavily padded blue bra. L.A. woman that Sunny was, she wondered why, if Kitty Ratte were so successful, had she not had a boob job. And anyhow why hadn't she had those buckteeth fixed? And the front two had awful cheap too-white veneers. Obviously whatever Kitty did, she wasn't making enough to keep up with the Joneses of Monte Carlo.

"I have a 'partner,'" Kitty explained. "Not a husband, you know, just someone I have an 'understanding' with."

"You mean you're a mistress?"

Kitty's forced laugh was a bit angry. "I suppose you could call me that," she said stiffly. "I prefer to call it, the way the Europeans do, an 'arrangement.' He travels a lot, but there are many things, when he is here, that we like to do together. Special things," she added with a reminiscent little smile. "But then, there are also many things I prefer to do on my own. So, what about you, Sunny Alvarez? Why don't you tell me your story? I'm here just for you, just to listen to you."

"Oh my God," Sunny said, suddenly so grateful to have someone—anyone—to talk to that the story simply came spilling out: about Mac Reilly, TV's star detective. All of it. All the hurt. All the pain. All the love. "And all for nothing."

"But you're so wonderful, so beautiful," Kitty breathed admiringly. "How could Mac *not* want you?"

Sunny choked back more tears. She hid her face in Tesoro's already tear-damp fur, aware that the eyes of the beautiful Indian woman were also on her.

"But now you tell me, Kitty," she said, speaking as she always did as the thought flashed into her head. "With all your friends, what are *you* doing, alone in a hotel bar on Christmas Day?"

Kitty's eyes took on that secretive look again. "I'm on my way to a party. In Cannes. In fact I must leave now."

"A Christmas party?" Sunny felt a pang of envy for this unknown woman.

"I told you I have many friends. And now with you, perhaps I have a new one. I understand what you are going through. Why don't you and I have lunch tomorrow? Go shopping? You know, just fun, girl talk, that sort of thing?"

Loneliness was like a disease, it overtook you in weak moments and Sunny found herself agreeing almost too eagerly.

Kitty patted her hand again, so sympathetic Sunny felt grateful. Clutching her black Chanel bag and with a flash of naked thigh, Kitty unhitched herself from the stool. "Tomorrow then. I'll pick you up at noon."

Sunny watched her walk from the bar, an odd little knees-together trot in the black leather, red-soled Louboutin pumps that were too high for her and that did not go with the flimsy shirtdress, that Sunny noticed was unbuttoned to midthigh. She wondered for a quick moment if Kitty was a hooker, but then dismissed the thought. She was just too ordinary.

Maha watched Kitty leave. She didn't know what she was up to, but she knew it was not good, and sensed also that Sunny was vulnerable. She got up and went over to Sunny. She looked at the little dog lolling on her lap. "I would guess you were French," she said, in her sweet singsong voice. "The French always have their dogs with them. But by your bearing, I can see that you are not. You must be American."

"I am," Sunny admitted, warily.

"Excuse me for interrupting, and allow me to introduce myself. My name is Maha Mondragon."

"Sunny Alvarez."

Maha gave her an intense, assessing look. Then she said, "I felt it necessary to come here and warn you. Take care with that woman."

Did she mean Kitty Ratte? Nonplussed, Sunny stared back at her.

Maha said, "Some of us are able to sense corruption. It has a particular unmistakable aroma. It permeates the atmosphere. Trust me."

Stunned into silence, Sunny took a nervous sip of champagne.

"My dear, I have something else of importance to say to you. Remember this. You must not be afraid of the future. Take whatever chances life might offer you."

Maha's hand sat lightly on Sunny's shoulder. "Trust me," she said again. Then with a bow of her beautiful head, she returned to her table and the trio of waiting friends. She did not look back and they left together, heading, Sunny guessed with a knife blade of desolation stabbing her chest, for a wonderful dinner together. After all, it was Christmas Day. And *she* was alone in a hotel bar.

Then in walked Prince Charming.

chapter 12

A weight lifted from Sunny's chest. "How did *you* get here?"

"Magic." He took her hand in both of his, bent and kissed it. His sun-streaked dark blond hair slid over his eyes as he lifted his head and looked at her.

"Did I tell you you were very beautiful? Even in those awful boots?"

"My comfort boots."

"Now I'm here you won't need them anymore."

His look was hopeful. And Sunny had been right, his eyes were a sort of greenish hazel. Funny, she had no idea who he was, what he was, where he was from, what he did. And she didn't care. *He* had cared enough to seek her out again. *He* was here. And Mac, the famous private detective who could locate a criminal at fifty paces, was not. Despite the fact that there were two dozen missed calls on her phone from him.

Anyhow, this was definitely not the time to be thinking of the man who had left her at the altar. Well, almost. Besides, what was it that Maha Mondragon had just said to her—that she should not be afraid to take the chances life might offer her? Prince Charming was definitely one of those "chances."

He was wearing a black cashmere jacket and a white linen shirt open at the neck. The French cuffs were left loose and tucked up without any links. His skin had that overall tan glow that came from the surf and the sea and, golden California girl though she was, Sunny felt a pale winter waif in comparison. She wasn't missing any small detail about him: his hazel eyes, his dark blond hair, his firm mouth, the strong chin, the faint lilt of a foreign accent. She still knew nothing at all about him and somehow that was part of the charm.

"Come with me," Prince Charming said and Sunny slid off the stool, tucked the dog under her arm and went.

She wasn't thinking of Mac, she wasn't thinking of anything. All she knew was that she was in Monte Carlo sitting next to this attractive man on a gray suede banquette, in a half-empty lamp-lit restaurant late on Christmas Day. For now she did not have to think about Mac and the fact that they were through. She was not "Alone." Prince Charming was all she needed. Someone to be with "for the moment."

"You must be a magician. To come to find me, turn my day—my *life*—around."

His smile was a heartbreaker. "Sorry but I'm a mere mortal. There's no 'magic' involved. I knew where you were. I followed you from Paris, I couldn't stand being on my own."

She nodded. "Alone is too painful."

"So exactly *who* are *you,* magical princess?" he asked as the waiter poured pale gold wine into tulip-shaped glasses.

"Are we allowed to tell the truth now?"

"I know *I* am allowed. You are looking at Eduardo Johanssen, usually known as Eddie, half Brazilian, half Swedish. Choose whichever half you like better."

"Interesting name," she said. They looked at each other for a long silent moment, side by side in the booth.

"Here's to you, Sonora Sky Coto de Alvarez." He touched his glass to hers.

"You already know my name."

"I couldn't forget you, sleeping on the plane. You were so vulnerable, so hurt, with the tearstains still on your cheeks. I didn't know whether it was all that champagne, or if I'd bored you to sleep. All I knew was I needed to find out."

"Do you know *why* I was alone and crying?"

"If you want to tell me, then I'm happy to listen. I promise I will understand."

Somewhere along the line they had ordered food, and now the waiter placed steaming bowls of *soupe au pistou* in front of them. The scent of basil wafted up. Neither of them picked up their spoons.

She said, "You knew I'd run away though?"

"It was apparent, from what you told me on the plane: buying a ticket at the last minute, throwing a few things into your case, packing up the dog, not knowing where you were going when you got to Paris. And the fact that you were so obviously upset."

"The red eyes, I suppose."

"Red but beautiful."

This time Sunny laughed. "Of course, you were right, I was running away. I am still. I'm running away from a marriage that will no longer take place."

"He left you at the altar?"

It was Sunny's turn to shrug, and this time the V-neck of her dress, unlike Kitty Ratte's, revealed a hint of firm rounded breasts. Nothing to do with Hollywood implants, Sunny had grown them herself, to her chagrin, at the age of thirteen, when she was horse-mad and a tomboy and hated being female. Of course she had changed her mind since then, since she had discovered the power of breasts, what they did to a man, and certainly what they did to a woman, under a man's, especially Mac's, touch.

She said, "Mac had important work to do, he canceled the wedding. It wasn't the first time, but it was the last."

"You still love him though."

"I don't know," Sunny said in a small strangled voice.

"Yes, you do. It's part of what happened, who you are, what kind of woman. I'll bet you don't give up on love so easily, Sunny Alvarez."

Her head drooped on her long neck, her hair, silken and black, swung forward to hide her face.

"You know what?" Eddie pushed her hair gently back behind her ear, disentangling a strand that had caught on her diamond drop earring, which, of course, were the ones Mac had given her last Christmas. "We have similar stories, you and I."

Her eyes slid toward him. She held back the tears. Just.

"My home is Stockholm, but my business takes me around the world. Too much travel. Too much separation. Finally, my wife couldn't bear the loneliness. She found another life. Now we are in the middle of a divorce."

"Do you still love her?"

"I always will."

"Then why are you letting her go?"

"Because, my sweet Sunny, she deserves her freedom with a man who can make her happier than I ever could."

"You must have been happy in the beginning?"

"Beginnings are always happy. Love, lust, insane longings for each other."

His eyes linked to hers. Sunny recognized that look and felt that warning flutter, that dangerous delightful flutter in the pit of her belly. Don't go there, she warned herself, *don't go there, Sunny, you're too vulnerable, too "Alone"* . . .

He patted her hand, turned and spoke to the waiter who'd brought a bowl of chopped chicken for the dog, who was sleeping peacefully. Sunny was still thinking about what Eddie had said. She knew she'd better change the subject. "So what do you do, Mr. Johanssen?"

"I'm in the shipping business, tankers, containers, that sort of thing. Quite boring for someone like you, involved in Hollywood showbiz."

Sunny laughed. "Did no one ever tell you the truth about

Hollywood? That more often than not it's even more boring than shipping containers and just about as mundane."

"But you love it."

"I admit, I love it. I love California, I love Malibu, and my home in the marina with its view of all the boats I've even dreamed of sailing away on."

The vibrating of her cell phone brought her out of the trance she was falling into. It was Allie. She answered it.

"Allie, oh Allie . . ." she said.

"What's up? *Really* up? I mean, have you truly *left* Mac?"

"I have. And I need you. Can I come and see you tomorrow?"

"Where are you?"

Sunny told her.

"I'll come to you. I'll be there tomorrow evening, I don't think I can get out of here earlier. Listen, book me a room, a double."

"Is Ron coming with you then?"

"No, I'm bringing a friend from my school days. I haven't seen her in years, then she called me just before Christmas and said she needs help. She's done nothing but cry since she got here and I'm afraid to leave her alone. Anyhow, I'll tell you the story when we get there. Just know that you're not the only one needing help at the moment."

"Oh, Allie, you talk like the new *You*. I know you'll sort us all out."

Allie's laugh would have been familiar to millions of moviegoers. "Hey, remember me asking you, only a couple of years ago, *Sunny, have you ever been heartbroken?* You said you didn't think so. But *I* had, my darling Sun. And I remember what it feels like. I'm there for you, whatever it takes."

Sunny sniffed, remembering. She looked at Eddie. He was obviously trying not to listen. "Thank you, Allie. I knew I could count on you."

Cutting off Allie was like cutting off a lifeline. "Reality" swept back in full force. Sunny looked at the stranger she was having dinner with. The man who had come to find her. The man with magic in his eyes and she somehow knew, magic in his touch. She knew she had better leave. Go to bed. *Alone.* That dreaded word that tonight she had to face up to. She apologized, said, it must be jet lag, but she suddenly felt exhausted and needed to go to bed.

Oh God, she hoped he didn't think that was an invitation. A few minutes ago though, it might have been. She was a woman at a vulnerable point in her life, with feelings, emotions.

He signaled the waiter, signed the bill, took her arm, walked her out of the beautiful golden-lit restaurant.

Sunny didn't believe how nice he was, how thoughtful. How handsome. And how sexy. There it was again, that flutter in her belly. She said, "I have a lot to thank you for, rescuing me twice."

He smiled. "Perhaps some other time, we can try again. Tomorrow I have to leave for Paris."

"You will come back though?" There she went again, that impulsive voice, anxious this time, saying exactly what she was thinking.

"Yes. I will."

Against her better judgment, Sunny leaned in to kiss him. His mouth gently drew her lips into his. A lingering soft kiss.

"I'll be back as soon as I can," he promised. Then he walked through the grand foyer and out through the glass doors.

A short time later, tucked into that huge mint-green bed with Tesoro arranged neatly on the pillows, exhausted, Sunny fell instantly asleep. Her last waking thoughts were of Mac. And of Eddie Johanssen. Yet, oddly, she dreamed of neither man. It was Kitty Ratte who was in her head, and the strange warning from Maha Mondragon. And of Maha telling her that she must take the chances life offered her.

chapter 13

This was the most important "case" of his life and Mac Reilly, super-detective, was stumped. He had no idea where Sunny was.

He had just gotten off the phone with Sunny's charmingly hippie, beautiful mother, whose name was Flora and who wore hibiscus flowers in her blond hair and communed with nature under the Santa Fe moon. She would wander amid the desert cactus and wildlife and coyotes and rattlers who apparently found her unthreatening and left her in peace. And of course, he'd talked with Sunny's papa, the handsome Mexican rancher who looked like a Latino actor in a Western movie, with his thick silver-gray hair and trim mustache and his polished-tan skin.

They'd always been there for Sunny and Mac: Mom otherworldly; Papa earthy and direct. And they were concerned when Mac asked if they knew where their daughter was.

"You mean she's not with *you*?" Flora sounded astonished. "But she told us she was going away, somewhere special for Christmas. She said it was a secret."

"We assumed she meant with you." Papa's voice boomed.

"Of course you two have had a fight." Mothers always knew.

"Kind of, well not really a *fight*; call it a disagreement."

Mac was not usually evasive but he didn't want to upset them and he certainly didn't want to tell them their daughter had disappeared. "Don't worry," he said confidently, "I know where she'll be. I'll get back to you later."

"You make it up now, you hear me?" Flora's voice was sharper. "Let me tell you something, Mac Reilly, you and Sunny are too good together to let things simply fall apart. Take it from me, when you have it this good, never let it go, because there's some sort of law in love that says you will never find again what you've got now."

Mac put down the phone. It was still Christmas Day in Malibu.

The sea pounded on the rocks outside the window and rain spattered on the glass, causing Pirate to lift a curious ear. A small fire flickered hesitantly in the grate, not enough to really warm the room, and certainly not enough to bring a Christmas glow to Mac's heart.

He slung an arm over Pirate who snuggled deeper into the curve of his body. He thought about where Sunny might have gone. To a spa perhaps? But what could be more depressing than a spa at Christmas, a time of festivity that Sunny loved. A Caribbean island? She wasn't a St. Bart's kind of woman, and there were so many other islands. Paris, where they had been so happy just a few months ago? But Paris was a long haul simply to run away; it would have been easier to head for Vegas or the Napa Valley. But Sunny had no friends in those places, and she did have a friend, a very good friend in France.

Without even considering the nine-hour time difference, Mac picked up the phone and dialed the Perrins' number.

"Yeah?" Ron Perrin's voice had more than a hint of fatigue to it and Mac was instantly guilty. "I might have known it would be you." Ron added, "What took you so long, Detective?"

"You mean Sunny is there?"

Ron heaved a sigh. "Look, I don't know what's going on, only that Allie said Sunny's left you. Mac, you got another woman, or what? Okay, okay, you don't have to tell me *why,* you fuckin' idiot. What's *wrong* with you? You straighten everybody else out yet you can't get your own personal act together—*plus* you happen to have one of the best girls in the entire world, *and* one of the most beautiful. And I'll tell you what, while I have you on the phone Mac Reilly, if you don't want to marry her then fuckin' tell her so, don't keep stringing her on like this. Plus I'll tell you somethin' else, buddy. She won't have to wait around long, somebody else is gonna grab her and you'll never see her again."

Ron spoke the truth. Mac ran a distracted hand through his hair, eyes scrunched in desperation. Next to him, Pirate whined soulfully. "I'm sorry," Mac said.

"Don't tell *me* you're sorry, asshole," Ron roared. "Tell *her.*"

"How can I? I don't even know where she is."

Ron sighed again. "All right, jerk. I shouldn't be doing this, but in the name of friendship and all that you two mean to me, and to Allie, all that you've done for us—"

"Saved your lives," Mac reminded him, putting on the pressure.

"*Including* that, I'm gonna do it anyway. Sunny called Allie in deep distress. She's in a hotel in Monte Carlo. Allie's meeting her there—plus Allie's taking along another friend, from her high school days, who is also in despair and who, in fact, looks like a case for *Extreme Makeover.* So the two of them are on their way to save Pru, and to save Sunny."

Ron told him the name of the hotel, then said, "For old times' sake, you want me to send my plane for you?"

"Thanks for the offer, but I can probably get on the Air France that leaves tonight. Nobody flies Christmas Day."

"Think of the carbon footprint you're saving me," Ron said, with a grin in his voice. "And listen, bastard, this time do the right thing. Okay?"

chapter 14

The morning after Christmas Sunny was awakened by the stream of sunlight coming from a gap she had deliberately left in the curtains. She had also left the window open, just enough to let in the cool breeze. Unlike the Pacific the Mediterranean did not have that crashing boom of waves. It was an almost tideless sea, blue as the sky, sometimes even bluer, especially in the evening right after sundown when the sea and the sky blended and the very air seemed to have the same neon-blue glow.

She stepped out onto the small terrace and looked down at the armada of white yachts cramming the marina; at the enamel sea glittering with diamond points of light, at the palms and the plane trees and the bustle of activity near the famous twin-domed casino. Tesoro waggled next to her, whining. Dragging on a pair of sweat-pants and a T-shirt Sunny slammed a baseball cap over her tangled hair, grabbed the dog and took the elevator down to the lobby.

The bellboys smiled, the doormen said, *"Bonjour madame, et ça va la petite?"* Which, from Sunny's sojourn in the South of France the previous year, she knew meant "how is the little one." The dog loved all the attention the French gave her and wagged her whole behind in delight.

They jogged across the square and onto the promenade alongside the yachts. Sunny wondered why Mac had not found her. Had he even gone looking for her? Fear at losing him burned equally with anger in her chest. Nobody knew, she thought sadly, that "heartbreak" was exactly what it meant: it was so physical she could feel the two pieces of her heart, heavy as lead.

When she left the hotel she didn't think to look at the time, she had not even put on a watch and was simply enjoying the heat of the winter sun on her back as she trotted along with the dog. Then she saw a clock. It was eleven-thirty and Kitty Ratte was to pick her up at twelve to go shopping.

She stopped to look at a yacht where crew members were washing down decks, brushing off cushions, sprucing up for the owner's arrival. She wondered if Eddie was in Paris now and when he would come back. As if on cue her BlackBerry rang.

It was him. She clutched the phone to her chest. She should not answer. It was all too difficult, and, she knew, too dangerous. Turning, she jogged back to the hotel.

Fifteen minutes later, showered, hair barely dry, a dust of blush on her pale face, a gleam of her daytime lipstick, L'Oreal British Red on her lips, in a pair of white jeans, a black T-shirt, a white cashmere sweater slung French-style over her shoulders, feet thrust into black mules, gold hoop earrings her only jewelry, and with Tesoro waiting on her lead, she finally allowed herself to listen to Eddie's message. It was brief.

"The bar. Tonight. Eight-thirty."

Sunny clutched the BlackBerry to her chest again. Should she go, or should she not? was the question as she took the elevator down to meet Kitty.

Kitty waited outside the hotel in a small white Fiat with Spanish number plates.

Kitty knew all the hotels, all the bars along the Côte d'Azur, where she sought out her targets; men, or women. So far though, blackmail had not been successful enough for her to retire to that bar in Marbella, Spain, she lusted after. She did not even own her own apartment and she owed three months' rent. Besides, she needed Botox and Restylane and her dermatologist needed to be paid. There was no time to lose.

Monte Carlo was a long way from Vilnius, the capital of Lithuania, that was Kitty Ratte's place of birth, but that was a long time ago, more years than she cared to admit. She lived much of her youth on the Baltic Sea coast, freezing her butt off while the man her mother lived with—marriage was never an option—fished for whatever half-frozen-to-death fish came out of that icy sea. Kitty's first memory was of being cold. Her second memory was of hating the woman she called Mother. And her favorite memory was of the day she left that Baltic seaport, on her way to find a new life with a young man who claimed to have fallen madly in love with her, and to whom, aged fifteen, she gave her virginity though not her innocence, because Kitty had never been an "innocent."

The act of "love"—as the young man whose name she had by now forgotten had called it—meant nothing to Kitty. It was merely a commodity to get her from point A to point B, and when she reached point B, at that young man's expense, she moved quickly on, without even informing him she was going.

By then she was sixteen years old. Just.

A trail of men—young, old, good-looking and eager, or fat and married, it didn't matter—marked Kitty's progress through the escort clubs and sex clubs of those Baltic countries, all the way through Poland and the Ukraine, Hungary and Croatia, and finally to Paris, where she had taken up with a professor of medical science at the hospital where she had managed, through lies and false references, to get a job as an assistant in the pharmacy. By then her brown hair was dyed red, though not as bright as the present day. With her pink cheeks and bucktoothed smile, as yet without the two cheap veneers on the front, her sturdy peasant arms and thighs, plus her extreme youth and obvious sexual availability she had a certain appeal.

She stayed with the professor for six months, finally running off to London on her own in search of better pickings. She took with her several bottles of the pharmaceuticals known as date-rape drugs, that she'd learned, from the professor, who was a good teacher, could render a person semicomatose, and highly susceptible to sexual exploitation. In fact the "victim" would be incapable of constructive thought, and unable to take physical action to defend themselves, unable to move or think. Anything could be done to them while in that sedated state.

Kitty was never sexually satisfied, but now the use of these drugs gave her a sense of power that was both heady and frightening. She could kill someone in that sedated state. It would be easy. Kitty had no feelings for anyone but herself. She knew what gave her pleasure. And killing just might.

Now, she smiled eagerly as Sunny walked toward her, instinctively understanding her vulnerability. With a woman as vulnerable as that, anything was possible.

"Hiii." Kitty's twin veneers gleamed whitely in an ingratiating grin.

Sunny wondered why the woman had not done something about them. "Hi," she called back, running down the steps and climbing in next to Kitty, who was wearing a pink jersey wrap dress that rumpled over her white thighs.

"I think you look better today," Kitty said, throwing Sunny a quick glance as they sped off. "I hope you had a good night's sleep?"

"As a matter of fact I did."

"And did he call you? The absentee lover?"

"He called many times."

Kitty slammed on the brakes at a red light, making the tires screech. "But you didn't answer him?"

Sunny shook her head. "No."

"Is he handsome, your lover?"

"*I* think he is."

Kitty's head swiveled Sunny's way as she dodged through traffic. "And do other women think he's attractive?"

"I don't ask other women how they feel about him." Sunny did not like the way this conversation was going. She didn't want to talk about Mac to this woman with her pointed questions. Yet wasn't that the reason she was here? To try to talk it out, get Mac out of her system, try to decide what to do, where she was at? Try to deal with being alone again, after four entire years spent in Mac's company?

"I guess they do," she admitted. "Mac is a celebrity because of his TV show. He's got those kind of rumpled good looks detectives in fiction are supposed to have: deep blue eyes, crazy black hair, always standing on end because he pushes his hand through it so much. And he has wonderful hands, slender, tanned . . ."

"A tight body?" Kitty asked.

Surprised, Sunny admitted that yes Mac did have a tight body.

"Then you must be missing him. Missing having sex with him, I mean." Kitty glanced sideways at Sunny as she parked at the Gray d'Albion lot in Cannes. She laughed and added in a mischievous tone, "If you are missing him like that, then I know exactly how to take care of it. I mean, a woman can't go without sex simply because she leaves a man. No reason for that now, is there?"

"I really hadn't thought about it." Sunny's back was stiff with embarrassment. She hardly knew this woman. What exactly did she mean, she *knew how* to take care of it?

"Well, here we are," Kitty said. "Let's start with Gucci. They're all here. There are other shops just off the main boulevard, we can do them all and fit in some lunch in between."

Adjusting her white sunglasses, Kitty took Sunny's arm and they walked into the sunshine. They drifted in and out of the stores, but

Sunny's mind was not on shopping. She was thinking about Allie, who was to arrive that evening, and also about Eddie and how she was going to manage that situation with both of them there. Allie would never understand about Eddie. In fact she wouldn't dare tell her.

An answer came as the BlackBerry buzzed. "We have people for dinner tonight—I can't just cancel. Will you be okay if we come tomorrow?" Allie said.

"Who is 'we'?"

"I'm bringing Pru Hilson, an old friend from my school days. I told you about her. She's going to need our expert Hollywood makeover help."

"How about making over my heart?"

"That's my priority, baby. I'll see you tomorrow. Behave yourself. I love you."

Sunny found herself having lunch with Kitty on the terrace of the Hotel Martinez, sipping a glass of rosé and tucking into a hearty roast chicken, then, because she'd hardly eaten the previous night, and was suddenly starving, following it with delicious cheeses, a soft Banon wrapped in chestnut leaves; a Saint-André, her favorite; and a hard sheep's milk cheese that tasted of rosemary, served with a heavenly crusted golden baguette, the kind she and Mac sometimes dreamed of, on their Malibu deck, and sometimes wishing they were in France. Oooh . . . how she wished Mac were here now, eating this *fromage de Saint-André,* and the Banon, a contrast in cream and suppleness that, simple though it was, somehow hit that satisfying spot.

Kitty's flame-red hair glittered in the sunlight as she bit inelegantly into a burger. Her plump peasant hands gripped it like paws, and she smiled up at Sunny as she chewed.

"*Soo* good," she said. "I didn't realize I was quite this hungry."

She looked at Sunny from behind the white sunglasses with the intertwined Gucci *G*'s on the sides in gold. Her Chanel purse was on the chair next to her and her Dior earrings swung like signs in her ears. "I feel so sorry for you," she said, patting Sunny's knee gently. "You are going through so much, and I was hoping this little diversion would help you forget. Well, perhaps not *forget,* but help you not think about what happened, for a short while at least."

She said it so kindly Sunny was touched. In fact, apart from a penchant for luxury stores and a taste for sex talk, Kitty Ratte was innocuous. Yet, at the back of Sunny's mind was Maha Mondragon's strange warning. *"Corruption has its own particular aroma."*

Kitty dropped her off at the hotel with a kiss on each cheek. She gave Sunny her phone number, waiting while Sunny put it on her BlackBerry, then said, "Perhaps I'll see you later. I might have to come by the hotel, you never know."

But Sunny's thoughts were already flitting to her date with Eddie that evening. Would she or would she not go? And was Mac even trying to find her? She wished Allie would get here and rescue her.

chapter 15

Eddie Johanssen had not heard back from Sunny agreeing to meet him. Of course, he should have stayed in Paris, he had work to do, but there was a pull, a connection that had brought him back to Monte Carlo.

Truth was, Eddie thought, sitting at the hotel bar that evening, fifteen minutes early for his hoped-for date with Sunny, he had never met a woman who exposed her feelings so dangerously. Most of the women he met were concerned only about themselves: about the way they looked, what they wore, worrying about every detail. He included his about-to-be-ex-wife in this category. Jutta was a woman he'd once loved very much, and somehow he still loved her, though he could no longer live with her. The divorce had turned out to be messy with accusations and claims on Jutta's part that Eddie was determined not to defend. Let her have whatever she wants was his theme with the divorce attorneys, though of course they insisted on protecting him. Now matters were in a highly inflammable state, with Jutta determined to take him to the cleaners, and keep custody of their two children.

Eddie was at a vulnerable point in his life too. Lonely, he was emotionally open to the soft looks, the delicate dark beauty, the *trust* that Sunny Alvarez had placed in him, right from those first moments on the plane. It felt good to have a woman treat him like that; a woman running away from a man—he had guessed that immediately; and a woman who trusted enough to fall asleep next to him. There had been other women in his life besides Jutta, of course. But none like Sunny.

The hotel bar was busy. The after-Christmas sales were on and groups of women perched on the gray suede chairs surrounded by shopping bags, drinking pale pink martinis, exclaiming about their bargains, laughing with the exhilaration only shopping seems to give females. The elegantly beautiful Indian whom Eddie had noticed last night was alone at a table in the corner, being served champagne. La Grande Dame, Eddie observed. A nice wine. He hoped she would have someone to share it with. For a second her eyes—her beautiful dark eyes—connected with his, then she glanced away leaving him with the unnerving impression that she could read his mind. More . . . that she *knew* him.

In another corner, a group of men clustered together, heads down, listening intently to whatever business scheme was being discussed. There were two barmen tonight: the same silver-haired one from last night, and a younger man, tall, skinny, his wrists sticking out of his sleeves as he shook more of those girly martinis.

Eddie nursed the vodka on the rocks he'd ordered, more because he was propping up the bar alone than for the alcohol. He already felt drunk enough at the thought of being with Sunny. He glanced at his watch. Eight-twenty-five. He loosened his tie, dark yellow with a muted pattern and unbuttoned the top button of his blue shirt. He wore the same cashmere jacket as before and his dark blond hair was still wet from the shower. To the women sitting on those gray suede chairs, interestedly watching him over the rims of their martinis, he looked pretty damn good.

For once, Sunny had left the Chihuahua, exhausted and sleeping on the bed and she was alone. She walked into the bar as the minute hand of the clock moved to exactly the half hour.

Eddie's face lit with a smile as he saw her, and she strode, in that lovely long-legged way she had, toward him. Just as all hell erupted outside the hotel. The shriek of police sirens, fire trucks; more police.

Frightened, the women gasped, asked each other, "Is it terrorists? A bomb? Surely not here in Monte Carlo."

Sunny ran to Eddie; he put his arm around her and she leaned nervously into him. This wasn't the entrance she had expected to make; she'd thought they would be alone and could talk, quietly. She meant quickly to tell Eddie that even though she was attracted to him, she would not see him again. She'd tell him he was her savior, that he'd kept her sane these past couple of days; she would say how lucky she was to have known him, and how lucky to have that kiss. Their one and only real kiss. She'd tell him she would never forget it, or him.

Sighs of relief fluttered through the bar, as the sirens faded. The Indian woman signaled the waiter to pour her a second glass of champagne.

"What do you think happened?" Sunny asked, breathless from the scent of Eddie's skin as she kissed his cheek.

"Probably just some false alarm." He didn't want her to think about terrorists tonight. He wanted her to think of him. She sat next to him on the tall gray chair at the bar, lovely in a simple black dress. Instead of the boots she wore high satin sandals with a perky bow on the front. Her ankles looked fragile as a racehorse's and her feet good enough to kiss. He asked what she would like and when she said champagne he ordered the Grande Dame.

"Extravagant." Sunny smiled as the waiter opened the wine.

"It's a night for extravagance." He lifted his glass, meeting her eyes. "I haven't forgotten that kiss last night," he said. "In fact, Sonora Sky Coto de Alvarez, the memory of it was what brought me back here."

Sunny took a breath; she was getting in too deep when what she'd meant to do was to put a stop to it, before it really began. "I can't guarantee any more kisses," she said quickly.

He nodded. "Okay. Then where would you like to dine? I know a wonderful Japanese place in Cannes, or we could try the fish place on the beach in Golfe Juan. Or if you're tired, then right here in the hotel again."

His phone gave a muted beep and he excused himself and turned away.

The young bartender poured the champagne and said to Sunny, "There's been a robbery, at the jeweler's, La Fontaine." He frowned, worried. "I grew up here in Monte Carlo, things like this never used to happen. That's why people live here, they're not afraid the way they are in places like Mexico City or São Paulo."

Sunny turned as Maha Mondragon said hello. "Remember me, Madame Alvarez," Maha said, "I spoke to you last night?"

"Of course." How could Sunny forget the mysterious warning and the advice for her future.

"This may sound strange, *madame,* but allow me to explain. I am drawn to you because I see you are troubled. Your vulnerability reminds me of myself, many years ago. It is a dangerous place, emotionally, to allow yourself to be. Let me just say, Madame Alvarez, that if you need help, then I—this *stranger,* you might say—will help you."

Sunny looked into her beautiful eyes, saw something she knew was goodness, as well as mystery. Maha Mondragon had read her situation perfectly; she knew Sunny was in trouble; knew she was on dangerous ground with Eddie; and also with Kitty.

"I don't know what to say, except—thank you," she murmured.

"Though we do not know each other, think of me as a friend you can trust," Maha spoke softly.

"But *who* are you?" Sunny asked.

"I am a jewelry designer." Maha indicated her fabulous necklace, a heavy piece studded with cabochon rubies swirled in gold and studded with tiny diamonds, like stars around the planets. It was spectacular.

"My jewelry is one of a kind. It's handmade by superb Indian artisans, men whose families have been working in the same craft for a century or more, and believe me they are true artists. I sell to exclusive stores in Europe, but now my business is expanding and I need some help. Remember I told you last night to take the chances life offers you? Well, tonight, *madame,* I am offering you that chance."

Still on the phone, Eddie raised an apologetic eyebrow at Sunny, excused himself again and went back to his call.

Maha said, "I'm looking at you and seeing a woman in trouble, a woman in need. But I also see a woman who is trustworthy. That is why I'm offering you a job. It will be very different from what you are used to, but very exciting because it involves traveling back and forth to India."

Sunny said, astonished, "But I already have a job. I have a PR company to take care of. I should go back to L.A.—"

"This will not take all of your time. You could certainly combine both. Only if you wish to accept, of course," Maha added, with a smile that showed perfect white teeth. "I must be in Europe for longer periods, and what I need is a trusted go-between, someone to pick up my jewelry from Rajasthan—don't worry it will all be declared to customs, it's all quite legal. And also to return other pieces that are not quite right, or perhaps not selling, so the jewels can be recycled into new designs. Naturally, all of the pieces are very expensive, though perhaps not as expensive as the diamonds I've just heard were stolen from La Fontaine."

Maha looked at Sunny's stunned face and laughed. "I can see I've overwhelmed you. And your companion is waiting. I'm sorry to disturb your evening, but promise me one thing, Madame Alvarez, that you will consider my proposition. And in turn I promise you it will be lucrative, as well as exciting." Her beautiful dark eyes met Sunny's. "Besides," she added gently, "I know I'm looking at a woman desperate for some excitement in her life. Trust me, you will find it in Mumbai."

With a stroke of her silky hand along Sunny's bare arm, Maha walked back to her own table, gorgeous in a deep blue chiffon sari bordered with aqua beads that slid around her body as she walked. Beauty was Maha Mondragon.

chapter 16

Allie and Pru had managed to arrive on the day they had first planned and would surprise Sunny.

"Listen to me, Pru," Allie said, as she dragged her friend by the hand through Nice airport. "You're in the South of France. You are about to meet my dearest friend, a woman who not so long ago saved my life, when a killer was stalking me."

"I read about it in *The New York Times*," Pru said, out of breath and huffing as Allie hurried her on. "For God's sake, Allie, slow down."

Allie slowed to a regular walk instead of the fast gallop she had adopted years ago in an effort to outrun the paparazzi. They still caught her though, even now, when she was no longer a "movie star." Well, except here in France where she'd played a couple of roles in small French films whose scripts she'd really liked, and with directors she admired. Oddly, to her they were the most rewarding movies of her career, though her vineyard was now her true "love." Along with Ronnie.

Darling Ron Perrin, her husband, who was ready to drop anything and everything to make her happy, to take care of her, to love her. Ronnie was the only man who could make her feel like a girl again, that young girl he had met and helped up the ladder of fame more than twenty years ago. He was a bastard, but she loved him.

Tonight she had called Ronnie who, because his Cessna was undergoing repairs, had immediately chartered a small plane and had them flown directly to Nice. He said it wasn't worth getting the big plane out for such a short trip, though he would if she wanted. Allie hadn't wanted. All she wanted was to get to Sunny as soon as possible. And now here they were, earlier than Sunny expected.

She kept telling herself what had happened couldn't be true; that Sunny would never leave Mac. Mac and Sunny were a pair, a duo, true lovers in the best sense of the word. Sunny was ditzy and funny and clever; she rode a Harley, she had a business degree from Wharton, she ran her own successful PR company. And she loved Mac Reilly to death. Had done since the moment they met at a Malibu party, "eyes across the room," that sort of thing. And Mac was a goner from that moment. He loved his Sunny, even more than he loved his dog Pirate, and that was saying something. Mac would have died for Sunny, but he would not give up "detecting" or whatever he called it, helping victims, finding killers, reuniting lost souls on his TV show . . . solving crimes that other people had given up on, including in many cases the police. For Mac, that came first, as it always had in his life.

"I think he's a man afraid of commitment," Allie said to Pru, as they walked out to where several drivers stood holding cards aloft with clients' names written on them.

"Who is?" Pru asked, thankful to have stopped for a minute. She had put on so much weight in the last few months she no longer felt like herself. She was inhabiting somebody else's body. Even her hair did not seem like her own anymore. And her face resembled the full moon she could glimpse outside the glass doors, shining down over the Riviera.

What was she *doing* here in the Riviera? Land of bikinis and babes, hot women and even hotter men? Why hadn't she just told Allie she would stay home and not have to juggle her way through the chic town of Monte Carlo, with only a drab caftan to wear. Even a nondrab caftan, perhaps soft and velvety, or thin and flowing in gauzy pink lawn or something, would still be a caftan. And she would still be the overweight lump of a friend of the glamorous movie star.

But that was why Pru had called Allie in the first place. She'd known instinctively Allie was the only one who might be able to help her. Allie had always been beautiful, even as a kid in high school she was a knockout. And how Allie had hated all those trashy small-town boys hitting on her, talking about her, saying bad things that Pru had known were lies. Allie was as "pure as the driven snow," as the saying goes. And then she made a bad marriage to a rich older man, and later, humiliated and saddened, divorced and moved on. "Hopefully," Pru had said, "to bigger and better." In Allie's case, after more than a few adversities with her career and men, as well as with Ron, that had come true. Not so, though, for Pru.

"There he is." Allie waved at the driver holding the card that said PERRIN and the man hurried forward to take their bags. A small one for Allie, a larger one for Pru. Paparazzi flashbulbs went off in their faces and Allie grabbed Pru's hand again and made a run for it.

Pru climbed thankfully into the car, tucking her long skirt underneath her legs, which, oddly, were the only part of her that had remained thin. She still had good legs though now they were hidden, like the rest of her. She hated that red caftan; it was meant to be Christmassy and now it only reminded her of cranberry sauce. And it certainly did not go with her complexion, which had now somehow become too pink.

"Tomorrow, we are going to get you some new clothes," Allie said, turning to look at her.

"Hah! A horse blanket would be about right I think."

"At least it'll be a chic horse blanket." Allie laughed and Pru, always verging on tears of self-pity, found that she was laughing along with her.

Pru rolled down the window and sniffed the air. "I could swear I smell jasmine."

"You do," Allie agreed.

Pru sniffed again. "But it's December."

"And this is Nice, one of the great flower capitals of the world. Stuff grows here that you'd never find in the States at this time of year. Oh, Pru, this place, the Riviera, the Côte d'Azur, whatever name you want to give it, is special. It has a magic that can cure all ills. I swear it can, as they say in the Bible, *restore your soul*. Believe me, Pru, and believe in yourself, because you will leave here a new woman."

Pru shook her head. She was cautious now. No more flights of fancy for her. Her man had cheated on her, he'd ditched her for another woman; and now she had no hope of finding anybody else to love her, because she was so overweight and unlovable. Oh God, she would never be loved again! Never sleep in a man's arms again, never know the intimacy of a hard body on hers.

"It won't happen," she said flatly.

"Trust me." Allie looked at her, without touching. She did not want Pru to burst into tears again. Not now when the car was pulling up in front of the hotel and young men in white uniforms were rushing to open their doors.

"Welcome to Monte Carlo," the doorman said. "Welcome back, Miss Ray."

"Madame Perrin." Smiling, she corrected him. "And thank you."

There was no need to check in. The manager himself in a black suit and bow tie, came personally to greet Allie.

"We have given you a penthouse suite, Madame Perrin. It's charming, I think you will like it."

"Why, that's very kind of you." Allie smiled her thanks. She was still treated as the movie star despite her "retirement" from Hollywood.

"I saw your last movie, the French one, *Les Étrangers sur la Plage*. It was very moving, your performance."

Allie nodded her thanks again. "I'm so glad you enjoyed it."

The lavish Sun King penthouse suite was, Pru said, looking around, stunned, magnificent.

"I should travel with you more often," she said, walking onto the terrace that swept round the corner suite. The insistent sounds of police sirens and ambulances shattered the silence again. The manager apologized.

"Some trouble in Monte Carlo tonight, a robbery at a jewelry store. I'm so sorry, this never happens here."

"I've been to New York," Pru said, "I'm used to it."

But Allie wasn't. Allie was a country girl now, the true country girl she had always wanted to be. She loved the absolute silence of a country night; a silence that, if you stood still and simply listened became full of noises: the rustlings in the grass; the coo of a dove; the wind in the tree, the flutter of leaves spiraling to earth. "The country," it had turned out, was never truly silent.

Allie asked the manager for Sunny's room number. He gave it to her and he told her that he understood Madame Alvarez was in the bar. "With a companion."

Allie wondered who the *companion* was? Had Mac beaten her to it? If so then Ron must have told him. Dammit, Ron should *not* have done that. She'd needed to talk to Sunny first; now her chances of finding out the truth would be ruined.

She turned and looked at Pru, still out on the terrace, still in that awful cranberry frock that in fact would have fit a woman twice her size. Pru had brought along a suitcase that Allie knew must contain similar enormous clothes, enough for a month.

She shrugged, she didn't have time to argue clothes right now. "Come on, Pru," she called. "Powder your nose and comb your hair. And put this on." She handed her a gossamer shawl, woven of cashmere so fine it must have been made from the combings of the tiniest baby goats, in a pale gray color that Allie hoped would tone down the cranberry caftan and Pru's pink complexion.

"Where are we going?" Pru stared doubtfully at the gray pashmina. She'd hoped for a shower and room service.

"No time to argue," Allie said, throwing a black cardigan over her T-shirt and buttoning it to the neck. With her blond hair pulled back, black pants and ballerina flats, she looked all of eighteen.

"We're off to the bar."

chapter 17

Back at her table in the bar, Maha glanced at her watch, then checked the entrance. A small frown creased her perfect brow. From where she sat she could see part of the foyer, plus the doors to the restaurant, and also keep an eye on Sunny sitting up at the bar with the very attractive man, who's name Maha had found out, was Eduardo Johanssen.

Maha read Sunny's body language perfectly as she leaned into him. Interested, but restrained. She wondered why so restrained, with a man that attractive. Perhaps Eduardo was married and this was a secret assignation, a winter rendezvous, in the South of France. She thought it interesting, but hopefully not interesting enough to ruin her plans for Sunny.

Her assistant, Sharon Barnes stalked into the bar. Sharon was Australian, over six feet in her heels with the striking looks of a model, which she had been at an earlier point in her life. Now, though she was hitting forty. She didn't look it but it was still too old for a model who had never really, or at least only for one season, been the hit of the runway. Since then Sharon had traveled around, working the Eastern European countries, organizing model searches, running her own small agency in Prague. It had not been very successful though, until she had met Maha three years ago.

You could never call Sharon beautiful, not with her strong features, her short buzz cut, and too-long skinny limbs, but she had beautiful eyes, dark green with winging brows.

Sharon cast a glance at Maha and without so much as a hello or a kiss, threw herself into a chair and signaled the waiter. "Scotch," she barked. "On the rocks. And make it a double."

Maha said nothing.

Sharon's hand tapped nervously on the chair arm.

Maha said nothing. "So?" Sharon asked finally, one brow raised.

The waiter brought the Scotch and poured more champagne. Champagne was Maha's only addiction. Besides money, of course.

"So. Everything is fine," Maha said.

"God, I'm dying for a friggin' cigarette." Sharon threw her head back, an anguished look on her face. Sharon's addictions were quite clear.

"You could always go outside and smoke."

"You've gotta be kidding." Sharon took a gulp of the Scotch. "Stand outside, like one of those Russian hookers with skirts up to their bums and no knickers, smoking and eyeing the blokes. I don't think so."

Maha laughed at her description and her Aussie accent.

"You're always so fuckin' calm and happy," Sharon grumbled.

Maha adjusted her blue sari over her olive-tan shoulder. "I see nothing to be unhappy about."

Sharon shifted her handbag and the shopping bag that said JOSEPH on it, from her lap to the adjacent chair. "Look what I bought," she said, fishing out a plain cashmere sweater. "Gray, like these chairs."

"Interesting," Maha said, not meaning it and Sharon grinned. Maha was a master of understatement.

"On sale," she said. "Forty percent off."

Maha nodded as she raised a welcoming hand to the two men from the previous night, accompanied by a short, brown-haired woman, expensively dressed and toting an orange Hermès Birkin bag. The men carried her many shopping bags.

"I see that the sales won you over too." Maha dropped a quick kiss on the woman's powdered cheek, catching the scent of her freshly applied perfume.

"Sales make a good diversion," she said, embracing Sharon, while the two men shook Maha's hand. They did not kiss her, treating her with respect, as their employer.

"Where did you park?" Maha asked.

"At the Casino," the tall man said.

Maha watched Sharon, who, giving in to her cigarette addiction, fished a pack and a lighter out of her bag and made for the door.

"I'm joining the hooker brigade," she called over her shoulder, making Maha laugh and the others stare, astonished.

Then, like the other groups of businessmen in the bar, they leaned their heads together to talk, ironically, considering what was going on just down the street, about the jewelry business, though Maha's jewels were never sold in classic stores like La Fontaine.

Outside, where Sharon was smoking her cigarette, strolling nervously back and forth across the square, the sound of police sirens and ambulances still wailed into the night. After a while, she lit a second cigarette from the stub of the first, told herself she was gonna die of friggin' tobacco-induced lung cancer, added that she didn't give a shit, then shut her eyes and covered her ears to stop the screaming of the sirens in the night.

chapter 18

There was a police cordon round Nice airport when Mac arrived. Soldiers toting weapons inspected every passenger. Sirens wailed in the distance and helicopters hovered overhead. There was no doubt something was seriously up.

A bank robbery? Mac wondered. But this was one of the safest regions of the world. Surely nobody would attempt such a thing. He thought about it while waiting in line at immigration. It was Christmas, and everybody would have been off guard, celebrating, with the spirit of goodwill in their hearts. Except the bad guys. And bad guys always knew how to take advantage of a slack situation.

"It's a jewel robbery," someone in front of him said. The rumor spread quickly down the line. "Monte Carlo. One of those expensive shops, like Cartier or Fontaine."

Interesting, Mac thought, a jewel robbery at Christmas. Somebody was going to get a nice gift. But he was not going to get involved in any robbery, be it bank or jewelry store. He was only here to be with Sunny.

When he walked through the green light at customs, carrying the small bag he had packed hastily before the quick trip to the airport—it was Christmas Day and there was no traffic—he was stopped along with everyone else, and had to wait a frustrating ten minutes to be searched before being waved on.

He was hurrying through the main arrivals hall, heading for the taxi rank when he spotted the Police Inspector, whom he knew from last year, when they had worked together on the series of art thefts taking place along the Riviera. The Inspector looked harassed and tense and whatever had happened Mac knew it must be big and probably dangerous.

He called out to him and the Inspector swung round, throwing his hands in the air, saying, "I might have known I would see you here. Back like a bad penny to haunt me again."

"No more hauntings." Mac grinned, referring to Chez La Violette, the villa he'd rented the previous summer. "This looks like more trouble than that."

"It is, *mon vieux,* trust me, it is." The Inspector gave Mac a sharp glance, but did not ask why he was here without Sunny. He was a Frenchman and too discreet for that. Instead he said, "All the roads are blocked, you'll get nowhere."

Mac told him where he was going. "Then you had better come with me. I'm driving back there now. They've worked over another La Fontaine. That place must have nothing left by now, they already did the Paris store on Christmas Eve. Come on, Mac, ride with me. I'll drop you off at your hotel."

Speeding past the outlying cop wagons, waved through red lights, the Inspector brought Mac up to date on the robberies. "Two, here in France," he said, "plus one in London, one in Rome, Berlin, Milan . . ."

"You're looking at a lot of loot to be disposed of," Mac said. "You have any idea who they are using?"

"None." The Inspector gave an angry shrug, then smoothed his smart uniform jacket back down again. He adjusted his cap to a better angle, peering out the window at the helicopter lights sweeping the coastline. "Nobody knows how they can get away with those diamonds without cutting them and that will more than halve their value. The other stuff, emeralds, rubies, they'll get rid of easily enough, they'll already have men in place for that. But the diamonds are another matter."

"How much do you reckon they're worth?"

The Inspector took a deep breath. "In Paris, one necklace alone was worth over twenty million. They took rings, each worth many hundreds of thousands. And the unset stones," he shrugged again, "well, La Fontaine is still guarding their real value even from us, probably because they had more than the tax man knew about. But trust me, Mac Reilly, we are talking hundreds of millions."

"But *here*, in Monte Carlo?" Mac couldn't help adding, "Of all places, surely the safest on earth."

"Certainly, along with Zurich, it's one of the safest in Europe. As yet we have no knowledge of exactly what was taken tonight. They used the same format, expensively dressed women shoppers wearing masks, Marilyn Monroe if you can believe it. They hijacked the security doorman, shot out the security camera, took all the mobile phones, cut the lines and locked the door after them. There was no alarm, no sign that anything was wrong until somebody walked by, saw lights on and people lying on the floor. That was when she called us."

"She?" Mac looked at him curiously. He would have thought it would have been a man who sounded the alarm.

"A female. Anonymous. Said she didn't want to be involved, but that something was wrong at La Fontaine. My men have the place surrounded, the area's cordoned off. We sent ambulances."

Mac's eyebrows rose. "There are casualties?"

"It would seem so." The Inspector's voice had a grim edge to it. "Here we are," he added as the big car swept past the square and along the boulevard to where an area was roped off with yellow police tape. Emergency vehicles stood by along with dozens of cop cars, blue lights flashing. A couple of fire trucks waited on the other side of the street and police photographers busied themselves taking shots of the storefront. Lights were on in the shop and Mac could see uniformed men inside.

"Sorry I won't be able to get you to your hotel," the Inspector said, talking on his mobile at the same time to somebody inside the store. "I'm needed here."

Mac thanked him as he climbed out of the car. Halogen lights suddenly bathed the scene in hard white industrial light. As he watched, a black body bag was carried from the store and loaded into a dark van Mac knew must be from the coroner's department. He felt a familiar clench of anger in his stomach. The bastards had killed someone, probably the security guard or some innocent store assistant. God, what men would do for money. For some, life was meaningless in the face of millions of dollars.

He turned and walked quickly away, waved through by the cops who had seen him arrive with their chief, hearing the wail of even more sirens.

The hard white light disappeared into the soft melting darkness of a Côte d'Azur night as he quickened his step, thinking only of Sunny. Sunny was here. They would find each other again, he would tell her how much he loved her; what she meant to him. He would marry her whenever she wanted. Just please God let her still love him. Let her leaving him not be the end.

Pacing the square, smoking her second cigarette, Sharon debated the rival lures of the bar and a double Scotch on the rocks against another cigarette. She shivered, hearing the sirens, seeing the halogen glow to the sky in the east. She was both drawn to it and repelled by it.

She saw an attractive man carrying a bag, making for the hotel. In an almost reflex female action, she smoothed her skirt, settled her little black fur jacket more closely around her face, holding it with an unbejeweled hand. Her large diamond studs glinted in the lamplight. Her eyes followed him. He had not even noticed her.

Sharon's eyes narrowed as she watched him striding in an easy lope up the hotel steps. She knew him from somewhere, she could swear she did.

Kitty Ratte had been forced to park a couple of blocks away due to the police cordon and had to walk to the hotel. She too saw the man and guessed immediately from Sunny's description that it was Mac Reilly. She eyed him appreciatively. He was too good to miss; as good as the "companion" Sunny was with the other night. Maybe even better. Great. Two men were always better than one. And with Sunny either too innocent or else too dumb, the field was clear for a little play. And "play" was what Kitty really loved. In fact she made her living from it.

chapter 19

Pru was starving, as always, and Allie knew she'd better get her some dinner, and also get some food into Sunny, who was probably starving too, only in the opposite way to Pru; from not even thinking about food instead of the desire for it. She couldn't believe her eyes when she saw Mac walking across the foyer.

"Oh my God." Allie clasped Pru by her plump shoulder. "He beat me to it."

"Who?" Pru folded the flimsy gray shawl over her bosom in an effort to look thinner.

"Mac Reilly, of course."

"You are kidding me!" Pru peered shortsightedly across the spacious marble hall. "I always watch his show. He's so cute . . . I mean in the nicest possible way, not sort of jerky or showbiz or anything. Just, well you know, *nice.*"

"He is that," Allie agreed. "Except when it comes to pinning him down to marriage. And now what do I do? Look, he's giving the bellboy his bag, he's not even going to his room, he's heading straight for the bar."

"But that's where *Sunny* is."

Pru was so excited her soft brown hair seemed to stand on end all on its own without any of the vigorous back-combing and spray she usually gave it. Pru had been back-combing her hair for two decades and still couldn't accept the fact that a great fluff of teased hair was not where it was at these days. Now, of course, she no longer bothered and her hair simply hung, stringy, around her shoulders.

Allie and Pru watched Mac walk toward the bar. A young woman preceded him; a slender young blonde in a short white dress carrying a bouquet of lily of the valley. Her hair was pinned with a diamond crescent and a spray of jasmine that Pru could smell from fifty paces.

And behind Mac, hot on his heels, in fact, came another woman, this one with flame-red hair that reflected the light in a halo of dazzling color. She hurried in a fast knock-kneed trot, the skirt of her orange shirtdress riding up on plump thighs, Chanel purse swinging from her dangling arm, Dior earrings swinging in her ears.

Behind *her* came another woman: tall, stalking on towering heels, little black fur jacket clutched to her throat and with a smoker's cough that could be heard from where they stood.

"Well. How about that," Allie said. "Mac has a female escort."

"What shall we do?" Pru asked, thrilled at the thought of meeting Mac Reilly.

Allie considered. Should she let them meet, let them talk to each other, work it out alone? But she was worried. Sunny had told her it was finished. Over. Sunny was distraught, not in her right mind, and Allie knew that when a woman's heart was broken she could not think properly. In that state thoughts just milled around women's heads . . . *he said this . . . he did that . . . I told him . . . he told me . . . I should have done this . . . that . . . whatever . . .* She couldn't just leave Sunny alone feeling like that. She would have to help her.

"So, okay," she told Pru. "We'll sneak into the bar and sit in a corner at the back, where they won't see us. If I think there's trouble we'll go help."

chapter 20

Sunny couldn't believe "the bride" was running into the bar again, still in her white shift, still clutching her posy of now-wilting lily of the valley. Again, she climbed onto a chair and demanded, "Martini. On the rocks. *S'il vous plaît.*"

The young bartender gave her an appraising look and shrugged; they got all sorts in bars, even ones as classy as this. The bride tossed back the drink in one long swallow, took a deep breath, stuck her chin in the air and stalked back out again, passing Mac Reilly at the entrance.

Surprised, Mac turned to look, wondering what a bride was doing alone in a bar. His glance caught that of a middle-aged woman with fiery red hair behind him. She gave him the eye and a come-on grin.

Eddie Johanssen knew he had fallen hard for Sunny. It was difficult not to. Sunny was beautiful but it was more than that. She had a natural charm, an ease, a flirty, girly air that took him out of his divorce troubles and into another world where life was fun. He wanted to hold her, to kiss her full lips that he knew would taste so sweet. He had not felt this way about a woman in forever. If only he could get Sunny to believe that there was life after the detective fiancé and perhaps a future for them . . .

Sunny was leaning into him, telling him how much she'd enjoyed being with him. "But . . ." She hesitated, and looked sadly at him.

Eddie hated that *but*. "But *what*?" He placed his hand over hers. "But *what*? Sunny. You told me you'd left Mac, that it was over. I saw how unhappy you were. Can't I be the one to console you?"

"Believe me, you're the only man who could." Sunny was aware of the pressure of his hand on hers. She could not allow this to go on. She must not. She turned her eyes away. And shocked, saw Mac.

How could it be anyone else in that faded T-shirt and the old black leather jacket? His chin was blue with stubble, his hair was rumpled and his eyes were tired.

Eddie realized who it must be. He took his hand away from Sunny's but she didn't even notice. She was looking at Mac. It was as though Eddie were no longer there.

Sunny's eyes linked with Mac's exactly the way they had the night they met at the cocktail party in Malibu. Time had stopped at that moment and it stopped again now. There were only the two of them in this room, in this hotel, in this world.

Kitty Ratte watched. She quickly took in the situation, saw the possibilities of the game. Her serpent's eyes hardened. "*So*," she whispered to herself. "*This is just perfect.*"

Eddie got up and walked to the far end of the bar. Kitty hurried after him. In their dark corner, watching, Allie and Pru held their breaths, afraid of what might happen.

Maha, flanked again by Sharon and her other employees also watched the little scene taking place; a scene so fraught with sensuality it hung in the air like an aura around the main players.

Mac walked over to Sunny. He held out his hand and she took it. She slid off the stool, adjusted her skirt, then, forgetting all about her purse which she left lying on the counter, and forgetting all about Eddie, with whom she had been so involved just minutes ago, she walked hand-in-hand with Mac Reilly, out of the bar, and through the marble foyer to the elevator.

They stopped and looked at each other.

"Room ten-oh-one," she whispered, and he pressed the button. He opened his arms and she fell into them.

"What took you so long?" she said.

chapter 21

Allie ran after them. Sleek as a greyhound, Pru thought watching. And twice as gorgeous, even dressed so simply. No flashy jewelry, no look-at-me over-the-top style. Allie Ray the woman was the same girl she had been in high school: modest, unassuming and almost totally unaware of her good looks. While Pru, of course, was now a fat unattractive female in her early forties, in a dreadful red caftan and Allie's very expensive cashmere pashmina that could have swaddled a babe, if Pru had had a child that is. Which now she would not. Never. Have children.

Her sigh was strong enough to have swept the erring husband out of bed along with his mistress, his new woman, whatever she was. All Pru knew was that she had worked in the same office. That's how they had met. The whole situation was one long cliché. Didn't they always say it was the coworker, the neighbor, the best friend? Now Pru knew only too well they were right. Proximity, availability, opportunity. The "come-on," and no consequences. Only now there were. Consequences. One of them being that she had eaten herself into a decline and didn't know how to get out of it.

In the foyer, half-hidden behind a giant floral display on the large round table, Allie saw Sunny in Mac's arms standing by the elevators. Then Sunny suddenly stepped back and rushed outside, with Mac hurrying after her.

Fingers crossed, Allie decided there was nothing she could do to help right now. She would call Sunny later, tell her she had gotten there earlier than expected, had seen her with Mac and to please call and tell her what was going on.

Meanwhile she'd better get back to Pru Hilson or she would probably faint. If ever a woman needed straightening out it was Pru. She had lost her man, for whatever reason, and Allie did not believe it was all Pru's fault. From what she could gather (she had never met the husband, had only seen the photograph that Pru still carried in her wallet, staring at it like it was the holy grail, touching his imprinted face with a finger, still in love, or so it seemed) the husband was a shit. Anyhow, Allie had seen his photo and she did not care for what she saw. An arrogant red-faced man, the kind who always wore dark glasses so you couldn't read his eyes, a smile on his fleshy lips, a hand resting on a dark green Jaguar sport car that Allie would bet he was wishing was a Bentley.

"Come on, Pru," she said, back in the bar. "Let's go get something to eat." And she swept Pru quickly out in front of her, telling her what she had seen as they went.

Maha watched her go. "That's Allie Ray," she said, and the others swiveled their heads to look.

"Still beautiful," Maha commented.

Maha was also thinking about the little scene in the bar. The emotions had been palpable between Sunny and the man who had suddenly taken her over. Eddie Johanssen had been left in the dust. Sunny had not even excused herself, not even said goodbye and good luck. Still, you never knew, it might not be over with Johanssen; the game might continue. Maha hoped whatever was going on would not divert Sunny from the plan she had in mind for her. Sunny Alvarez needed a new life and Maha knew exactly how to give it to her. Besides, interestingly, Kitty Ratte had already moved in on Eddie.

Maha watched Kitty giving him the same sweetly sympathetic glances she had given Sunny just the other night, from eyes as hard and shiny as blue sea glass. Corruption is a form of evil and instinctively, Maha knew Kitty Ratte was a professional in corruption.

The bar felt suddenly too stuffy, too filled with perfume, too many nerve endings twanging. As when the bride had galloped in for her martini and left, angst trembled again in the air.

The bar was quiet now because all roads had been cordoned off due to the robbery. "Why don't we go up to my suite," Maha said to her companions. "We'll send down for dinner and talk some more."

Leaning on the bar, Eddie cradled his drink between cold hands. He had not realized how strongly he felt about Sunny until she walked out on him without so much as a backward glance. Not even an excuse me. Not even, oh by the way this is my ex-fiancé. Not even wait here, I'll be back. Not a promise of anything more between them. Yet he knew she felt the same strong attraction he did.

Now he did not know what to do, except just stay here and hope she would return.

"You should be angry," the woman sitting next to him said. "Sunny should not have left you like that."

Eddie swiveled his eyes to her, then turned away. He did not answer.

Looking at him, Kitty knew exactly what she was dealing with and knew he was exactly what she wanted. A rich man. A man with a past; a man in the throes of new love and lust; a man dazzled with new possibilities; a *vulnerable* man.

"I am a friend of Sunny's," she said, hitching herself higher on the chair. Her orange shirtdress slid open to midthigh. She noticed his sideways glance and smiled.

"I know Sunny so well," she added, speaking softly. "Sunny is an emotional woman and not responsible for her actions. I mean, how could she leave you, just like that? She told me you have been together for a while now, long enough to know that you care. Oh don't worry," she added quickly, pressing a gentle hand on Eddie's arm. "Sunny told me everything. But of course, I will never repeat it."

Eddie wondered what it was Sunny could have told her.

Kitty lowered her chin and gave him her demure up-glance smile filled with sympathy, as were her eyes. "Look, why not let me buy you a drink? Tell me your troubles? I promise, I'm a very good listener." She signaled the barman and ordered a Red Bull and a glass of red wine for herself and another vodka for him.

It was the older of the two barmen, the one with the silver hair. He deliberately avoided her eyes as he set the drinks in front of her. He knew what she was and he did not like women like Kitty bringing down the tone of his bar.

And Eddie did not notice the pill Kitty slipped into his drink. He turned to look at her.

"Here's to you." Kitty lifted her glass in a toast.

He stared at her, trying to take in the reality of her: the flame-red hair sweeping over blue eyes under puffy lids; the milkmaid cheeks; the prominent teeth; vulgar Dior earrings; the fleshy naked thighs. And, most of all, the sympathy that seemed to shine right out of her. And right now Eddie was a lonely man in need of consolation.

Kitty gave him an even broader smile. "Here's to good luck," she said, lifting the glass again, and this time he lifted his in response.

Suddenly, Eddie felt the need to talk and Kitty proved to be a good listener. She knew how to pat a man's hand, how to be sympathetic, letting him know at the same time that she found him very attractive.

An hour went by, maybe two. They were still at the bar and Sunny had not returned.

"I don't understand how she can't want you," Kitty was saying, running a hand lightly down Eddie's arm. "You're *so* attractive. So . . ." She smiled at him with her small secret blue eyes. "So *sexy*."

The pill she had slipped into his vodka was working. Eddie was staring at her, hypnotized, exactly the way Kitty wanted him.

"Believe me, Eddie Johanssen," she whispered. "I know what I am talking about. You don't know what you are missing. Sunny is a simple woman. There are things that a woman like me can do that would surprise you. After all, you and I both love sex, don't we? Come on now, admit it. Sunny will never do to you what I can."

The mention of Sunny's name jolted Eddie back to reality and away from Kitty's pinpoint eyes. He got unsteadily to his feet. "I have to leave." He felt very drunk, though he'd had only two vodkas. "Thank you for your company, Kitty." He didn't know what else to say. "You were good to listen to my . . . my . . ."

"Your *emotional* problems," Kitty said, so softly again he had to lean across to hear her. Then, quickly, she kissed him, a flutter of her open lips against his, a tiny suggestion of tongue that he could believe he either had, or had not, felt. That was Kitty's style. She was a professional, she knew her job and exactly how to play him.

"See you tomorrow," she called as he turned and made for the exit. "I'll be here." She did not add, "Even if Sunny is not," but she knew Eddie would get it. Blackmail was on her mind and she'd bet her last buck she could get Eddie.

chapter 22

When Sunny left Mac at the elevator, she ran outside, shivering in her little black dress.

Lights glittered on the boats and in the Casino, and the castle glowed on its rock like something from a fairy tale. The curve of the bay was a bejeweled necklace strung into infinity to the west, fading into the sweep of mountains to the east.

Mac stood looking at her. The distance between them was more than a mere few feet; it was a deep moat and he did not know if Sunny would let down the drawbridge so he could cross to the other side.

He said, "You asked what took me so long."

She did not reply. She did not even turn her head to look at him. Worried, he ran his hands through his already-rumpled dark hair.

"Sunny, let's go back inside. We can go to my room, and talk. You'll catch your death out here."

He put his hand on her shoulder and Sunny jumped. His touch was like an electric charge through the silken fabric of her dress. It was as though Mac were putting his brand on her again. He had already done that the first time they made love, when even the air around them had seemed illuminated from the electric shock of their kisses.

She turned and walked away. He followed. The police sirens still howled and the halogens pooled in a white glare. Helicopters clattered noisily overhead, catching them in their beams.

She stole a look, to see whether he was keeping an eye on the police activity that was so much a part of his life, but his head was down and for once he seemed oblivious. God, he was so handsome in his own particular roughed-up way, the way she loved. But she had left him for a good reason and she must keep to that resolve. It was time to become her own woman and not merely a permanent fiancée. Even though she wanted to, she couldn't simply fall into Mac's arms the way she had by the elevator and say, as she always did, exactly what was on her mind. Like, *what took you so long.* When what she should have said was *you bastard, go marry somebody else. I'm gone.*

But she knew Mac was not going to marry any other woman. The truth was, Mac was "married" to his work.

Mac saw her shiver and took off his leather jacket. He swung her round, stuffing her arms into the sleeves, rolling the cuffs. He put his hands on her shoulders. His grip tightened as he said, "You are the love of my life, Sunny, I'll never let you go. I'm so sorry. I am so *so* sorry. I behaved selfishly, I didn't think of you, I put myself first."

The wind blew Sunny's long dark hair into her face and she put up a hand to push it away, along with the tears.

Mac was thinking of her falling into his arms just minutes ago by the elevator. "What took you so long," she'd said, and he had been swept with relief. She had not really run away, he'd thought, closing his arms around her; she had simply been upset, she'd felt rejected. And he *had* rejected her, putting off the wedding once again.

Truthfully, he had not thought marriage meant that much to Sunny. The idea of marriage had always been like a game between them. Last year, after all the murder and mayhem in St. Tropez, when they were back home, he had asked her to marry him. "Right here, right now," he'd said. "Marry me." But she'd thought the timing was wrong, or something. Who knew with women? And so their delightful game of Sunny and Mac had continued, until this fixation of hers with getting married in the New Year had come up. Of course he'd agreed. He wanted to stay with Sunny forever, however long life gave him, but when it came to setting a date, something else always came up. "Someone always needs you more," Sunny had said, with an edge of sadness in her voice that had never been there before.

Normally, Sunny was like her name; a sunshiny person, a woman who radiated joy of life, a woman who understood love, who understood Mac, who loved him. But right now she was a woman radiating indifference, and right now, Mac could not blame her.

"Sunny," he pleaded.

Sunny turned to look into his familiar face, wondering if what he had just said was true. If she did agree to return to L.A., to their life, to her work, his work, their dogs, the Malibu beach cottage, would it be the same all over again? She recalled what Maha Mondragon had said about taking the chances life offered her, and that she should not be afraid of the future. There was something mystical about Maha that drew Sunny to her. Perhaps Maha really could see into the future. And if so, had she meant her future with Mac? But oh God, she loved him.

Her eyes reflected the lamplight as she looked at him. "You bastard," she said.

Mac hung his head, acknowledging his guilt. He said, "But I still love you."

"Even though you don't want to marry me?"

"I can only repeat, I love you Sunny. I always will."

"I bought the wedding dress," she said. "Lace."

"But you're not a 'lace' girl."

Sunny smiled. Dammit Mac knew her too well. Or thought he did. Right now she had something he didn't know about her, and his name was Eddie Johanssen.

Shocked, she remembered she had simply left Eddie without so much as an "excuse me I must go," or even "I'm sorry." She wondered whether he had waited for her to return, and if he'd guessed who it was she had walked off with.

He must, she supposed, with a tinge of regret because, with Eddie, everything had been so simple, so outside the realms of everyday reality, right from the beginning on the Paris flight, alone together for all those hours. It had been a relief to have a man's complete attention and interest. After all she was a woman alone. And vulnerable.

But Mac knew nothing of her "romance" with her new savior; Mac had always been that savior. Mac had been her entire life. They were two as one. Together. Forever. Or so she had thought.

"I already knew about the dress," Mac told her, still standing a couple of feet away, though it might as well have been a thousand miles. "I went to your place, looking for you. I found it hanging in the closet. I brought it here."

Stunned, she reached across that thousand-mile gap, touched his face, felt the harsh stubble under her fingers. *"You brought my dress?"*

"It's your wedding dress," he said softly.

"I never really liked it," she said.

He caught her hand, turned it palm up, kissed it.

"Oh God." Sunny shook her head. "You know me too well, Mac Reilly."

And she crossed that chasm between them and stepped into his arms.

Their kiss was "a thousand kisses deep," as Leonard Cohen had sung, so often, about the emotion they now felt. A thousand kisses deep, a thousand touches, a thousand words of love were between them as their lips met.

Sunny felt that kissing Mac was a line to the real life she had envisioned for them, the life they had enjoyed so much; being together; always laughing; keeping Tesoro from fighting with Pirate; dinner on the deck of his tiny Malibu cottage in a bikini, or wrapped up against the wind or the summer fog, she playing Lady Detective to his Private Eye.

She pulled away, ran her hand down his rough cheek, looked sadly at him.

"What is it?" he asked.

Sunny was remembering the "bride" storming into the bar and demanding a martini. Had that bride been stood up too? Not once, but twice? Sunny could never put herself in that position. She knew Mac's life's work would always come first. She understood, but this time she was determined to do something about it.

"We need to start all over again," she said. "Love isn't all it's about. We need to really talk, to really see each other, to evaluate our love."

"Evaluate our love," Mac repeated, uncomprehendingly. "But I told you, Sunny, *you* are the love of my life."

She shrugged off the leather jacket, pushed it back at him. "It all depends, Mac Reilly," she said. And she turned and walked quickly back across the square.

"Sunny." Clutching the jacket, Mac yelled after her.

"I'll speak to you tomorrow."

Her voice floated toward him under the rustle of the wind in the trees, and the wail of the police cars and ambulances.

The Inspector's car stopped next to him with a squeal of tires.

"Get in," the Inspector said. "I'll take you back to your hotel."

Mac shrugged. "Thanks, but no need, it's just across the road."

The Inspector gestured to the activity behind him. "One woman killed," he said. "It's not a good scene, my friend. Call me tomorrow, perhaps you can be of help."

"I'll think about it," Mac said, as he began to walk back to the hotel.

chapter 23

Maha Mondragon's friends were looking a little wilted. They were in her suite and had eaten a little, drunk a lot, though Maha herself was always careful and anyhow only ever drank champagne. Besides, they were here on business.

The windows were open but now there were only the normal sounds of city silence: cars, voices, laughter and the faint hiss of the sea.

Maha had summoned the room service waiters and two of them were clearing the table. Sharon was smoking out on the terrace because Maha could not stand the smell of cigarettes in her room. The brown-haired woman was sitting quietly, eyes half-rolled in her head as though about to fall asleep. A plain woman, Maha thought, watching her, with her round face and too-short chin, but when she tried she could look expensive, which was always a plus.

Giorgio, the older of the two men, always looked good: tall, narrow-hipped, extremely well-dressed; a man who could go anywhere. Italian, of course. Only Italians looked like that. And then there was Ferdie. Argentinean, an ex–polo player fallen on hard times. No more polo ponies for Ferdie, no more royal invitations; no more blondes lining up, champagne glass in one hand, the other held out for the Cartier baubles, the black American Express card, anything they could get.

Maha felt quite sorry for Ferdie, who was a man used to the best and who had now to settle for a lot less. He was useful, though. Men in his position always were. They were willing to do anything for instant rewards.

The waiters bowed a polite good night and Maha walked into the bedroom, picked up a large canvas travel bag trimmed with tan leather, returned and put it on the dining table.

She unzipped the bottom section of the bag, which was about twenty-inches-by-twenty, the correct size for a carry-on when flying, detached it, then began to take out most of its velvet-wrapped contents.

She unwrapped them and put them on the table. There were a dozen gold bejeweled necklaces fashioned in the famous Kundan style from Rajasthan, where instead of "claws" or "prongs" the gold was wrapped thickly around precious stones, so they appeared to be embedded. Earrings, bracelets, brooches, all gleamed under the chandelier, like a display in a store window. One necklace featured large rubies of a color that used to be called "pigeon's blood," though Maha thought they were more the rosy-red of a fading sunset. There were emeralds too, for which Rajasthan was famous, more precious even than the rubies. And of course, there were sapphires, blue as Maha's sari; as blue as the summer Mediterranean in the deep of the evening and bluer than the eyes of the man she remembered had come into the bar and taken Sunny Alvarez away, as though no one else existed.

With a pang of alarm, Maha suddenly realized who that man was. She had seen him on television. His was not the type of docudrama program she usually watched; she was more into romance, society romances where everyone was well dressed and the fights were "civilized." Unlike real life, of course, but what mattered was that they took her mind temporarily off reality, and that was all she asked. What worried her was that Mac Reilly was concerned with real life, and with death, and that he was very good at what he did.

"My God, Maha," Sharon exclaimed, coming back in from the

terrace, where she had carelessly stubbed out her cigarette. To the Sharons of this world, every surface, be it beach, terrace, or street, was an ashtray. "Do you mean to tell me you lug all that pricey jewelry around in that *bag*? It should be in the safe!"

"I have no faith in 'safes.'" Maha said. "Out in open view is much better. Besides, nobody is going to steal anything in this hotel except maybe iPods and cell phones, and anyhow my designs are too identifiable for a petty crook to dispose of. No, I think a bag, zipped and locked, of course, is much the best way to keep anything really valuable."

She arranged the jewelry on the polished tabletop and her employees grouped round as she produced a set of drawings.

She looked at the four, assessing them, wondering about their worth to her now.

"Congratulations," she said. "This was the most important night of your lives. You are already winners. Now we must get to work. This jewelry is the key to your future. Without it you do not exist."

Sharon had caught Maha's hard assessing look and she fixed it in her memory to be brought out later. Much later, when things needed to be finally sorted out between them. Now, though, like the others, she paid full attention to what Maha had to say.

chapter 24

In her Sun King suite, Allie was waiting patiently for Pru to emerge from the bathroom. She glanced at her watch one more time, pacing back and forth, mentally thanking the management for the suite because the two of them together in a double room might have been hard to take. The fact that the suite had two bathrooms might be its biggest asset because Pru had been in hers for at least an hour, splashing around in the tub, and buzzing the hair dryer, over which Allie had heard her alternately sniveling and cursing the husband. Whose name, she had been informed, was Byron.

"Like the lord," Pru told Allie.

"You mean the Lord *God*?" Allie asked, astonished.

"*Lord Byron,* the poet, silly." Despite her woes Pru had laughed which instantly changed her face to the merry imp Allie remembered from school. "Forgot all those poetry classes, didn't you?" Pru added. "The Romantics. Hah! Little did we know!"

Allie guessed she meant little did they know what effect "the Romantics" would have on their lives.

"I've come to believe in romance," she told Pru, who'd said "Hah!" once again before she'd disappeared into the bathroom. And that was over an hour ago.

Allie was worried about Pru, but she was more worried about

Sunny. All she wanted to do now was get Pru into bed with an Ambien, hope she'd get a good night's rest, then she'd call Sunny. She needed to know her friend was all right and exactly what had happened between her and Mac tonight. To say nothing of what had gone down earlier to make Sunny take the drastic step of leaving him.

She had too much on her mind even to think about Ron until her BlackBerry rang.

"Oh, it's you," she said when Ron said, "Hi, what's goin' on."

"Well, excuse *me*," Ron said. "I thought at least I'd get a 'Hi, hon, I miss you.'"

"Hi, hon, I miss you."

Allie had a giggle in her voice that Ron loved. "I should fuckin' think so," he said, with a laugh in his own voice.

"Don't curse at me, please," Allie said coldly.

"Hey, I seem to remember you are the same woman who likes my cursing. At other 'special' times, of course."

Allie laughed and said, "Oh, shut up, Ron, I'm in trouble here. Nothing's going the way I want it."

"Hmm, that's my spoiled little movie star," Ron said affectionately.

"Pru's been in the bathroom forever. I know she hasn't drowned because I can hear her. I can also hear her cursing but since it's the husband she's cursing that's okay."

"I must remember to watch my step," Ron Perrin said, sounding thoughtful.

"Plus I saw Sunny take off outside the hotel with Mac. In fact I saw him arrive, saw a scene so hot between them in that hotel bar, you would not have believed it. Sunny was with another guy, and when Mac walked in and held out his hand, she just got right up and took it and walked out with him, without so much as a by-your-leave."

"Jesus," Ron said.

"I thought they were getting into the elevator, going to her room—or his—then all of a sudden she ups and walks out the door."

"He followed her, of course."

"Of course he did. And I haven't seen them since, but I know if she's still out there she'll be freezing her butt off. December nights are a touch chilly here in Monte Carlo."

"You want me to come there?"

"What?"

"You want me to come join you, help out with all the dud romances et cetera."

"I think you've done enough damage." Allie laughed, "Oh, Ronnie Perrin, the knight in shining armor, coming to the rescue of the fair damsels. Now I know why I love you, jailbird though you are."

"Now, honey, you know that was all a mistake."

Allie shook her head. "Liar."

"Well, almost a mistake. It could have happened to anyone. A mere slip of the accountant's pen. Tax evasion is always the accountant's fault."

"You bet," Allie said, smiling. "And the big shots always get to pay the price."

Ron's sigh made her laugh. She said, "No, you need not come here, at least not yet. And I must go because, finally, believe it or not, one of the damsels in distress is emerging from the bathroom, pink as a peony in full bloom."

"You'd better take care of that tomorrow," Ron said. "It's unbecoming."

"Trust me, I intend to. Meanwhile, I have work to do. Talk to you tomorrow, Ronnie Perrin."

"Talk to you tomorrow," he said. "And Lovely sends a big kiss." Lovely was like their child.

"Kiss her back for me." Allie switched off her phone and turned to look at Pru who was wearing madras plaid pajamas that might have belonged in a boys' boarding school. Her stringy hair was pulled back in a rubber band and her face was shiny as Snow White's apple. Allie knew she had a job on her hands if she was to turn this woman from Snow White into Eve, with a much tastier and unpoisoned apple.

Pru plumped on the edge of her queen-size bed and automatically reached for the chocolate on the pillow.

"Oh, Pru, when will you ever learn. Just because it's there does not mean you have to eat it." Allie snatched away the chocolate, and the one on her own bed, then went to the minibar and removed all the packets of nuts and candy and sweet drinks.

"Only water," she said, ringing for room service to come and remove temptation.

Pru swung her legs into the bed and pulled up the sheet. "I'm sorry," she said meekly. "It's just habit, I suppose."

"That's okay. We'll talk about it tomorrow. And by the way, tomorrow, we're going to buy you some shoes."

She handed Pru a glass of water and watched her swallow the white pill that hopefully promised a good night's sleep, with no thoughts of her husband with the "other woman."

"Why shoes?"

"Because you have great legs and pretty feet. A woman must always emphasize her best points."

"I wish it were my tits." Pru gazed gloomily down at her spilling bosom.

"Shapelier tits can be achieved with weight loss and exercise. Most of what you have there is fat, Pru Hilson. I remember you in school, you had very nice breasts. *Cute,* I think the word was."

"Did Teddy Masters tell you that?"

Teddy Masters was the high school heartthrob and of course champion football player, with all the privileges and access to pretty girls that led to.

"Darn right, Teddy did." Allie crossed her fingers behind her back. Encouragement was the name of her game and she hoped God would forgive the lie.

"Imagine that. Teddy Masters." Pru slid down in bed. Her eyes were already closing from exhaustion, emotion and the sleeping pill.

Allie saw her face relax, freed from the tightness of stress and pain and anger. Somewhere in there was a lost little girl, a woman in need. Somewhere, Allie would find her. But now it was time for Sunny.

chapter 25

Sunny answered on the first ring. "Allie," she said, sounding either out of breath or choked up.

"What room are you in?" Allie asked.

"Ten-oh-one."

"I'll be there."

Sunny was waiting at the door. She grabbed Allie's hand and pulled her inside. Her room was in its usual chaos; Sunny never unpacked; she simply took things out and left them on chairs or even the floor.

"Oh, *Allie,*" she said.

"Oh, *Sunny.*"

The hugged, tight as two bugs, arms gripping, eyes streaming.

"You want me to sic the dog on Mac, or what?" Allie said, and Sunny gulped a laugh.

"You mean that Lab? She'd lick him to death."

"Not a bad way to go," Allie said and they fell back on the bed, hands clutched, laughing hysterically. Tesoro hovered worriedly over them, yapping.

Allie pulled herself together first. This was serious and she said, "You know I'll do anything. Just tell me what's going on."

"Mac opted out of the marriage?"

"He *dumped* you?"

"Well, the wedding."

"Oh. The *wedding.*" Allie had heard Sunny and Mac's "wedding" stories a couple of times before and couldn't help being a bit skeptical.

"He said he was too busy, we would have to change the date."

"You mean that's all? Change *the date*?"

"Dammit, Allie, I'd bought *the dress.*"

"Yeah, well it does sound a bit last minute," Allie admitted. She glanced thoughtfully at her. "Anyway, if you were having a wedding why wasn't I invited?"

"Nobody was. No family, no friends. Just us, the dogs and the preacher. A woman."

"Don't tell me Mac ran off with the preacher?"

"Of course he didn't." It was Sunny's turn to look thoughtful. "She's not bad though, you know in that buttoned-up-cassock kind of way."

They giggled, and held hands again.

"Want a drink?" Sunny suggested.

"You bet I do."

Sunny went to the minibar and produced small bottles of vodka, scotch, rum, gin. "Whatever?" she asked, waving the vodka that seemed to be everyone's favorite right now.

"Got a splash of cranberry?" Allie asked.

Sunny knelt at the minibar, shuffling through the contents again. She was still in the smart little black dress, though now she was barefoot, and despite her swollen eyes and tangled hair, she managed to look sexy.

"Remember when I ran away from Ron?" Allie said. "And you came to see me."

"You'd been to see Mac first," Sunny reminded her.

"Oh yeah. It was about Ron's mistress," Allie said thoughtfully. "The one who was murdered."

Sunny shuddered, remembering the story and her and Mac's romp through Italy in search of the killer.

"But then you came to see *me*," Allie said. "And *I* asked *you* if you'd ever had a broken heart, because my heart was surely breaking, as though it had been dropped on the floor and stomped on."

"Which in a way it had," Sunny agreed, handing her the glass of vodka. She splashed cranberry juice into it, along with a small scoop of ice. Then she filled Tesoro's water bowl and gave her a doggie treat.

"The thing was," Allie said, taking a gulp, "I always loved the bastard."

"Still do," Sunny said.

"Always will." Allie took another drink. "What about you?"

Sunny sat on the bed, legs sticking out in front of her, an elbow propped on the pillows, gazing at the pink drink, remembering all those pink Cosmopolitans she had drunk just last summer at the charming little hideaway in St. Tropez that had sheltered her and Mac as well as a bunch of misfits, including a couple of lonely children, too old to know heartbreak and too young to understand danger.

"How quickly time moves on," she said. "How quickly things can change."

"They needn't change, Sunny. Believe me, you two just need to work it out."

Chin balanced in her hand, Sunny stared into her pink cocktail. "He broke my heart," she said. "I had the dress. Cream lace."

"But you *hate* lace."

"It seemed right at the time. Besides, white is no good in winter, the light is too harsh."

"Spoken like a true publicist. Except in this case, Sunny Alvarez, you are talking about yourself. What's so goddamn fantastic about a wedding anyway? And correct me if I'm wrong, but did you, or did you *not*, turn down Mac Reilly last summer when *he* asked *you* to marry him? And tell me again if I am wrong, but when you said no Mac did *not* burst into tears and say you had rejected him. And did Mac ever say to me, 'Sunny turned me down and she knew I had bought a white linen suit and we could have gotten married right there and then at the beach, we could have called Allie and Ron and they would have been there in an hour. And we could have decked Tesoro out in a little white tulle skirt with a flower tucked into her red harness, and given Pirate a doggie bow tie and white collar.' Did Mac say *any* of those things to you, when *you* turned *him* down, last summer in St. Tropez, Ms. Sunny Alvarez?"

"I'm a selfish bitch," Sunny agreed mournfully. "Why did I do that?"

Allie sighed, staring into her own pink drink. "Who knows why we women do anything," she said. "Men always think we know exactly what we're doing, and the truth is few of us even have a clue."

"It's all instinct," Sunny agreed. "Reacting to circumstances."

"Aren't we supposed to be above all that? Weren't we emancipated in the sixties?"

"Seventies, I think."

They sat quietly for a minute, then Sunny said, "There's someone else."

"*What!*" Vodka shot over the edge of her glass as Allie sat upright. "*Mac has another woman?*"

Sunny glanced guiltily up at her. "No. I have another man."

"*Oh. My. God.*" They stared at each other for a long moment. "This changes everything," Allie said. "Why did you let me go on like that? When you *knew.*"

"I didn't . . . I mean I don't really know. I mean it's just someone I met on the flight to Paris. He was sympathetic, we didn't even tell each other our names, he let me cry on his shoulder, I think. And then he found me a hotel here instead of Paris, because

I didn't know where to go and it was snowing, and then he showed up here."

"You bet he did," Allie said. Then, realizing, "Oh my God, it's the man in the bar. The one you left sitting there, staring after you when you took off with Mac."

"Like I was hypnotized."

"Like *he* was hypnotized."

"What will I do, Allie?"

"Oh hell, Sun, let's just get some sleep." Allie was too weary to cope with this new turn of events. "Tomorrow, we'll talk. You and me. Oh, and Pru."

"Who is Pru?"

"You remember, the school friend I told you about. We're all going shopping in the morning. Shoes."

"I went shopping this morning," Sunny said. "With Kitty Ratte."

Allie thought for a minute. "I'm willing to bet that's the flaming redhead who took over where you left off with the mystery man."

"His name is Eddie Johanssen. He's getting divorced. And yes, that's Kitty. She's a bit odd-looking but quite nice."

"Quite nice" was a phrase Allie had never heard Sunny use before, and she thought as far as Kitty Ratte was concerned she'd certainly gotten it wrong.

"Let's stick just to me, you and Pru," she said. "That's about all I can cope with. Besides, we need to talk some more in private."

"Stay with me," Sunny pleaded. "In the morning we'll send down for breakfast, invite Pru over."

Allie hugged her. "It's time you got some rest. I think you need to be alone for a while, think things out."

Aware of Sunny's pleading eyes as she walked to the door, she added, "And by the way, do not answer if Mac calls. Not in the state you're in. We'll talk about it in the morning. Okay?"

"Okay."

The door closed and Sunny sank back onto the bed. She stared up at the ceiling, looking for answers to a dilemma of her own making.

She closed her eyes and Maha Mondragon's face floated into her mind . . . Maha telling her to take the chances life offered her. And to beware of Kitty Ratte.

chapter 26

Mac stood for a long time with the shower turned to hard-pulse, his head down to receive the punishment, water sluicing from his loins, cool, refreshing but still not taking away the stiffness and fatigue of the long journey, the weariness of his estrangement from Sunny, and the silence of a room that, with her, would have been cluttered with her "stuff," and buzzing with life.

Mac's TV show was not merely "a job." To him, he was fulfilling a need desperate people could not find anywhere else, lost as they were in the meshes of old police files, or even in those of more recent vintage, but always lost, their loved ones demolished at the hands of some psychopath, cold-blooded killers all.

It was true, his job did intrude on his life the way he imagined a dedicated surgeon's must, because, as with a patient, when someone was suffering and needed him, he had to be there. Long hours, time spent away from their own loved ones were all part of the game. And yes, he loved what he did and believed he brought some semblance of life back to people who had given up hope. *Closure* was a word that featured large in Mac's show.

He also had his "day job" as Sunny liked to call it, when he was hired by people in trouble, like Ron Perrin who had called him in when he was being accused of murder. Mac had searched for and found runaway movie star Allie, blond hair cut to the scalp and dyed brown, turquoise eyes hidden behind dark glasses; he had discovered she was in danger, and the identity of the true killer. There were many more people who had cause to thank him, and somehow he had become known, because of his show and the publicity, as the Hollywood Private Eye.

Mac always smiled at that description. To him, Private Eye meant films noir and Raymond Chandler and the Black Dahlia murder case, stuff from the thirties, forties, even fifties with detectives in snap-brim fedoras and slouchy suits with wide shoulders. A far cry from Mac in his faded T-shirt and jeans, and the soft black leather jacket that Sunny had bought him, telling him it was Dolce & Gabbana, laughing at him when he'd said he thought that was some kind of Italian ice cream. That's how much Mac knew about designer labels.

He cared nothing for the trappings of success and still lived in his tiny one-bedroom wooden shack overlooking the Pacific, with the four-foot-square "entrance hall," the small living room opening through glass sliders onto the wooden deck where the Pacific sometimes thundered under the wooden pilings; the old sofa where the dog, Pirate, his dearest friend, sprawled at his ease, when he wasn't on the bed that is, shedding of course and inclined to snore, but hey, Mac loved Pirate and he could do no wrong. Though he did sometimes wish Pirate would take on Tesoro. That Chihuahua could use a nip on her tiny three-pound behind, just to keep her in her place and not on Mac's back, claws out, when he made love to Sunny.

Mac turned off the shower, stepped out, toweled himself vigorously, then wrapped himself in the hotel's oversize terry robe. He didn't bother to look at the clock on the bed table. Time had gotten lost somewhere between Malibu and Monte Carlo. It no longer mattered.

He opened the glass door onto the terrace and stepped outside. The same cold wind that had chilled Sunny raised the hairs on his arms. He leaned on the rail looking at the distant still-halogen-lit crime scene. He felt sorry for the woman who had been shot, a life taken for a bag of diamonds.

He guessed that right now, in a forties or fifties crime novel, the Private Eye would light a cigarette, dragging deeply on it while figuring out exactly who had done the evil deed. Of course the answer would come to him in a flash, and all the conspirators would line up, pistols at the ready, while he told them exactly who had done the robbery or the evil deed. And the Private Eye always won.

Not this one, though. Despite his friendship with the Inspector, and his sympathy for the victim Mac had no interest in this robbery.

All his attention, all his emotion, all his . . . *his life* . . . was focused on getting Sunny back. He missed Pirate, though.

chapter 27

It was late when Kitty left the sex club in Cannes she often frequented, the kind of club where swingers, men and women, or sometimes men with men, or women with women, or all together any-old-how, got together for the purpose of sex, or simply to watch. Whatever their pleasure.

The "club" was one large room, the center a crowded dance floor, the music retro-disco. Black velvet curtains swathed most of the walls as well as the windows. Leather couches, some with amorously occupied couples, lined the room. There were "private" rooms, with enormous gilt four-poster beds, some round, some hexagonal, where a couple or several together might indulge in groups, though the doors were never shut to allow the voyeur customers to indulge in their own singular dreams. Large bowls of condoms were placed on tables and a bar supplied any kind of drink, while the clientele ranged from raunchy suburbanites out for a night on the town, to serious sex addicts and voyeurs and sadomasochists seeking their like among the well-dressed crowd. No jeans were allowed, cocktail attire was preferred with obligatory no panties for the women, and "no restraints," as the brochures so amusingly phrased it, for the men.

Men alone, without a companion, were allowed only once a

week, on Friday nights, though women alone were always welcome. For a little more than the entrance fee, dinner could be had while observing the antics, and making a choice, and maybe joining in a little.

Strobe lights licked at the half-naked bodies and every now and then someone sprayed perfume into the air.

Kitty needed the sexual contact of strangers she found at the clubs. It gave her a strange satisfaction to be taken by men who were as emotionally unaffected as she was, though unlike them, she never found it sexually satisfying. Power was what she felt, even though she was often the one being degraded in some sadomasochistic act, handcuffed and collared, men grouped around her, watching her moan and scream in a pretend ecstasy she never felt. *That* was her power. The men thought they owned her with their sex. She knew they did not. It was weird but she was addicted to it, the way others were addicted to cocaine. Though of course, she wouldn't say no to a line or two of that either.

Kitty was well-known at all the clubs, but her "act" and her body were becoming tired. Kitty could no longer undress completely. She had to rely on attracting tourists or businessmen who had not been there before, who had never seen her trolling for customers, one or two or more at a time, unfastening her dress to display herself. Now she was ashamed of her pear-shaped middle-aged body and her pancaked breasts. She always kept on the padded bra and a camisole that covered the folds in her belly, though not her private parts, her *chaton* as she called it in French, making a little pun on her name, "Kitty."

No panties of course, that would hold matters up. Which phrase meant a great deal to Kitty. "Getting it up" was her job. And the truth was she *was* getting a little old for it. The hair on her head might be dyed red, but her pussy was waxed, and with her plump cellulite thighs, naked she looked like a plucked chicken.

Teenagers with bodies to die for were taking Kitty's place, and what man would not prefer their young flesh. She now had to rely on flattery, charm, sex talk and acts so outrageous with promises to do whatever the men or women, or both together, wanted.

There were also, of course, her ads on Craigslist and on Eros. com, with photos of her in exotic poses, always in the upholstered bra and cami, but looking magically younger, and extolling her sexual expertise. And then there were the adult ads in the local papers: *"Mature foreign woman. Expert in all forms of massage. Natural redhead, willing to experiment any way you like to bring you happiness."* "Natural" of course was pushing it.

And then there was the escort service from where she was sent to the lesser hotels because she had never been in the category of the expensive "high-class" call girl; she was merely "an escort." For a modest amount of money she would meet unimportant businessmen at their hotels, slipping in head-down in an attempt to be discreet, though of course there were always security cameras, positioned in every hotel lobby and on every floor, that recorded exactly who came in and out and where they went at any given moment. Those records, of course with Kitty on them, were microchipped and stored by the hotels for easy identification, in the event of any police trouble later.

So far, though, Kitty had avoided that kind of trouble. She never stole from her businessmen and she never cheated on their fees, though she did try to charge for "extra" services, about which she would whisper in their ears, while dangling a pair of handcuffs, *"Come on, everybody does it. It's fun."* Sliding her hands over her body, rubbing in scented oil, she would ask, *"Does it excite you when I do this?"* And, *"Do you want to hurt me? Anywhere except the face."* And in the little overnight bag she carried, she would have her special "sex" outfit: the leopard bikini pants, the padded push-up bra, the cheap blue silky camisole. She wore this same outfit on all her sexual encounters, and of course always her precious Louboutin heels with the identifiable red soles that she believed gave her an expensive air of class. Also in her little overnight bag were lotions and lubricants, a vibrator, handcuffs and studded collars in leather with metal spikes;

and sex toys, masks, and a sweet little whip as well as a paddle, for those kinds of services. It didn't matter to Kitty. She never felt anything sexually anyway. Not a thing. Although of course she always moaned a lot so the men would think she did.

Kitty's "partner" was James Franklyn, whom she called Jimmy, a married Englishman with whom she had an ongoing relationship. When Jimmy got mad at her he told her she was a true nymphomaniac. *"Multiple partners,"* he yelled, ticking off the list on the fingers of one hand. *"A constant need for masturbation.* And never, *never* any feeling or satisfaction."

It was true Kitty never climaxed. In fact she was secretly deeply disinterested in sex though she tried every morning with her vibrator to satisfy herself personally. It never worked. What Kitty liked was the attention. She was a sexual predator who sought out men vulnerable to her brand of flattery. She liked to turn on a man by talking sex, by offering it, but at heart she was a voyeur. Kitty Ratte was as cold as meat in a meat locker, and as manipulative and scheming as any criminal. Kitty still denied being a nympho, but when Jimmy Franklyn, failed accountant husband of Martha Franklyn of suburban Surrey, England, called her a psychopath, she felt like killing him. And she might have. Instead, she went to a therapist.

Only once though, because the woman had looked into her eyes, asked a few pertinent questions about her lifestyle, about what she felt when she was with a man, about who she thought she really was, and then dismissed her. "You lie even to yourself. You need more help than I can offer," she had said as coldly as her professional manner would allow. It upset Kitty, being despised by a therapist. She'd paid good money only to be insulted.

Getting up to leave, Kitty had stopped at the door. "So?" she asked, in that middle European lilt. "Am I a nymphomaniac?"

The therapist looked at her from behind her desk, hands steepled together, cool. "Absolutely," she said.

"And a psychopath?"

"Ask yourself that," the therapist said. "And see what answer you come up with. Meanwhile, there's a place in Switzerland. I suggest you consult the psychiatrists there. Perhaps they can help you." And she wrote down the name and address on a piece of paper and walked across and handed it to Kitty.

Kitty put it in her Chanel purse, looking hard into the therapist's eyes all the time, her blue pinpoints furious under her lowering brow and the fringe of red hair. "Bitch," she had said as she departed, slamming the door behind her.

chapter 28

Jimmy was at Kitty's apartment that night when she returned from the club.

He got up from the sofa where he had been stretched out, tall, emaciated-looking with sunken dark eyes, clean-shaven, thin brown hair and as unremarkable as Kitty. It was his interest in sex that had drawn them together. She had given him the sex chat in a hotel bar, about how much she loved sex; how sexy he was, how attractive, and how much she wanted him. Jimmy had fallen for it like a ton of bricks, because like her, Jimmy was a voyeur. He enjoyed watching Kitty do her "act," which meant provocative poses in the leopard bikini pants, legs apart, wiggling her plump bottom, using her vibrator while he watched, asking if she was turning him on. The cami never came off though, and certainly not the bra.

"I'm ashamed of my body," she told Jimmy later in their relationship. "It's getting old. But my other longtime lover says I'm beautiful. And our sex together is great." Of course there was no other "lover" but Jimmy did not know that then.

Jimmy thought Kitty was far from beautiful but he got off on the show and the stories she told him of her other sexual exploits. Over the past couple of years they had become close, and Jimmy left his suburban life in England behind more and more often to tend to the new "business" of blackmail he and Kitty had developed together. They had done well, but only in a small way, with small-time targets, married men afraid of being caught by their wives who'd paid up and moved on. Kitty was too afraid to keep up the demands, though, and they soon went through the cash, which anyhow, had not been enough to buy Kitty her jewelry and watches, or her apartment, or the bar in Marbella they longed for.

"You're late," Jimmy said now, not touching her.

"I went to the club."

Kitty unhooked her bag from her shoulder and threw it onto a chair. Her ground-floor apartment in a converted old house was smaller than she would have liked, with glass doors leading onto a tiny garden with a gate set in a hedge at the far end. The decor was an attempt at a Mediterranean theme: seashell cushions, blue-and-white cotton-duck curtains, silvery bits and pieces and cheap crystal figurines of fish and seabirds, things like that, that Kitty "collected" on her travels. Not that she traveled anymore. She couldn't afford it.

There was a small living room with a couple of beige couches and matching chairs set around a glass coffee table; a commercial painting or two and a gold sunburst mirror over the fake fireplace, where a red glow emanated from an electric bed of logs. And, unnoticed by her "visitors," hidden in the ceiling and aimed directly at one of the couches, was a professional video camera, the size of a nail head. Like a nanny-cam but very powerful. No detail escaped it.

The apartment was a month-to-month rental and Kitty had to work to pay that rent. She *hated* not owning it. It drove her nuts, boring into her brain as she struggled to come up with the money each month. She could not even afford another pair of the Louboutin shoes, let alone the Hermès bag she craved. Now, at last she was about to do something about that situation.

She went into the bedroom, kicked off the stilettos that were killing her; threw off her dress, the chemise and the bra, put on a robe and walked back to the living room where Jimmy was pouring himself a vodka soda. Kitty could be naked only with Jimmy, who knew and understood her.

"Come with me," Kitty said, leading the way into the kitchen where a computer sat on the counter under a bank of cupboards.

Jimmy followed her. "Drink?" He lifted up his glass.

"Red Bull." Kitty settled herself on a metal chair in front of the computer which was tuned to Skype. When Jimmy was back in England, it kept them in touch sexually, with both of them naked on the screen, as well as keeping her "in touch" sexually with plenty of others. But sex was not on her mind now. She gulped down the Red Bull, waiting for a caffeine rush which, since it was her sixth of the night, she had no problem achieving. Then, "Look," she said, beckoning Jimmy over.

She had Googled Eduardo Johanssen. Google gave them, or anyone who cared to Google Eddie, a great deal of information on him, more than most would have needed to know. But for Kitty it was important and she was about to tell Jimmy exactly why.

"I was with Eddie tonight," she said. "I spent a couple of hours with him. He's lonely. A new girl left him for someone else. Her name is Sunny. I know her. Don't worry, she's an easy one; simple or dumb, or maybe both. Anyhow, I became her new best friend and I have her under control. Now I'm also Eddie's friend. I have him bewitched. He told me his wife is divorcing him and it's very messy. She wants to keep the kids. He won't allow that. He's rich and he's a loner." She turned and beamed her bucktoothed grin at Jimmy. She said, "Any evidence of Eddie's lack of moral standing and he loses those children. Plus most of his fortune. He's ripe for the taking."

Jimmy nodded, then drained his glass. "I'll find out everything else there is to know about him. By tomorrow, you'll have all the information you need."

"As well as these." Kitty took a bottle of pills from the counter and held them up for him to see. "My secret weapon."

Date-rape drugs and Ecstasy were only two of the secret weapons in Kitty's new blackmail game.

chapter 29

Sunny woke, heart pounding. A crack of light came from the bathroom door because she couldn't sleep in a room that was totally black. Mac had laughed the first time they had slept together when she'd confessed that she had always been afraid of the dark. "Sunny Alvarez afraid of the dark?" he'd asked, kissing her neck where the pulse fluttered under his lips.

"Hey, a girl can't be brave about everything," she'd retorted.

"Not this gal, though," he'd said. "Not the one who rides a Harley like a man and drives a car like a racing pro; who surfs and swims like a porpoise; and who faced danger with me. Not the woman who found a body in a refrigerator in Tuscany, and another under a cactus in the California desert; who walked into a Halloween party that turned out to be not so Halloween and she was the only one in costume."

Sunny had dressed like a lady vampire for that party, not so ladylike though in fishnets and stilettos and fangs. And Mac had been embarrassed in his own vampire outfit, though it was less revealing than hers. She'd faced down the stares of those country-club ladies in their St. John suits, martinis in hand. She had stuck her chin in the air, given them her best vampire smile and walked right out of there—and into even more danger than she had ever expected. But that was another story.

Right now, in the hotel room in Monte Carlo, Sunny was afraid of the dark.

She switched on the bed light and Tesoro growled, blinking from the pillow, grumpy at being disturbed.

The gap in the curtains showed a gleam of gray light. A glance at the clock showed it was five-thirty. Too soon for the sun, too late for the moon. Night and darkness were being dismissed and Sunny could breathe again.

In the bathroom, blinking in the sudden bright light, she took a quick shower, threw on jeans, a shirt, an oversize hoodie; brushed her hair into a ponytail and put on the baseball cap.

"Come on, Tesoro," she said briskly. "We're going for a walk."

Eyes still tight shut, the dog shoved her nose deeper into the pillow.

Sunny put on her harness and picked her up, and walked out to the elevator.

As the doors slid shut, she had a sudden memory of her and Mac together in another elevator in this very same city, Monte Carlo, just last summer. She had been wearing a short black chiffon dress that fell in narrow pleats, sashed at the waist with satin ribbon, and held loosely at the back with three tiny crystal buttons.

"Have you ever made love in an elevator?" she'd asked Mac, unhooking those tiny buttons and sliding the dress down over her naked breasts, laughing at Mac's shocked face. There was nothing that delighted Sunny more than being naughty.

Panicked, Mac had hauled her dress back up, just as the elevator stopped at another floor to admit a surprised-looking couple, who stared suspiciously after them when they got out and raced, laughing, down the corridor.

"Naughty," Mac had said, when he'd caught up to her.

"Isn't it fun?" she'd replied, tumbling onto their bed, still laughing as he pulled off the black chiffon and they made love.

This morning though, in Monte Carlo, the wind was gentle, almost springlike. It was too early even for the crews of the fancy yachts to be out cleaning and polishing and fluffing nautical-looking cushions. Massive-hulled super-yachts, too big to fit into the marina, were moored beyond the harbor, pennants fluttering, helicopters poised on top like giant seabirds, all steel and white. Their absentee owners would show up again in May for the Cannes Film Festival, when they would entertain Hollywood royalty in the manner to which they believed Hollywood royalty were accustomed, though in all probability most of them, like Allie Ray, longed for a simpler life.

Sunny knew she had shocked Allie with her confession about Eddie, though it was really quite innocent. Well, almost. She and Eddie had not even kissed. Well, only that time at the airport in Paris, the two kisses on the cheek, then the extra one "for friends." And of course the soft lingering kiss on the lips when they said good night in the hotel lobby.

Sunny remembered Allie saying Kitty Ratte had moved in on Eddie and she frowned. That couldn't be true. Kitty was her friend.

She walked along the harbor with Tesoro dragging reluctantly on the lead, stopping every few feet for a long sniff.

Kitty was so bourgeois, so innocuous she was almost boring, and always wanting to please. But wait a minute, hadn't Kitty talked sex to her? Asking if she missed sex with Mac because if so Kitty could "take care of it." Sunny had dismissed it then as silly "woman talk." Now, though, she wondered.

Seeing the yellow police tape and the cop cars still outside the scene of the previous night's crime, she ducked down a side street and found a tiny storefront café open early. The aroma of coffee lured her and she sat at the counter, dunking a flaky croissant into a *café crème*. Memories of the past summer in St. Tropez with Mac opened floodgates of tears that rolled down her cheeks into the hot coffee.

The waiter, a white apron wrapped around his waist and tied at the front, white shirtsleeves rolled, a cigarette burning in a nearby saucer, even though smoking was forbidden in public places in

France, eyed her then leaned across the counter. "*Madame?* Do you need help?"

She shook her head. "I'm okay."

He took another drag on his Gauloise Bleu, stubbed it out in the saucer and shunted the remains into the trash can underneath the zinc counter.

"It's a man, of course," he said, understanding immediately. "But *madame* is too beautiful to cry for any man."

He set a small glass of brandy in front of her and drew espresso from a hissing machine, strong enough Sunny thought, sipping it, to fortify even the weakest of nerves, if not also to destroy the liver. The brandy made her choke.

"You are very understanding," she said, managing a smile.

"Go back, tell him he is a fool," he advised. Then with another of those little Gallic one-shouldered shrugs Sunny knew meant *what the hell,* added, "But then all men are fools."

She pushed the euro coins toward him in payment. He pushed them back, and said it was on him.

"Trouble is," Sunny said, turning at the door to look at him, "there are *two* men."

"*Mon Dieu.*" The waiter's face expressed his astonishment. "*Eh bien, madame. Bonne chance.* Good luck," he called after her.

chapter 30

The Inspector had had no sleep. He sat at his desk in a normally tranquil *préfecture,* tranquil at this time in the morning anyway, before the latest bunch of ruffians were arraigned and sent before a judge and on to prison where they could no longer disturb the elite population of the small elite few kilometers of the French Riviera, that were home, some of the time, to some of the richest and most elite people in the world.

The criminals were usually minor: pickpockets, credit card scammers, shoplifters, but security was tight and they rarely succeeded in getting away with anything.

Of course in the twenties and thirties, there had been the daring kind of cat burglaries where jewels were stolen from a safe in the master bedroom of a grand pink villa; and of course there was the time when there was a fire in the penthouse apartment of a very rich man who had perished in the flames under what, some had suggested, were suspicious circumstances. This had proven to be true and a culprit was arrested. Anyhow, real crime was rare in these parts. And a job like the La Fontaine robbery was unthinkable. Just as it had been unthinkable at the Paris store, and in Milan, Berlin, London, Rome. And probably even more cities. The Inspector was too tired to think about it right now.

All the Inspector knew was that he had a murder on his hands. A young woman was dead and a small child—a two-year-old boy—left motherless. From what he had gathered in his questioning of the distraught shop assistants, there had been no reason for the robbers to kill her. They had obeyed orders, handed over keys, phones, diamonds. It simply did not make sense, they had said, though of course, they were all suffering from shock and had been taken off to the hospital. Except the one who had been carted away in the black body bag.

The Inspector slumped wearily in his chair, his cap on the desk alongside his feet, his smart jacket slung over the chair back, arms behind his head, thinking. He looked up at the knock on the door and an officer entered.

"The crime scene photographs, sir." The officer handed over the printouts of the pictures the Inspector had already viewed on his computer. He did not, at this moment, choose to look at them again. Instead, he put them in a blue folder, marked with the young woman's name, MADAME YVONNE ELMAN, DECEASED, stood up, put on his jacket and cap, tucked the folder under his arm, told the officer he was going out for coffee and could be reached on his mobile if needed, then walked out and round the corner to the nearest café. It was eight A.M., and he had been thinking about Yvonne Elman for more than twelve hours.

He took his usual seat at the café and ordered his usual breakfast: one hard-boiled egg, two croissants and a double espresso. He would have liked a brandy but he was still on duty. He took out his phone and called his wife, told her to expect him home for a fast ten minutes, when he would shower and change his clothes then get back to business.

His wife had listened to his telephoned reports through the night and she understood. *Serious* was not word enough to describe this situation and her heart bled for the young mother who had met her unwarranted and unexpected death.

The Inspector cracked open his egg, peeled it, sliced the contents, then ate them slowly in between sips of the strong espresso. He signaled the waiter for a *café crème,* double, then dunked his croissants in the creamy froth, looking like an aging bloodhound with his long lined face, large ears and droopy brown eyes.

He wondered if it was too early to telephone Mac Reilly, decided that it was not and placed a call to the hotel.

Monsieur Reilly was not accepting calls yet, he was told. He opened the file and studied, one more time, the shattered face of Madame Yvonne Elman.

chapter 31

The rock on which the Grimaldi castle had stood for more than seven hundred years—up-and-down years, both financially and scandalously—loomed over the tiny principality of Monaco. Much of its almost four hundred acres had been built on landfill to expand its territory and also to enlarge its harbor into one of the smartest ports of call on the oceangoing planet. The Greek, Aristotle Onassis, before he had a falling-out with the then prince of Monaco, had come up with the idea of this expansion; he had known exactly how to carry it out and take the principality from near ruin to one of prosperity with a tax haven status that had no equal.

Millionaires were common in Monte Carlo but the newer, smarter description *billionaire* guaranteed access to every grand party, while also guaranteeing that everybody who was anybody would also attend, be it on a yacht, or in a penthouse overlooking the marina, or in a villa set back in the foothills, though many also owned villas close to St. Rémy or in St. Tropez, where they escaped Monaco's somewhat claustrophobic atmosphere and the constant danger of bumping into the same people at the same events.

The Monégasques, the hometown citizens of Monaco, lived real lives amid the grandeur and the hubbub and influx of tourists and sightseers, protected and cared for as perhaps in no other country by their rulers, with job security and no taxes, and celebrations for almost any festive occasion.

Monte Carlo had been famous for several decades not only for its Casino but also for its pricey shopping, and La Fontaine, the jeweler's, had a historic place on one of its prime boulevards. It had been there as long as the Casino itself and owed its success to those Belle Epoque years and to the twenties and thirties and the men bent on blowing their Casino winnings on extravagant jewels for a courtesan or a new girlfriend.

Even though the Paris store had been robbed and a sadistic act of violence committed against a young woman assistant, no one ever imagined this could happen in Monte Carlo, the city of rosy dreams.

"That's exactly *why* it happened." Mac finally answered when the Inspector called him for the third time at ten minutes after nine the day after the robbery, the day after Yvonne Elman's murder, and the day after Mac had arrived in Monte Carlo and Sunny had told him they needed to reevaluate their relationship.

"Right after Christmas," Mac said. "Everybody's relaxed, their shopping's done, and of course grand jewelers like Fontaine do not have 'sales,' so there was no business pressure. In fact I'm willing to bet there wasn't much 'business' being done that day, except women returning gifts, exchanging them for the piece they'd really wanted all along."

"You mean the one they'd hinted about to the husband for months and which he was too dumb to pick up on."

Mac laughed. But then Mac had not seen Yvonne's death photographs. "You're probably right," he said, thinking of Sunny buying the red dress and the boots before he'd gotten around to it.

"It's an expensive street," the Inspector said. "Pricey boutiques, all of them. You wouldn't get the kind of customer, 'clients' they prefer to call them, going in there not properly dressed."

Mac assumed he meant women dressed in Dior and furs. Monte Carlo was different from L.A., where nobody ever wore fur, and those with money strolled the best stores in shorts or in jeans and T-shirts and flip-flops if they wanted.

"So why this call, Inspector?" he asked, though he got the feeling he knew the answer.

"Mac, a young woman was murdered last night. The mother of a two-year-old boy, the wife of a crew member on one of the yachts. A nice young couple, Mac. A toddler left motherless."

"I feel for them," Mac said. And he meant it. "I've encountered this situation before," he added. "It's never easy. In fact, Inspector, it's the kind of hell no one should be put through."

"I knew you, of all people, would understand. And it's because of what you just said, because of your experience in this kind of strange murder, that I'm asking for your assistance. Off the record, of course."

Mac looked out the window, coffee cup in hand, thinking about the unknown Yvonne Elman. "Inspector, why did you use the word *strange* to describe the murder?"

"Because, my friend, it was entirely unnecessary. There was no need to shoot the young woman. She and the other four salespeople, one of whom was the manager, had handed over the jewels, the keys, the phones. The security cameras had been shot out, the alarm disabled, the guard disarmed. All the three female robbers were wearing surgical gloves, masks and blond wigs, and were therefore unidentifiable. They had what they wanted. All they had to do was walk out of there, lock the door behind them and drive off in the vehicle that I'm sure was waiting for them. They knew it was unlikely anyone would even realize the place had been robbed until later, and by then they would be long gone. Which in fact is exactly what happened. The staff were locked in there with that dead girl and no way out and no passersby to summon help."

Mac thought about the Paris robbery and the act of violence against another innocent female saleswoman, and knew there was more to this affair than stolen jewels, though of course they were at the heart of it. In the end, money was always involved and this was big international money, in a case involving at least five countries and a network of thieves who knew how to play their game. Not anymore though. He knew this would be their last. No jeweler in the world would allow fur-clad expensive-looking women inside their doors without checking and double-checking. He was sad for the young woman's family and for the Inspector's dilemma, but because of Sunny he could not get involved.

"You have to understand, *mon vieux,*" he said, calling the Inspector "my old friend," though in fact their friendship went back only to the previous summer, but because the Inspector had helped Mac, he needed to soften the blow. "I can't get involved. I'm here on private business. Personal business." He hesitated, then added quietly, "*Very* personal. In fact to me, right now, nothing is more important. I'm sorry."

The Inspector's sigh came down the phone. "I'm sorry too, Mac," he said. "Of course, I understand."

Mac thought he probably did. In affairs of the heart few understood as well as a Frenchman.

But the Inspector had not given up. "At least come down and take a look at the crime-scene photos," he pleaded. "Give me your thoughts on what and why this happened."

"Let me call you back," Mac said, as the room phone rang. He clicked off his cell phone, picked it up and said hello.

"Ooh, hello," a woman's voice said, a little breathlessly. "Am I speaking to Monsieur Mac Reilly?"

Her voice was not familiar and she had an accent Mac could not place.

"You are."

"*Ooh,* Mr. Reilly. My name is Kitty Ratte. I'm a friend of Sunny's. And Mr. Reilly, I need to speak to you. Quite urgently."

Mac had taught himself always to take a beat before he replied to a leading statement like this one.

"Mr. Reilly?" the woman's voice sounded anxious now. "Are you still there?"

"I'm here, and since I don't know you I'm wondering exactly what you need to tell me that's so urgent."

"Well, then, Mac Reilly," the woman murmured in a voice more like a purr now, despite its guttural edge. "It's about Sunny. I'll be on the terrace, to the left as you come out the doors. I have red hair. You can't miss me."

"Red hair," Mac said.

"I'll be waiting," Kitty said.

chapter 32

After Kitty returned from the club she and her partner, Jimmy, had spent what was left of the night discussing not only Eddie but Mac Reilly.

An Internet search had revealed more about the world-famous detective. She and Jimmy had discussed how his presence might affect their blackmail plans and decided they needed to do damage control. Now Kitty was taking action. Like Eddie, Mac Reilly was vulnerable. His woman had dumped him. He was a man in need of consolation, and who better than the expert Kitty. A detective was not immune to the lure of sex, or to blackmail and Kitty knew the woman he loved would dump Mac all over again if she ever found out he'd had sex with her.

In Kitty's psychopathic mind, she was cleverer than any detective; and so far that had proven true. Apart, that is, for a small sojourn in a Spanish jail on charges of extortion, but that was a minor matter, long forgotten. At least by her.

Besides, it gave Kitty an illicit little thrill, moving in on Sunny's fiancé. Her own life was a long way from the lives of women like Sunny, or Allie Ray. Beautiful women with charm and talent who used their brains to get where they were, women who did things, had real lives. *Real women,* while she had only a façade, a woman who offered so little she gave it away for free. "Honor" was something Kitty had never had, and never aspired to.

Kitty saw Mac before he saw her. She thought he was surely attractive. Lucky Sunny, she got all the men; they all fell for her dumb charm, because Sunny was dumb, Kitty was sure of that; too dumb to see what might go on before her very eyes. He walked to the table where she was sitting with a cup of coffee in front of her. It was still only nine-forty-five A.M., and but for a few hearty breakfasters in nautical-looking navy sweaters there were few people about.

Kitty had dressed carefully that morning, choosing a floral dress with a V-neckline almost to the waist and a demure white cami beneath. She'd sprayed on fake tan and where the skirt fell away, her thighs had a golden glow. She wore her precious black Louboutins and carried a black nylon Prada bag with the triangular insignia prominently displayed, and wore the white dangly earrings that spelled out DIOR. Startlingly, she had pulled her hair into two pigtails that stuck out like small red missiles behind her ears, and fluffed her fringe over her eyes in what she believed was a way that made her look more girlish and sweet.

The toothy smile she gave Mac and the delicate wave of the hand in greeting was as sweet and open as she could make it.

"Ms. Ratte?" Mac took her in, in one comprehensive glance.

"That's who I am. And I'm so glad to meet you, Mr. Reilly. *Mac,* as Sunny always calls you."

Mac said nothing.

"Please," she waved delicately again, indicating the chair next to her, "won't you sit down, Mac? Here, next to me, so we can be absolutely private."

"I can't think of any reason we need to be private."

"Aah, but you see, I know *Sunny.*" Kitty patted the chair again. "*Please,* Mac," she said, wistful now. "Sunny told me you were such a nice man. A good man, which I see you are. Won't you be nice to me now, indulge me just a little? Who knows, we might even become friends."

Curious about what she had to say about Sunny, Mac sat.

Kitty waved over the waiter and ordered him an espresso. "Make that two," she added. "I fancy another." Her sideways glance took in Mac, who was looking at her.

"Why don't you tell me what it is you want to say?" He glanced pointedly at his watch. "I have an appointment."

"I'll bet it's not with Sunny," Kitty said, watching for his reaction. He did not reply. "You're a very attractive man," she added softly. "Though I'm sure I'm not the first woman to tell you that."

Mac sighed, exasperated. He had no time for this strange woman whose only claim on his attention was that she said she was Sunny's friend, and that Sunny had talked to her. Despite his misgivings, he was vulnerable, and he needed to know what Sunny had said, and espccially if she had, by any small chance, said she still loved him.

The coffee came in dark green bistro cups with tiny gilt spoons, a froth of richness on top of the deep brown espresso. Kitty put two sugars in hers and stirred it thoughtfully. Mac ignored his. He didn't want to be here drinking coffee with this woman at ten in the morning, or any other time.

"Sunny told me she'd left you," Kitty said at last. "I understand how hurt you must be, and now I've met you, I'm asking myself how could she do that? How could she *not want* you? You're so *attractive*. I know all about you," she added, resting her hand lightly on Mac's knee. "And what I really meant is you are so *sexual,* Mac Reilly. You know something? You and I are creatures of the same breed. Of course it was Sunny who told me you were like that. 'Sexy,' Sunny said. 'Good in bed.' She said you were everything she wanted, except you didn't want to marry her. Now, looking at you, I'm asking my-self why you would want to get married anyway, when you can have exactly what you want without that silly piece of paper and the gold band."

Shocked, Mac wondered if Sunny could really have talked about him, about their private times together? He looked into Kitty Ratte's serpent's eyes. Had she really allowed this woman into their personal lives?

There was something in Mac's gaze that caused Kitty to remove her hand hastily from his knee. She knew instantly that Mac saw her for what she was: a small-time suburban hooker on the make, and it made her furious.

"Of course, Sunny told me all about Eddie." Kitty stuck the verbal knife in viciously. She stirred the remnants of undissolved sugar at the bottom of her cup, as if reading tea leaves.

"Eddie Johanssen, I mean," Kitty added, glancing up. "The man she met on the plane, the man who booked her into this hotel. The man who came here to be with her."

Mac got to his feet.

Kitty smiled up at him. "Trust me, I'm on your side," she said, anxious now. Had she gone too far? "I'll do everything I can to get you two back together. I'll talk to Sunny, tell her how much you care."

Mac stopped her. "Let me ask you something, Ms. Ratte. How do you *know* how much I care about Sunny?"

Wide-eyed, innocent, Kitty said, "Oh, but of course, Sunny told me everything."

Without another word, Mac turned and left her sitting there.

She watched him walk away, a lithe easy lope that guaranteed a good body underneath the jeans and leather jacket. A man like that was too good to let get away. This time jealousy as well as blackmail was her motive for stealing someone else's man.

chapter 33

At ten-thirty that same morning Sunny finally checked her BlackBerry. Mac of course. Twice since eight-thirty.

In the first message he said, *"I love you, please call me."* In the second he said, *"I love you. Please marry me."*

There was a note of cool confidence in his voice and Sunny could not decide whether it was confidence in *his* love for *her,* or confidence in *her* love for *him.* Or whether he was just confident that she would come around and fall into his arms. Which, she remembered, was exactly what she had done last night.

There was a third message. It was from Allie. "So how are you this morning, Miss Lovelorn, Runaway, Two-Timing Woman? I hope you are up for shopping? Don't they always say a little shoe-shopping is good for all that ails a woman in trouble? Personally, I've often wondered who 'they' are, who said such a damn silly thing, but today I'm putting my trust, as well as yours, and Pru's, in them. Remember Pru? Well, when you meet her you will not forget her, which is something I have to work on. Meanwhile, meet us on the terrace at eleven o'clock. I'll have a car waiting. And do not, I repeat do *not,* Sunny Alvarez, hide behind a veil of tears and let me down. Remember. I know about the other man, so you had better come clean. See you at eleven."

Shopping was the last thing in the world Sunny wanted, but Allie was in charge so of course she would be there.

A couple of morning newspapers, along with a pot of coffee and a basket of croissants had been delivered to her room, but she had already breakfasted at the small café on the side street with the understanding waiter. She settled with the papers in the sofa by the open window where the sunlight warmed her, looking at the headlines. They were in French but there was no mistaking the words ASSASSIN . . . TUÉ, and MORTE . . . *Murder . . . dead.* There was a wedding photo of an attractive dark-haired young woman, happy with her bridegroom; and a picture of a scowling baby.

She picked up the English-language newspaper, the *International Herald Tribune*, and read that a young woman assistant at the exclusive jewelry store had been shot. A murder of "startling indifference," the report said. The salespeople had obeyed the robbers' instructions, given them everything. There had been no need to kill this mother of a toddler, working for her living. Why? was the big question on every newspaper reporter's mind. And one to which nobody seemed to have the answer.

Sunny recalled the halogen-lit scene, the helicopter lights and the long stretches of darkness across the sea to the mountains; the *blah-blah* wail of dozens of French police sirens. A woman had been murdered and all *she* had been thinking about was herself and Mac and her so-called on-off marriage. As well as, she admitted it now, Eddie her would-be lover.

She did not say Eddie's name out loud, even alone in her room. Anyhow, there was no message from him on her BlackBerry; he had not called, and she could not blame him. She had publicly embarrassed him walking out with Mac without even a please excuse me, I'll call you later.

Would she though? Have called him later. Would she call him now? She hurried to change her clothes to get ready for Allie's shopping expedition. She was definitely not calling anybody. *Shoes* were all that were on her mind.

Her phone buzzed. She glanced at the name and sighed. *Kitty Ratte.* The last person she needed. But then she remembered guiltily that the woman had befriended her on Christmas Day when she was alone and had needed someone to talk to. She was a perfectly nice woman, though hadn't Allie told her Kitty had moved in on Eddie?

The phone stopped buzzing, then started again.

Sighing, she picked it up.

"Oooh, *Sunny* . . ." Kitty always seemed breathless, as though she'd been caught unexpectedly doing something wicked. "I'm out here on the hotel terrace and I was just thinking about you. I'm having coffee. Would you like to join me? After last night, I thought you might want to talk."

Sunny remembered Kitty had been there for her before. She had been a good listener, anxious to help, to "take her out of herself" with their little shopping expedition; a girly lunch. And in a way she had. Just as she had tried to help Eddie when he'd been left so publicly. Besides, she wanted to know what Eddie had said to her.

Anyhow, she owed her. She said, "Just for half an hour. Then I'm going shopping."

"Ooh," Kitty said again, sounding disappointed. "With Allie Ray, I suppose? You are lucky to have such a good friend. Okay, I'm here, waiting for you now, Sunny darling. And then I'll tell you all about Eddie."

Kitty always knew how to bait the trap.

chapter 34

When Maha Mondragon was at her palatial white stucco many-pillared home in Mumbai, on the western coast of India, a city with a population of more than eighteen million, she had a slew of servants to take care of the menial tasks. Now though, she was tidying up her hotel suite prior to the chambermaids coming in to clean.

Mumbai, where she had lived since she was born, thirty-eight years ago, and which used to be known as Bombay and in fact still was called that by many of its inhabitants, was her favorite home, though there was also a recently purchased small mews house in London's Kensington, not too far from Harrods, where Maha found neighboring Harvey Nichols more to her liking, shoppingwise. Except for food that is. In her opinion there was still nothing to beat Harrods' Food Hall, not even Fortnum's, especially for their pastries; the tiny artistic *mélanges* of chocolate and raspberries on a creamy custardy base. Maha's downfall was chocolate, although she kept herself severely in check. The fact was, Maha would rather eat chocolate than caviar, though she did love champagne with anything.

Her wonderful jewels were still on the dining room table. Now she rewrapped them in their black-velvet sleeves and put them in the canvas travel bag on top of the several other objects, also wrapped in black velvet. Maha zipped the bag, locked it and hefted it from the table, pulling a face at its weight.

Wherever she traveled, New York to Tokyo, Maha always stayed in top hotels. It would not do for a woman selling quality goods like hers to be seen at a lesser venue. In Maha's opinion, quality always spoke of quality, meaning she lived in a top place because she had top-of-the-line jewels. Soon, though, she hoped to make a permanent move to New York. In fact she already had the condo picked out, in the upper eighties where everyone of "quality" lived or wanted to live. She had been puzzling for years on how to achieve that ambition, stymied at every turn by careless employees without sufficient brains or strong enough nerves to carry through what she demanded from them.

Maha had long ago decided that in her line of work innocence was the best quality a woman could possess. And Sunny Alvarez possessed exactly that innocence.

Maha's exotic jewels were already sold at top stores and boutiques from Tokyo to Paris. Harrods had turned her down, saying they were too flashy for their clientele, something that, since many Indians lived in London, had surprised Maha, whose custom designs were made by craftsmen in Rajasthan and were sold wherever well-heeled tourists shopped. But somehow, however much she had made, it was never enough.

Now, she picked up the discarded shopping bags from Sharon and the Bulgarian's previous day's forays at the sales and stuffed them into the wastebaskets. With a flicker of distaste she tossed in Sharon's lipsticked cigarette butts, and the Bulgarian's tissues. The woman had a terrible cold and in Maha's opinion should not even have been within twenty meters of her hotel suite, but there had been nothing she could do about it.

Next, she checked her closet, noting that her large garment bags and twin suitcases were still locked, and that the clothes she intended to use here in the South of France were newly pressed and hanging neatly on the rails, the saris shelved equally neatly, with a rack of delicate shoes along the bottom. No mere Louboutins for Maha. Her shoes were handmade on her own last by an exclusive shoemaker in Milan, where she went twice a year to pick out a new collection. For her, Louboutin was merely commercial.

In the spacious marble-lined bathroom she began arranging her cosmetics, and perfumes—actually, perfumed oils brought from India and which she found more subtle, personally blended to her exquisite taste. She put them in neat rows on a clean washcloth, something the chambermaids usually did but which she had told them she preferred to do herself. She did not want their hands touching her personal things.

There was the black kohl she used to emphasize her eyes, the bronze dust with the hint of sparkle for her cheekbones, the subtle understated tinted moisturizer and the deep cerise and bare-beige lipsticks that she alternated, depending on the color of her sari.

Maha wore a sari only in the evening, or for business lunches where she was expected to look more alluringly exotic. At other times, she wore a white linen blouse, black pants and a short black jacket, along with her beautiful shoes, made without exaggerated points and with heels just high enough to enable her to walk elegantly without breaking her neck in stilettos. Warmer days, she wore sandals studded with turquoise or other stones, and in winter, elegant calf-length boots. She almost never wore a skirt, having been brought up in a society where it was proper for a woman to keep her legs covered.

Maha did not care anymore about those rules, she simply preferred her own way of dressing, and the black-and-white regime was easy for travel, no need to worry about what to wear since it was practically interchangeable. And for night there was always that gasp of color, the soft swish of silk chiffon, the blaze of a distinctive jewel, sometimes even a flower, an orchid or hibiscus, whose color was reflected in the shine of her glossy black hair, pulled severely behind her pretty ears.

Maha Mondragon was quite something and she knew it. She

was a beautiful woman. A successful woman who had worked her way up from the dire poverty of Mumbai's garbage-ridden slums, and one who was about to become even more successful and attain her dream of joining that upper social strata that, up until now, had managed to exist without her. And she knew that Sunny Alvarez could help her achieve that. It was simple: Sunny needed her; and she needed Sunny. How could her plan fail?

chapter 35

Sunny was in jeans, a white tee, a drapey red cardigan that matched her daytime red lipstick, and the black sheepskin comfort boots. She also wore medium-size diamond stud earrings that she had bought and paid for herself years ago, and a Cartier tank watch with a white alligator strap. No rings, no other jewelry. Tesoro was with her, tugging on her lead.

Simple good taste, Kitty thought, putting up a hand to touch her own Dior earrings and looking her enviously up and down, wondering why she somehow could never quite achieve that. In her flowery jersey frock and the Louboutins, she felt overdressed. She gave Sunny that little here-I-am wave, hand fluttering, two front teeth gleaming.

Sunny dropped kisses on her cheeks and placed Tesoro on the chair between them.

Kitty's eyes were filled with false admiration as she looked at her. "Beautiful," she murmured. "Perfect."

"I don't know about that," Sunny said, embarrassed. "I just threw on the nearest clothes."

"But you are *always* perfect," Kitty said, her eyes still gleaming with something other than admiration. Hatred, perhaps?

"In fact," Sunny said nervously, "I don't feel perfect or wonderful or beautiful or any other of those adjectives right now. I kept waking in the night, frightened. I don't know what I was frightened of, just of the dark, I suppose. I was up at five-thirty. I took Tesoro out for a walk and had breakfast at a small café near the scene of the crime."

"The scene of the crime?" Kitty carelessly dismissed the events of the previous night. She waved over the waiter and ordered a café crème for Sunny and a Red Bull for herself. "Oh, you mean the jewel heist?"

"I mean the *murder.*"

Kitty drank the Red Bull straight from the can. "Murder happens," she said with an indifferent shrug. "Though not usually around here. I'll bet if you were in New York you wouldn't even have noticed it."

"Well, I'm not in New York and I am noticing it." Sunny was offended by Kitty's indifference. "Especially since it happened just down the street from here, while we were in the bar drinking champagne."

"With Eddie Johanssen you mean." Kitty took another slug of the Red Bull then wiped her mouth delicately with a paper napkin imprinted in dark blue with the name of the hotel.

Sunny sighed. "I'm sorry for what happened."

"What's to be sorry for?" Kitty shrugged. "Your lover came to find you and you went off with him. And by the way, I happened to run across Mac a short while ago, right here on this terrace. I hope you don't mind, Sunny, but I took the liberty of telling him I was a friend of yours. I said of course I understood, and I would do anything I could to help."

Angered, Sunny slammed her coffee cup into the saucer, sending the little gilt spoon tinkling. Tesoro gave a nervous bark. "*You did what?*"

Kitty threw her hands in the air, looking shocked. "Did I do something wrong? Ooh, Sunny, I'm sorry. All I wanted was to help.

And after all you *had* left Eddie sitting there, in the bar, with everyone looking at you and Mac, looking for all the world like lovers, and knowing you had simply walked off and left him."

"I heard you were quick to give him some consolation."

"Who else was going to pick up the pieces? The poor man looked shattered, as well as embarrassed."

Sunny hung her head. All Kitty had tried to do was save a bad situation. "Sorry," she said again, leaning across Tesoro to take Kitty's hand. "I know you were just trying to help, and I know I behaved badly, but it was as though I was in a dream . . ."

"So, did you make love with Mac last night?" Kitty asked, smiling her predatory smile. Tesoro leapt up and bit her wrist.

"Ooh, *look*," she yelled. "Now I'm *bleeding*."

Sunny passed her a couple of napkins to blot up the tiny drops of blood where Tesoro's teeth had nicked Kitty's wrist. "Bad dog," she said, but she thought Kitty deserved it.

"I'm mortified you think I did the wrong thing," Kitty said, with that little upward glance, easy tears trickling. "You know I would do anything to help you, Sunny. And Eddie."

"So what did Eddie say? After I left?"

Kitty's small blue eyes hardened. "I shouldn't really tell. Not now you're back with Mac."

She was right. Sunny knew she should go and apologize to Eddie, say she was sorry and take it from there. My God, what did she mean, *take it from there* . . . was she crazy?

Maha came out of the hotel and walked past the terrace to her waiting car. In one quick glance, she took in Kitty Ratte sitting next to Sunny. Ignoring them, she stepped into the car and was driven off.

Kitty did not even notice her because right behind came the famous Allie Ray. And with her was an overweight woman in a green plaid skirt, green blouse and a gray cashmere shawl. Kitty decided she must be Allie's assistant and therefore unimportant. She dismissed her from her radar.

"A day shopping together," Kitty said, wistfully. "How wonderful. Just the way *we* did, Sunny. Was it only yesterday?"

Guilty, of course Sunny had to ask her to join them. All she'd really wanted was to be alone with Allie so she could sort out her love life. Now not only would Allie have Sunny to sort out, and Pru, she also had Kitty.

chapter 36

Eddie was on a flight to Germany where a new tanker was being built for a client; not a Greek, they were not so prominent now in the tanker business, but an American of Middle Eastern origins, who had money to spend on such things since he made a fortune from oil.

Eddie's job was to broker such deals. His own family still owned small shipyards in Holland and Scandinavia, where they too had built great ships. Not so many now, though, since deals were so tight, but certainly more than enough, along with the commissions Eddie made around the world and the oil deals, to keep him and his family in style, both in a weekend house on their own small island off the coast of Sweden, and also a large town house in the historic part of Stockholm. The town house was conveniently close for his two small children, a boy, aged five, and a girl, six, to attend one of the best day schools in the area. And also close enough to the action for his wife to spend a great deal of her time hanging out at parties with "friends."

When Eddie first met her, the pretty Jutta looked like every man's dream of a Swedish girl, a natural almost-white blonde, with large blue eyes fringed with blond lashes that gave her a look of perpetual youth and on which she never used mascara. She had an even smile and a lean athletic body. Jutta was a champion skier and looked wonderful on the slopes, a blond vision in the marine-blue ski suits she always wore because they matched her eyes. With her handsome husband, they looked the perfect couple.

That was why nobody could understand when they split up. "Why?" her friends asked Jutta. And "Why?" his friends asked Eddie.

"Because it's over," Jutta told them with an indifferent shrug. "Because it might never have been," Eddie had said, with a slightly different perspective on things.

He didn't blame her; he traveled so much, and as a woman left alone with two small children Jutta was forced to become independent. Such love as they once had for each other had dwindled and on Jutta's part disintegrated into anger. Now, even though she no longer loved Eddie, she did not want him to be with someone else. Jealousy, not love, was making her vindictive.

Eddie did not understand that. He was willing to be generous, give her the house on the island, as well as the town house, and a great deal of money, though she wanted a lot more. All he wanted was shared custody of his beloved children. That was the catch. Jutta was claiming *sole* custody, with visiting rights only one weekend each month for him.

"After all," she had said in her written statement to the court, "Mr. Johanssen is away so much he barely sees the children anyway. Why should anything change now? It would only upset their routine. Their emotions are involved here."

Matters were now in deadlock. Eddie loved his children. They were the most important part of his life. He had his work, and he had his kids. And that was it. That is until he met Sunny Alvarez on a flight from L.A. to Paris and his life took a U-turn. She wasn't the first woman he'd become acquainted with since he and Jutta had split up a couple of years ago, but she was different.

The flight attendant stopped to ask if he would like something to drink. She was attractive, with a warm look in her eyes as they met his. Eddie thanked her, refused the drink and, leaning back, thought about Sunny.

How was it possible, he asked himself, to feel so strongly about a woman he had met only a few times, and who he now knew for certain was in love with somebody else? He had never believed in love at first sight, but now he was considering it. Was what he felt for Sunny love? It was certainly lust, because she was a beautiful and very sexy woman. Was it merely the attraction of opposites? And timing? Eddie, so deliberate, so attuned to his business life, with the dregs of his marriage getting him down, and Sunny, so vulnerable, so open in her emotions, so eager to laugh again, so cast down at the end of a long affair.

Last night's scene played out again behind Eddie's closed eyelids. Mac walking into the bar, holding out his hand to Sunny, and Sunny without a single word, a second glance, taking that hand and walking away with him.

That was painful. And even though the redhead, Kitty whatever her name was, had plied him with drink and sympathy, Eddie had returned alone to his room and spent the night slumped in a chair, feeling as though he'd had too much to drink, wondering what the hell Kitty was all about and asking himself why Sunny had done that, and suspecting he knew the answer.

The plane was coming in to land. He looked out of the window at the checkered blur of the sprawling city; at the giant derricks in the shipyards; the blaze of fires where rivets were tortured into steel; at the gray pall of the northern climate on a bad day. He wished he were back in Monte Carlo. With Sunny.

chapter 37

Allie said to Sunny, "I want you to meet my friend Pru."

Impulsively, Pru reached over and kissed Sunny. "Lovely to meet you," she said.

"Wonderful," Kitty said, when Sunny introduced her to Allie, eyes shining in that wide admiring way she had. "I'm so thrilled to meet you." She totally ignored Pru.

Sunny explained that Kitty was a new friend and that she had invited her to join them on their shopping expedition.

"It wasn't meant to be *entirely* shopping," Allie pointed out to her because she wanted them to be alone so they could talk. Especially about the "other" man. Besides, there was something in Kitty's eyes that made her uneasy. Kitty was pleasant, though, chatting on about where the best deals were to be had in Cannes and her favorite shopping area. Somehow, though, Allie did not think they were on the same wavelength, clotheswise. Allie was into the simple things of life, and Sunny had her own very distinctive half-biker-girl, half-romantic-sylph look, depending on the occasion. Or more usually on her mood, because Sunny didn't give a damn about "occasions."

Pru climbed into the limo first and sat in the corner. Kitty got in and sat next to her, completely ignoring her. Sunny and Allie got in last.

When Sunny took off her dark glasses, Pru noticed her eyes were swollen. She'd heard the story about Mac from Allie last night, and had gotten an update when she'd been woken with a cup of hot coffee that morning and denied even a single croissant. Her coffee somehow tasted very French and not at all like the coffee-shop stuff she was used to. She wondered how on earth she, a hometown gal from the depths of Texas who had never really been anywhere in her life and who, if she had not known Allie in high school, would never have even met a movie star, let alone become involved with glamorous people in a fabulous place like Monte Carlo, a place everybody knew about but only the lucky few ever got to visit. She sneaked a look at Kitty, who was telling Allie that she lived in Cannes and that she was involved, in a small way, in the modeling business.

"How interesting," Allie replied, uninterested. She turned to Sunny, who despite her promises was fighting back the tears.

"Pull yourself together," Allie scolded. "We'll never get anywhere like this." Sunny sniffed and Allie put an arm round her. "I love you," she whispered.

"Love you too," Sunny said, gripping her friend's hand tightly.

Watching them, a steel band wrapped around Kitty's heart, it tightened her throat so she was unable to speak. *She* wanted to be the one Allie Ray was talking to; *she* wanted to be the movie star's best friend; in fact right this minute she wanted to *be* Allie Ray. Hatred for Sunny shot through her. She glanced angrily out the window and she saw Mac Reilly on the hotel steps, watching their car pull away.

She saw that Mac had spotted Sunny getting into the car.

Kitty hated women like Sunny, who were so effortlessly comfortable with themselves, so easily able to charm. She envied people like Allie who had it all: looks, fame, money. Now she was determined to get the better of Sunny, the woman she could never aspire to be, and she had a *double* way to get even with her. Blackmail was on her mind, but murder lurked in her heart.

* * *

Mac watched them drive away. Sunny had not even bothered to answer his messages. He hoped Allie could talk some sense into her.

She had never stayed away from him this long, even when they'd had a fight, which, like everybody else, they sometimes did. Even Tesoro had not given him her usual woof of recognition. He was shut out of Sunny's life and he had never felt more lonely.

He thought about calling Ron Perrin, asking him to come down to help, or even driving up to see him in the Dordogne cottage and vineyard the ex-Hollywood mogul now called home. But it was too late.

Instead he dialed the Inspector's number on the cell phone. "I'm coming over to take a look at those photos," he told him.

chapter 38

"Where to first?" The limo driver was heading on the auto-route to Cannes.

"The Presunic department store," Pru said quickly, because she'd heard it was inexpensive and department stores were the only places she'd ever shopped. She'd never dared to enter the intimidating portals of the expensive boutiques.

"Hermès," Kitty said at the same time.

"Chanel," Allie decided firmly, because she liked classic things with a slight edge that she felt Pru needed.

Sunny said, "But isn't there a street market this morning? I hear they have great clothes there."

"How did you know that?" Kitty asked, surprised.

"I remembered from last summer."

"You were *here*? Last summer?"

"With Mac," Sunny said, tight-lipped.

"Make it Chanel, driver, please," Allie said with a touch of authority.

"But I can't afford Chanel," Pru said.

"I can," Allie said. "And you will do as I say. Okay?"

"Okay." Pru looked down at her green plaid outfit wishing she had had something more chic to wear to such a chic store.

Kitty turned her shoulder so that her back was to Pru. Fixing her beaming smile on Sunny, she said, "I just know you'll look wonderful in Chanel."

"Sunny looks wonderful in anything, including black leather on a Harley," Allie said.

"Is that so?" Kitty's accent emerged in the lift at the end of the sentence. The thought of Sunny in black leather interested her. Her first "sexual" outfit had been a black leather bikini that she had worn at a sex club in Budapest. But that was a long time ago.

Pru sat silently on Chanel's softly padded chair while an assistant brought shoe after shoe for her to try on. The other assistants were grouped in a corner and she guessed they were talking about the jewel robbery and the murder of the young woman assistant who, like them, worked at a boutique.

"Those look wonderful," Allie said. "Get up and walk around, see how they feel."

The shoes were black suede with three-and-a-half-inch heels, and a slight platform.

"*Madame* has pretty feet," the saleswoman murmured. "Perfect for our shoes."

"They *are* perfect," Sunny said, as Pru's ankles wobbled.

"You just have to learn to walk in them." Allie was determined she should have them. "What about red? Red shoes always make a girl feel good."

The very idea of red shoes, which she knew would draw attention, terrified Pru. Allie got up to have a look around and Kitty walked behind her. Pru saw Kitty lift her cell phone and realized she must be taking photographs of Allie the movie star. She understood immediately that Kitty meant to sell them to the tabloids. She could just see the headline in the *National Enquirer* and *People*: SHY ALLIE RAY SHOPPING AT CHANEL IN CANNES, and Allie's hard-earned privacy in France would be gone.

She got up and grabbed Kitty's phone. Kitty snatched it back but it slid off the photo she was taking and onto another. A picture of a naked man with a studded leather collar round his neck. He was holding a whip and there was no doubt he was ready for action.

"*Oh my God,*" Pru whispered, shocked. "*Who's that naked man on your phone?*"

Kitty quickly stuffed the phone in her Prada bag. "*What* naked man? What are you talking about?"

"The one whose photo is on your phone. *Before* the ones you took of Allie just now."

"I wasn't photographing Allie, I was taking a picture of some shoes. I'll look at the picture later at home and then decide if I want to buy them."

"Liar," Pru said, under her breath, not wanting to make a scene.

Kitty gave Pru a venomous stare. "You look like a housewife on a day trip."

"And you," Pru hissed, "are like a bourgeois older woman on the make. And I'll bet any man will do."

"*Bitch,*" Kitty snarled.

"*Bitch,*" Pru whispered back.

War had been declared between Pru Hilson and Kitty Ratte.

Much later (in fact four pairs of shoes, including the red Chanel ones later, plus a pair of jeans that to Pru's amazement fit like a second skin—in fact they almost *became* her skin, holding her in and lifting her butt amazingly), they were on their way to a café. En route they had bought a few tops and a couple of sweaters from an inexpensive backstreet boutique (Chanel's clothes did not fit Pru and besides, she wanted to pay for things herself and not take advantage of Allie's generosity). They had also visited a local lingerie store where Pru had been fitted with a bra that not only lifted her to amazingly delicate new heights, but somehow looked soft and sexy. She had not been able to resist their lacy underwear which Sunny assured her would make her feel like a new woman. Sunny had even made her buy a lacy garter belt and black stockings.

"After all, you never know when opportunity—in the form of a handsome man—might present itself—*himself*," she corrected with a grin. "A girl has to be ready for that, you know, Pru."

Pru looked doubtful. Handsome men did not just spring off the streets where she lived. Or if they did they were not springing at her. But then, she was not going to live there anymore. Definitely not. She did not yet know *where* she would live, but it would be a fresh start. That's exactly what she needed: a fresh start. And watching the salesgirl stuff shocking-pink tissue paper into the bag containing her new and sexy underwear, Pru smiled. Man or no man, she would feel good, wearing it. It was like a secret, kept all to herself.

And now Allie had made a hair appointment for the next morning and they were sitting at a café sipping glasses of rosé, nibbling on sweet French radishes, watching the passing sideshow.

"What a wonderful day this was." Kitty beamed at Allie, humble with gratitude. "I can't thank you enough for inviting me."

In fact Allie had not invited her, but she merely smiled. She said, "Pru, that was just a start. Did buying the shoes make you feel a little better?"

"I think so," Pru said, still worried about the expense, though she knew Allie took pleasure from treating her. "And thank you."

"So, Pru, we're starting you off on salad," Sunny said, caught up in the makeover of Pru Hilson, who was after all a jilted woman, much like herself. Well, not quite. Sunny had not been jilted. *She* had done the jilting.

"Stop thinking about Mac." Allie tapped Sunny's hand to bring her back to her senses. "We'll talk about him *and* the 'other man' later. When we're alone."

"And after a couple of glasses of wine," Sunny said. "You know Mac always loved this South of France rosé."

"Mac always loved *you*," Allie said. Then she added, "In fact I've never seen a man so in love with anybody."

"Except Ron Perrin with you."

"And look how nearly I lost him; how nearly we lost each other." Allie's gaze was serious. "Just think about what you're doing, Sunny. Promise me you will."

Sunny promised.

Bored with Pru, Kitty stored the previous conversation about Mac in her mind for further use. She had already drunk a couple of glasses of wine and now she ordered another bottle. "My treat," she said, beaming.

Pru looked up, saw Kitty looking at her, saw the scorn in her eyes. *Cheap bitch,* she thought, deciding she had better warn Allie and Sunny against her later, when they were alone.

Sunny had noticed before that Kitty drank too much, but she said nothing. That was Kitty's problem; Sunny had enough of her own to deal with.

"Pru," she said. "We've decided tomorrow you should be a blonde."

"You're kidding!" Pru had never thought of changing her mousebrown, ever.

"Get ready for the new you," Allie said, smiling, as they ordered lunch.

A few minutes later, Pru stared dismayed at the small portion of lobster fettuccini in front of her. In her opinion it was barely enough to keep Tesoro alive. Understanding, Sunny said, "Do you ever wonder why, with all the wonderful food in this country, Frenchwomen look so good? And yet they always seem to be in restaurants and cafés, always eating?"

Pru had never thought about Frenchwomen and their diets. In fact she never thought about Frenchwomen at all.

"What Sunny means is, it's the *way* you eat, not *what* you eat," Allie explained. "Frenchwomen don't merely *eat* their food, they *taste* it. They make each mouthful count. Take a bite of that lobster fettuccini now, Pru. Really savor it, then tell us what you think."

Pru looked at the three women looking at her, and then looked

down doubtfully at her plate. She liked lobster; she liked pasta—
though this sauce was pale and barely there, and certainly was not
the tomato variety she was used to. An unknown sprig of greenery
adorned the side of the plate. She picked it up and sniffed.

"Pru, how can you have gone through life and not smelled tarragon?" Sunny said exasperated.

"Easy. Nobody eats tarragon where I live. *Lived*," Pru added
quickly, because she was certainly never going to live in that town
again.

"It's one of the most fragrant herbs. Mac loved to cook with it."

"But it's licorice." Pru sniffed again.

"Uh-uh, it's *tarragon* and it goes with the lobster. Now, taste it
before it gets cold."

Pru speared a piece of the lobster, half-afraid to put it in her
mouth because she'd already decided she did not like the licoricy
tarragon and couldn't say so.

"It's like sex," Allie encouraged. "Close your eyes, and just think
about what you are doing."

Eyes closed, Pru thought. She knew instantly that the sweetness
of the tiny Mediterranean lobster was different from the Maine variety she was familiar with, usually eaten smothered in drawn butter
and with a bib around her neck to catch the drips.

Quite suddenly she understood. Her eyes opened. "It tastes like
the Mediterranean sea," she said, amazed she could be that specific.

Sunny grasped her hand. "Of *course* it does," she said. "And that's
what you need from it, Pru. To *really* taste. It's not about the quantity,
about filling up the gas tank, it's about taking your time, savoring the
pleasure the food gives you. The pleasure of the moment. That's what
good food is about. It should be all *pleasure*."

"The sauce is a very delicate Alfredo," Allie added. She was eating the same thing. Just a hint of it, a fresh light pasta, a delicious
taste of fresh-from-the-sea lobster.

"And there we are." Sunny was beaming. "A whole new food

philosophy, Pru. You don't need quantity to feel good, and you don't need to *diet* diet. You need to eat like a Frenchwoman. And I promise, if you tell me when you're finished that you really enjoyed each mouthful, I'll order you some cheeses. Just three, I think, a sliver of each so you can tell us after which you liked best and why."

"Is this an education?" Pru asked, a little affronted, even though she was enjoying the lobster and truth to tell, the plate was almost empty and she badly wanted more.

"Think of it as 'the Monte Carlo makeover,'" Allie said, and everyone, even Kitty, laughed.

"I like it," Pru decided. "And you know what, I think those jeans will fit even better tomorrow."

chapter 39

Mac sat at the Inspector's desk with the death photographs of Yvonne Elman spread out in front of him. He was no longer looking at them. He stared out of the window at the tops of the trees where the leaves rustled in the light breeze. The Inspector looked down at his hands, fingertips steepled together, as though in prayer, though in fact he was not praying. He was merely hoping.

"Terrible," he said, breaking their silence.

"An understatement," Mac said.

It was not easy looking at what was once the face of a young woman and that was now merely a bloody mask of scraps of flesh and shattered bone. And embedded in the remains of that face were shards of diamonds. A hundred minuscule pieces of what had once been a twenty-carat stone that, fragmented by the bullet, had imploded and caught under the camera's lights, sparkled and glittered through the pink froth of brains and blood that was all that was left of Yvonne's head. A once valuable and now worthless diamond was the price of this young woman's life.

"I figure the victim—I mean Yvonne"—Mac hated to depersonalize a dead woman into merely a corpse—"was holding up the stone for the gunman to take. Instead he shot her."

"And hit the diamond instead."

"As well as."

"You mean the robber intended to 'kill' the stone."

"Probably just for the hell of it, show his power, show that he had more than enough and didn't need anything from her, or from society."

"Then our robber is a sociopath."

"Could be. A sociopath cares for no one but himself, or herself, yet he moves in society, gets through the world on a certain amount of charm and normal behavior. He has a strong desire to be accepted by that society while at the same time descending into the depths of cruelty and depravity without any feelings for others. He could easily kill and not feel a thing. You might call him a 'murderer with charm.' Most con men are sociopaths; they become your 'friend,' that's how they get away with it. Look at all the financial misdoings recently.

"A psychopath is similar, but more antisocial, more immediately dangerous. He's like the sociopath, though, in that the only person who counts is himself. *He* is the most important. He will have no real friends and will usually live a lonely life, half-hidden in normal society. And then he'll go out and murder, go on killing sprees, often beginning with small animals when he's still a child, feeling the thrill of power at that killing, progressing to sexual power always followed by the killing, and usually leaving his victim hideously disfigured, maimed, disemboweled, literally cut from top to toe.

"And then," Mac continued, "we have a third type; the oddball, that combination of the two, the one with face-value charm, at ease with society, though always with a hidden past, yet still with that urge to kill."

"And I've noticed they often kill at the time of the full moon," the Inspector said, recalling the moon shining behind the helicopter beams and the halogens.

"Could be. The tides are in tune with the phases of the moon, why not the minds of men."

"Are we now assuming the shooter was a man?"

Mac wasn't assuming anything. He said, "This type of needless killing was very male, but from the descriptions of the robbers, their approximate height, weight, clothing, we must still assume they were women."

"They carried very small semiautomatics, the kind a rich female might carry for protection. Though she would need a permit of course, and a good reason."

"Like for instance she was rich and frightened and thought somebody might try to kidnap her?"

"Perhaps."

"If she were that rich she'd have hired a bodyguard." Mac was remembering hiring Lev Orenstein just last year. Lev was simply the best security man. He knew the Riviera coast better than the back of his own hand. He knew every nook and cranny, every slip road and minor highway. Lev could get a woman out of trouble faster than she got into it. There was no excuse for women toting guns, in Mac's opinion. The victim had certainly not carried a weapon. But that was always the way it was; the victim lost her life then got lost in the courtroom shuffle while the killer got sympathy, blaming it on his terrible upbringing, or parental abuse, or having a crack mother and living on the street. They gave a bad name to all those kids with similar backgrounds who picked themselves up, survived, took their lives into new areas, along with their dignity and self-respect. Mac had no time for killers, whatever excuse their defense lawyers gave in court.

He took another look at Yvonne's death pictures. "I'm hoping her husband did not have to see these."

"He identified the body by the rings she was wearing. These copies are for you," the Inspector said, collecting them and putting them in a folder, slipping in a photo of Yvonne when she was still an attractive young married woman and not merely a faceless body. "It's against the rules, but there are no rules in matters like this. I need your thoughts, Mac. That's all. You cannot take part in anything that might go on here, that's a police matter. But you have the ability to see the quirkiness in things, the odd, the strange, something different that might lead to the perpetrator."

"Not always," Mac said, recalling the times he had failed. "I'm not perfect."

"But then, which of us is?" The Inspector was just glad that Mac was walking out of there with the folder of pictures under his arm. Mac had not turned him down this time, and perhaps, only *perhaps,* something might come of it.

chapter 40

Maha was wearing an exquisite sea-blue sari this evening, fashioned of the most delicate silk chiffon and clasped at the shoulder by an immense aquamarine with a mountain-glacier glimmer about it that drew the eyes of everyone in the bar. Which seemed, Maha thought, irritated by the crowd, to have become *the* fashionable meeting place since the jewel heist down the road. It was as if everyone wanted to see the scene of the murder. She shuddered delicately as she sat at her usual table and ordered her usual bottle of champagne. No caviar tonight, though. She was not in a caviar mood. Instead she ordered a plate of petit fours, the chocolate kind with cake and cream underneath and icing draped thickly over the top. Maha could not control her sweet tooth to-night.

She glanced round, thanking God the redhead was nowhere in sight. The woman disturbed her deeply. Maha understood Kitty Ratte. She knew she was corrupt and like all corrupt people was on the hunt for victims. Maha did not know what her game was, but she recognized a predator and knew instantly that this predator had Sunny in her sights. Exactly why, she wasn't sure.

Anyhow, Maha was not about to let that happen. If anyone was going to corrupt Sunny Alvarez it was herself, and in ways she was sure were completely different from the sexual ones the redhead had in mind.

Sharon Barnes, Maha's number-one assistant, stalked into the bar, followed almost immediately by Sunny Alvarez's ex-fiancé. Maha felt suddenly chilled. She had made it her business to find out all there was to know about Mac Reilly. She knew exactly who he was, and what he did, and knew he did it well, following a gut instinct that was very much like Maha's own when it came to assessing people, knowing who they really were. Now she was nervous.

Sharon covered the ground between the entrance and the table in a few swift strides, threw her new Valentino jacket, which was almost the color of Maha's rubies, onto the chair next to her, fishing immediately in her tote for her pack of cigarettes. "Ciggies" as she liked to call them, as if the diminutive lent the cigarettes a sort of feminine charm.

"Shit." Sharon remembered there was no smoking. She flung the pack back in disgust, signaled the bartender and ordered a double shot of Scotch on the rocks and some olives.

With her close-cropped dark hair, winged brows and wide sullen mouth Sharon looked as though she were playing a role in a French movie, and indeed she spoke French like a native from all her years of living in Europe. Prague was now the city Sharon called "home" but she had always been restless and home was wherever she chose to make it. Or at least it had been until she joined forces with Maha three years ago.

Sharon's eyes were on Mac, who was standing at the bar. She heard him order a beer, a Stella, then she saw him turn and survey the scene. For a second her eyes met his, then he glanced away.

Sharon liked the way he looked, with that nice lean body. She could not abide fat men, none of those "love handles" for her, she wanted to count every rib, thank you very much, and she'd bet this guy was good in the ribs department.

"Know who that is?" Maha asked.

Sharon turned to look at her.

"Sunny Alvarez's ex. One of the foremost American detectives, with his own successful TV show. Mac Reilly succeeds in solving crimes when others, including the police, have failed."

Sharon's brows rose in shock. Maha thought she really was attractive when that hard-boiled shell dropped away. Maha knew all about that hard-boiled part of Sharon. It was why she employed her.

"Ex? What?" Sharon asked, taking a gulp of Scotch and pulling a face. The spirit always caught the back of her throat at first taste and she often wondered why she drank it. Except after the second she knew why. It made her feel good. Like the fuckin' cigarettes. Hey, she was an addict. So what?

"I believe he is her ex-fiancé, and the reason Sunny is here is because she ran away from him."

"How do you know that?" Sharon bit into an olive. The juice squirted onto her new Valentino blouse. "Shit," she said again, on the verge of losing her temper.

"Barmen always hear everything," Maha said, though anyway Maha also made it her business to know what was happening around her. She knew every detail of the jewel heist and the murder, including the fact that a very large-carat diamond had been involved. A famous stone, it turned out, known as the Babe Bailey diamond, more than twenty carats, flawless, D color and extremely valuable. Maha also knew its history. It had been cut by an expert who was now dead, an Iranian who'd known more about diamonds than any man Maha had ever encountered.

"I heard the Babe Bailey diamond was shattered in the jewel heist," she said, taking a minuscule bite out of the miniature chocolate petit four and washing it down with a sip of champagne.

Sharon's face expressed her indifference. "I don't give a shit about diamonds," she said, matter-of-factly.

Maha wished Sharon would control her language. Even though Maha had been brought up in squalor on Mumbai's streets where cursing was an everyday event, along with violence, brutality and death, she was a refined woman. Now, of course, the beautiful jewels made by her craftsmen in Rajasthan had replaced those terrible childhood scenes in her mind's eye, but it was also the reason Maha knew evil when she saw it. And she saw it now, entering the bar, one more time. It was as if the redhead could not keep away. Was it only Sunny who lured her? Maha wondered.

"God, there's that bitch, again," Sharon said, reaching over and snitching one of Maha's petit fours. "I wonder who she is and what she wants. Other than a man." Since Sharon was a woman who had been in the fashion world and who now ran a model agency in Prague, she knew a lot about females.

"Only we women see that aura of corruption about her," Maha said, watching as Kitty got Mac Reilly in her sights and, in her knock-kneed cutesy trot, thighs flickering through her wrap skirt, hurried toward him. "Men just get her come-on; the I'm so sexy and you're so wonderful chat. And I'll bet you most of them fall for it."

Sharon laughed. "You mean she's getting more than I am?"

Maha glanced at her. "And are you 'getting any,' as you so crudely put it, Sharon?"

Sharon shrugged. "I guess I could if I put it out like the redhead. It's as though she's wearing a label round her neck with 'available' written on it. I mean, she's so middle-aged suburban and with that ghastly hair and those thighs, in that cheap wrap dress, you'd think guys would give her the brush-off."

"What Kitty has," Maha said, watching corruption taking place before her very eyes, "is knowledge. She knows how to flatter, how to sympathize, how to let a man believe he is wonderful, and that she needs him and wants him."

"Well, he's not bad," Sharon said with a grin that did not reach her beautiful eyes.

"Pity about that Babe Bailey diamond," Maha said again, and

again getting no reaction from Sharon, who instead asked where the others were.

"Lisa left for wherever it was she came from. Ferdie and Giorgio are driving to Budapest."

"And where does that leave me?" Sharon asked, looking angry.

"On your way back to Prague," Maha said, softly. *"Bitch."*

chapter 41

Mac had left messages for Sunny, asking her to meet him anywhere she liked, just name it, only please agree to see him. Yet despite what she had said last night—that they must talk, reevaluate their relationship, Sunny had not called him back. So now Mac waited at the bar, with a beer he did not really want, hoping his phone would ring.

He leaned an elbow on the polished wooden counter, not seeing anything because his mind was still filled with the horrifying reddish blur that was Yvonne Elman's brains with the shards of diamonds spattered across them, tiny stars in a lost kingdom of the soul.

Mac had seen some horrifying sights in his career but figured this was one of the worst. And all for the lure of big money. *Fast money.* Or maybe not so fast. Eastern Europe was being touted as the new El Dorado for diamond trafficking, but he still could not figure how and where the stones would be cut. He knew many of the larger ones were identifiable and would certainly need to be recut before they could be sold on the open market. Perhaps they would try to sell them immediately on the underground market, which would be faster, though less profitable.

Profit from murder. Profit from a woman's life. Profit from a motherless child. From a bereft young husband.

"Ooh, *Mac,* there you are."

There was an intimate squeeze of his forearm and he turned his head just in time to catch the brush of Kitty Ratte's lips against his.

"Ooh, Mac," Kitty said again, her tiny blue eyes aglow with admiration and sympathy. "I just thought you looked so *lonely,* standing there. *So all alone.* I just felt you *needed* a little comfort."

Mac removed Kitty's hand from his arm and placed it carefully on the wooden bar. "And exactly what 'comfort' do you have in mind, Ms. Ratte," he said, in a voice so cold it would have left any normal woman out in an ice field.

"Ooh, well, I know how much you care, about Sunny I mean. And she is so *beautiful.*"

"Sunny is beautiful," Mac agreed.

"I mean, how can she not *want* you." This was a favorite line of Kitty's.

"Y'know what, Ms. Ratte, whatever it is you're after, I'm not interested." Mac stepped back but Kitty reached out for him again.

"Don't. *Please* don't go," she whispered, easy tears glinting. "I'm so lonely . . . and Sunny has become such a good friend." Her eyes sharpened. "She tells me everything."

Mac was used to reading people like Kitty, experienced in dealing with the sociopath, the psychopath, the cold manipulating natures of people who felt nothing for others. He had heard the same line before from Kitty, but again because of Sunny he could not let it go.

"Please, *please,* sit here, next to me, so we can talk quietly. You know I was with Sunny today." She put her hand on Mac's arm, linking them. "We had lunch together. She is very . . ." Kitty hesitated, as though searching for the right word. "Very independent in her thinking." She caught Mac's eyes and brushed away another tear with a trembling finger. "It's as though this nonwedding has changed her character. I don't think you would even know the new Sunny, the way I know her now. Sunny wants to find a new life, perhaps even a new . . ." She left the sentence dangling. "Well, no, I won't even go there . . ."

She ducked her chin and gave Mac her upward glance from beneath the red fringe, full of sympathy, making sure that, without her having to say another word, he understood that what Sunny wanted was a new man.

Mac got up and walked away.

Kitty's hard eyes followed him. For a minute, just a minute there, she'd had the great Mac Reilly in her power. Just watch out, Miss Alvarez have-it-all smarty-pants-better-than-everyone Sunny, she thought vengefully. I'll get your man yet. I'll make him squirm with delight and you will suffer the pangs of hell. Women like you, who saunter through life with everyone falling at their feet, always suffer the worst when their man betrays them for a woman like me.

Out it the foyer, Mac called Sunny again. There was no reply. In his heart he felt something that was close to grief. He placed another call, this time to Ron Perrin.

"Get down here, Ron will you," he said abruptly. "I need you."

"Y'do? What about Allie?"

"What about her?"

"I told you she's there, with Sunny. And the friend."

"Jesus," Mac said. He'd forgotten all about Allie.

"It's not only Sunny," he said to Ron. "I've got a murder on my hands."

"Not *again*," Ron groaned. "Will you never learn?"

chapter 42

Mac was outside the hotel when he heard Sunny's voice. He looked at his phone, thinking he must be dreaming.

But she was just steps away. She had Tesoro on the lead and was looking at him with a half-pleading, half-stubborn expression, as though determined not to give in, even though she might want to.

He walked over, picked up her hand, held it to his lips. That invisible wall was still between them.

"Sunny. Please, let me tell you how much I love you." He wasn't pleading, it was a simple statement of fact. "Love like ours doesn't just disappear." He felt her hand grip his and breathed a little easier.

"No," she said.

He gazed into her face, wondering did she mean love like theirs did disappear? Or no, it did *not*? How had he ever become a detective when he couldn't even figure out what a woman meant when she said something this important.

"Help me out here, Sun baby," he said, running his hand gently up her forearm, which tonight was covered in a lavender-gray wool sweater that fit her body so perfectly he figured some expert little knitter in the English countryside must have fashioned it specially for her. The neck exposed her throat where he saw a bluish vein that almost matched the shade of the wool. A man in love, he missed no detail.

"You braided your hair," he said, touching the glossy plait that lay across her shoulder. He so wanted to kiss her.

But then suddenly Sunny leaned across that chasm that lay between them and kissed him. And for a minute life suddenly became normal again. Until she pulled back and said, "Mac, why don't we talk?"

"Okay." He would have agreed to anything right then. "Just don't let go of my hand."

Sunny did not let go and they walked hand in hand with the little dog trotting between them, back into the hotel. She led him into the bar. Mac wondered why they hadn't gone to her room where they could be alone, but then he guessed right now "alone" wasn't what Sunny wanted.

She paused to say hello to the beautiful Indian woman, who was drinking champagne, along with a tall model-type with a sullen face.

A dozen bracelets jangled as Mac shook Maha's slender hand. Novice though he was jewelwise, he would be willing to bet they were expensive. Especially that huge gold-clad aquamarine brooch. He thought Maha was not only beautiful, there was an air of mystery about her that did not allow you to see the real woman hidden behind the smile, the gleaming dark eyes, the glamour. Sunny was smiling warmly at her as though they were old friends. Then Maha introduced them to her associate, Sharon Barnes.

"I feel as though I already know you," Sharon said, looking Sunny up and down. "Maha's told me so much about you."

"Ooh, *Sunny* . . ." Kitty's voice came from the bar where she was still sitting, a beer in hand. "I *hoped* I would see you here tonight."

Sunny stopped to kiss her too and to introduce Mac.

Kitty gave him her best grin. "I'm so happy to meet you, Mr. Reilly," she said, when just minutes ago she had kissed him.

Sunny excused them and they went to sit at a lamp-lit corner table. She put the dog under her chair and smoothed her black pencil skirt over her equally smooth golden knees. With a pang, Mac noticed she was wearing the tall black leather boots he'd wanted to buy her for Christmas.

He said, "Tell me how you know that red-haired woman."

"Kitty? She was here, in this bar, Christmas Day evening. I was alone and so was she. She wished me Happy Christmas and came over to talk. She was pleasant; we had lunch the next day. She said she understood my loneliness, and I felt she was . . ." Sunny stopped and stared blankly at Mac; she realized she had no idea what she had thought about Kitty then. But now she knew. "I thought she was *needy,*" she decided.

"And Maha Mondragon?"

Sunny smiled. "You're jealous because I made new friends."

"That's true."

"As a matter of fact Maha spoke to me that Christmas night too. It was so strange. She actually *warned* me against Kitty. *'Take care with that woman,'* she told me. *'Corruption had its own unmistakable aroma.'* I couldn't understand what she meant by it."

"Maha is a clever woman," Mac said.

Sunny decided not to tell Mac what else Maha had said, about her taking the chances life offered her, nor about Maha's offer of a job. Which, because she really liked the mysterious Maha, and with her new desire for independence, she just might consider accepting.

Suddenly nostalgic for their summer in St. Tropez, she ordered a Cosmopolitan. "I know it's not fashionable," she said, smoothing her skirt nervously again.

"And since when did you feel the need to apologize for ordering a girly drink?" Mac asked. He took her hand again. "Oh God, Sun baby, I love you so much. You can drink a dozen pink cocktails and I'll kiss the taste from your lips when I tuck you, intoxicated, into your bed . . ."

"*My* bed . . . ?"

Their eyes linked with that magical connection of chemistry, attraction, sex; memories of each other's bodies.

"*Our* bed," he said, holding both her hands tightly in his now.

"With Tesoro biting your ears," she whispered back.

"Or even worse places . . ." They grinned at each other.

She said, "And poor sweet Pirate, afraid to jump on the bed in case Tesoro chased him away . . ."

"Until you took pity on him and picked him up and put him there . . ."

"And Tesoro growled and the wind howled outside sending the waves slamming up the beach, frothing over the rocks sounding just like Niagara . . ."

"And the fire burned low in the grate and the house smelled of Mitsouko, your perfume, and apple logs and wine, and your lips tasted . . ."

"Of the peaches we had just eaten and the juice was running down your chin . . ."

"And of grapes and more wine . . . and . . ." Mac had no need to say "of sex." The look in Sunny's eyes told him she remembered.

"So, what now?" he asked, looking at her.

She was so coolly simple, with her hair pulled back in that braid and the gleam of diamond studs in her ears, reminding him of the tiny crystal buttons on the black chiffon dress she'd almost removed that night in the elevator. She was wearing her red lipstick, one he knew well because he often carried it in his pocket when they went out in the evening and she didn't want to take a purse. There were so many small intimacies between them. He was in love with the golden glow of her Latina inheritance, her skin; with the sweet curve of her cheek; the amber eyes that looked copper in the lamplight; the long legs with the smooth knees and a hint of even smoother thigh beneath that black skirt. And those boots, his would-have-been Christmas gift meant to be placed under the ratty fir tree that always listed to one side because they could never get it into the holder straight, needles already dropping but its piney scent filling the house, along with all those other scents . . .

He said, "Sunny, what are we going to do?"

The question hung in the silence between them, along with the memories.

Then, "All I know is I love you, you bastard," she said.

They gripped hands under the table, their eyes were hot for each other, his leg pressed against her thigh, her lips trembled as she took a sip from her glass.

"It's hopeless," she said with that unexpected smile that lit her face and lit a flame in his heart, the way it had from day one. "I just fuckin' love you."

"And I love you, but I don't curse about it."

She was smiling at him. Her hand was on his thigh. "If *fucking* is a curse word then I want to curse with you a lot. And right now."

Mac leaned in and kissed her. He breathed in the subtle scent of Mitsouko and her warm skin.

His hand on her knee sent electric shocks through her; her lips drew him into another world.

"I want you naked," he whispered. "Right now."

She gave him that smile. "Room ten-oh-one," she reminded him. "In ten minutes."

He watched her walk away. So did Kitty Ratte who had not missed a second of the sexy little scene. Jealousy had a burn like acid; she would take care of little Miss Sunshine soon. Meanwhile, she had work to do.

chapter 43

Pru Hilson was wearing her new shoes, the scarlet sling-back Chanels she had finally been talked into because they reminded her of the women on reruns of *Sex and the City,* a favorite program on those long nights in front of the TV when "the husband" was off on his "travels," or whatever he cared to call it. Finally knowing the truth about him had not made the memories of those nights any easier, but what women always said about buying shoes had turned out to be true. Pru felt better, if a little weak since all she had been living on since the Christmas turkey sandwich was a few olives and the small plates of food that though delicious, did not always fill her needs, especially at a moment like this. Right now, she needed *real* food. And lots of it. Desperately.

In fact what she really longed for was a good old-fashioned all-American hot dog. How the hell had she ended up in France anyway? Hah! All it had taken was one phone call and Allie saying of course you must come, I'll help you, and she had been there like an arrow flung from a bow.

She stepped from the elevator and cast a quick nervous glance around the foyer. No one in sight. Well, at least no one she knew. But oh my God there was someone she would *like* to know. A tall gorgeous man whose dark blond hair flopped silkily over his eyes, and who was striding in an easy manner toward *her.* Eddie Johanssen.

"Good evening," he said.

He stood politely to one side, smiling questioningly while Pru just stood there. Then she realized, Oh, oh my God, he was simply waiting for her to get out of the elevator so he could get in!

Mumbling apologies she hurried past him, forgetting all about the new three-and-a-half-inch red Chanels. Her ankles wobbled and she almost fell. Cheeks flaming she drew herself to her full plump height of five-four and strode on.

She loved those gosh-darn red heels, though. They made her feel better. Allie was right, her legs sure did look good in expensive designer shoes. Pru guessed that was why women mortgaged their houses or sold their kids to buy them. Just joking.

Another quick glance and she scuttled unobserved into the brasserie at the rear of the hotel, where she took a seat in a quiet corner and ordered a Diet Coke, a club sandwich and fries. She shrugged off the guilt. What the hell, the Coke was "diet." And the french fry or two couldn't do her any harm. Could it?

She glanced down at her still ample bosom, captured this evening in a shapeless black silk top—expensive she'd have you know—with a black cardi slung over to hide any flaws. Of which there were many.

Like many French brasseries, this one's walls were lined with mirrors and there was no getting away from herself. There she was, life-size, reflected a hundred times. She sighed. Maybe she should rethink those fries after all. Besides, if Allie found out she would kill her. She was watching her like a hawk, not allowing a single extra morsel to find its way between her teeth. Very good teeth by the way, she thought, catching sight of her mirrored face. They were a little large perhaps, but white and even, and all her own, thanks to a mom who taught her how to take care of them. She had been a cute teenager then with a normal size-eight body—or was it even a six?—which Allie had told her hotshot high school footballer Teddy Masters had said was *really* cute.

Giving herself another little secret look, Pru thought maybe, just maybe there might even be a hint of a cheekbone under that pink flesh. Which anyhow looked less pink because Allie had given her the correct tinted moisturizer and a tan blusher instead of the pink she had been using. Soon, she might even progress to mascara and lip gloss. Well, perhaps not lip gloss; she didn't feel like a "glossy" person. She wished she could wear red lipstick like Sunny Alvarez, who, along with Allie Ray, was the most lovely woman she had ever met. Anyhow, tomorrow she was to get her hair done. Allie had booked her in at Jacques Dessange in Cannes. She was to become a blonde.

She wondered hopefully if blondes really did have more fun. Perhaps it was just an old wives' tale, like the shoe-shopping thing. She patted her hair doubtfully in the mirror. Somehow she had never envisioned herself as a blonde and now wondered if, with her ample curves, she might look like the classic image of a barmaid. She grinned; that might not be all bad; maybe she'd get herself a new job!

French Coke was different from the homegrown stuff she was used to. Sweeter. In fact so sweet she could almost taste the sugar.

"This *is* Diet Coke?" she asked the waiter as he set the bowl of fries and the sandwich in front of her.

"Certainly, *madame.*"

"Well, then, I've changed my mind. I'll have Perrier please. And I'd like some lemon with that."

Tasting a fry Pru felt better but still guilty.

She ate a quarter of the sandwich in the time it took for the waiter to bring the Perrier, pushing away the fries as she thought of the gym she was going to with Allie tomorrow, and then the spa where she was to receive thalassothérapy treatments, whatever that meant—something to do with seawater she believed; and hot stone massages, and derma-something . . . "The works," Allie had promised her.

Somehow the sandwich didn't look so tempting anymore and Pru sat looking at her mirrored reflection, sipping her Perrier with lemon, wiggling her pretty toes in her expensive new shoes. For once she was thinking about tomorrow instead of only today. It was still hard though. For a woman to change her ingrained habits, that is.

The fries seemed to gaze back at her as she stared at them. An entire three quarters of a club sandwich was still on the plate. She knew she'd better get out of here before she ruined everything. Besides, guilt was not a good feeling. And in truth, she had not even enjoyed it.

Pru signed her name to the check, scrambled to her feet, left the food on the table and walked out. It was a small triumph, but still, a triumph.

She wondered if she would see the gorgeous man in the elevator again.

chapter 44

Mac and Sunny were in room 1001, lost in her downy, mint-green, silk-damask bed with the curtains closed around it, shut off from the world. Sunny thought that two alone was a lot different from being one, alone. Two was perfect.

Mac's tongue moved lazily from her lips and down her taut arched neck. His hands circled the pouty coral nipples, then smoothed down her long golden body, her oh-so-familiar, oh-so-loved golden body, until finally, he lifted her into his face, to his mouth, his tongue.

He heard Sunny giggle. He lifted his head. She was *laughing*.

"I'm sorry," she gasped. "Truly sorry, I didn't mean to laugh, but it's just all so . . ." She was laughing so hard, she had to bury her face in a pillow to hide the yelps.

He sat back, staring at her. *"What?"* he asked, baffled.

"What, *what*?" Sunny's muffled voice came from under the pillow.

"I've never had this happen to me before," Mac said, sounding wounded.

"Hah, hah, hah! That's because you never made love to a woman this crazily happy before."

Sunny clutched the pillow over her breasts. Her eyes were alight with laughter. Seeing his downcast face, and his downcast member, she bit her lip to stop further giggles escaping. "I apologize," she said, reaching for him. "I was just so happy in that moment, just so wonderfully not 'alone,' except all alone with you. Ooh, Mac, I'm so in love with you, it makes me want to laugh, even at all the wrong moments. You can't know what I went through without you."

He took her in his arms and they lay body-to-body alongside each other. "Oh yes I do know," he said. "Oh yes I do know, and I'm telling you now, I won't ever let you leave me again."

"You shouldn't have *let* me leave," she objected. "You should have said, 'Don't even think of leaving me, Sunny Alvarez, you belong right here.'"

"I'm saying it now."

She pulled her face back from his. "Say it," she demanded. "Say it now. *Swear* it."

"I swear it," Mac said. "You are the love of my life, I will never let you go."

"Oh God, oh God." She relaxed, at peace in his arms, all laughter gone. They looked deep into each other's eyes. "I won't go, Mac," she promised. "I won't ever run away from you again."

"I guess that means we have to get married."

Sunny hooked him with a long brown leg, pulling him closer. "Maybe," she said. "Maybe we will, and maybe we won't."

"But I'm yours." He put his hands under her. He was hard again, ready for her, for anything she wanted. "I'm your sex slave," he murmured, his face half hidden under her long tangle of glossy black hair at the nape of her neck. "Do what you want with me."

Sunny began to laugh again, and this time Mac joined in. "Oh God, I love you," she said. "You always make me laugh."

His cell phone vibrated on the glass coffee table. Sunny glanced up. She saw the chair where Mac had thrown his pants, next to her skirt and sweater. His shoes were by the door next to her boots, the black leather jacket was over the back of another chair, her lace panties on the floor, her bra on the coffee table, next to his phone.

"You'd better answer it," she said. "You always do."

"Not this time," he said. And he took her lips in his, sending those urgent electrical impulses that hot wired her until she vibrated like the cell phone. Only with a lot more pleasure.

chapter 45

Mac's phone had continued to buzz at ten-minute intervals but they had managed not to hear it. Finally, he lay back. His right arm was round her, and his left hand stroked her tangled black hair. Her head was tucked into his shoulder, her right leg slung possessively over him, her inner softness pressing against his hard thigh. It was her favorite position because with her head on his chest she could hear the beat of his heart, the rhythmic thudding of life and love.

The phone buzzed on like a demented fly.

Sunny lifted her head and looked at him. His eyes were closed and by now the dark stubble on his chin had taken on a bluish look. A faint smile lifted the corners of his mouth. She leaned over and kissed it.

She loved Mac's body, long, lean and muscular, though she never saw him work out, unless walking the beach at Malibu counted as a workout which, since he often walked for miles while thinking about his next case, it probably did.

She said, "Don't you think you'd better answer it?"

Eyes still closed, his fingers tangled in her hair. He pulled her back into him. "Why?"

"Ma-a-ac . . . you *have* to answer it."

"No I don't." He dropped a kiss on her shoulder, still lost in the moment. "Smooth," he murmured. "So smooth."

The phone stopped buzzing. Sunny stared warily at it. That phone ruled Mac's life and therefore it ruled hers. Always, at the other end, there was trouble. Now she was nervous. What if someone was in danger? What if they needed help? An inner voice told her she should leave this alone; she had gotten what she wanted. She was with Mac, he was not answering. Finally, she came first.

It buzzed again. She couldn't stand it. She ran to pick it up.

Out of the corner of her eye she saw Mac raise himself on his elbow, watching her. The number on the screen was not one she knew. "Hello?" she said cautiously.

"I wish to speak to Monsieur Reilly." The masculine voice sounded very surprised that a woman had answered.

She walked back to the bed, handed it to him.

He took it, looking at her, puzzled. "Why did you answer?"

She shook her head, she didn't know. She went into the bathroom and put on the hotel's dove-gray terry-cloth robe then went to the window and pulled back the curtains. She stood looking out into the sparkling night, a night just as clean and clear and beautiful as she knew Paris must be overcast and cold, and very possibly still snowing.

She heard Mac say "Hello Inspector." Trying hard not to listen, Sunny bent to pick up their scattered clothing. A manila envelope fell from Mac's jacket pocket, and she picked that up too. Somehow the photos slid out and she was looking at them. A blown-apart head, a nightmare of what used to be a woman's face. She knew of course who it was. Who it had been.

"*Oh God, oh my God . . .*" She covered her eyes. "*Oh no, Mac, please, no.*"

She heard Mac quickly tell the Inspector he would get back to him. He came and knelt beside her, took her hands from her eyes and held them tightly. "You were not meant to see those. I'm so sorry, I would give anything for you not to."

Tears splashed from the tip of her nose onto the gray robe. He wiped them away with the sash.

"Who is she?" Sunny asked.

"Don't ask. Just put it behind you. Tell yourself we are not involved because we are not."

"We're not?"

"Absolutely not."

"Then why was the Inspector calling you?"

"He asked for my help. I refused. Of course there's nothing I could really do anyway; it's up to the *brigade criminelle,* the French crime police, not a foreigner like me."

"A well-known detective like you."

He frowned. "It's none of my business."

"Is that what you told the Inspector just now?"

"Yes, it was."

"What was her name?"

"Yvonne."

"I remember. I saw her picture in the newspaper, pretty, with a husband and a small child."

Mac said nothing.

"She worked at the jeweler's and the robbers killed her," Sunny said. "They shot her face away."

"One of them did, yes."

"And you are going to do nothing about it?"

"I came here to be with you."

Sunny saw compassion for the dead woman in Mac's eyes. She knew that, as he always did, Mac had to go where the truth took him. That was simply the way he was.

She said, "It's what you do, and I'm sure you'll be able to help."

Mac understood what she was telling him. The love between them locked them into their own space. He took her in his arms, held her close, mopped her tears and said, "So how can I work without my Private Eye assistant?"

She managed a grin. "You mean you've fired me?"

"Get your clothes on," he said, "we're going to the *préfecture.*"

Ten minutes later though, Mac changed his mind. Sunny had seen the photos but he didn't want her to hear the details of how Yvonne died. He didn't want her upset more than she was already.

When he told her, Sunny seemed relieved. "I'll go find Allie," she said, kissing him lengthily in the elevator. Then, "Do you realize how much of our sex life takes place in elevators?" Laughing, she added, "I'm going to tell Allie and Pru our good news. After all, they came here specially to help me.

"Good luck," she called after as Mac walked away.

chapter 46

Ron Perrin was not amused when Mac was not at the airport to meet him. He got on his iPhone immediately. "I'm standing outside fuckin' Nice airport, so where the fuck are you?" was his greeting.

"I may be a detective but unless you tell me your time of arrival I don't know when to expect you."

"Ah. Right. Well then, I'll get myself into a limo and be with you in half an hour."

"I'm not at the hotel. I'm at the *préfecture,* alone with the Police Inspector. I thought it was better if Sunny didn't join us."

"Sunny?" Ron was baffled. "How did I get the impression I was on my way to save your relationship with Sunny?" He could almost see Mac's grin.

"It's saved," Mac said. "But thanks anyway. Come right over." Mac gave him the address of the *préfecture.*

"Why don't you just send a cop car for me," Ron joked. Last thing he wanted was to be in another cop car, even if he were not handcuffed this time.

Fifteen minutes later he was drinking coffee—not bad coffee for what he would have called in the United States a precinct house, listening to an Inspector who looked like one of the bloodhounds from a Sherlock Holmes movie, telling about the murder a couple of nights ago; exactly what had been stolen, the destruction of the Babe Bailey diamond; the shards of which had ended up embedded in the dead woman's face.

Ron knew what it felt like to be shot at, though his attacker had fortunately missed the target—namely his heart, which was a good thing because now that heart belonged permanently to Allie. In fact it had always belonged to her, though neither of them had realized it then—"due to circumstances," as Ron liked to say when they reminisced about the bad old days. But because Mac had saved Allie's life Ron was prepared to do anything to help him, including lending him Allie for Sunny-support, or flying to Nice in his small Cessna in turbulent weather with cumulus attacking him at every thousand feet.

"So, what're we gonna do about it?" he asked, one leg crossed over the other knee, Styrofoam cup of now-cold coffee still clutched in his hand.

"You mean what am *I* gonna do about it," Mac said.

"*Actuellement*, the position is that it is *I* who must do something about this case," the Inspector said, jowls drooping even more sadly. "The staff at the Paris store, as well as the staff here, have already been interviewed, except the woman who was injured in the Paris heist. She has only today been released from hospital. She claims she remembers nothing. I am hoping, Mac, that you might be able to get through to her, trigger her memory."

"Mac doesn't speak French," Ron said. "But that's okay, I'll translate for him."

Mac threw him a skeptical glance. "And when did you learn to speak such good French?"

"Remember me? The French landowner? I have to get along with my neighbors, don't I?"

The Inspector said, "The story is the same in all the other targeted jewelers'. The three women in Marilyn Monroe masks, two tall, one shorter, all with long blond hair, in very good fur coats, mink but top of the line, though not identifiable by designer even to the connoisseur-eye of the store manager, who knows about such things. The coats were long, to the ankle, and of a dark color. They wore surgical gloves. A single strand of blond hair was found on one of the glass counters. It was human hair but probably from a wig."

"They never took off the masks, even on the street after they left?"

"Not that any of the staff saw."

"And they didn't see the getaway car?"

"No one saw it perfectly, though the manager believes it was some kind of van, the type with the sliding doors. You must understand the staff were all in shock; their friend was lying on the floor with her face shot away, blood was sprayed everywhere, even onto their own clothing. They were hardly in a state of mind to be noticing details, they were afraid for their lives."

"I'll bet they were," Mac said. "Did anyone describe the gun?"

"Shiny. Very small. A pistol, was how they described it."

"A pistol with a powerful punch," Mac said, remembering the results of that bullet.

"Ballistics are working on it, but the word is it's probably a 9mm."

Ron was on his iPhone again. "What are you doing?" Mac asked.

"Getting the Cessna refueled. I guess we're off to Paris."

Mac thought about Sunny and how they had left things between them. Could he simply leave now? "Good luck," she had said. He knew that of course she would understand. And he would need that luck.

chapter 47

Eddie had returned early from Hamburg. He showered off the grime of travel, put on casual chinos and a navy cashmere V-neck. Without looking in the mirror he combed back his still-wet hair that was long enough to lie smoothly on the nape of his neck. There was no doubt Eddie was a good-looking man. Not that he thought about it much, and since his marriage had disintegrated and Jutta distanced herself, there had been pleasant diversions but no one involving his emotions the way Sunny had.

Sunny had not called him back. He guessed that meant that what had never really been, was over. It still didn't stop him from hoping to see her in the bar and talk to her, but when he got there the place had already emptied out, just a few couples and business groups. It was still early and the bar was quiet. He saw the redhead whose name he couldn't remember, sitting up at the bar, waving him over. He saw her turn to the bartender, order something, then she waved at him again, tilting her head appealingly.

Wanting to avoid her, Eddie hesitated. Which gave Kitty enough time to slip the small pill into the vodka on the rocks she had already ordered for him. The pill was known for good reasons as the "date-rape" drug, because after only several minutes the victim would become dazed. She knew Eddie would be like putty in her hands. He

would feel weak and as though he was drunk. He would have difficulty thinking coherently, or even moving and talking. Of course the
drug was also dangerous; the drop in blood pressure could cause
sudden death. Kitty put this out of her mind though. For her purpose, it was ideal. The pill in the drink always did the trick, it fizzed
for half a second then disappeared, untasteable and undetectable.

Kitty had almost given up hope when Eddie walked in, exactly
as she'd wanted because her trap was set, and tonight she was ready
for action. Kitty was a professional; she knew exactly what to do.

She slid from the stool and walked over to Eddie. Her silky
dress clung to her broad hips and flurried around her knees. She
put her hand on his arm. "You look like a man in need of a woman
like me," she said softly. "Come, Eddie, sit with me. Let's talk."

Tired, sad, world-weary and vulnerable, Eddie went with her.

"You were away on business?" she asked, ordering a third beer
for herself and a third Red Bull. Kitty knew she drank a lot but
swore it never affected her, except to make her tongue looser, which
made Jimmy mad because he said she ran off at the mouth and that
was dangerous. But tonight, that didn't matter. She knew exactly
what she was doing, and the endless Red Bulls gave her a caffeine
high that sent adrenaline pumping through her veins and along with
her usual beers, which she loved and drank from the bottle, had
her on a terrific high. Watching Eddie sip his doctored vodka, Kitty
smiled.

"I was in Hamburg," Eddie said. The redhead had her hand on
his arm again. He stared disapprovingly at it but then he shrugged.
The woman was only being nice to him. He caught her glance then
she looked demurely away.

"Hamburg," she said, speaking so quietly he had to lean closer
to catch what she was saying. "That's a very sexy city, I know it well.
There are swinger clubs there that take care of all your needs." She
lifted her eyes and met his again. "All your desires," she added softly.

Her face was suddenly all Eddie saw, all he could focus on. After a long moment he pulled his eyes away. He seemed to have drunk the vodka very quickly and he saw that Kitty had gone through the beer like it was Coca-Cola.

He said, "I don't go to sex clubs."

"But Eddie, you don't know what you're missing. I love going to those clubs, I love it when men I don't know, total strangers come on to me, I love it when they touch me sexually . . . of course I never wear panties. I'm so sexy, Eddie. Doesn't it excite you when I talk like this? Don't you want to hear about it? I know you're really a voyeur, a man who would like to watch me do that."

Eddie could not believe what she was saying; he couldn't even remember how he had gotten into this conversation or what he was doing here. He knew he needed to leave, yet he had no will. He let her order another drink.

"That's half the fun," Kitty said, fluffing her flame-colored hair and taking another gulp from the beer bottle. "But why are you and I talking sex, Eddie Johanssen, when I'll bet what you really need is food." She watched Eddie pick up his glass and drain the second vodka. His hand shook.

"I'll tell you what," she said in that urgent whisper, pressing his arm close to her breast. "We'll go back to my place. I'll fix you a real home-cooked meal. I'll bet you didn't think I would be a good cook, did you? But I make the most delicious meatballs you've ever eaten, even in Sweden. We'll put on some music, drink some wine and I guarantee soon you'll feel good again."

Right now all Eddie felt was tired. He wanted to get up and leave but his legs did not want to move.

Kitty flung some euros on the counter. She had to act quickly to get him into the car. She put an arm around Eddie and hauled his around her waist. Together they walked from the bar.

The bartender's eyes followed them. He wondered what was going on, but anyhow figured he knew.

chapter 48

Kitty drove to her apartment. She put on all the lights and lit every lamp. The overhead tracks delivered a glare that hurt Eddie's eyes. She had left the curtains open and the garden was also lit up.

"It's like a film set in here," he protested, but Kitty only laughed and said she liked to see what she was doing.

She put her arms round him and pressed her lips on his. And this time it was not just "a hint" of tongue; it was definitely tongue. She rubbed her body against him. "You are so wonderful," she whispered, her breath hot in his ear. "I'm so attracted to you." She took his hand and put it up her skirt. "Feel how hot I am for you, Eddie?"

He stared, stunned, into her blue serpent's eyes.

"You like this, don't you?" Kitty said. "I know you do. You're like me, a voyeur at heart. I want you to watch what I do Eddie. Then I'll teach you."

He pulled away from her, and, worried, Kitty thought he seemed to be getting stronger. She had to give him more drugs. She would crush them up and put them in the meatball. Anyhow, she'd really like to fuck him, just for the experience.

"A shy boy," she laughed. "Or maybe you're just hungry."

She led him to the white couch to the left of the coffee table. Eddie dropped into it but she pulled him back up. "No, not there," she said firmly. "Sit right here. This is the place I want you." She arranged him carefully on the other sofa on the right so the video cam would have him in direct focus. "Now I'll go put on some music, I'll get you a drink and bring you my home-cooked Swedish meatballs. Odd you being Swedish, that it's my specialty, don't you think?" she added, bending to stroke Eddie's confused face.

Staring vacantly up, Eddie found himself thanking her. She went to put on a CD. He groaned. Was that *really* Engelbert? He hated it but couldn't even get up enough strength to change the CD. What was he doing here? He certainly didn't want to fuck her.

Kitty reappeared from the kitchen carrying a glass of red wine and a big white plate containing a single meatball to which she had added the ground-up drug Rohypnol.

"Taste this one," she said, giving him her best bucktooth smile. "If you like it, I'll serve you more."

She hovered over him and unknowingly, he ate it. Already drugged by the pill she had slipped in his vodka, he was a man with no will of his own. He would do whatever she said.

Kitty knew that soon he would be completely in her power. She could do whatever she wanted. She would arrange him in compromising positions in front of the hidden video cam. Eddie would awake on her sofa the following morning, none the wiser and she would simply tell him he'd had too much to drink and had fallen asleep. Now, the video cam was on, the lighting was strong; Eddie had taken the drugs. The rest was up to her.

"Make yourself comfortable." She hitched his legs up onto the sofa and put the glass of wine in his hand. Then she left him.

Eddie felt very strange. Had he had too much to drink? He should ask for some water, that would make him feel better. His thoughts were slow; it was as if he were living in a dream. He wanted to get up but was incapable of even moving his legs. He did not like the way he felt.

He heard Kitty call his name and looked up. She was posing in the doorway in leopard-print bikini pants, a skimpy blue satin cami and a cushioned bra that pushed up what little she had. Incongruously, she had on her daytime black leather Louboutin shoes with the red soles. Her legs gleamed with oil and she was holding a small travel bag.

She adjusted her sexy pose, right knee in, then she swung round and gave him the back view. Cellulite, emphasized by the harsh lighting, rippled her thighs.

"This is all for you, Eddie, baby," she whispered throatily. "I'm so attracted to you. I'm falling in love with you. You are so wonderful. I want you so much. I *need* you."

She knelt before him, took the wineglass from his hand, leaned over and kissed him. Lingeringly. Eddie did not kiss back. He could only stare as she stripped off the panties and posed in front of him, smiling.

"Doesn't this excite you?" Kitty was in charge now, displaying herself to him.

Stunned, Eddie stared at her hairless crotch, her plump thighs and skinny calves. Kitty looked like an overweight plucked old chicken. Suddenly he exploded in laughter.

Kitty seethed with anger. *This was not the way it was supposed to happen.* He was still helpless with laughter. She pushed him back down into the sofa. Her small blue eyes stared malevolently into his, pinpoints of venom.

She opened the little overnight bag that contained her arsenal of sex toys: a blue vibrator; lubricants; oils; lotions; handcuffs; a whip; a leather mask and studded collar; sadomasochistic magazines and sex toys.

Eddie had difficulty focusing. Kitty was about as erotic as the Ratte she was named for and yet somehow he could do nothing. He was helpless and could not get away from her. Then, quite suddenly, he fell backward, into darkness.

Kitty checked his pulse. A little slow but not dangerously so.

Still, Eddie was a fit man, he was stronger than her other victims and she wasn't sure how long he might be out. She had to work fast.

He was almost too heavy for her to handle as she stripped him down, maneuvered him into the special place on the sofa in front of the camera, then arranged herself with him.

She took Eddie through enough poses that she was sweating at the end of the fifteen minutes of sexual labor, before finally giving up. She was wishing she had insisted Jimmy hide in the bedroom so he could have helped her. Why did she have to do all the work? Jimmy could easily have been edited out of the video later. Though of course Kitty could not be edited.

It was important for her blackmail plan that *her* face be right there next to Eddie's; that whoever saw the photos or the video, it would look as though Eddie was fucking her and that sadomasochism was involved. Especially, that is, to Mrs. Jutta Johanssen, mother of Eddie Johanssen's two precious children. Eddie would die for those kids. Or if not die, then certainly he would pay a great deal of money to save them from the shame and humiliation. The media just loved a good sex scandal involving a rich and powerful man. Eddie was Kitty's jackpot.

Looking at him, she half-wished he'd been awake long enough to be even an unwilling participant. She was humiliated by the knowledge he had not wanted her. She would have enjoyed playing him along, letting him think he was a sexual demi-god and the only man she'd ever really wanted. She was getting too old for that to work anymore. It was no use telling the men she picked up at the club that her "partner," Jimmy, thought she was beautiful and that he loved her body; and that the sex between them was "wonderful." The truth was all Jimmy wanted was to watch the videos of her having sex with other men at the clubs. He liked taking pictures of her there to look at later. Jimmy was too much like Kitty.

These photos of Eddie were money in the bank. She and Jimmy could go back to Spain, to Marbella and open that little bar he often talked about. She would meet lots of men there, playing hostess. She could even start her own swingers' club. Kitty laughed as she thought how it would suit her perfectly.

She was still laughing when Eddie came round. She slumped next to him on the sofa, half-naked though still wearing the bra and cami because she was ashamed of her aging body and small slack breasts, a glass of red wine clutched in her hand.

When he saw her Eddie thanked God she wasn't totally naked. Then, as consciousness began to return, he asked himself *why* she was *half*-naked? He shook his head. He wouldn't want this woman even if she threw herself at him. Which ominously, he now began to believe, was what she had done.

"Stay right there, Eddie," Kitty whispered. Her breath smelled of stale red wine. "You've had too much to drink, *chérie*. Go back to sleep, let Kitty take care of you. Later I'll help you remember what a good lover you are, and how good I am."

She laughed as Eddie thrust her away. Somehow he managed to haul himself to his feet. She watched as he pulled on his clothes.

Her laughter was all Eddie heard as he staggered out the door and began to walk. He did not know where he was. He did not even know *who* he was. An hour passed, maybe two. It was still quite early but he had no clear knowledge of time. Eventually his head cleared sufficiently for him flag down a taxi and give the driver the name of his hotel. It was a night he would never want to remember.

And in fact, when Eddie awoke in his own bed, he would have no memory of the previous night, nor of what had happened. It was as though when he tried to think back, his mind had a black hole in it.

Which because of the date-rape drug Kitty Ratte had given him, was exactly what she had known would happen.

* * *

The returning Eddie was a sight that startled Pru Hilson, who was sneaking down in the elevator in search of a snack. A *French* snack, a small piece of good cheese, a thin slice of baguette with French butter. Small is beautiful she reminded herself, thinking of the new jeans, at the same time her mouth watered for the taste of the cheese. The way it used to for that hot dog. She still did not dare to remember hot dogs. They were locked away in her memory bank along with the once-upon-a-time husband. Pru was no longer eating to fill her fantasy life; she was enjoying food and felt no guilt about this little snack. She had left Allie sleeping, and in only her bathrobe and not expecting to meet anyone, Pru ran the elevator heading for the pool area where she knew there was a snack dispenser, when the elevator stopped, the doors opened and the gorgeous blond man stumbled in.

Pru put her hand out to stop him falling all over her. He was disheveled; his sweater was on backward and she couldn't help but notice his pants were not zipped.

Worried, she said, "Do you need help?"

"Ninth floor," he said. His voice was a rough whisper.

She pushed the button and the elevator rose again.

"Really, can I help you? Do you need water, or something?"

His eyes focused on her but Pru realized he was not seeing her. "Thank you," he said.

The elevator stopped and Eddie Johanssen got out. Pru got out too. She watched him stumble slowly down the empty hallway. She thought he must be dead drunk. But then she wondered. A man like that? The *perfect* man. He would *never* get drunk.

Something was definitely wrong.

chapter 49

It was getting late. Sunny was with Allie and Pru (who had given up on her snack after meeting Eddie in the elevator), when Mac called.

Looking at her glowing face, Allie said, "It's him, I can tell."

Sunny gave her that secret smile. She had not yet had a chance to tell them she and Mac were back together, that they had spent the past few hours making wonderful love, and all was right with their world.

"Hiiii," she whispered into the phone.

"Hi, there, baby . . ." Mac's voice was one of the elements that had made her fall for him; light and low and sexy.

"I'm in love with you," Sunny whispered.

Allie and Pru didn't even bother to pretend they weren't listening. Eyes goggling, Pru clasped a hand to her heart and sank backward onto the bed.

"I'm in love with you too," they heard Mac say.

Sunny was twirling a strand of her long dark hair, smiling a secret little smile. Pru looked at Allie who rolled her eyes.

"I need you Mac," Sunny whispered. "I want you. I want to be in bed with you. I'm away from you for ten minutes and I go crazy . . ."

"Oh God, Sunny, you know I feel the same way, you know that . . ."

Sunny closed her eyes. Allie and Pru glanced apprehensively at each other.

"There's a *but* in there somewhere," Sunny said, suddenly suspicious. "What are you going to tell me?"

"I'm at the *préfecture* with the Inspector, and Ron."

"*Ron?*" Allie repeated her husband's name wondering what he had to do with anything anyway.

Mac said, "Ron flew down here to help me sort things out with you."

Pleased, Sunny said, "Well, it seems he didn't have to, but I'm sure Allie will be happy he's here."

Allie stood, arms folded across her chest, looking puzzled.

"Tell Allie Ron says hi and he'll see her when he gets back from Paris."

"*Paris?*" Her heart sank.

"Sunny, honey . . ."

Sunny did not want to hear what she knew Mac was going to say next.

"Listen, babe," he said anyway. "I'm talking about Yvonne Elman. There's a woman in Paris, she worked at the jewelry store. One of the robbers struck her with the gun. Her face was damaged pretty badly. She's just out of hospital and doesn't want to talk to anybody, says she doesn't remember a thing. I'm hoping there could be something subliminal she might know, something she wants to hide even from herself, because she doesn't want to remember the pain."

"So you told the Inspector you would go see her, see if she would talk to you . . ."

"Babe, what else could I do?"

Sunny took a deep breath. Hadn't she just told him she understood what he did? She said, "Of course you must go. I only hope there's something you can do to help the police find the murderer."

"Believe me, it's not what I came here for, Sunny, you know that. I came because I wanted to find you, I wanted to be with you."

"Mac." Her voice was a whisper that even Allie and Pru, all agog, could not hear. "I only ever want to be with you. I love you."

Relieved, he said, "I'll call from Paris."

"Okay."

"If you need me, just call me, okay?"

"Okay."

"And I love you. Remember that."

"I will."

She closed her phone.

Allie folded her arms tighter over her chest. "So, okay. Two things. Are you back with Mac? And what's Ron doing here?"

"Yes, I am. I was just going to tell you when he called. And Ron came to Monte Carlo too, to help Mac get back with me. Now they're both going to Paris to investigate the jewel robbery."

Allie sighed, "And I thought I'd left him at home looking after the dog. I might have guessed he'd find trouble."

Pru slumped on the edge of the bed. "Be still my heart," she cried, clasping a hand to her breast. "I'm living in a romance novel."

They all laughed, then Allie said she was so happy for Sunny, so happy for Mac and what the hell had they been thinking anyway to ever be away from each other. She gave Sunny a hug and Pru got up and did the same, and then they all cried a bit and Allie suggested opening a bottle of champagne.

"Let's go out to celebrate," Pru said, surprising them. They agreed and quickly looked each other over deciding whether they needed to change.

Allie was wearing Levi's rolled over spiky ankle boots, a white tee and a furry vest that looked as though it had been removed from a fake Mongolian lamb in the sixties. Allie was into vintage and the rock-and-roll era was her favorite. The shaggy grayish-white strands of "fur" tangled with her fall of long straight blond hair, which she clipped hastily back without so much as a thought to how she might look.

Sunny was all in black: leggings, a long V-necked sweater dress and the famous black boots; not the UGGs, but those almost-Christmas-present ones. Her makeup had worn off and her hair still had a sexy tangled look. She ran her fingers through it, uncaring. All she felt was great.

Pru was wearing a sweater too, one Allie had found for her. Hyacinth blue with an empire waist, tight under her breasts then looser over the bits that were still what Pru termed "a nuisance." Since Pru had fallen for the unknown Eddie Johanssen she was determined more than ever to rid herself of that "nuisance." There was nothing like a man to make you want to look good, even though Pru knew she had a long way to go. Still, her red Chanel shoes looked terrific with the new black pants that did not squash her thighs and somehow made her look slimmer. Allie had given her one of her own lipsticks, Yves Saint Laurent's Nude Blush, which Pru had told Allie was the only bit of her that was going to be seen in the nude for a long time. After seeing Eddie even in that weird state, she was wishing it would not be quite so long.

Holding Tesoro on the lead, waiting for the elevator, Pru said to them, "Something very strange happened to me tonight."

"To *you*?" Allie was astonished.

"Well, not exactly to *me*, but that gorgeous Swedish man. Eduardo Johanssen."

Sunny glared guiltily at Pru, who went on, "I've seen him before, getting in and out of the elevator, in the foyer, that kind of thing, and I mean the man *is gorgeous*. Do you think you can be in love with a man you've never even met? Or at least not *really* met?"

The elevator came and they stepped into it.

"Pru, for heaven's sake stop gabbling and tell us what exactly you mean, 'in love' and 'something strange,'" Allie said.

"I'll tell you later," Pru muttered, aware of the other couple in the elevator.

"Thank heaven too that we're not going to that hotel bar," Allie said as they walked through the foyer, though Pru did cast a longing glance in that direction, thinking perhaps Eddie might have gone there. They dropped the dog off to be walked by the bellman.

It was impossible for Allie Ray not to be recognized. They had only to walk under that famous art nouveau glass canopy when the Casino doors opened magically, a table was found, champagne presented. Sometimes being a celebrity was okay, Allie said, smiling her thanks, though Pru thought anyone who acted less like a celebrity than Allie did not exist. Her friend was straight-ahead, unpretentious and anxious to keep her privacy, which was the reason Pru had been so angry when she had caught that bitch Kitty Ratte snapping pictures of Allie on her cell phone.

Pru stared at Sunny as they sat scrunched tightly together on a small banquette. "You look wonderful tonight," she said, sincerely.

"You have that 'glow.'" Allie smiled.

"*What* glow? What do you *mean*?" Pru asked, then blushed when they just smiled at her. "Ooh, oh, sorry, I didn't realize . . . oh hell, Sunny, lucky you."

"Your turn will come," Sunny said, holding Pru's hand tightly. "You're already looking different."

"And tomorrow you'll be a blonde," Allie added encouragingly.

It was true, Pru did look different. Her face was less round and her bosom was now contained in the snug sweater that did more for her shape than those God-awful baggy caftans ever had. "If you've got it, flaunt it," was Allie's new motto for Pru, and while not actually *flaunting* her breasts, at least now Pru acknowledged their existence

"Does anyone ever drink anything but champagne in Monte Carlo?" Pru asked. Champagne had not featured largely in her previous life; the odd glass at weddings, occasions like that, but never just for the sheer pleasure of it. She ran a hand through her limp brown hair wondering what she would feel like tomorrow when she was a blonde.

Sunny answered. "They drink Cosmos in the summer. In St. Tropez. Or at least I did."

"So what happened with the handsome stranger?"

Pru said, "I was in the elevator alone tonight when it stopped at the lobby."

Allie held up a hand. "Excuse me, but what exactly were you doing alone in the elevator?"

"I was just so darn hungry," Pru said defensively.

Allie put her face in her hands and groaned.

"I was only going to see if I could get a little cheese, a *tiny* slice of baguette. I needed the taste . . . I mean, Allie, I wasn't just friggin' hungry . . ."

Allie lifted her head and stared hard at Pru. "You *never* curse," she said. "So you must have *really* wanted it."

"Believe me, I was hungry."

"I know the feeling." Sunny was sympathetic. "Trust me, I've eaten bags of M&M's when all else seemed to fail. Somehow they slide right down, just that little crunch first and then you feel you've eaten nothing. Cheese is so much healthier. See, you've learned, Pru."

"So what about Eddie Johanssen?" Allie took Pru's hand encouragingly.

"Well, here's the strange thing. This beautiful man, you know how he looks, so handsome, so man of the world, so in charge . . . Well, let me tell you tonight he was not. Eddie Johanssen *staggered* into that elevator. I had to put out my hands to stop him falling all over me." Pru paused while they waited eagerly for what she would say next. "His pants were unzipped," she said.

Allie groaned. "And why were you looking down there anyway?"

"Ooh, you know it was just one of those passing glances, I mean the guy almost fell on me. Also his sweater was on backward.

And he slurred his words. In fact he could hardly stand up straight. And when I asked if he needed help he simply said thank you. He couldn't even focus. I don't think he even saw my face or knew who I was. I pushed the button for the ninth floor for him and he stumbled out. I watched him stagger down the corridor to his room."

"And then what did you do?"

"Then I went back down in the elevator and got my cheese and crackers."

"Both!" Allie said, mad at her now.

But Sunny was thinking of Eddie, not of cheese and crackers. Darling Eddie; her savior, her mentor; a man with whom she had half-fallen in love, and who she believed had fallen for her too. It was a "what-might-have-been" situation, and she had not yet even called him, not even left a message, apologized, thanked him, said goodbye-and-she-would-never-forget-him. She had just simply left. Selfish bitch that she was, how could she have been so cruel? *So* cruel Eddie went off and got drunk and all because of her.

"Eddie and I know each other," Sunny said in a small voice.

They turned to look at her.

"What do you mean 'know'?" Allie said.

"I was in love with him, a little bit, just for a few days . . ."

Allie groaned. "Sunny, are you telling us he was the other man?"

"I met him on the flight to Paris, he let me cry on his shoulder, he wouldn't let me stay in Paris because of the snow, it was Christmas and I was all alone and so was he. He booked me into the hotel in Monte Carlo, and then . . ."

"And then what happened?" Allie held out her hand, palm out to stop Sunny from answering. "No, no, it's better I don't know so I don't have to lie to Mac."

"But you *don't* have to lie, I mean nothing happened . . . Well nothing more than a kiss. Between friends, of course."

"Of course." Allie glared at her. "Why the fuck didn't you tell me all this earlier, Sunny? I thought you were dying of love for Mac."

"I was. I *am*. Nothing happened."

"You *kissed* Eddie Johanssen," Pru said, in a voice that was half a sigh. "Oh my God, you *kissed* Eddie Johanssen . . ."

"Just between friends," Sunny said firmly. Then, more honestly, "It could have been the beginning of something but then Mac arrived . . ."

"Mac came to *find* you," Allie reminded her.

Pru said, "Oh God, I remember the scene in the bar. Mac walked in and you walked over to him without a backward glance. It was almost as if there was a sign over your heads saying, 'We are lovers.' And you left Eddie sitting at the bar without so much as a backward glance. And then Kitte Ratte moved in on him. I *saw* her."

"Poor bastard," Allie said, realizing just how badly Sunny had behaved.

"I'm so sorry," Sunny said. "I couldn't help it. Eddie is kind, he's gentle, I was all alone, lost . . ."

"*And* he's sexy as hell," Pru said. They turned to stare at her and she added quickly, "At least he looks that way."

"Are *you* in love with Eddie too?" Allie asked, throwing her hands in the air.

Sunny said quickly, "*I* am definitely not in love with him. I mean, I could have been . . . but now I'm not."

"And I don't even know him," Pru said virtuously, smoothing down her hyacinth-blue sweater. "It's not possible, is it, to be in love with a man you have never actually spoken to?"

"Not unless you're a fan of a movie actor," Allie said. She knew all about crazed fans.

"So anyway, Sunny, what happened with Mac?" Pru hastily changed the subject.

Sunny shrugged, half-smiling as she remembered. "We just fell into each other's arms, the way we always do," she said dreamily. "Throwing our clothes off on the way. Making love with a man you really love is different, Pru. It's more than just the sex, *wonderful* sex, God I could just eat him up; but it's about that special chemistry, the bond that brings you together, the things that don't need to be said, the holding each other, my leg over him, his arm around me. And afterward . . ."

"Afterward . . ." Pru whispered. In her few married years she had never felt any of what Sunny had just described; had never had the sheer joy of lovemaking, never been held like that . . . *afterward* . . . "How wonderful," she said, wistfully, longing for that afterward.

"So, now what are you going to do about Eddie?" Allie asked.

Sunny took out her BlackBerry. "I'm going to call him right now. See if he's okay. And then I'm going to meet him, explain everything . . . You know. And thank him for just being the man he is. A strong man and a good friend in time of need."

"Lucky you," Pru said softly.

There was no reply to Eddie's cell phone. It was late now. Sunny would have to try him again tomorrow.

chapter 50

Paris

The woman injured in the jewel heist had refused to come to the *préfecture*. She had told them everything she knew, now she wanted to forget. But when Mac called her personally and asked if she would speak with him, because she knew his TV show she agreed to meet at Deux Magots, a café on boulevard St. Germain. Her name was Danielle Soris.

Mac waited alone at a table on the covered patio. It was very cold though the sun shone brightly from an azure-blue sky, gilding Paris in eternal beauty despite the eternal traffic. Danielle had only agreed to speak to Mac alone so Ron went and sat a couple of tables away, perusing a copy of the *International Herald Tribune* and wishing Allie were with him.

An old hand by now at all things French, Ron ordered hot chocolate to warm himself up, something Allie would never have allowed him to do. Allie kept him in shape, saying now they had worked things out she wanted him around for a lot more years, and he'd better let her worry about his cholesterol. He was enjoying the hot chocolate immensely. A guilty pleasure.

He looked up from his newspaper, caught Mac's eye and winked. Lifting his cup for Mac to see what hot chocolate in France was all about, he said, "Real melted chocolate. Real cream. Real heaven."

Mac ordered a double espresso. He had not slept, he was worried about Sunny.

He threw the coffee down his throat and ordered another. Ms. Soris was late; she was supposed to be there at three and it was already three-twenty. Traffic? Or a change of mind? He thought of Yvonne Elman and hoped it was traffic. Ms. Soris was their only real witness and even that was in doubt. He needed to know what else she had seen, perhaps only subliminally, besides the masked figure who'd dealt her a blow that could have been fatal.

"Monsieur Reilly?"

Danielle Soris was wrapped in a black woolen trench coat, wore flat black suede boots, a Russian-style fur hat and sunglasses. The scars on her face were a dark pink.

She had entered from the square on the other side of the boulevard, the one with Paris's oldest church, l'Eglise St. Germain des Pres. Mac wondered if she had been praying.

"Of course I know it's you," Danielle Soris said, in English. "I recognize you from your TV show. I admire you very much, Monsieur Reilly."

Mac got to his feet and shook her hand. He said he was glad she could come and held a cane chair to the tiny bistro table for her. He looked at her face then quickly looked away. Surprisingly, she laughed.

"Don't worry, everyone does the same thing. I'm getting used to people not looking at me anymore."

"Then do you mind if I ask you about the surgery? What exactly happened?"

"What happened, Mr. Reilly, was that my right cheekbone was fractured into tiny pieces. Some of the bone splinters penetrated the orbital area. I don't remember the pain because I have deliberately chosen not to, otherwise I would not be able to get on with my life." She put a hand to her eye where the delicate tissue was pulled upward so the eye could close.

"I have bone grafts in my cheek," she said. "They tell me that one day it will all smooth out and the right side of my face will begin to resemble the left again. Until then, this is how I look."

She took off her dark glasses and faced Mac. He looked back at what was obviously once a very pretty woman. Despite the grafts, the right side of her face had a caved-in appearance.

Danielle Soris brushed her long brown hair forward, replaced her sunglasses then pulled her fur hat lower over her forehead.

"Like this," she said with a smile, "I can almost get away with it."

"You're still a beautiful woman, Madame Soris."

She shrugged. "That's what my friends tell me. I'm allowing myself to believe it might be true, because you see, *monsieur* . . . Oh please allow me to call you *Mac*. And of course I am Danielle. You see, Mac, it's the only way for me to get through this *event,* as I call it now. I have to put it out of my mind, away from my sleeping thoughts, forbid the bad memories, the dreams, the fear. I cannot allow the fear to have access."

"I understand."

A waiter came and she ordered a glass of champagne. "You don't mind, do you?" she asked, raising her glass in a toast. "I feel the need for something festive. After all, in a few days it will be the New Year."

"Then may I be the first to wish you a Happy New Year." Mac raised his coffee cup. "You are a remarkable woman."

She laughed. "No, I'm simply a woman attempting to keep her sanity. And sometimes succeeding. But you see now, don't you, Mac, that I cannot talk about what happened. I cannot revisit that event. I never want to hear about it, think about it, allow my mind to wander into it. I simply cannot."

"I understand," Mac said. "But there's something I need to tell *you,* Danielle. About a young woman, like yourself, who was not so lucky when the robbers came calling in their Marilyn Monroe masks. Yvonne Elman had no face left. Someone shot her, took her life the way they almost did yours. Yvonne left a two-year-old son and a husband who is mourning her. I promised I would do my best to find her killer, and so far all I have to go on is what you can, or cannot tell me."

Danielle put down her champagne glass. The air was cold and she had kept on her bright red gloves. Now she took them off and lay them on the table, smoothing the soft kid leather. Mac noticed that her fingers had a slight tremor and that she wore no rings.

"Believe me, I understand," he said gently, putting his hand over hers to stop the trembling. Hers was cold.

"You are so kind," she said, still not smiling. "To warm me up."

"It's the least I can do."

"Human contact is very necessary, very . . . soothing," she said, sighing. "And you have made me feel very selfish when I suppose I should be feeling grateful."

"You need never feel grateful for what happened to you."

"Then I am bewildered. What *should* I feel, Mac? Guilt, for the poor dead Yvonne? You know I do. I just don't know how to deal with it."

He held her hand tighter across the table. "You are not compelled to do anything. I will understand."

She nodded, brushing her hair back again. "I can tell you only one thing. It comes into my mind when I'm not thinking about it, when I'm in my kitchen preparing coffee, or a sandwich, it's behind my eyes when I close them to sleep. I'm not even sure if what I think I saw is true, or a figment of my imagination, which is why I have never spoken of it to the police. It's all a haze, a blur . . . But the Marilyn Monroe woman was holding the gun, pointing it at me. It was a very small, very shiny gun. Steel, or perhaps chrome. I remember thinking, the way you stupidly do when you are looking disaster in the face, how very pretty it was." She smiled sadly at Mac. "You must remember I am in the jewelry business. I notice things like that."

"I'm glad you told me. Yvonne's family will appreciate your help."

"One more thing." Danielle took her hand away. She pulled on her gloves, then drained the champagne. "I'm remembering it now, I can see it perfectly in my mind's eye. There was a long-stemmed rose engraved on both sides of the barrel of the gun, cut very deep into that shiny steel. It stood out, that's why it's coming back to me. A black rose picked out in gold. It was quite beautiful. Really, quite lovely."

Her eyes linked with Mac's as she stood to leave. He got up and took her hands in his. "Yes, now I am sure that is what I saw and I'm not simply dreaming. I imagine it must be a connoisseur's piece," she added quietly. "And that is all I can tell you."

Mac stared into the face of this once-lovely woman, now scarred for life. "You are very brave, Danielle. And I thank you."

She nodded, and gave him a little goodbye smile. The right side of her face did not move.

"*Bonne chance,* Mac Reilly," she said, turning and making her way through the forest of small tables, out onto the street, where she was soon lost in the crowd.

Ron came up behind Mac. "Any luck?"

"Better luck than poor Madame Soris." Mac sat back at the table and ordered another espresso. His nerve ends jangled with the stress of unanswered questions, unsolved problems, the sight of a woman's ruined life.

He said, "The gun was a Kahr Black Rose. The PM 9 I'd bet. It's exactly the kind of gun a woman would like, small, easy to handle, powerful as hell and with little recoil. That black rose stands out against the steel, shiny as a mirror, so shiny in fact a girl could fix her lipstick in it. The rose is picked out in twenty-four carat gold. Exactly what a fashionable woman would enjoy."

"A gun like a piece of jewelry," Ron said.

"Exactly," Mac replied.

chapter 51

Paris

Later, Ron and Mac were having dinner at the bar at La Coupole, not in the main dining room with the tables with the white cloths. They ordered oysters—Belons—Ron's favorite and beers, not champagne.

"Goes much better," Ron said, tilting back his head and sliding a silvery mollusk from a pearly shell down his throat. "Oh God, the brine is wonderful, I feel I've just eaten the sea."

"At least it was protein," Mac said. "You can discount the salt factor, it's natural."

"More where they came from," Ron said, ordering up another dozen. "These creatures must multiply worse than rabbits."

"I wasn't aware that mollusks had a sex life," Mac said, grinning.

"You should be such a lucky mollusk." Ron grinned back. "But I can see you no longer have problems on that score. Sunny's got you by the balls again."

"Jesus, Ron! If you weren't such a friend I'd be tempted to ram that mollusk down your fuckin' throat."

Ron shrugged, he took a sip of his beer, making a pleased face. "God that's good. Now all I need is a good cheese, some good bread and a glass of deep dark red wine that tastes better than the stuff I'm producing at the moment, and I'm a happy man. Meanwhile, no need to lose it, Mac. Sunny's your woman and that's all there is to it. It's the only reason I'm here with you, and my wife is there with her, and now, mission completed, I'm on my way home."

"Home? Why? We have a crime to solve."

"That's your job, not mine. Never was. I'm no longer a mogul business tycoon, I'm a vintner. I'm not a detective."

Mac glared at him. "I thought you were in this to the end."

"I've got a wife to go home to, friend. And you have a woman you were always going to put first. What happened to that little idea?"

"Sunny does come first. She understands about all this, about the senseless murder, about the two-year-old with no mother . . ."

"Understand *this*, Mac. They're *all* like that."

Mac downed his beer. He nodded. "I understand. And Sunny understands too. We have come to an agreement. She comes first and my job comes first."

"First of equals, huh?" Ron nodded back, knowing what he meant.

"The Black Rose is an American gun," Mac said, "made in Worcester, Massachusetts. It had to have been imported."

"Legally? Or illegally?"

"That's the question, but my bet would be illegally."

"Mine too. So how do we find out who bought it?"

"We ask illegal questions," Mac said with a grin.

Mac's phone vibrated. He took it from his pocket, checked it. It was the Inspector.

"*Ça va, mon vieux,*" he said, hoping for good news.

"Mac, I have something to report. As you already know there are rumors, more than rumors, *indications* I should say, that the center of illegal diamond selling has moved from Amsterdam and Istanbul, to the Balkan countries, specifically, Hungary, Poland, the Czech Republic."

"I'd heard that." Mac was looking at Ron who was looking questioningly at him.

"There's news, undocumented, that perhaps Prague is the new center, that all the robberies are organized from there. My informant is a member of a gypsy tribe. No doubt he will be killed if he is discovered to have told."

"Is he involved directly?"

"He claims not to be."

"And do you believe him?"

"I do not. But you understand there is nothing I can do. I want the information, he wants freedom. He was picked up dining in a very grand restaurant, very well-dressed, flashing money, big tips, champagne . . ."

"He's hot stuff," Mac said dryly. "And by the way, was he alone?"

"No. Not alone. And by the way, just so you know, our gypsy is a woman. She had a male guest, someone she'd picked up in a bar, a rent-boy, ready for anything as long as he was paid."

"Charming couple," Mac said.

"Looked like a million bucks," the Inspector said. "Or maybe even more."

"And you've set her free?"

"To my regret, yes."

"Any idea where she went?"

"Our gypsy woman took the next flight out to Prague. And by the way, gypsies like her no longer live in caves or caravans. Our gypsy lives in an apartment in New Town, Prague."

The Inspector gave Mac the address. He noted it down.

"I'll be there tomorrow," he said.

Then he told the Inspector about the Black Rose gun and what Danielle Soris had to say, and the Inspector said he would get right onto it.

Mac closed the phone and looked at Ron. Ron's eyebrows were in his hair. "So?"

"So. We have a lead. A gypsy woman, lives in Prague, says that's where the robberies emanate from."

"Emanate," Ron said, thoughtfully. "A big word for a bunch of killers."

"I'm going there tomorrow," Mac said

"And I'm going home," Ron said. "Sorry, *mon vieux*," he laughed. "See, I speak French just as good as you do."

"Just as well as I do," Mac corrected him.

Ron gave him an annoyed shove so Mac almost choked on his beer. "Oh, have another fuckin' mollusk and shut up," Ron said. "I have to go home. My dog needs me. My horse needs me. My wife, if she ever decides to leave the love of your life, hopefully still needs me."

"She always will." Mac knew.

"I'm a lucky man." Ron wasn't grinning now. "Thanks to you, Mac Reilly. And listen, I'll fly home tomorrow, first thing. I'll go back, check on my animals and my vines, see the cottage hasn't burned down, talk to my woman. Then I'll meet up with you in Prague the next day. How's that?"

"A true friend," Mac said, high-fiving him. And then Ron ordered a cheese platter that stank to high heaven and tasted like paradise. The red wine was deep and dark and good. They had a clue; a destination; life was looking up.

Just one thing. Mac had to tell Sunny he wouldn't be back the next morning.

chapter 52

Sunny stood in front of the bank of French doors leading to the terrace in Allie's Sun King suite. Allie and Pru sat on the edge of the bed, skidding on the slippery silk comforter, stopping their slide by jamming their feet, heels down, toes up, then looking expectantly up at her.

Sunny was on the phone with Eddie Johanssen. Or at least she had called his number and now she was listening to his message. She had not realized before that Eddie had such an accent; his voice was charming, soft-spoken, clear, calm. Like the man himself.

She fiddled nervously with the end of a massive tassel that clasped the golden silk taffeta curtains, wondering what to say. She could not tell him she wanted to see him, though in truth, she owed Eddie that courtesy. But it was better for everybody, for her and Mac and Eddie too, if she did it this way.

"Eddie, oh, Eddie, it's me," she said quickly after the tone. "I mean, this is Sunny. I meant to call you before, *earlier* I mean, but I was, well I was sort of caught up in things and . . ." She took a deep breath. "Well, Eddie, I just want to say thank you for helping me when I needed help so badly. And thank you for being so kind, and so . . . thoughtful, and . . . well, everything that you are. I'll never forget that, Eddie, truly I won't. But, you see, now my life is back to normal, back on track I suppose you could say. I'm back with Mac anyway. And you know he's the love of my life. I just needed to tell you that, Eddie, and to say thank you for being there, for being you . . ."

The message cut off and Sunny thanked God. She might have gone on too long anyway, said too much. As it was she heaved a sigh of relief. Now there were no more secrets.

"Was I okay?" she asked the two women, who were sitting, open-mouthed, staring at her.

"*Okay?*" Allie said finally. "You sounded like a woman in love."

"I did not!"

"Yes, you did so." Pru ran a distracted hand through her short honey-colored hair.

"Pull the bangs more forward, Pru," Allie instructed, running her own fingers helpfully through Pru's new crop. "It really looks great."

Pru peered into the mirror on the wall opposite. "Do you *really* think it's okay?"

"Oh for God's sake!" Sunny yelled. "We're talking about Eddie Johanssen!"

"*You* were talking about him," Allie said. "And it's a good thing you left a message and didn't go and see him because I just know you would have given him a big kiss goodbye."

Sunny went to sit next to them on the bed. They slumped in a line, staring at the dark blue horizon that was the Mediterranean.

"I don't love him, of course," she said after a long silence. "I love Mac. I can't live without Mac. I am not complete without Mac. With Eddie, I would have had to be another Sunny, a different woman." She turned her velvet eyes mournfully on them. "I couldn't do it. I couldn't be Alone. And being without Mac was being Alone. I never knew the meaning of the word until I left him. We were always together, the two of us, never just one. Always."

"And now you always will be again," Pru said, wishing she

could feel like that about somebody. "Anyhow, when's Mac coming back from Paris?"

"Tomorrow morning." Sunny smiled at Allie. "With Ron, I guess."

"I guess." Allie's smile linked with Sunny's.

Left out, Pru watched them enviously. She wanted to understand these feelings, to know why someone was so alone when the man she loved was not with her; why the two women were linked in their knowledge of their love. How, she wondered, did you get that, get there, get to love and be loved?

Sunny's phone rang and she grabbed it quickly, smiling. Of course it was Mac. "Hey," she said, the smile still in her voice.

Shameless, the other two listened in.

"Prague?" they heard her say. A frown creased the space between Sunny's eyebrows. "A day? *Two?* You're not sure. But is it that important?" She nodded, swishing back her long dark hair, frowning down at the golden rug. "I know, I know I agreed and I do understand. And of course, Mac, darling, it's exactly what you should do. Believe me, I mean it."

The two women glanced meaningfully at each other.

Sunny was saying to Mac, "So Ron is returning to the vineyard. Yes, I'll tell Allie he'll call her later. Okay, Mac. Yes, of course I love you." She smiled and lowered her voice. "I'll always love you, you're my lover boy, who else would make love to me like that?"

Pru's brows rose. She looked at Allie. "Like *what?*" she whispered, but Allie just smiled.

Sunny closed the phone. "So," she said flatly. "Mac's not coming back tomorrow. He's off to Prague instead."

"*Prague?*" Allie asked.

"He has a lead, something the Inspector told him. He didn't go into details."

Pru heaved a giant sigh and said, "So, what do you do now? Just sit here and wait for him to come back?" Actually, what Pru was hoping was that Sunny wasn't going to change her mind and say the hell with it, and go see Eddie again. There was a blank look on Sunny's face, as though she were thinking inner thoughts. They waited silently for whatever was going to happen.

What Sunny was thinking about was Maha. Everything that Maha had ever said to her flew into her mind, from that first time on Christmas Day evening, in the bar when she had warned her against Kitty Ratte; to her oblique counseling about "men." Maha *knew* her. She understood that right now something else was needed emotionally, besides simply a desire to assert her independence. Sunny had always been independent, except in the ways of love. And what she needed, now, for her *own* good, not to prove something to Mac, was to take that "chance" in life that Maha had offered her.

"That's it." She got up and began pacing the room, over to the window then back again.

"You're getting me dizzy," Pru complained.

"But, I *know* you, Sunny," Allie said. "What's going on? What are you up to?"

Sunny stood in front of the bank of windows, silhouetted in the lamplight. "I'll tell you what I'm up to, my darling friends. I, Sunny Alvarez, am finally taking the advice another woman offered me. You know what she said? 'Take whatever chances life offers you.' And that is exactly what I'm going to do. No more waiting around for Mac. I am going to become my own woman."

"And how are you going to go about that?" practical Allie asked.

"I, my beautiful, lovely, movie goddess, am going to Mumbai."

"*India?*" Pru gasped.

"Oh no you're not." Allie got up and took Sunny by the shoulders. "You can't do what that woman asked you."

"*What?*" wailed Pru, still in the dark.

"She's going to act as a courier for Maha Mondragon smuggling jewels into India."

"It is not *smuggling,* it's all perfectly legal. Maha has everything documented. You know I would never jeopardize Mac's career by doing something that wasn't legal. You can only imagine what that would do to his credibility!"

"I don't trust Maha," Allie said, giving Sunny a shake to try and force some sense into her. "There's something wrong about the whole setup. Anyhow, why can't she just take the jewelry to India herself?"

"She's too busy, she has to go to New York, to Hong Kong."

"Then what about those satellites she has around her?" Pru asked. "You know, the two guys who look like extras in an Italian movie, and the tall woman who's so full of herself she acts like no one else exists. Why don't *they* take the jewelry back to Mumbai."

"I guess they're doing other work. Anyhow, it's all documented," Sunny explained patiently, though privately she thought she had better check again with Maha and make sure. "Everything is aboveboard."

"And shipshape," Allie said, defeated.

"It's only because I need to prove myself, just for once," Sunny said, though it seemed to Allie she had proven herself many times in the past, including when she'd found the woman's body in a refrigerator in a Tuscan villa. Sunny had a knack for trouble and Allie was worried.

But there was nothing she could do; Sunny was already on the phone to Maha.

"Maha, I'll do it," she was saying, listening as Maha said how wonderful, and please come to her suite right away. They would organize everything. It would only take half an hour, an hour at most. She would leave tomorrow, first thing.

chapter 53

"*You will never regret* this," Maha said, taking Sunny's hand. "You are a clever woman. There will be no problems, I promise you."

"Mac isn't coming back tomorrow," Sunny explained. "So I thought I would take the opportunity."

Maha's shrewd eyes assessed her. "It's the correct move. You will feel better doing something completely on your own. Something more daring. An adventure."

"Instead of Mac having all the adventures."

"And where is Mac?" Maha was already taking out the travel bag with the zippered compartment containing the jewelry.

"Prague. He'll be gone a few days."

Maha's back stiffened. "Will he, now? Well then, that will give you just enough time to complete your mission. You will leave early tomorrow morning on a private plane, destination Brussels. From there you will fly Air India first-class to Mumbai."

Sunny thought India suddenly seemed so far away, and Mumbai so exotic; an enormous city, teeming with millions of people; the smell of spices; the heat; the animals; sacred cows that you should not touch; the smell of dung, of sweat, of mimosa, of the sea; and visions of white marble palaces . . .

"It's a long journey," Maha was saying. "But you will be comfortable. My assistant will meet you at the airport. His name is Rahm Singh. He will be wearing a traditional white Indian caftan, and a red-and-yellow turban. He will be holding up a card with your name so you cannot miss him. Rahm Singh will drive you to my house, there will be no chance of you getting lost."

"And the jewels?" So far they had hardly been mentioned and Sunny was getting anxious. "How do I get through customs and all that?"

"First, and most important. You will never let the jewel case out of your hands, or your sight. It must stay with you at all times. You go to the bathroom on the plane, it goes with you. It rests under your seat, not in the overhead compartment. Under no circumstances must you hand it to a steward or any other person. As for security, you will be met and walked through." Maha handed over a dark blue zippered leather folder. "All the necessary documents are in here for customs leaving Brussels, and then for customs in Mumbai. You will be expected. Everything is arranged. Your import documents will be stamped, and of course in reality you are not importing anything. We are merely returning the jewels to India. So there can be no problem now, can there?"

She smiled her beautiful smile; her teeth were so white and even, her fuchsia-lipsticked mouth so lush and pretty Sunny wondered why she didn't just give up the jewelry business where she seemed to have to work so hard, and simply become a Bollywood movie star.

"You must go get your passport, bring it here," Maha said. "We need to stamp it."

"Stamp it?"

"A visa," she explained. "You need it for India. I will have someone from the consulate come round and take care of it."

She took Sunny by the shoulders again, looking deep into her eyes. "You are doing the correct thing," she said gently. "This will make things better between you and Mac, make him see you as a different woman. A new woman, perhaps. Anyway, one who can stand on her own two feet and who doesn't need a man to prop her up."

"A woman like you," Sunny said and Maha laughed.

Then, "There's one thing you have not asked me, Sunny. One important thing. Which is exactly how much am I going to pay you for this work."

Oh my God, Sunny hadn't even thought about the money.

"You'll never be a businesswoman if you don't ask about the remuneration up front and come to some agreement," Maha chided.

"So much for the Wharton business degree," Sunny said, cast down. "I was just too excited, too anxious."

"No need to be anxious. I will pay you ten thousand dollars for your three days' work. I trust that is acceptable to you?"

Acceptable! Sunny was stunned.

"Very well. Now you must go, bring me the passport. I will have the money and the jewels ready for you tomorrow. You will leave at five A.M. The weather is pleasant in Mumbai, hot but no monsoon yet. Take a shawl for the evening."

Maha was suddenly all business, back behind the table.

"I will call Mumbai, make sure you have arrived safely," she said. "And give you the rest of your instructions, about where to deliver the jewels, and to whom. Rahm Singh will keep me informed. And of course, India is a place where even the tiniest villages have cell phone contact. In that sense it is one of the most developed countries in the world."

"You mean I can call Mac?"

Maha hesitated. "I would rather you did not. Not only for me, for my business privacy, but because you are temporarily my employee. I need you to respect that and not discuss where you are and what you are doing."

"Of course," Sunny promised.

"Besides," Maha added, turning away with a smile as Sunny

hurried out to fetch her passport. "It'll be fun, keeping the detective guessing. Keep him on his toes."

Sunny laughed with her as she closed the door.

Back in the Sun King suite, the two friends were waiting for her.

"Well?" Allie said.

"You'll have to take care of Tesoro," Sunny said. "I'll be gone three days. She's paying me ten thousand, and if you are both very good and stop bitching, and promise never to tell anyone—and that includes Mac and Ron—where I am and what I'm doing, I'll bring you back a souvenir of Mumbai."

Allie gave her that deadpan look known to millions of moviegoers. "All I can say is it better be good. A ruby for my silence."

"You're right. A ruby," Pru added, grinning as they followed Sunny to her room to help her pack.

chapter 54

Mumbai

Getting there was so easy Sunny figured it had to be legal. The small private plane flew her from Nice to Brussels, then Air India took her first-class to Mumbai. Sari-clad women with glossy black hair pulled back into a bun handed out jasmine-scented hot towels and served almonds dusted with spices on filigree silver dishes, with crystal glasses of French champagne. The soothing Indian whine of sitar music played in Sunny's headphones, and later, the vegetarian *thali* she had ordered came on an indented silver dish, each section containing a different curried vegetable, including her favorite yellow lentil *dal,* and cauliflower cooked in hot spices, and the heavenly Bombay curried potatoes, along with a cucumber, mint and yoghurt sauce called a *raita,* which hit her with a cooling glow after the subtle heat of all the spices. Dessert was the wonderful Indian rice pudding, so different from the ones she had eaten as a child; this was cold with the lemony hint of cardamom hidden in its creaminess.

Later, stretched out in her own little private compartment, snuggled down in her soft blanket, with the scent of jasmine in the air bringing a promise of the exotic India at the end of her journey, Sunny could not wait to get there.

When she awoke they were skimming over the glittering lights of civilization at dusk, over miles of devastating blackened slums

piled against modern steel towers and crumbling Victorian Raj buildings, seemingly just thrown away by uncaring mankind.

Mumbai, city of contrasts, of eighteen million people, the richest
to the poorest; of Bollywood and high-tech; of scavengers and beggars; expensive shops and fine cuisine; once a group of marshy
islands landfilled to form the city on the bay.

Emerging from the plane, fatigued and apprehensive, clutching
Maha's bag of jewels, Sunny stood in line at immigration where her
passport was inspected and she was waved through.

At customs, Sunny was shown into a small office off to one side
of the customs hall, where a man in a crumpled white linen suit
invited her to sit on a rickety plastic chair, while he casually inspected Maha's documents. A fan turned slowly overhead, moving
the dust around.

After a while he lifted his eyes and looked Sunny up and down.
Her heart jumped; she felt guilty as hell of something. She only
prayed it was not smuggling. The man said nothing, instead he ex-
tended a thin brown hand and pressed a number on the phone.

Oh my God! This was it. She should never have agreed to do
this, never have done it, Mac would tell her how foolish she had
been to trust anybody . . . all she had wanted was to prove herself,
in some stupid fashion . . . and now what . . . ?

The man in the crumpled white linen suit spoke in an Indian
language to someone else. He put down the phone and sat looking
across his scruffy desk at Sunny, saying nothing. Sunny was sweating. She decided she had better meet his eyes and do her best to look
innocent. Suddenly furious, she told herself fuck it, she *was* innocent.
All she was doing was ferrying Maha's jewels back to India where
they came from.

A breeze wafted through the tiny room as the door swung open
and another man came and stood behind the one in the white suit,
gazing stonily at Sunny.

"Your passport, please," he said, in English.

"But I already came through immigration," Sunny protested.

"Nevertheless, your passport."

He held out his hand and Sunny took the passport from her pocket and gave it to him. She hated to see it go. She might never get it back . . . she would be stuck here in India forever . . .

The man looked at the passport then lifted his eyes and met hers. His were deep brown, the whites very white, his skin dark honey, his luxuriant hair silvered black.

"Thank you, Ms. Alvarez." He handed back the passport.

She sat clutching it to her chest, wondering what next. Was she free to go?

The passport man nodded to the white suit and left the room. The draft of cooler air wafted through again as the door swung shut behind him.

The white suit looked at Sunny, then at the two bags on the floor next to her: the small hastily packed one that contained a few items of clothing and Maha's heavy zippered bag with the jewels.

"Thank you, Ms. Alvarez. Have a pleasant visit to Mumbai," he said in suddenly perfect English.

He got to his feet, picked up Maha's bag and handed it to her. Unsmiling, he held open the door. Sunny thanked him and walked through it, certain he could feel the fear coming off her in great wafts, like the air-cooled draft into his hot little room.

On shaky legs, she strode as fast as she could through the green customs area and into the terminal. *Oh. My. God.* She would never do this again. *Never.* Not even if Maha promised her the biggest jewel in the crown of some decadent Mumbai Rhanee; not if she offered to have someone replicate the Taj Mahal in marble to commemorate her visit; not to prove herself to Mac, or to anybody— even her own self—that she was up to any chance life offered her.

Quite suddenly, Sunny was not sure about the new chances life offered.

The hell with this, she thought, the bag clutched in her sticky palm as though it were cemented to her hand, sweat trickling down her back, as she emerged into the noise and the smells and the throng of people, thick as a forest, pushing, shoving, shouting in her ear, touting bicycle-rickshaws, taxis, time-shares, hotels, spicy snacks, sweets, tours, trips.

There was no man amongst the crowd, though, holding up a card with Sunny's name on it. Uncertain, she stood for a few minutes, scanning the scene, then she made her way outside.

The tropical night seemed to fold over her, heavy with the scent of flowers and gasoline fumes. Palm trees waved on the ink-blue skyline, brightly lit towers glittered in the distance, and somehow, over it all, was the scent of the sea. Not crisp and salty like the Pacific, but strong and sultry with a hit of the marshes on which the city was born.

Taxis and buses lined the sidewalk and people pressed past her, a tidal wave of humanity and all of them, it seemed, wanting to get out of the airport and to the city.

Sunny checked the sheet of paper with Maha's typed instructions. She was definitely to be met by Maha's assistant.

Panic hit her: she was a woman alone in India with a bag full of jewels. Something had gone wrong. Yet how could it? Maha had been so certain, so careful, every detail taken care of. Maha was a woman who crossed her *t*s and dotted her *i*s . . .

"Madama Alvarez?"

He was there after all, right beside here, a tall, dark, thin man with piercing black eyes and a red-and-yellow turban wrapped around his head. He wore a long white Nehru coat over narrow black cotton pants and leather sandals. Dazed though she was, Sunny had time to notice that his toenails were polished. And that he was, after all, holding the card with her name on it.

"At last." She beamed up at him, relief shining in her eyes. "Yes, I'm Sunny Alvarez."

"So sorry, *madama*, not to be there the very moment you arrived." His voice had a singsong lilt and he was very serious. "But the traffic is very bad tonight in Bombay . . . Mumbai as you call it nowadays."

Sunny grinned. "For a moment there I thought I'd come to the wrong place."

He did not crack a smile. "I shall take your bags, Madama Alvarez," he said, reaching for Maha's bag.

"No!" At least she still had enough wits about her not to part with the damn bag after practically sleeping on top of it all the way on the plane, and now that it was stuck to her palm with sweat. "I'll carry this one."

"It is as you choose it," he said, in his quaint English. "Please to follow me to the car."

Sunny was very pleased to follow him. She couldn't wait to get to the car, couldn't wait to sink into the seat and let Mumbai flow past the windows.

It was a black Mercedes 600; one of the most expensive models. The interior was cool cream leather and, in an old-fashioned touch, there were twin crystal vases clipped to the sides, each holding a spray of tiny white star-shaped gardenias whose fragrance permeated the air, sending a shiver of pleasure along Sunny's sweaty spine. This was a car for a woman in a silken sari, a bejeweled perfumed woman, an Indian beauty. A woman like Maha Mondragon.

A console fashioned from dark burled walnut held drinks and pretty glasses, etched with a silver pattern of leaves. Bottled water chilled in a small cooler.

Sunny smiled at her rescuer as she settled back against the cushioned upholstery. "I'm sorry, but I forgot your name," she said.

"My name is Rahm Singh, *madama*. I am the Mondragon's chief assistant."

"Thank you, Mr. Singh." Sunny thought it was strange that he called his employer "the Mondragon," but figured that it was probably the custom here, in India.

They were already weaving through the airport traffic, down a seemingly endless harshly lit road, past garbage heaps like small mountains and half-naked shockingly emaciated children scurrying like tiny rats, amongst them; past honey-colored Victorian mansions, leftovers from the Raj, aflutter with lines of multihued washing; past blank-faced government buildings and into the city, along the Marine Drive, where bicycle-rickshaws pulled couples on an evening's outing; past a beach with crashing waves and more children running on thin reedy legs in and out of the water; past the palm trees and lantern-lit stalls with vendors selling *papadums* and breads filled with spicy meats and vegetables and sticky sugarcane; past beggars without feet or hands, reputed to have been mutilated as children in order to earn more from the pity of their indifferent public; past splendid hotels aglow with warm light and cool air, and past mansionlike homes, fastened in with strong metal gates where the old-rich lived; and past towers of condominiums where the young new-rich lived; past offices still lit and active though now it grew late. It seemed, Sunny thought, that Mumbai, shocking and exciting, never slept.

The big car slowed as they approached a pair of tall iron gates through which Sunny could see a small guardhouse. A man in a long white cotton shirt and baggy pants, tight at the calves, emerged. Recognizing the car he opened the gates and waved them on.

Sunny rolled down her window the better to see the view of sparkling lights strung along the coast, exactly like Malibu and Santa Monica. The Queen's Necklace of Mumbai, viewed from the top of Malabar Hill. The unexpectedly cool air rushed in and the scents of India came at her, enveloped her. At that moment it seemed India offered itself to her and quite suddenly she fell in love with it.

Five shallow marble steps led to a single-story many-pillared white house. The long narrow pool in front was edged in papyrus grass, its dark cobalt waters afloat with pink blossoms. At the far end, as though guarding the house, was an immense gilded statue of a goddess.

Rahm Singh opened the car door and Sunny stepped out, still holding on to the bag. She stopped to look. "But who is she?" she asked, staring at the statue.

"That is Mahalakshmi. The goddess of wealth and prosperity."

Mahalakshmi . . . Maha . . . goddess of wealth and prosperity . . . Of course, that must be where Maha had taken her name . . . from the goddess . . .

Smiling, holding on to the bag of jewels, Sunny walked up the steps. All fear left her. She was at Maha's house. She was home free.

chapter 55

Monte Carlo

Pru woke alone in the Sun King suite, with the three-pound Chihuahua on her chest. She opened her eyes and gazed directly into Tesoro's round bulbous ones. She wondered how a little dog could express so much sadness, evoking her pity simply because her beloved mistress had gone away for a few days. Plus she was sure Tesoro understood she was the most loved dog in the world, except maybe for Mac's Pirate, or at least that's what she had heard.

Tesoro's nose touched her warm cheek, icy as a fresh martini in the bar last night and Pru grabbed the soft sleek three-pound mutt and held her close. Of course Tesoro was no mutt, but, to Pru because she had never had one, all dogs were mutts. Why, she asked herself now, had she not had a dog? It would have gone a long way to comforting her when she got rid of the awful Lord Byron husband. And Tesoro adored her, she could tell because she never tried to bite her.

"Tell you what, sweet, softie, smoothie little baby," she whispered in Tesoro's delicately lifted ear. "You and I are going to have fun today. We'll go for a walk. I'll buy you lunch. I know you like chopped chicken, and, if you promise not to tell Sunny, I'll even give you a lick of my ice cream." She thought about the ice cream and quickly decided against it. "Not good for either of us, sweetheart," she said, sighing.

Tesoro snuggled into her, snuffling her hair. *Oh my God! Her hair!* The blond short cap of hair that she had been assured just a couple of days ago had transformed her into a new woman. Pru had not been certain then and she was even less certain now.

With Tesoro tucked under her arm she faced the gilded mirror opposite the windows. Shards of honey-blond hair fell across her forehead. Unsure, she put up a hand to touch, ran her fingers through the crop of gold that had taken the place of the shoulder-length stringy brown. "Short" made her nervous but both Allie and Sunny had told her it was wonderful. "Now everything works," Sunny had said. "Your skin color, the slight tan, the bronzer."

"You're starting to look like a South of France woman," Allie had said, pleased that her plan had worked out.

Still. Pru was left with the underlying insecurity that maybe it wasn't as fabulous as they said and that they were simply being encouraging to make her feel good.

Nervous, she put Tesoro down and went and took a shower. The little dog howled mournfully outside the glass door and she was forced to open it so at least it would not feel abandoned by everyone it knew. Pru thought it was certainly different, looking after someone other than only oneself; it made life more interesting somehow. And now she had a duty to take the dog for a walk, make sure she was safe, to help Sunny, who was on her important mission to Mumbai that was so secret no one but Pru and Allie knew about it. And Maha Mondragon, of course, who had planned the whole thing and gotten Sunny out of there with her bag of fabulous jewels without any delays for visas. Maha had everything under control, though Pru did still wonder why Maha could not have taken the jewels back to Mumbai herself. Too busy, Sunny had told her cheerfully, as she threw a few things into a case, ready to leave.

And then the same day Sunny left, Ron fell off his horse and broke his leg and Allie was on the next flight out of Nice. She'd said she would find out if he was okay, make sure he was comfortable and that the obstreperous Lab understood to calm down and not knock him over and break the other leg. Then she would be back, probably around the same time as Sunny. And also maybe as Mac, whom Sunny was again so passionately in love with, it made prickles rise on Pru's neck, just thinking about how sexy they were.

The truth was Pru had never been intimately and emotionally or even *sexually* really involved with anyone. Oh, a few high school romances, but in her day sex was something you thought about more than you did. Sex was a mystery, despite her marriage, and because of the husband-who-shall-be-nameless's selfishness, and also, Pru guessed, because he had not cared and probably hadn't really ever fancied her. Even in her honeymoon pale blue silk-chiffon very expensive nightie and robe, the one with the satin ribbons that she'd thought was sure to turn any man on, he'd barely looked at her. It wasn't until later, when she became more aware, that she realized a scarlet-and-black Victoria's Secret garter belt and push-up bra might have worked better, and by then it was too late, and anyhow she didn't care anymore either. Or at least she told herself she didn't care, but really, she did. And the hurt went deep.

She saw the glow Sunny carried like an aura; the heightened awareness of her body, of her being; the look only a woman fulfilled had. And now, dammit, Pru wanted that look. Only trouble was she had no idea how to find it.

She laughed at herself thinking about being sexy as she pulled on the narrow blue jeans Allie had chosen that made her butt look tighter and smaller and somehow more "rounded." And the soft brown flat suede boots with the fringe up the side, and the chocolate cashmere sweater that cost more than any sweater ever should but hell it made a difference, softer than silk and clinging in the most appealing way exactly where it should. The fact was too that after only a few days, there was less of Pru to cling to. She wasn't a skinny bitch yet, but she was on her way.

The little dog perched on the dressing table while she applied a touch of mascara, a hint of bronzer to her cheeks and the new nude lipstick that went perfectly with the new blond hair and the some-how new mouth that had a better curve to it. That was because she was smiling, and smiling was something she had not done in a long while.

"Okay, so here we go, Tesoro," she said clipping on the dog's scarlet jeweled harness. "The South of France woman out for a walk with her exquisite little international dog. Shall we stroll together along the Croisette in Cannes? Maybe even spot a movie star or two, though of course, as a Hollywood dog you're used to that. Then we'll have coffee somewhere, perhaps think about lunch. And there'll be no time at all for worrying about Ron, and wondering why Maha sent Sunny to Mumbai. And none at all for thinking about Eddie Johanssen who probably skipped town when he heard Sunny was no longer interested."

Oddly, as Pru and Tesoro stepped out of the hotel into a glowing blue day and a silver rented Renault convertible, Kitty Ratte was the only person not on Pru's mind.

chapter 56

Pru was not used to being on her own anymore. After years of being left alone while the erring husband "traveled" or more likely lived a whole second life, you would have thought she would be accustomed to it, but after a mere few days in the company of Allie and Sunny, she felt lonely without them.

Girlfriends, she thought, as she mooched slowly along the Croisette in Cannes with Tesoro dragging reluctantly behind, and the winter sun so hot she needed a cold drink, preferably champagne of which she had all of a sudden become fond, and the hell with Diet Coke. Anyhow, "girlfriends" were the best life had to offer. Unless life also offered a lover of course, but then Pru had never had a serious "lover," meaning a man who was so crazy for her he wanted to make love to her all the time and couldn't live without her. Truth to tell, she had never really had a man "friend," either. The husband was never her "friend."

They'd met at somebody else's wedding where Pru was a guest, not even a maid of honor or a bridesmaid though she and the bride lived in the same small town and had known each other since childhood. Pru wasn't the kind of girl who got asked to be bridesmaid, though she was not overweight then. She was just the nice ordinary girl with the good skin, whom everybody liked and no guy ever

came on to. But the fact that her father, the local small-town building baron, had left her money was well-known, and the husband-
who-shall-be-nameless because Pru could no longer even bear to
think his name, had known that. He'd sought her out, swept her off
her feet and before she knew it it was *her* wedding and they were going on a honeymoon to Florida, driving a brand-new Cadillac Esca-
lade she had paid for and that was big enough to seat eight. Later the
husband graduated to foreign cars, with the British-racing-green Jag
being his absolute favorite. Pru guessed that had the marriage lasted
he would have progressed to a Porsche. Men like that always wanted
a Porsche. Red, of course. And with vanity plates. And of course, he
had also managed to get through a lot of her money, leaving her
alone in a small apartment with a view of a parking lot.

Pru had had enough of men like her husband. She only wished
she had not begun her descent into eating because of him. Rats like
him should not cause the downfall of women and ruin their bodies,
just when they needed that body most!

She felt a tug on the lead. Tesoro had stopped dead in her tracks
and sat gazing beseechingly up at her.

"What?" Pru asked, exasperated.

"She wants to be carried."

It was a man's voice. Pru swung round. "Ooh," was all she managed to say.

"That's a very small dog, they tire quickly," Eddie Johanssen said.
"Such short legs, you know."

"Yes. Of course." Pru swept Tesoro up, clutching her to her
bosom. "Thank you. Why didn't I think of that?"

"You were obviously lost in your thoughts."

He wasn't moving on, he was just standing there, talking to her,
handsome as all get out and looking a lot more in control than he
had the other night.

"I think I know you, from the hotel," he said. "I seem to remember meeting you in the elevator."

"You weren't feeling well," Pru said, helpfully jogging his memory. Then, embarrassed, she knew she should not have said that. What man wanted to be reminded that he had been drunk?

"I don't recall," he said. "I just remember your red shoes."

Pru's "Oooh . . ." was doubtful. She had not been wearing the shoes that night, she'd been barefoot in a bathrobe. Obviously he must be thinking of their *first* encounter. "The shoes were brand-new," she said, pulling herself together. "And cost twice what I thought they should have."

"A good investment." Eddie's eyes twinkled, he was intrigued by her openness.

"I'm hoping so." A grin lit Pru's face too. A handsome man had noticed her shoes, he'd remembered they were red. Allie was right; she must have good legs.

They stood, looking at each other. Eddie liked her, he liked her open, unthreatening attitude. *Simple* was not the word to describe her but for the life of him right now he could not think of the proper one.

"I'm Eddie Johanssen," he said.

"Pru. Prudence Hilson."

He said, "I'm alone too. Could I buy you a cup of coffee?" Pru's instant beam delighted him.

"You are the first person in France to offer to buy me a cup of coffee," she said. He lifted an eyebrow in surprise and she quickly added, "Mostly people just want to offer me a glass of champagne. I thought it was all anybody drank in France."

She was rattling on nonstop, so nervous and so thrilled she couldn't bear herself.

Eddie took her arm and guided her across the road to a red-awninged café. Tables spilled out onto the sidewalk and there was the buzz of conversation.

There was a big smile on Pru's face. Here she was with the handsomest man in the café, with an aristocratic little Chihuahua on her lap just like any smart Frenchwoman, and her feet tucked into the gorgeous new brown suede boots. Her suede jacket toned perfectly and her new cap of short blond hair stirred in the breeze as though it had a life of its own. She felt so chic she laughed.

"What are you laughing at?" Eddie asked.

"Just at my being here, in France, sitting in a sidewalk café."

"And where would you usually be?"

"In a small town in Texas you've never heard of, probably watching *Entertainment Tonight* on TV and wishing I could be part of that glamorous unattainable world."

"And so now you are." He looked her over seriously. "Your hair is different."

She put up a hand, patted it. Tesoro rustled, watching her uneasily. "Blond." She was still nervous about it. "And *short*. Is it okay?"

He reached out and touched a strand. "It's wonderful. See how it catches the light. It brightens your whole face."

"Really?" Pru knew she was blushing.

"Such a charming face," Eddie said, delightedly watching her blush some more.

He ordered cappuccino for her and a double black coffee for himself, and asked the waiter to bring water for the dog.

Then, "Why do you have Sunny's dog?" he asked.

Pru's heart sank. Was this the real reason he had stopped to talk to her?

"Sunny had to go away. She couldn't take the dog with her." She was certainly not going to tell Eddie Sunny had gone to Mumbai, not only because she was sworn to secrecy, but because it was none of his business. Sunny had told Eddie goodbye; though admittedly it was on the telephone. She had said it was lovely to know him; thanked him for helping her, and that she would always consider him a friend. Still, the lingering sadness in Eddie's eyes touched Pru. She decided, though, it was time for him to bite the bullet.

"Sunny and Mac are back together," she said, as gently as she could. "You know they'll always love each other."

Eddie's smile was rueful. "Sometimes we like to think about what might have been, and not what is." He shrugged. "Sunny came into my life at a moment when she needed me, or perhaps just some-one like me."

Pru reached out and patted his hand, a narrow, tanned hand, long-fingered, dusted with a few golden hairs. A slight shiver ran through her, enough to raise the hairs on her own newly blond neck. God, he was attractive. She had never felt this kind of attrac-tion for a man before and was beginning to understand how Sunny was with Mac. But she couldn't let Eddie know this, after all, he was simply being friendly. "I understand," she said, with the sweet smile on the newly curved nude-lipsticked mouth that, had she only known it, was tempting enough to kiss.

And Eddie Johanssen did just that. He leaned over and kissed her, gently, on the lips, practically knocking her socks off with the shock. "Thank you," he said. And then he smiled too, and asked if she would have lunch with him.

So she did.

And that's when he told her the mysterious story of his "forgot-ten" night, and she told him that she had seen him in the elevator and thought he must be drunk. She said that she had wanted to help him, but was puzzled because she didn't think a man like him was the kind to get drunk.

It was two o'clock by now and they were sitting in a tiny bistro in the plaza of the hilly village of Mougins, elbows on the table, leaning into each other, still talking quietly. Tesoro was asleep on the chair next to Pru, having polished off enough chicken for two Chihuahuas. They had lunched on grilled *loup de mer,* a fish of surprising delicacy, fresh from the sea, along with a salad dressed with local olive oil and a gentle balsamic vinegar. Plus they were already on their second bottle of rosé, well, only a half bottle this time, most of which she had drunk, since Eddie was driving. She guessed it was the wine that made her so uninhibited, bold even. She'd told him the story of her disastrous marriage and unfaithful husband, and how she was in the process of moving on; and he'd told her about Jutta and the bad divorce and how much he loved his children.

There was a silence and she looked at him.

"Eddie," she said, leaning closer until their faces were almost touching. "Do you really like my hair?"

His eyes considered her for a long moment. Earlier, he had not been able to think of the proper word to describe her, but now he knew. *Innocent.* A true "innocent" was what Prudence Hilson was. And he liked that. He said, "I think you are a different woman with blond hair. But you know, Prudence, it's what a man *sees* in a woman, not always what she looks like. In you, I see a kind, caring person, a woman who thinks of herself last, a woman who gives friendship easily but will no longer be fooled by a false image of friendship, or even love. I think you are a cleverer woman than you believe you are, Prudence Hilson, and I'm glad I met you. I'm happy to be having lunch here with you, in this charming French village, in this good little bistro where they cook fish so sublime I want to eat it all over again. You—your company—has made me a happy man today. I want you to know that."

Pru knew the fiery blush must show under her bronzer but hell she didn't care. This beautiful man had just told her he was glad to be in her company and that she made him happy. She suddenly thought about him and Kitty Ratte. She wondered if he had been with her that "lost" night; and exactly what had happened. She recalled that Maha had told Sunny Kitty was corrupt, that she was evil. Pru could believe it. Now, she wondered what Kitty had really been up to.

Pru might be an innocent but she wasn't dumb; she knew about the effects of drugs and alcohol, and she knew what she had seen that night was wrong. Eddie Johanssen was simply not that kind of man. What had Kitty Ratte done to him that lost night? What drug had she given him to make him lose all memory of it?

Guessing right, she said, "You'd been with Kitty Ratte the night I saw you inebriated in the elevator."

Eddie frowned. "I seem to remember meeting her in the bar. Not on purpose, she just happened to be there."

"Isn't she always. And no doubt looking for trouble. *Her* kind of trouble."

Eddie smiled. "I'm hoping she didn't find it with me."

Pru wasn't joking when she said, "I wouldn't bet on it. I don't trust her, and let me tell you there's not one woman among us that does." She shrugged. "But anyway, it's over. And I don't want to spoil our lovely lunch talking about someone so unimportant."

Impulsively, she reached for his hand. "Are you okay now? About Sunny, I mean."

He nodded. "Sunny was lonely. I was the man who happened to be there."

Tesoro raised her head and gave a little wail.

"Uh-uh," Pru said. "I'm not experienced with dogs but I think that means she needs to go for a walk." And getting up, she took Tesoro off around the cobbled square, while Eddie took care of the bill.

Back at the hotel, Eddie told her he was leaving for London that night. "I have to be in Glasgow tomorrow," he said.

"Business?" Pru asked, hoping it wasn't a woman.

"It's always business. That's what's wrong with my life." His voice had an edge of bitterness as he remembered his divorce and his lost family.

They said goodbye in the lobby. He was heading out to the terrace to make phone calls, and Pru was going to her room to call Allie and tell her everything that had happened. And also find out if she had heard from Sunny.

"Prudence, I made a new friend today," Eddie said, taking her hand in both of his.

He bent to kiss it, and Pru felt that fiery blush again; he'd quite taken her breath away.

"Thank you for a lovely day," she said. "In fact it was one of the nicest in my life."

"Then may there be many more."

His eyes met hers in a smile; there was an understanding between them.

"Friends," Pru said, turning to walk away. "So call me, friend."

"I will," he promised.

chapter 57

Prague

There was a message waiting at the hotel when Mac arrived in Prague late the next day, much later than he had expected. His flight had been delayed. Worse. They had boarded then sat on the lifeless plane while outside important-looking things were being done to the engines by men in orange overalls. After two hours they were disembarked from the plane, nerves rattled, anxious to find another flight to Prague, only to find more long delays. He surely missed Ron and his Cessna.

Mac was lucky to get one of the last seats on a flight leaving five hours later, with the result that he ended up late in the chilly airport, thanking God he had a carry-on and did not have to wait like the others, whose bags anyway were probably still on the original flight. There were definite benefits to traveling light, though try to tell Sunny that when she was packing and he would come across stubborn resistance.

"I have to have these shoes," she would say, clutching them to her chest, dark eyes flashing. "You must understand Mac, a woman *needs* her shoes."

"But *six* pairs?" he remembered complaining when they were off to the Riviera on vacation. He'd thought it would be a shorts-and-flip-flops deal, which it was, except when Sunny felt the need to get dressed up. And she looked so great when she did, how could he grumble about having to wait for the bags to come down onto the carousel while the rest of the world just got on with living.

Where the hell *was* Sunny? Allie wasn't telling, and nor was Ron, although he guessed both were in on the secret.

"I'll tell you when I get back," Sunny had said. Now, sitting in an overheated taxi on his way to an unknown Prague hotel, Mac knew he should have insisted she tell him. Uneasiness accompanied him all the way. And then there was the message from Ron.

It was on the room phone; Ron had not been able to reach him on his cell. "Fell off the fuckin' horse. My fault. Broken leg," he said.

Mac checked the time. Nine-thirty at night. Same as in France. He checked his room. It was barely okay; kitschy, chintzy, flowery slipcovers, dark green carpet and a musty smell. A bit like grandmama's house in a bad fairy story. He peeked into the bathroom; the shower looked decent though; efficient.

He took off his jacket and sat on the edge of the bed, cell phone in hand. Ron answered immediately.

"I could have been in Australia," Mac said wearily. "The time it took to get to Prague."

"Australia's sunnier," Ron said. "Anyhow, I'm *hors de combat*, as they say."

"Who's 'they'?" Mac asked and they both laughed.

"I'm sorry, my friend," Mac said, seriously. "Take care of yourself, or I'm sure Allie will anyhow. Meanwhile, I'm gonna get myself a sandwich, I seem to remember I haven't eaten all day. And while I think of it a drink wouldn't be a bad idea. I wonder if there's a bar in this hotel."

He glanced again round the room with its granny furnishings. "Jesus, if there is I'll bet it has women in dirndls and guys in lederhosen playing accordions and singing in a language I don't know, and what's more right now, I don't want to know."

"The joys of foreign travel," Ron said. "Call me tomorrow, tell me about the gypsy."

"Will do," Mac said.

He wasn't far wrong about the accordions; just no lederhosen. Wrong country he supposed. But the beer was cold and the bratwurst sandwich hot and the waitress's smile friendly.

In less than an hour, he had eaten, showered and was fast asleep in granny's pink-peony-flowered bed.

The Czech Republic in winter was not like California, or even Monte Carlo, where gentle winds softened the air and sunshine gilded the ornate pastel buildings, where pretty women swung their hips feeling sexy in little skirts and cute boots. Prague had a harder wintry edge; gray skies, a chill that crusted on the skin, making Mac shiver. It was a beautiful city but Mac had no eyes for it right now. He was on his way to an address in New Town, to the apartment of a gypsy named Valeria Vinskaya. He would bet his last buck that was not her real name, but Valeria was an entertainer, a gypsy dancer, and he guessed a melodious name went along with the act.

She claimed to be an "international artiste," the Inspector had told him, which simply meant she went wherever she chose and did whatever she wanted, crime being her operative word. So far her crimes had been on the smaller level: street theft, confidence trickster in a minor way; conning men into parting with their wallets while they were asleep. Her biggest deals, though, were auto thefts, where the gypsy team whisked stolen vehicles into warehouses, stripped them of their parts, then shipped those parts on to be resold in other countries.

Valeria made a living, but now suddenly she seemed to have hit the jackpot. And like all small-time thieves, the money burned a hole in her pocket. She'd had to spend it, flash it around: new clothes, a fur coat, a boyfriend. Only temporary of course, but that was all Valeria knew.

The apartment was on an anonymous street of gray cement buildings, flat-fronted, small windows, not even a shutter to add a hint of charm. An iron grill covered the entrance. Mac knew Valeria's apartment was on the first floor. He had not called ahead to make an appointment; in his experience surprise was his greatest asset. Of course, whether she would open the door to him was another matter, but he was betting on the Inspector's name to get him in.

He pressed the buzzer, huddling in his long black overcoat, waiting. To his surprise a response came immediately.

He did not understand what she said in Czech, but anyhow he announced himself, said he knew she spoke English and that he needed to see her.

"Why?"

The voice was deep, dark. Exactly, Mac thought with a smile, the way a gypsy woman's was supposed to sound in movies. He told her he was a friend of the Inspector's. There was a long silence.

Then again, "Why?"

"I would be much more comfortable talking to you inside," he said, shivering. "It's cold as hell out here."

"And I always thought hell was supposed to be hot." He heard her laugh, then she said, "I can see you, you know. I'm looking at you as we speak."

Mac looked up, saw a dark shape at the window, then the iron security gate swung open.

He was in a narrow lobby with walls painted institutional green. A chandelier glimmered in the interior gloom, as out of place as a bunch of stolen diamonds. There was the sound of a door opening and he turned to look. He had expected a dark Romany woman, all long black hair, big gold earrings and a swirl of many-colored skirts. What he was looking at was a young woman, maybe in her twenties, petite, with short black hair. She was looking back at him through a thick dark fringe that fell into eyes that were a strange light color. Gray, he thought. And she wore jeans and a heavy gray sweater.

"Mac Reilly," he said, walking toward her, hand outstretched. She did not take it.

"I know," she said, stepping back so he could come in.

He was in an all-purpose room; fuchsia-pink walls, a small kitchenette to one side, a pink plastic curtain separating a shower from the black futon in the corner; messy with rumpled sheets. A tiny TV sat on the shelf opposite. There were no books. A small table stood under the window from where she had watched him. It was the only window in the studio apartment. A closed door hid what Mac guessed was a toilet, and a clothes rack ran the length of one wall, crammed with spangled red and black skirts, the swirling gypsy ones he had expected, as well as ordinary everyday stuff. A fur coat, mink he supposed, was on a hanger at the end of the rack. It looked new and it also looked expensive.

"Good coat," he said appreciatively.

She shrugged. "Get on with why you're here."

"Mind if I take off *my* coat?" Mac glanced round, taking his time. He did not want to miss anything.

"Oh, too bad! I'm forgetting my manners. Mr. Reilly, please allow me to take your coat. May I offer you a drink? Slivovitz is good on a cold day like this. Warms those places that need to be kept warm, or so I've heard."

Her light gray eyes mocked him as he laid his coat over the back of one of the two chairs at the round table which was covered in a long fringed pink cloth. Suddenly from beneath, emerged a small cat. Silver-gray, spotted darker at the sides, charcoal rings around its tail.

"A beauty," Mac said, putting out a hand to it. The cat hissed and struck out at him.

"She drew blood," Valeria said, smiling. "Just the way a woman should."

There were two club chairs in front of a sixties oval glass coffee table. The chairs were black, which was a relief from all the pink.

Mac took a tissue from his pocket and mopped the blood from the cat scratch. He sat in one of the chairs, then carrying two small glasses, Valeria came and sat next to him. She gave him a lengthy look, taking him in boldly, head to toe.

"Well?" Mac asked.

She grinned and suddenly looked very young and pretty. He could see her collarbones sticking out under the gray sweater and her face was thin, pale.

"I like what I see," she said. "Here's to us, Mac Relly."

"Reilly."

She shrugged. "Mac is better." She was flirting with him.

He said, "Valeria, you know I am not with the police."

"I know who you are. We get your show here."

"Then you also know why I'm here."

"I admit to nothing." Her small face folded into a sulk and her eyes hardened.

"I'm not asking you to admit to anything. All I want from you is some information. Not enough to put you in danger, just enough to help find a killer who had no emotion about killing. Someone who kills for the bitter thrill of it, not for financial gain, or jealousy."

"Not a crime of passion then," she said, thoughtfully, tucking her legs under her in the chair and taking a sip of the Slivovitz, or whatever the colorless liquid was in her glass. She looked at him over the rim, all big gray eyes and sharp cheekbones. "Too bad. Crimes of passion are the only ones to interest me."

"And what about love. Let's talk about that, Valeria."

"Are you in love then?" Her eyes were big now, interested.

"That's a very personal question." Mac was too smart to answer or take a sip of the Slivovitz.

"And I ask it for a very personal reason."

He knew he shouldn't but he asked anyway. "And what is that?"

"Because I find you very attractive, Mr. Relly."

"Reilly. And the name is Mac."

"Like macaroni and cheese."

"Mackenzie, actually."

"You're not drinking, Mackenzie. Think I've poisoned the wine?" She laughed out loud now as he set the glass down on the coffee table.

"I wouldn't put it past you."

She nodded. "Quite right. Nor would I. But I am no cold-blooded killer, Mackenzie. That's not my style. I'm just a cheap dancer who picks up a living wherever she can. I'm a gypsy, a Romany, despite the way I look, and that makes it easier for me to get jobs, dancing, in Poland, Hungary, Germany . . . You name any small club in any small town and I've danced in it."

"So you are not a criminal."

She took a sip and eyed him again. "What do *you* think?"

Mac laughed. "I think you are charming, I think you are a flirt and I think you know exactly what you are doing, Miss Valeria Vinskaya. And no, I do not think you are a killer. But before you get carried away on the Slivovitz, let me tell you a little story, about a jewel robbery. About a murder."

She was quiet while he told her, curled up in her chair like a small gray mouse while he talked about the fur-coated killer. Only her eyes were alive, staring into space. At least Mac thought she was, but following her gaze he saw she was looking at the fur coat.

"Pretty coat," he said into the silence.

"It used to be," she said, and getting up she took it off the hanger and slipped it on. She twirled in front of him. It was way too big, and came all the way down over her feet.

"I was going to have it altered," she said, "but there's nobody here I can trust. It'll just get stolen and sold on. That is how everybody makes money."

"Stealing," Mac said.

She slumped back into the chair, wrapping the soft fur around her. The cat came soundlessly running, jumped onto her furry lap, curled up and tucked its head down to sleep. They looked, Mac thought, like a drawing from a child's storybook. An enchanted waif, a silver cat, a stolen fur coat.

"Where did you get it?"

She glanced at him, shrugged. "It was hanging in a cloakroom in a restaurant. My friend enticed the coat-check woman away, I took the coat. When I got it home—back to the place I was staying—I found something in the pocket." She looked fearfully at him now. "It was a diamond ring. A large diamond. Yellow, but beautiful. So I sold that on and kept the coat." She shrugged. "And that's the way it was Mackenzie Reilly. I'm a bad girl, or maybe a good girl gone wrong. Take your pick. But I'm no killer."

"Who did you sell it to?" he asked, and got no reply.

They sat in silence for a while. The only sound was the cat purring. Outside the sky grew even grayer. Mac wondered how she stood it, confined in this room, jazzed up in pink to make its prisonlike structure more bearable. He wondered about her future.

He said, "Give me the name of the restaurant." She was silent.

"At least the city." Silence.

"Is that all you have to tell me?" he asked finally.

"That is all I am *going* to tell you," she said firmly.

"Then there is more? You know who the coat belonged to, don't you? Whose the diamond ring was?"

Maybe she didn't, but if she would only tell him the name of the restaurant he could check for a reported stolen fur and trace its owner. He was sure the diamond ring was part of the La Fontaine haul in Paris, or the one the day after Christmas in Monte Carlo. He needed to know who she had sold it to.

She got up suddenly, unraveling herself from the fur and the cat. "Take it," she said, thrusting the coat at him. "I want nothing to do with it. I don't want it anymore. I don't want blood on my hands. I am a thief, Mackenzie, not a killer."

He took the coat, folded it carefully. It was soft as silk, delicate as the woman who was gazing at him now, tears oozing from her waif's gray eyes.

"Goodbye, Mackenzie," she said, striding to the door and holding it open. "Do not ask any more questions. Do not come and see me again."

He took his own coat, felt in his pocket for his business card; gave it to her as he walked past her. She leaned into him and quickly kissed his cheek. "You smell good," she said.

And then the door slammed behind him and he was out in the chandeliered hallway, out into the dark gray street.

He needed a drink.

chapter 58

Mac was not the kind of guy who spent a lot of time in bars, other than for work. They were not his milieu; he would rather be on his Malibu deck overlooking the Pacific than any bar in the world. Wasn't that almost a Humphrey Bogart quote? *Casablanca*?

He couldn't get the pathetic young gypsy out of his head; her pointed little face, her scraped-together lifestyle, the beautiful cat who was so like her. A pair of gray little waifs, beaten down by life. No wonder the cat spat and hissed. So did the girl.

He had to walk for a long time before he found a cab; there were not too many of them in the grim district where the gypsy lived. When he finally hailed one at a busy intersection, he gave the driver the name of his hotel, then asked him to wait. He went inside, collected his stuff, paid his bill, got back in the cab. He couldn't stand the dingy place anymore, it was as claustrophobic as her pink apartment.

He had the cab drop him a couple of blocks away. He needed air; he needed to walk. She was still on his mind; vulnerable, vivid. *Pathos* was the word he felt was needed to describe her. Carrying his small bag and with the fur coat tucked under his arm, he found a café. Golden light spilled from its large windows onto the cobbled street. Like a Van Gogh painting, he thought, as if he had stepped back into a different century.

He took a seat inside the glassed-in terrace and put his bag on the chair next to him, folded the mink and placed it carefully on top. The waiter was young, decent-looking, serious about his job. "Sir?" he said.

"A double brandy. Rémy please, if you have it."

"Certainly, sir." The waiter waited, pencil poised over his little pad, eyebrows raised in a question. "And for *madame?*"

Mac stared blankly at him. *"Madame?"*

The waiter gestured at the coat. "Another brandy, perhaps."

Mac understood. "Thank you, no. There is no *madame.*"

The young waiter was embarrassed. "I'm sorry, sir, I just thought . . . with the fur . . ."

"It's not a problem," Mac said, though it was indeed a problem and right now he did not know what to do.

He thought the Inspector was correct and gypsy Valeria would be in danger if she talked. He almost regretted going to see her. What if the people she was afraid of, the dealers to whom, he was sure, she had fenced the yellow diamond ring, which he was also sure came from La Fontaine's collection, thought she had talked?

He downed half the brandy in one gulp, shuddering as it seethed down his throat, savoring the after-sweetness. Then he dialed the Inspector.

He answered on the first ring. "So?" he said.

"So I met the gypsy."

"And?"

"She's merely a small cog in a big wheel, a by-chance thief who stole too much. It all got too big for her. That's my opinion."

"Why do you say that?"

"The fur coat she was flashing when you took her in for questioning was stolen by her from a restaurant coat-check."

"Which restaurant?"

"She wouldn't tell."

The Inspector sighed.

"It was either in Monte Carlo, or Paris though, because in the pocket was a diamond ring. A yellow diamond. Large, she told me. I'm willing to bet it was one of La Fontaine's."

"I'll have a check run on which city she was working in, though I'm guessing it was Paris, after the La Fontaine robbery. After all, she had to have time to go back to Prague and sell on the ring. Then she came to Monte Carlo to spend the money. And wear the fur. Flashy, was how I would describe her."

How strange, Mac thought. She was in fact so pathetic, so easily knocked off her high new-moneyed perch. "I'll bet she blew it all," he said. "And I'll bet she didn't get that much for it either. She would have gone to one of the smaller guys in the chain, he would have smelled its true value from twenty paces and cheated her, made money on it himself."

"What about the fur?"

"Haven't had a chance to check it yet, except for the pockets. Nothing there. And there's no label. I'll take a proper look when I get to the hotel."

"Which hotel?"

Mac thought about it, surprised. Then he said, "The Four Seasons." He'd had enough of lousy hotels, seedy apartments and the unattractive end of Prague.

He told the Inspector he would call him when he'd had a chance to check out the coat properly, then he called the Four Seasons and booked a room.

Sitting in the café, he chose something simple, and leaving the rest of the brandy, ordered a bottle of wine. It was local, the waiter told him. Who knew the Czech Republic had vineyards? He must remember to tell Ron about that. Mac was a bit of a wine connoisseur and was pleased when the wine turned out to be pleasant and aromatic. Relaxing, he tried once more to call Sunny. The phone's ring sounded as though it was in outer space.

Frustrated and worried, he ate the pork dish which was braised with vegetables, a hearty peasant dish for a cold Prague evening. In fact darkness had closed in. It was already night.

A cab took him to the hotel where he inspected his room, then took a shower, washing away the debris of a bad day. He wished he had never come to Prague. He tried Sunny again. No answer.

The mink coat was on the chair where he'd thrown it when he came in. Now he picked it up, ran his hands over the soft skins, pliable as a bolt of satin. It was a very expensive coat; anyone legitimately losing it, or having it stolen from a restaurant, would certainly have reported it to the police. He thought about the robbers, three smart women with their blond hair, their Marilyn masks and their long fur coats. And the diamond in the pocket.

He took the fur and pulled the sleeves inside out, felt them carefully, looking for a maker's name or initials in the silk lining. There was nothing, nor was there an owner's name embroidered inside, as was usual in a custom coat like this. He spread the fur on the bed, ran the flat of his hand over the lining, found a small pocket inside, fastened with a tiny jeweled button. Nothing there. But there was another pocket beneath it, a mere slit, edged discreetly with fine silk, a secret pocket meant, he guessed, to hold nothing more than a credit card or a hundred-dollar bill for those emergencies when a woman needed taxi fare. He put his fingers inside, still nothing. Wait though. His fingers closed over a piece of plastic.

It was one of those fancy business cards. Thin, opaque, off-white printed designer-style, in pale gray so you could hardly read it.

But Mac did. SHARON BARNES, it said. THE BARNES MODEL AGENCY. There was an address in Old Town, Prague.

Mac turned the card over and over in his fingers. He knew the name but could not remember where he had heard it before. One thing he knew, though, he would be visiting Sharon Barnes at her model agency the very next morning.

He decided not to call the Inspector again tonight and called Sunny again instead. Of course she did not answer and Mac fell asleep, still worrying about her.

chapter 59

Mumbai

Barefoot female servants, heads meekly bowed, waited for Sunny in the vast cool hall of Maha's house, hands clasped in front of them, wearing silky red tops that came down to their knees over the usual narrow cotton pants. Their hair was shiny, black, braided into a thick plait, tucked with a colorful blossom. Cool dark eyes surveyed her as Rahm Singh introduced her.

"You will take the *madama* to her room," Rahm Singh commanded. "Show her everything."

They lifted their heads and looked up at her; lamplight fell on their faces and Sunny choked back a gasp. Thick raised scars ran down the sides of their cheeks.

Seeing her shocked expression Rahm Singh explained. "The Mondragon took these women away from the slums where they were mistreated. She gave them a better life."

He indicated that Sunny should follow them, then left.

The three slender women led her down a hallway to the back of the house, passing a room that seemed geared to entertaining, with divans and silk-shaded lamps dotted around its vast space. The tall windows were uncurtained and Mumbai sparkled like La Fontaine's diamonds in the distance. A room to the right held a dining table that Sunny guessed would seat at least twenty, with silver urns of flowers set atop it and brocade-covered chairs around it. Beautiful carpets gleamed under the softly shaded lamps, in the gentle colors of old-style vegetable dyes, some intricately patterned; some telling a story; some modern and muted, and all beautiful.

The hallway led into a small library where unread books bound in leather lined floor-to-ceiling shelves and deep modern chairs were placed around small tables, with magazines and silver and crystal boxes of sweets and nuts. Beyond that, a garden room, light-heartedly furnished in wicker and English flowered chintzes, led out onto a flagged terrace with giant tubs of hibiscus and jacaranda and mimosa, the low walls aclimb with brilliant bougainvillea.

Sunny's room was down the corridor, past the library, in the guest wing. Double doors opened onto it and stepping through them she seemed to step into another world: a silken, brocaded, softly carpeted, marble-floored haven of multihued luxury; soft, cool and inviting after the long plane ride.

The four-poster bed, reached by a flight of five tiny steps, was huge and puffy and draped in white muslin. A white sofa and chairs were grouped around a coffee table, holding an old stone trough of gardenias. A table under one of the tall French windows was set for one with lovely dishes and exquisite antique silverware, a remnant, Sunny felt sure, of the days of the British Raj, and that had probably belonged to some important lady, maybe even the governor's lady. Curtains fell onto the floor in a heap of fuchsia silk; the carpets were also silken in turquoise and cobalt and cream and taupe; the paintings on the yellow-lacquered walls were modern Indian, bravura strokes of color; and the green-onyx bathroom, the color of a mermaid's lair, was so big Sunny thought she could get lost in it.

No time for getting lost, though. One of the women was already running a bath, spilling in handfuls of salts and pouring in sweet-smelling oil, while another folded towels and placed them on the edge of the circular tub, along with cakes of geranium soap and bath gels and lotions, scattering pink rose petals on the greenish water.

The third unpacked Sunny's small bag, taking away the crumpled clothes to be pressed, folding the T-shirt Sunny slept in, and arranging it on the bed, plumping up the pillows. Silent. Intense. And never a smile.

There was a knock on the door. Standing in the middle of all the splendor, Sunny called out to come in. Rahm Singh entered. He bowed and said he trusted everything was well, and that *madama*—as he called her—had everything she needed.

"What more can I want?" Sunny asked, smiling because he was so serious. "This is the best hotel I've ever stayed in."

"The Mondragon wishes for everything to be correct," he said stiffly. "After *madama* takes her bath and is comfortable, it is proposed that you be served dinner."

Sunny wondered who had proposed that. Maha, she supposed. "Thank you, Rahm Singh," she said, realizing that she was indeed hungry.

"If it is acceptable to *madama,* the cook suggests something light. A tomato soup, for which we are famous. A cauliflower dish made in the oven with tamarind and cumin, and paneer, our Indian cheese. A little sliced chicken, lightly seasoned with curry and of course, basmati rice, flavored gently with jasmine. And perhaps for after, our famous rice pudding, soft and creamy with the lemony hint of cardamom."

Sunny felt suddenly weak. The journey and the strain of ferrying the jewels were catching up with her. She almost fainted at the thought of more food. Sinking into the down-filled cushions of the white silk sofa she thanked Rahm Singh and explained that she would prefer, if possible, a little sandwich instead. "A BLT or tuna," she said, feeling ridiculous and all-American, but she had to eat carefully after a long-haul flight. "Oh, and a glass of white wine, please, Rahm Singh."

Minutes later, afloat in the immense round dark green bathtub, rose petals surrounding her, scented oils soothing her tired limbs,

Sunny wondered why Maha traveled so much when she had everything life could offer, right here in her own magnificent home with its band of servants to do her bidding.

Half an hour later, clean and fragrant, relaxed and wrapped in the softest cotton bathrobe, Sunny waited for Rahm Singh to appear with her sandwich. The three Indian women stood in line by the door, heads bowed. Awaiting orders Sunny assumed, though she had none to give and anyhow she did not speak their language. They were odd; so silent, so humble, with those bowed heads. And no smiles.

Rahm Singh appeared followed by another servant carrying a large silver tray on which reposed a platter covered by a silver dome; a fine crystal glass; a bottle of Evian water and a second glass. Rahm Singh carried a crystal wine cooler. The servant, a man this time, also barefoot and in the same kind of cotton clothing, said a respectful good evening and carefully set up the table. Rahm Singh placed the cooler to one side and skillfully uncorked the wine.

He held the chair for Sunny to sit, and feeling like the Queen of England, who probably lived like this every day of the week, Sunny sat. He held the bottle for her to approve. French; a white from the Loire Valley. Sunny remembered Maha drinking champagne every night, and smiled. That woman knew the good life.

She took a sip of the wine, thin, cool, light and absolutely perfect for the delicate way she was feeling. Lifting the silver dome, she inspected the sandwich. Round bread, puffy with air, deflated at her touch, smelling subtly of some kind of spice. Thinly sliced chicken, tomatoes, bacon strips and shredded lettuce topped with a dollop of mayo that when she put in a finger and tasted turned out to be a yoghurt-and-cucumber *raita*. If this was an Indian idea of a sandwich, it was her idea of heaven.

Rahm Singh had dismissed the three nameless women, and finally alone, Sunny sipped her wine, tasted her sandwich and then overcome by fatigue went to the window and stepped out onto the lamp-lit terrace. She breathed in the perfumed air, admiring a narrow rocky stream that meandered through the grounds. The bag with the jewels was safely on the floor next to the bed. She wondered when Maha would call with instructions for the next part of the game. Who she was to hand over the jewels to, and where?

Her thoughts turned to Mac, alone in Prague, just as she was alone in India. What fools they both were, she thought, going back inside. She tried his number on her cell phone but got only a beep. Oh God she missed him, *how* she missed him, she couldn't wait to tell him about her Indian adventure, about Maha's luxurious home; the muted servants; the BLT in the Indian bread and the white Loire wine she would love to have shared with him. She hoped he was safe in Prague.

Slipping off the robe, she climbed up the little flight of wooden steps and into the enormous fluffy bed. Closing her eyes she was asleep within minutes.

She left a light on, of course, because she was afraid of the dark.

chapter 60

Cannes

Kitty Ratte was sweating with panic. She was alone in the apartment because Jimmy had chosen this moment to go back to England. He said it was to try to coax money out of his wife and their ailing used-car business, or "pre-owned" as he called it, making it sound more important, and had simply left her to it. "It," being delivering the blackmail note. He had driven off yesterday morning and told her to call him when she had taken care of business.

"Taking care of business" was not as easy as Kitty had expected. In fact it was difficult because Eddie Johanssen had left the hotel in Monte Carlo the previous night and she did not have his cell phone number. Fuming, she sat on the beige couch—the very same couch on which she had "seduced" Eddie, "seduced" being what she now preferred to call it. And glancing through the still photographs taken from the hidden high-tech video cam, there seemed no doubt Eddie was a willing participant in a night of perverted anything-goes sex.

Kitty tapped the photos against her hand, frowning. She put a hand up to her forehead and groaned. She could *feel* those frown lines; she needed Botox; she needed the Restylane filler; she needed a goddamn face lift, her fuckin' chin was sliding into her neck, which was the same width as her face, giving her five chins when she smiled. She would have to remember not to smile so much, and besides the two cheap front veneers were looking decidedly suspect, overly white and bright and thick. She needed that fuckin' money; she was getting too old to work this game. She wanted that bar in Marbella; her own place; her own men to tease and hustle. She needed new swingers' clubs, new horizons for blackmail. She *needed* to be a predator, but she *wanted* to be *the* predator in charge. She was a woman who had always taken what she wanted, and now she wanted Eddie, and she was determined to get him.

Her cheap "gold" watch said five-thirty P.M. There was only one thing for it. She must go to the hotel bar and see what was happening. Perhaps Sunny would be there. Sunny would be sure to have Eddie's number and Kitty would plead with her, say it was important, that she had private news for him about his wife, Jutta. Sunny believed Kitty was her friend; she would give her the number.

Jutta and those two children were the answer to Kitty's prayers, and she knew exactly how to play Eddie. She had made sure her face was up-front and unmistakable in those photos. She would tell him it was *she* who was being blackmailed. *She* who was the poor sweet woman in trouble, only for making passionate love to a man she cared deeply about. Eddie would be forced to pay, to save *her,* and save *her* reputation. He could not betray her.

Half an hour later, showered, in a floral-print silky dress and the black leather Louboutins that were too high and that anyhow killed her; blue–eye shadowed and coral–lip glossed, Kitty put the incriminating photos in a manila envelope in her Prada bag and drove to the hotel.

She was so broke she could not afford to valet the old Fiat and she parked a block away, stumbling on the cobbles in the stilettos, cursing under her breath and sweating again. Who knew it would be this hot at the end of December? The silky dress was sticking to her cushioned bra by the time she climbed the hotel steps, just as a taxi drove up. Glancing over her shoulder she saw Eddie paying off the driver. A relieved smile beamed across her face and forgetting all about the five chins, she called out his name.

"Serendipity," she cried. "Oh, Eddie, Eddie, I've been trying to get in touch with you, but I didn't know how. And it's *so* important."

Eddie was not smiling as he walked up the steps to the hotel. "I can't think of anything that would be important between us," he said coldly, striding past her and through the swinging doors.

She hurried in after him. "Ooh but Eddie, Eddie, *please* . . . it is. It's so important you are going to *have* to listen."

He walked on. She followed at a trot.

"For the sake of *your children,* you are going to have to talk to me."

He stopped, stiffened, stood for a second, his back to her, then turned and met her eyes.

"And what, if anything, could you possibly have to do with my children?" He walked menacingly toward her, speaking so quietly no one else could hear. "They don't belong in the same world with people like you. Don't you dare even to breathe their names. Or . . ."

"*Or* . . ." Kitty heaved a tiny sigh. Tears squeezed from her small blue eyes and trickled down her cheeks, leaving faint mascara tracks. She searched futilely in her bag for a Kleenex until Eddie, ever the gentleman, felt compelled to offer her his handkerchief.

"Thank you, thank you so much." She sniffed back the tears and said, "It's all so awful, Eddie, I just don't know how to tell you. All I can say is that I love you, I love you so much since our precious night together. I want you so much. I need you, Eddie, darling . . ."

"What the fuck are you talking about?"

She glanced over her shoulder, putting on her best "afraid" look. "No one must hear this," she whispered, mopping the tears again. "We have to talk, Eddie. I have something you must see, you have to read it . . . it's all about us."

Eddie inspected her closely. Something was wrong and he knew he'd better find out what before she did something crazy. He didn't like the mention of his children. Not from a woman like this.

"We could go to your room," Kitty suggested, managing a smile. "We could be alone there."

"We can be alone in the bar," he replied curtly, leading the way without taking her arm, as he normally would have done with a woman friend.

It was six-thirty and the bar was filling up. Kitty led the way to a corner table at the back. A tiny amber-shaded lamp diffused a rosy light, the color of a South of France sunset. From the speakers a woman sang softly, in French, though the group, Pink Martini, was American. A waiter came to take their order. It was the younger barman, the one with the swagger who stared boldly into Kitty's face. Normally Kitty would have stared boldly back, but now she kept her eyes lowered and asked for a beer. "A Heineken," she said meekly. It wouldn't do for the barman, who knew exactly who and what she was, to get too familiar in front of Eddie.

When the beer came she drank it straight from the bottle, glugging like a whore at an Oktoberfest, almost draining it in one go. She called back the waiter and ordered another.

Eddie took a sip of his vodka on the rocks, watching her wiping beer foam off her lips with the back of her hand. There was not one iota of grace about this woman. She was cheap and so obviously available he was ashamed to be seen sitting with her. "Tell me what's going on," he commanded.

Kitty took a deep breath, then took out the manila envelope. She opened it, took out a piece of paper. Her eyes fixed on Eddie's, she handed it to him. "Read this," she said. "Then maybe you'll be ready for a second drink too."

Eddie smoothed the paper out under the pink light from the small table lamp.

Kitty watched as he read. She knew exactly what it said and she was looking for Eddie's reaction. She did not get one. He merely handed the paper back to her, saying nothing.

"Eddie, oh Eddie, but what do you think? What shall *I do*. It's a blackmail note . . ."

Eddie took another sip of his vodka. "I fail to see how it affects me."

"But look, *look*, Eddie." She smoothed the sheet of paper out again, staring down at the computerized message.

You have been observed. You are guilty. We will prove it in every tabloid on the planet and you will be ruined. You will lose every-thing. Isn't it better to pay two million euros in cash at a time and place to be appointed. Trust us, we know how to get you, in ways you will never expect. You will never know what hits you. You will be destroyed. Lose everything you've ever worked for. Including your life. And what's two million euros compared with a life? Ask your-selves that question, and come back to us with the answer so we can proceed. Kitty Ratte will be contacted later tonight. And yes, you are right to be afraid Kitty. And so is your man.

"My *man*." Kitty choked on the words, half-sobbing. "Don't you see, they mean *you*, Eddie. Oh God, some enemy saw us, spied on us that night we were together. That wonderful, wonderful night, Eddie. I can't forget it, I can't forget *you*. I can't get you out of my mind, I'm so *in love* with you. I *want* you, Eddie, I *need* you."

"What the fuck are you talking about?"

She leaned closer. Eddie's icy calm was cracking and Kitty wanted to smile with pleasure, but she did not. She had him, though; she could just feel it, see it in the set of his shoulders, his tight jaw.

She took the photographs from the manila envelope, handed them to him. "Look at these, Eddie," she said softly. "Just look at them. At you and at me. Look what you have gotten me into, Eddie. And I did it all for love of you."

Eddie slid the black-and-white pictures through his hands, taking in the fact that the man was himself, adorned with a spiked leather collar and handcuffs and nothing else, and that the woman on top of him, naked as a plucked chicken but for her cushioned bra and the camisole that, though he did not know it, she would never be seen without because she was so ashamed of her aging body, was Kitty Ratte. And in those photographs Kitty was sucking on him, licking him, straddling him, pushing his head between her legs, grinning in triumph, her head thrown back, holding a blue vibrator that was doing what apparently *he* could not do for her.

He gave her back the photographs, looked into her small predatory eyes, looked so hard he felt her recoil. *"You cheap bitch,"* he said. His low voice was filled with so much hate and menace, Kitty flinched.

"But don't you see," she cried. "It's *me* they're blackmailing. It's *me* in those photos, my face is *everywhere*. You have *ruined* me, Eddie Johanssen. I will be all over the tabloids and no one will ever want to know me again, I won't be able to go anywhere. You are destroying me." She reached beseechingly for his hand but he pulled away. "Eddie, oh *Eddie*, I was only making love to you, doing what you asked. You wanted the collar, you wanted me to whip you, you wanted the handcuffs . . . It was all *you*. I only did as you asked because I was a woman falling madly in love. Don't you see, Eddie, they are asking *me* for two million euros and I don't have it. If I don't pay, I am ruined. And maybe worse . . ."

She left the threat hanging in the air, watching to see how her ploy was going down with him. It had been Jimmy's idea to use *her* face, to say it was *she* who was being blackmailed, that Eddie was not the primary target, so she would never be thought of as the blackmailer.

"Someone wanted to get me," she whispered. "And now they have. And I only did it for love—and for the wonderful sex. Oh you are sooo sexy Eddie, *so* great. You are *perfect*. Can't you see how much I *love* you. How much I *want* you. How I *need* you? Eddie, oh Eddie, you cannot *betray* me. I'm a helpless woman whose life will be destroyed if you don't help me."

"And if I do?" Eddie's voice had that icy calmness again that got Kitty nervous.

"Then they'll give me the videos, they'll go away, leave us alone."

"And if I don't?"

Kitty slumped back in her chair, regarding him sadly. "Then I'm afraid we are both ruined, Eddie. You *and* me. I know you're in trouble with your divorce, and the custody of your children. It's such a pity. But you did what you did, you made love to me and someone took a video, and now we are there for everybody to see."

She slid the photos back in the envelope along with the note, licked the flap, sealed the envelope, then pushed it across the small table at him.

"I cannot bear any more right now," she said in that small teary voice. "I'm a woman who has been put in a terrible compromising position. And *you,* Eddie, put me there. Only *you* can get me out of it now. Please, do not let me down. Never betray me, Eddie. *Never.*"

Collecting her bag, Kitty got unsteadily to her feet. Eddie did not get up.

"And if I do 'betray' you, and don't pay, Kitty. What then?"

"Then they'll kill us both," she said simply. And with that she turned and walked out.

chapter 61

Back in his room, Eddie spread the incriminating photos on the desk. There was no doubt it was him, his face was lit as clearly as if he were making a movie, which unwittingly, he had. And so was Kitty's. Her unfortunate teeth stuck out like the rat she had been named for, her neck was as wide as her face and her small eyes were pinched in a grimace of pretend ecstasy.

But how did he know it was pretend? Perhaps he had really gotten so drunk he had fucked her and couldn't remember. Dear God, he had never been that kind of man; he loved women, loved making love, but not this . . . this *obscene* affair with the S and M collar and her wielding a vibrator. He gave silent thanks to the fact that in order to make love to a woman he had never been reduced to having her use a vibrator to get off. This woman was sick, she was crazy and she was so brashly unattractive to him, to everything he knew and treasured about women, their bodies, their love, their ability to make wonderful love, he knew he could never have been a knowing participant in this fraud. He had been duped, set up, ready for a blackmail attempt.

The phone rang. Automatically, he answered. It was Kitty. "I just wanted you to remember that night. I want you to know, darling Eddie, *you* are the only man who could make me come like that. The only one in a very long time. You can see the truth in those pictures. You were wonderful and I can't live without you . . . You must help me Eddie, you cannot betray me . . ."

He slammed down the phone, threw it across the room. Rage danced before his eyes, blackening the scene, his life . . . the cheap bitch had him by the balls, literally. For the first time in his life he was feeling a rage so blind he could have killed, killed to protect his children, his wife, his friends, his way of life . . .

He went out and stood on the terrace in the dark. He had never felt more alone in his life. Gradually, the blackness of the rage left him. His hands stopped shaking. He began to think more logically. He could not allow himself to become insane with anger because of this terrible woman. He must control himself. Figure out exactly what had happened. Then figure out what to do. He thought about calling his lawyer—but with what story? How was he to explain the photos that he had no knowledge of?

He went back into the room, poured himself a vodka. Drank it neat. He sat on the sofa, eyes closed, and willed his thoughts back to that night.

He saw himself entering the bar, the flaming redhead he knew as Kitty Ratte was smiling at him, her tiny eyes squeezed into slits, beckoning him over, asking him to join her in a drink, she had so much to tell him, about Sunny. Of course she had used Sunny as the hook. Kitty wasn't so dumb after all. He remembered that clearly now. He remembered her ordering him a second drink though he had not even finished the first, her shoving it toward him, saying drink this you will feel better . . . and then him thinking he must have had too much; feeling strange, elated yet weak . . .

Of course, *now* he remembered. She said he must be hungry, said she made the best Swedish meatballs in Monte Carlo, and since he was Swedish she would cook for him, they would be the best he had ever eaten.

They'd walked out of the bar together, her arm was around his waist. Oh God, they must have looked exactly like a pair of lovers on their way to a rendezvous. He wondered who had seen them, who had noticed? *Of course*: the silver-haired barman. Eddie had caught his skeptical glance. The barman had known something was going on . . . and Eddie would bet he also knew all about Kitty, who she was, what she was. She must be well-known in hotel bars around town.

Kitty had driven him to her house, she had eased him onto a sofa, put his feet up, a cushion behind his head, turned on all the lights until he protested it was like a film set . . . and of course that was exactly what it was. He saw it all now, every overhead light beaming into his eyes, the lamps lit, the awful Eurovision music; the way she arranged him so precisely on the sofa, obviously facing the video camera; her bringing him another drink, to make him feel better, and then her standing there, posing sexily, her cellulite thighs wobbling as she came toward him with a single meatball, on what seemed now to have been an enormous white plate. A single meatball that must have contained the final drug; the date-rape one that put him out of reality and erased his memory . . .

Whatever happened after that was documented in the photos in front of him. Looking at them Eddie thanked God he could not remember.

He got up, paced again to the terrace outside his window, thought again about calling his lawyer, about calling his wife, trying to explain. About calling Kitty telling her what a supreme cheap bitch of a lying whore she was. But what he really needed right now was a friend. He had plenty, around the world, but there was no one here, in Monte Carlo, who would understand. Except perhaps the one woman he had hurried back to Monte Carlo to see. It wasn't Sunny Alvarez, she was beyond his reach. It was the woman he had spent a calm relaxing pleasant day with and who had called him her friend.

He checked his watch. Ten-thirty. Was that too late to call? He paced some more, thinking about it, thinking about what to say, how to explain. Surely it was not too late to call a friend, someone he could pour his heart out to, who could bring some sanity to this terrible situation; someone who might understand because her very innocence would be a kind of protection.

chapter 62

Pru was eating an apple. At least she was about to eat it but looking at it she thought it was almost too beautiful to bite into and ruin. Red on one side, green on the other, exactly like Snow White's. She wondered if Eve's apple had also been like that.

Since the delicious lobster fettuccini lunch she had been really careful about whatever entered her mouth. As well as careful about whatever entered her thoughts, because she had to admit, she had thought about Eddie quite often. *Too* often, she decided, taking a bite out of the apple and settling back against the pillows.

Tesoro stretched full length next to her, front paws touching her arm, back legs full out. The dog looked like one of those pajama holders you bought little girls for a gift. Unzip its tummy and put your sleepover jammies inside. Pru smiled, remembering when she had done that. Did kids still do that nowadays? In this era of electronic games and text messages and Twitter and anything else that distracted the mind from the lovely everyday things. Like a beautiful apple and a dear little dog, who belonged to her friend Sunny.

And that was another problem. Pru had spoken to Allie yesterday, and again today. Allie had not heard from Sunny. Not a single word. She had tried calling her cell phone, texting, e-mailing. Nothing, and now Allie was worried. Especially since she had also called

Maha at the hotel only to be informed that Madame Mondragon had departed and there was no forwarding address. They had given her a cell phone contact number however.

"But when I called," Allie had told Pru, "that number had been disconnected. Turned out it was one of those throwaway phones, you know the kind you buy for twenty-nine bucks, the kind used by people who don't want to be traced, like erring husbands, or hookers."

Pru said amazed, "I'm sure Maha wasn't a hooker."

"Of course she wasn't," Allie agreed. "Maha was a lady. She would never do anything Kitty Rattish."

"Kitty Ratte?" Pru was getting an eye-opener.

"Well, what else could that woman be but a hooker, as well as a bitch." Allie thought for a moment then added, "I could think of a better word to describe her but I am too much of a lady to use it. Unless provoked, of course."

Pru laughed. She knew the word Allie meant. She had never used it in her entire life, though she had read it in books. And she surely knew its meaning.

"I'll see if I can find out where Maha went," she promised, but of course there was no further information at the hotel, and now Sunny was missing and Allie was afraid to call Mac because Sunny had wanted to keep her trip to Mumbai a secret, and surprise him with her new role in life. Neither Pru nor Allie wanted to ruin that for her, so they'd decided to give it one more day and if Sunny did not get in touch, then they would have to tell Mac.

"He's still in Prague," Allie told Pru. "I have his number. Of course Ron would have been with him if he hadn't fallen off the horse and broken his damn leg." She said Ron was doing okay and that she would fly back the next morning and together she and Pru would work things out.

Then, a couple of hours later, Ron had phoned. "Hey, Pru, you're never gonna believe this," he said, in a tone that was somewhere between stunned surprise and a laugh. "But Allie fell off her horse and broke her leg."

"The same one as yours?" Pru found herself asking, stunned.

"No. Mine's left, hers is right. Now we're both in casts and on crutches. Well, she will be when they let her out of the hospital bed. Godamit, we can limp along together, holding hands, good foot forward."

"I like that image," Pru said, grinning, though she felt terrible for Allie.

Anyhow, that had left her here, all alone in a hotel suite in Monte Carlo, except for Sunny's Chihuahua, who she was getting way too fond of to want to give back. Plus a head full of dreams of a handsome man with whom she had shared a delicious lunch in a sunfilled South of France piazza, and who had kissed her and called her his friend. She was a lucky woman, if a worried one.

She lay back in bed, blond head against the pillows, TV on without the sound, watching a French movie with Allie in a small role, called *Les Étrangers sur la Plage.*

Pru had almost forgotten she was now a blonde, she'd become used to it very quickly. And used to not having a double chin; used to clothes sliding over her body more easily. She surely wasn't thin but she had lost that awful bulk for which the ex-who-shall-benameless because she couldn't stand his name, was entirely responsible. Life dealt you things sometimes, jabs of pain, sorrow, defeat that sometimes women, and perhaps men too, did not know how to cope with. Dealing with deceit was hard.

Was that pain over now? Pru certainly hoped so. More, she believed it. The man did not deserve even a thought from her newly blond head, and the woman he had taken up with could have him. Let *her* pay for his new Jag, or even the red Porsche with the vanity plates, the Guccis on his feet, the Viagra he needed, the American Express platinum card with which he had taken her out to dinner. Paid for by Pru of course. No more, though.

She turned up the sound on the TV, enjoying hearing Allie speaking French so deliciously, with her slight American accent, that Pru was sure every man in France must be in love with her.

And then the phone rang.

chapter 63

"Prudence, this is Eddie Johanssen."

Pru caught an astonished breath. She'd thought it would be Sunny, calling at last.

"My friend," she said with a pleased tone to her voice that she knew he could not mistake. She didn't care, she *was* pleased to hear from him, even if it was ten-forty at night. "Where are you calling from?" she asked, expecting him to say Glasgow or Berlin.

"Room nine-thirty-three."

"You mean right here? *In this hotel?*"

"That's what I mean."

"Ooh," Pru said again.

"Prudence . . ."

No one but Eddie called her Prudence, not since her father died when she was six years old.

"Yes?"

"I was wondering . . . Well, I wonder if you would take a walk with me."

"Tomorrow? Of course I will." She was thrilled, already thinking perhaps they would have lunch, she would invite him, she would wear her jeans again.

"Not tomorrow. *Now.*"

"Oh." Taken by surprise, she stole a glance in the mirror, saw her empty night-creamed face. She couldn't go anywhere without at least her eyebrows on. And what about the nude lipstick that she was convinced had made Eddie kiss her?

"Why?" The question came from the insecurities deep in her soul.

"Because I need you," Eddie said. The simple words sounded like magic to Pru. "I need to talk to my friend. It's important. Serious."

Pru was already out of bed. "I'll meet you downstairs in five," she said, flinging off her pink cotton pajamas as she ran to the closet. There was no time for niceties and she pulled back on the panties she had just taken off, the same bra, a sweater, the jeans that even as she hurried she noticed were easier to fasten. Not perfect yet, but maybe soon . . . She ran into the bathroom, blotted her face with a tissue, penciled her eyebrows, flicked the nude Saint Laurent across her lips, ran a brush through her tousled blond hair, pushed her feet into ballerina flats, took a look at Tesoro still fast asleep on the bed, thought about taking her and decided against it, grabbed her key and made a run for the door.

The elevator was slow, stopping at every floor. Nervous, she paced back and forth, hurrying in when it finally pinged to a stop. She was down in four minutes but Eddie was there before her, a tense look on his handsome face.

He strode toward her, put his arms around her, held her close. "Prudence! Thank God," he murmured in her ear.

She smiled, thanking God too. This was too good to be true. She recalled all the dire warnings she had ever heard about "Too good to be true." It never was. Still, hope flared as Eddie held her away from him, looking at her. Could that be desperation she saw in his eyes? Alarm bells rang in her head as he took her hand and they walked together from the hotel.

The night was quiet, calm, so different from the night of the robbery with the wail of police sirens and the emergency fire trucks.

They walked, hand in hand, in silence, past all the yachts, some lit and festive, others silent and dark; past the still-open cafés where smiling people sat over drinks; down the fashionable boulevard and past the jeweler's, La Fontaine, where the woman had been murdered.

Pru could bear the silence no longer. She stopped, and still holding on to his hand, said, "What is it, Eddie? Something is very wrong, I can feel it. I'm your friend, you can tell me."

Eddie shook his head. He had been wrong to call her. How could he tell a woman like her about this sick scenario? He would have to show her the photos, see her shocked face, be disgraced in front of her. He sighed deeply; it was that or looking at disgrace for his children, his family.

"This is about Kitty Ratte," he said, facing up to it.

Pru nodded, but her heart sank. He was going to tell her he wanted to be with Kitty, not her. She could feel it coming.

"Kitty is a bad woman," Eddie said, still searching for how to begin.

"Evil. *And* corrupt," Pru corrected him. "Maha said so."

She caught his startled glance under the light of a streetlamp. The air was soft with just enough of a cool wind to stir their hair. Unthinking, she put up a hand and stroked Eddie's back from his eyes. To her astonishment he clutched her hand, held it to his cheek. He shook his head, eyes scrunched in a kind of agony she had not expected.

"But what is it, Eddie," she cried, frightened now. "What is it about Kitty Ratte?"

"She's trying to blackmail me," he said. "Oh she claims it's someone else and that they are trying to blackmail her, but why would anyone bother to try to blackmail a woman like that? A swingers'-club woman, a small-time cheap escort . . ."

"A whore," Pru said.

Again he nodded in agreement. "A whore."

Tucking her hand through his arm, he walked with her along the boulevard. The lights of a café overlooking the water beckoned, reflecting in the black sea. A waning moon shone down on them.

"Let's have some coffee." Pru guided him to a table under the awning. She ordered for them, waiting for him to speak. When the coffee came, steaming, dark, aromatic, she poured hot milk into hers while he drank his fast, and black. She signaled the waiter for another. And then Eddie began his story.

He told her exactly what he remembered; exactly what he did not remember; exactly what he believed had happened. Then he took the envelope from his pocket and laid it on the table between them.

Music filtered softly into the night air, laughter came from other tables, halyards clanged on the moored yachts, and the moon shone down just the way it had on the murder the other night, as Eddie opened the envelope, took out the ransom note and handed it to Pru, then laid the photos next to her on the table.

"I have to show you these because it's the only way you'll know what I mean, and how bad this really is. I understand if you choose not to look at them. I understand if you choose never to see me again. But I'm asking you, as a friend, to help me decide what to do."

Pru stared down at the photograph on top of the small pile. She was looking at a half-naked Kitty Ratte, a vibrator held to her hairless crotch while she straddled a completely naked and—Pru noticed—unexcited Eddie. Eddie's eyes were closed and there was a look of triumph rather than ecstasy on the Ratte's face.

Pru stared for a long time. Then without looking at the rest, she handed the batch of photos back to Eddie. His eyes met hers.

"Cunt," Pru said. The C-word just came out. She figured it was appropriate.

To her surprise, Eddie laughed.

"At least now you can laugh," she said, smiling at her own daring.

"It's just that I never expected to hear that word from you, Prudence."

She raised a freshly penciled eyebrow. "Am I wrong?"

He laughed again. "You are so right. But now what am I going to do? Look at me. In those photos I'm guilty as hell. And will the tabloid readers give a damn whether I was drugged? Whether I'm innocent? Of course not, they'll call me a fool, an idiot, a pervert. A guilty man. My children will be scarred by my actions forever. My wife, a good woman even though we are divorcing, disgraced. And I? Well, nothing good will happen to me, I can assure you of that. I lived all my life for my business. Now it will be gone."

They looked at each other across the little faux marble table. The cane chair creaked as he leaned into her, and their eyes linked.

"There's nothing else for it," he said. "I have to pay her."

Pru was silent. She knew blackmailers never gave up; once you paid they came back for more, and then more . . . She thought about her friend Allie, and about Allie's husband, Ron, who knew about things like this, a world where evil things happened. She thought about Sunny, lost somewhere in Mumbai and panic rose like bile in her throat. She thought about Mac, the man who truly understood people like Kitty Ratte and the corruption and evil they wore around them like an aura. And about Maha who had seen it all, right from the beginning.

"There's only one thing to do," she said, taking Eddie's hand in hers. "We must call Mac Reilly. Only he can help us."

chapter 64

Prague

Snow swirled over the steel-gray River Vltalva, minuscule flurries at first, of iced water that almost imperceptibly turned into flakes of crystal, competing with the silver Christmas decorations and tiny white lights strung across the Charles Bridge.

It was, Mac thought, stopping to admire the view, a thing of great beauty. A Californian, he rarely got to see snow unless on a special trip to the local mountains, to Big Bear, or farther into Tahoe or Sun Valley. Aspen was not a favorite, too smarty-boots for its own good; nature got lost in it. And if you wanted nature you were not going to find it here either, in the urban sprawl of old and new that was the lovely terra-cotta-roofed city of Prague. A city of spired medieval churches and gilded rococo theaters and pastel houses; of narrow cobbled streets that wound upward and skidded down again toward the river; of outdoor cafés protected now from the cold by heavy plastic shrouds, lit by glowing heaters that sizzled the head and left the toes weak with damp; of grand old-fashioned restaurants with waiters in tailcoats and snug local places steaming from the kitchen heat, red velvet walls closing round you and lamps like golden cherubs. And the food? Sublime, the simpler the better. The people? Friendly, handsome; classy-looking women in furs and tall boots; dark-haired, beak-nosed men in heavy green loden coats with small collars and a swaying pleat at the back, Dracula-like as they hurried purposefully, heads down, along the boulevards to secret assignations.

Why, Mac wondered, did he think everyone was on their way to a secret assignation? The reason could only be envy because he was missing Sunny so badly he'd almost gotten on a plane that morning and given up on this whole La Fontaine robbery case. Only the memory of Yvonne Elman's shattered face encrusted in shards of diamonds had kept him here. He could not, *would not* let this dead woman down. He owed it to her husband and to her two-year-old son. He did not want that child to be left with the memory of his mother killed senselessly, for no reason. Not that there was ever a true reason to kill anybody. But this kid was not going to remember his mother as a victim. He deserved the truth.

Justice was very much on Mac's mind as he crossed the bridge, beneath the towers, hurrying past the *alleé* of saintly statues that lined the balustrades, dodging the traffic as he crossed the road and turned into one of those charming cobbled streets in Old Town. Music came from the great wooden doors of a church. Its façade was crusted with the faces of angels, chiseled into the stone, and gargoyles floated over the roof. The snow led a pristine path to great wooden doors. Someone was playing the organ.

Intrigued, Mac climbed the shallow steps, leaving his own trail of dark footprints in the already-melting whiteness. He pushed open the door, stepped inside and was instantly enveloped in the smells of incense and musk; of heavily used worn hassocks, of vestments and candles and the roar of a great organ overall, thundering Bach's *Passion* into the soaring twilight, to the rafters forty feet above.

The sound of the powerful organ vibrated through Mac's body making him part of the music, part of Bach's vision, part of the organist's magical rendering. Up front, to the left of the altar, a row of young choirboys waited, white cassocks over their everyday sweaters, frilled collars with black velvet bows at the neck, gleaming hair neatly combed, hands clutching the open score, waiting their turn to sing.

When it came, their voices soared over the organ, delicate, penetrating, beautiful. A moment of peace, and yet of passion, in a strange city. A moment away from the ugliness of Mac's mission.

He left quietly, unseen, unheard. Back on the narrow street the snow was settling into tiny drifts, pristine, unshoveled, untouched yet by the blackness of trucks and cars. Just the way it must have looked a century, two centuries, ago. Prague was a city with a history, not all of it good, but it had survived wars, its people had survived, its buildings, its beauty, its great bridge. But Mac was not here for that.

He consulted the map given to him by the concierge at the hotel, checked the name of the street. It was a pretty street, charming in fact, its leafless trees rimmed with white, lights shining from the tall eighteenth-century buildings, red flowers shimmering behind glass in the florist's window; a pretty boutique, all space-age modern, steel and glass; pretty girls inside in short skirts and black tights, wondering no doubt if there would be any customers, and whether they might leave early so they could get home before the storm really hit.

The building he was looking for was plain, of a later vintage than the rest of the street, set slightly back. Three steps led to a black lacquered door next to which was a brass-encased list of names, each with a buzzer. Mac took the business card from his pocket and checked the name. The Barnes Model Agency was on the third floor. Mac pressed and was buzzed in immediately.

He pushed open the door and was confronted by another, glass-fronted one. Beyond that was a small foyer with one of those tiny ancient cage elevators he particularly disliked. He recalled getting stuck in one like it. Was it in Paris? Rome? The kind of elevator where a notice said ONE PASSENGER AND ONE PIECE OF LUGGAGE ONLY, or TWO PASSENGERS OF LESS THAN 250 KILOS.

Bypassing the cage, Mac strode briskly up the steps. This was a town house and the only windows were on the front of the building. There were merely yellow too-bright lights on each landing and the worn steps were gray marble. This was not one of your memorable Prague buildings. He wished Ron were with him, but broken legs seemed to be catching and now both he and Allie were on crutches.

He had one more landing to go for the third floor when his cell phone vibrated. He stopped, took it out of his pocket, flicked it open. *Let it be Sunny,* he was praying, *just let it be her, I'll take a plane out tonight, be with her in bed tonight, just let it be her.*

He had not heard from Sunny since she'd called him in Paris and said she was going on a quick trip, three days at the most. Her destination was a secret and she would tell him everything when she got back. Her voice had been full of excitement and pleasure and Mac had not had the heart to tell her he needed to know exactly where she was. Instead, he said *get back soon, think of me, don't forget us, I love you . . .* and she said the same. And, "Can't wait to tell you all about it, Mac Reilly." She'd given him his full Malibu TV show "PI" title, the way she always did when she was teasing him. "Have fun, baby," he'd told her. Since then, not a word.

It was not Sunny on the phone. Surprised, he saw the name Prudence Hilson, a woman he'd met briefly in the hotel in Monte Carlo. He knew she was a friend of Allie's and therefore of Sunny's. "Mac Reilly," he said.

"You don't know me," she said, speaking rather fast and, Mac thought, sounding extremely nervous. "My name is Prudence Hilson."

"I remember. You're a friend of Allie's. Ron told me you spent Christmas with them."

"I did?" She sounded astonished. Then, "Do you realize, that was only *days* ago? Oh my God, have you any idea how much has happened since then?"

"You're alarming me, Pru," Mac said, keeping a smile in his voice so she would know he was only joking. "Is this about Sunny?"

"Ooh. *Sunny.* Well, that's a yes and a no. First and foremost though, its about Eddie Johanssen."

Eddie Johanssen was the good-looking rich guy Sunny had met on the flight to Paris after she'd left him. Mac wasn't sure he wanted to hear what Pru had to say. "I know who you mean."

Her sigh was huge. "It's not what you think. Listen, Mac, Eddie Johanssen is a nice man, a decent man. He's a friend. A new friend I admit, but a good friend. He's not seeing Sunny . . . Look, I know you're in Prague. Where are you staying?"

"The Four Seasons."

Then, "Where *is* Sunny?" Mac asked, suddenly tired with talking around things. "Is she with him?"

"Good God, no. Of course she's not. The woman's crazy in love with you, always has been. Take it from a girlfriend, mister, that woman walks around in an aura of love and sexual fulfillment and *you* are the sole reason. She's not interested in anyone else. Eddie just happened to be there when she needed a shoulder to cry on."

"Okay." Mac wasn't convinced.

And then Pru said, "Eddie is in trouble. Serious trouble. He needs your help and I need to talk to you. I'm at the airport now, on my way to Frankfurt, and from there to Prague. I'll be at your hotel by eight tonight. Is that okay with you?"

"What?" He was stunned.

"Eight o'clock at your hotel. I'll be downstairs in the lobby. We have a lot to talk about, Mac. An awful lot. And it's very serious."

His phone went dead. She had cut him off. What the fuck was going on? What was there about Eddie Johanssen that didn't have to do with Sunny? He didn't give a shit about Eddie Johanssen and in fact he wished Eddie Johanssen had never entered his life. But then he remembered Pru was a friend of Allie's, and that Allie was

Sunny's best friend; and Ron, with the broken leg, was his friend. A circle of friends. Whatever it was, it was urgent enough for Pru to get on a plane and come here and ask his help. Whatever it was, he would do it.

chapter 65

The ribbed-glass door to the Barnes Model Agency led directly into a small office plastered wall-to-wall with photos of would-be models, though how many of them had gone on to a career in fashion, or swimsuit or even catalog was debatable. Sharon recruited from all the East European countries, the Balkans were particularly good for sexy unknown and eager girls, fresh from school and ready for anything. Sharon wasn't interested. She sent them on to other agencies who dealt in that sort of sleaze. What she was good at was getting roles in horror movies being made cheaply in Rumania, small-time stuff but she kept the producers and directors supplied and they kept her with sufficient money to run this small office.

The outer room, the one with all the model pics, was minimally furnished: a glass table on sawhorses; a Philippe Starck clear plastic Ghost chair; a faux zebra bench along the wall for waiting girls, kept busy filling out their resumes, or scanning their portfolios hoping they looked better than they really did. This was not a high-class business. To an outsider, like Mac, it looked as though it barely ticked over.

There was no receptionist in attendance behind the glass table; the computer was shut down. An old-fashioned telephone, a replica from the thirties, nickel silver with a big round black dial, was pushed to one side. A white leather appointments book was closed.

There was no sound. Yet, somebody had buzzed him in.

A door led to another office. Mac tapped briskly on it. "Ms. Barnes?"

Sharon Barnes froze in her position in front of the triple tall arched windows that were the only reason she had taken this cheap office. It gave her a dramatic backdrop and the light flooding in from behind left her face in shadow while illuminating those of her wannabe models and movie stars opposite, giving her a distinct advantage in that she could see exactly what was going on behind their hopeful greedy eyes; while they had no clue as to how she viewed them as potential clients. Right now the light from the windows had the opaque quality of falling snow, whiter than white and cold as the ice of fear that clutched suddenly around her heart.

She did not know who this man might be. He was definitely not the person she was expecting. She moved quickly. The safe was a big old iron model, an antique they said when she'd bought it, but it worked better than all the electronic ones whose codes were so easily broken. Sharon, with her old safe, had become quite the safe-cracker. Just one more of her hidden talents. She closed it now.

Was this man someone Maha had sent? Sharon knew she had been fired and she also knew why. That was okay. The money was in her secret account, as usual. She wanted revenge on Maha though, for cutting her off. She would get her eventually, one way or the other.

She scanned her desk, a narrow slab of steel like something found in a mortuary, quickly placed some papers in her leather Gucci tote, closed down her Mac laptop and lit a cigarette.

It had taken her less than a minute.

Arranging herself in her big pearl-leather executive chair, she dragged on the Gauloise, ran a hand through her black buzz cut, perched horn-rimmed glasses on her nose, smoothed her red suede skirt over her long thighs and said, "Who is it? I'm not expecting anyone."

That was a lie. She was expecting Ferdie and Giorgio, her co-planners. They were two hours late though and that made her nervous. Now this stranger brought a whiff of danger.

"May I come in?" Mac did not wait for an answer. He opened the door and, surprised, looked straight into Sharon Barnes's eyes.

Sharon felt the shock of recognition down her spine. She stiffened, her face tightened into a mask and then she said, "I don't know you. I was expecting somebody else, that's why I buzzed you in. Get out or I'll call security."

Mac knew she knew him. He also knew her. And that there was no security in this cheap office building. He said, "We were introduced a few days ago, in Monte Carlo. You were with Maha Mondragon."

Sharon changed her tack. "And you were with Sunny Alvarez."

Mac nodded. "My fiancée."

Sharon smiled. "I heard."

"I saw you outside, before that," Mac said. "You were smoking a cigarette and you were wearing a short black fur jacket. You clutched it around your neck as though you were cold."

Sharon laughed. "An observant man, but then you are a detective. And let me remind you it *was* cold in Monte Carlo that night. Only addicted smokers would feel compelled to go outside and half-freeze to death just for that cigarette."

"You should try Chantix." He was talking about the latest stop-smoking drug.

"Oh, *please*." Her tone was withering.

"Let me ask you something, Ms. Barnes."

She lowered her eyes. She was not about to ask him to call her Sharon; she wanted him out of here, and fast, before the other two showed up. If in fact they would, which was getting debatable. She did not trust them. She did not trust anybody. And especially this detective sitting so coolly opposite her, as though he had every right to be there.

"Why are you here?" She leaned angrily over the desk. She was not allowing him to question her. "Who sent you?"

Their eyes met over the slab of steel. Mac thought she had unusual eyes. Really quite wonderful. Dark green, very beautiful under winging black brows, set like Maha's jewels in her chiseled face.

Furious, Sharon pushed the horn-rims up again, pushed back her chair, leaned away from him, turning her profile to the window.

"I was in Prague on business," Mac said. "I came across your card and thought it would be interesting to meet."

"If you're looking for models to use on your TV show I can help you. If you are investing in movies in the Balkans I can find you would-be new stars. Young, attractive." She swung round to look at him. "Sexy."

"Is that what you sell?"

Sharon laughed. "You've got the wrong woman there, Mr. Reilly. I'm no pornographer."

"So what exactly were you doing with Maha Mondragon, in Monte Carlo?"

"What business is that of yours?"

"It's my business because I've been asked to help out in the La Fontaine jewel robbery. Not only the robbery and the murder that night in Monte Carlo, but the earlier one, in Paris."

Sharon laughed. "I get it. It's *The Pink Panther* and you are Inspector Clouseau. Right?"

"I wish." Mac took Sharon's business card from his pocket and put it on the desk. She stared at it. He said, "You've no doubt read how the robberies took place. Who the suspects are? Three women, long blond hair, long fur coats . . ."

"I read about it."

"Someone gave me one of those fur coats. Your card was in its pocket."

He shoved the card across the steel slab at her. She stared at it but did not touch.

"Anyone could have my card. Girls come in here all the time, looking for modeling jobs."

"I wonder if you had one particular model, tall, blonde, again wearing a very expensive mink coat, and who also happened to be in Monte Carlo the night of the robbery?"

Sharon turned her profile to the window again. "It was Christmas, nobody was booked. How should I know what models do in their spare time?"

"So what exactly were *you* doing there, Ms. Barnes?"

He had caught her out and she smiled, eyes glittering behind the glasses. "You're right, I *was* working, *Mr.* Reilly, with Ms. Mondragon. Maha is preparing to show her new jewelry line; a slightly less expensive one than the couture she normally does. It's to be a big event, Maha is going for the mass market, better than costume, but lesser than Cartier."

"Somewhere in between." Mac knew zero about jewels except for the pink diamond engagement ring and the small diamond drops he'd bought Sunny last Christmas.

"She needed models to show her jewels. Tall girls, very thin with long necks, like dancers. In fact that's what I suggested. Ballerinas are notoriously hard up and always looking for work. I could get them cheap. But Maha said she wanted more exotic girls. Gypsies, that sort of thing."

"Gypsies?"

Sharon understood that he knew more than he was saying. Disturbed, she got to her feet, towering in her red suede boots that she knew, with a flicker of distaste, would be ruined in the snow. Even at moments like this, moments of stunning danger, Sharon thought only about herself. She knew what to do next.

"I have answered all your questions, Mr. Reilly," she said coldly. "Though you had no right to ask." Her shrug expressed her indifference. "I was in Monte Carlo on business at Christmas. I work for Ms. Mondragon. I suggest you go to her for confirmation of the facts."

"Trust me, Ms. Barnes. I will." Mac knew there was nothing more to be gained. Picking up the business card from the steel slab he walked out.

He ran down the six flights of stairs leading from the third floor, footsteps ringing coldly on the marble. He turned from the last flight into the small lobby just as the elevator door clanged shut. In the cage he saw two men. They were the same two men he'd seen with Mondragon and Sharon Barnes at the hotel bar in Monte Carlo.

He stopped to watch as they sailed upward, closed into the cage like zoo animals on display.

He stepped out into the freezing evening that was already drifting into darkness. The leftover twinkling lights of Christmas reminded him that this was New Year's Eve. And that he was alone. In Prague.

chapter 66

Down the street from the Barnes Agency, music spilled out into Old Town Square. The pastel-colored palaces and Gothic buildings, the restaurants and cafés were alive with revelers. It was already New Year's somewhere in the world, as laughing girls reminded Mac, dancing past him, holding out their hands, inviting him to come and join them.

Mac walked down the narrow street to the river. Prague was a city of churches, so many their illuminated spires almost seemed to touch. He walked across the Charles Bridge with its ice guards to protect the old sixteen arches when the Vltalva froze. He stopped to inspect one of the great Gothic towers. The bridge was bustling with vendors manning their kiosks under the stony glare of the many statues mounted on the balustrades, while painters waited to sketch his portrait or sell an authentic oil of the city, or a pretzel, or a hot dog.

Mac bought a hot dog and ate it as he walked; it was spicy, hot and crunched as he bit into it. He thought somebody in the United States could make a fortune importing them, but then somebody could always make a fortune somewhere. Except the little gray waif, Valentina Vinskaya.

She had made enough to buy a few clothes, buy a boyfriend,

buy dinner in a smart restaurant. The yellow diamond ring had not made a fortune for her, but it might have made a good extra profit for Sharon Barnes, had she not been careless and left it in her coat pocket.

He was sure it was Sharon. Trouble was, he had no evidence. Unless he could persuade the little gray waif to tell the truth about who she had stolen the fur from and who she had sold the diamond ring to.

He wrapped his black coat around himself as he walked. He'd bought it in Charles de Gaulle airport, long, black, high-collared, not your average businessman's overcoat; but then Mac was not your usual businessman. Hugo Boss, and way too expensive, but it was that or freeze. It was cold in Prague. The coat swirled around his legs in the wind as he stepped into the lee of a vendor's kiosk and dialed Valeria's number. There was no reply. He left a message, saying simply, "Call me," but he was wary about leaving his name, just in case. He was worried, but it was New Year's, and he told himself Valeria probably had a job dancing in some club. Earning her living, one way or another.

Alone, in the middle of all the busy New Year's excitement on the Charles Bridge, Mac stared into the starless sky and thought about Sunny. He had to get in touch with her; he had to know where she was this New Year's Eve, what she was doing; that she was safe. He tried her number, got the same from-outer-space ring. He considered calling Allie but she had her own troubles, with the broken legs.

Then he remembered. Pru Hilson was coming. She would be here at eight. She would *have* to tell him where Sunny was.

Back at the hotel, Mac called the Inspector and brought him up to date on the gypsy, the ring, the card in the pocket of the fur coat and his visit with Sharon Barnes.

"I know she's involved somehow," he said. "What I don't know is whether she was one of the robbers."

He described her and the Inspector said he would have her checked. He would also check on Maha Mondragon, who was well known for her expensive jewels. "Not in La Fontaine's league," he said. "No diamonds."

"No diamonds," Mac agreed. "The gypsy fenced the yellow diamond ring. Probably got a couple of thousand euros. She didn't have the high-level contacts and anyway would have been too scared. This was high-class stuff, way out of her league, but she needed the money." Remembering her bleak pink apartment he added, "I can't blame her."

"A thief is a thief," the Inspector reminded him coldly.

Mac described the two men in the elevator and the Inspector said he would look into them.

"This all is involved with Maha Mondragon," Mac said. "I can feel it in my bones."

"Unfortunately, your bones are not enough," the Inspector said. "Proof, *mon vieux,* is what we need."

Yvonne Elman's dead face swam into Mac's mind. "Trust me, I'll find it," he said.

He checked the arrival of the flight from Frankfurt. It was on time and he sat in the hotel lobby, nursing a vodka and soda, remembering the tiny glass of Slivovitz he had not drunk that morning at the gypsy's, and waiting for Pru Hilson.

New Year's Eve was swirling all around him: the hotel throbbed with music and partygoers in black tie and backless satin dresses; lovely blond Prague women and their beak-nosed dark men, exotic, like something from a thirties movie. Perfume hung in the air and there was the sound of popping champagne corks. Mac had never felt so unfestive in his entire life. Except for Christmas of course. And now it was New Year's. Why didn't Pru get here? He would *force* her to tell him where Sunny was.

He heard a sharp high bark and looked up, startled, expecting to see Sunny. But it was Pru Hilson with the Chihuahua.

"I'm dog-sitting," she explained. "I couldn't just leave her behind."

Mac was on his feet, helping her off with her coat. Her wheat-color hair was dusted with melting flakes of snow and her cheek felt cold when they kissed. "Like old friends," she said, smiling.

It was, Mac thought, a charming smile. He didn't remember her looking like this; he remembered a brown-haired lumpy woman in a flowing cranberry caftan who looked as though she'd been left over from the Woodstock era.

"You look wonderful," he said, sincerely, smiling as he saw her blush.

"That's thanks to Allie and Sunny," Pru said. "They gave me the Monte Carlo makeover."

"It worked," Mac said. Then, "About Sunny . . ."

Pru looked at him, then looked at her watch. There were still almost ten hours to go before she and Allie could break their promise. Maybe Sunny would be back by then. "I can't tell you. Not now. Later, perhaps . . ."

Mac looked at her and she sighed.

"I promised," she explained.

The dog jumped onto Mac's lap. He called over the waiter, Pru asked for a Cosmo.

"Sunny's drink," she said. "She taught me."

"I'll bet she did," Mac said.

Pru told him she had a room and he got the bellman to take her small travel bag. "You must be hungry?"

"Not yet." She sat there in her brown sweater and jeans, legs crossed, looking very nervous.

"This is hard to explain," Pru said. "It's so terrible, I didn't know what to do. But then I told Eddie, we must go to Mac. He's the only one who can help."

Mac wasn't smiling, just listening, cool, guarded. Pru hoped she was doing the right thing. What else could she do if she were to save Eddie and his family, and their future?

She took the envelope from her purse and pushed it across the table. "There's a letter in there," she said. "Blackmail. And some pictures. Let me tell you first that those photos were taken without Eddie's knowledge."

Mac opened the envelope and took out the note, but before he could read it he heard someone say, "Pru, I couldn't let you do this for me. I have to take care of it myself."

Eddie Johanssen was standing next to Pru, his hand on her shoulder.

chapter 67

"Oh, Eddie," Pru said, beaming at him and shaking her head at the same time.

"It's my responsibility," Eddie said. He reached out his hand to Mac. "I'm sorry to trouble you with this problem."

"Problems like this are my job." Mac shook Johanssen's hand, noting that he was a very good-looking man. Handsome with that shock of hair, the slight tan, the long lean body. Any woman would have been pleased to be with him, including, he thought with a pang of jealousy, Sunny.

"Sit down, Mr. Johanssen," Mac said, watching him closely. "Would you like a drink?"

"Vodka, same as yours."

Eddie took the chair next to Pru. Mac thought he looked tired and strained. A man in trouble. And the woman with him was obviously under his spell, eager to help, anxious to prove his innocence in whatever little caper this turned out to be.

The vodka arrived but Johanssen ignored it; he'd picked up the manila envelope and was turning it over and over in his hands, as though he wanted to just throw it away. Throw away all it contained. Evidence of something he did or did not do.

Mac wasn't sure which option was true. Was the man playing

innocent? Recruiting a truly innocent woman to help him; make him look better, her being on his side?

"I know what you're thinking," Johanssen said. "I can only leave the answer up to you. If you choose to believe me, I will be grateful. If not, I will understand."

Mac dealt with criminals for a living, he knew all the telltale signs of guilt; knew how the eyes challenged or avoided; keeping their secrets. He understood guilt but right now he did not believe he was looking at it. But then, he had been wrong before. Nobody was perfect.

He said to Eddie, "Allow me to read the blackmail note first." He scanned it quickly, then put it on the table between them. He took a sip of his vodka. "So, what can you tell me about this?"

"I cannot remember clearly, any of the events. I will tell you all I have managed to salvage from the wreckage of that night."

Mac knew Eddie was not being dramatic; he was simply stating his position. He noticed that Pru put her hand over his as he talked, and that Eddie did not remove it.

It was an old story. Mac had heard it all before. Drugs. Ecstasy for the uninhibited high; then GHB or Rohypnol for the date rape that left the victim helpless against whatever took place, and with no memory afterward of what had happened, only a dark blank space where time used to be. He held out his hand for the photographs. Pru turned away, unwilling to look, but Eddie's eyes remained fastened on Mac.

Mac shuffled quickly through them, then put them back in the manila envelope. "I know this woman," he said.

"Kitty Ratte," Eddie said.

Mac said, "She was so obviously bad news I'm stunned Sunny even talked to her."

"Sunny told me it was because it was Christmas and she was all alone, and so was Kitty," Pru explained quickly, anxious to defend her friend. "Sunny was Alone, with a capital *A*. She simply couldn't stand it. She meant being without you, of course."

Mac knew exactly what she meant.

Eddie said, "Kitty claims it's *she* who is the blackmail target, *she* who's being blackmailed, and it's my fault. I have to pay or she will lose everything, her good name, her reputation."

"Hah," Pru said. "That's funny."

"What's more, it's stupid." Mac looked at Eddie. "You were duped, my friend. She didn't take you into her bed, did she? Oh no. She arranged you on that particular sofa, facing the video cam. She turned on all the lights, fed you the drug and away she went. No holds barred."

"Literally," Pru added, stroking Eddie's nerveless hand. His face was pale under the tan and she understood how much he hated this conversation, how he hated Kitty Ratte, how he hated himself for being involved. "It wasn't your fault," she whispered.

"Yes, it was. I allowed it to happen. I drank with her at the bar even though I knew what she was."

"You were lonely," Pru said.

"It's an old story," Mac said. "And one we can do something about, but first we need to nail her on the blackmail."

"I can't allow my family to find out . . ." Eddie was panicking.

"Don't worry, we won't go to the police. At least not yet." Mac knew exactly what he was going to do.

Eddie put his head in his hands, shoulders stooped. "What a New Year's Eve," he said hopelessly.

"Don't worry, the New Year begins tomorrow," Pru said, patting his bent shoulder. "Mac will take care of everything and nobody will ever know."

"Know *what*?" a voice said.

Mac turned at the sound of canes tapping on the marble floor. Legs in plaster, Ron and Allie swung toward him.

"Couldn't let you celebrate New Year's all alone," Allie said, laughing, as Mac got up to hug her.

"How did you find me?"

"The Inspector." Ron slapped him on the back in a bear hug.

"And anyhow, how did you fly that plane with a broken leg?"

"Just for your information, a Cessna is not flown by the legs. It takes hands and brains. And a computer."

"Right," Mac said.

"Hello, Pru." Allie was hugging Pru now, and waiters were hurrying with more chairs.

"Make sure the walking wounded are comfortable," Mac said to them. "I don't think there'll be much dancing this New Year's Eve."

Passersby on their way to parties turned to stare. "It's Allie Ray," they exclaimed. "The movie star . . . Allie Ray. Look how beautiful she still is . . ."

"You'd think I'd been gone decades instead of a mere couple of years," Allie said, looking like a mischievous teenager.

"You look wonderful tonight." Ron clasped her hand tightly in his. "You've always looked wonderful, always will."

She smiled at him. Her pale satin miniskirt came about ten inches above her knees, allowing room for the plaster cast that held her right leg in its grip. "I know, I know, its *very* short," she said, catching Mac's glance. "Don't worry, I'm wearing something underneath."

"But *what*?" Pru whispered. "How could you get anything over that plaster cast?"

"Spanx," Allie whispered back. "You just have to grit your teeth and pull like mad and then *oomph* they just go on."

"Ooh, *Spanx*." Pru had learned a lot in a few days.

"By the way, you look gorgeous," Allie said, amused because Pru still blushed at the compliment.

"Oh, do you know Eddie Johanssen?" Pru said, remembering.

Eddie had pushed his chair off to one side, feeling like the intruder on the friendship. He shook hands and said he would go, and wished them a Happy New Year anyway.

"Sit back down, Eddie," Mac said. "We haven't finished."

"Finished what?" Ron's dark eyes were on the alert for the trouble that just seemed to follow Mac around.

"Eddie's having a blackmail problem," Mac said. "We need to deal with it."

"I'll bet its Kitty Ratte," Allie said, arranging the sleeves of her black chiffon top and adjusting it farther off one shoulder.

"Sexy," Ron whispered, and she giggled.

"How did you know?" Eddie asked.

She shrugged. "All you needed to do was look at that woman. Those tiny eyes are like heat-seeking missiles; a predator on the prowl for matching heat. A victim. Or a loser."

"Well, she found it." Eddie's voice had a bitter ring.

"I told Eddie she was a C-word," Pru said primly, making them laugh.

Ron asked the waiter to bring a magnum of champagne. He checked his watch. "After all it is New Year's Eve," he said. "Only a couple of hours to go."

Pru glanced meaningfully at Allie. "It's already the New Year in some places we know. Does that count?"

"I'm worried to death," Allie whispered back. "What are we to do?"

"Let's tell Mac," Pru said. "Oh, Allie, *please* let's tell him."

"So, all business is over between you two?" Ron asked Eddie. "Is it okay to drink a celebratory glass?"

Mac nodded at Eddie. "Drink," he said. "It will be okay. She— and whoever she's working with—will be taken care of. And by the way administering drugs is a federal offense. As is blackmail. Trust me."

The champagne was poured, platters of hors d'ouevres, Czech-style, appeared: smoked beef, tiny pork chops with sauerkraut, minuscule sausages, cheese on little skewers, nuts and coconut-spangled dates and sweet rose-colored crisp ladyfingers, all the way from Rheims, where the champagne came from.

They toasted, then Mac had had enough of the talking and the subject. "Okay. Where is Sunny?"

In the silence that followed, his phone rang. Groaning, he answered. "Yes, Inspector?"

"The gypsy," the Inspector said. "I sent the local police to check her out. They found her sitting in a chair with a cat curled up on her lap, and a neat bullet hole in her forehead. Very neat, very small. Except at the back where her head was blown away."

"Tell me it was the Black Rose," Mac said. "The PM 9."

"Made in Worcester, Massachusetts. From the crime photos on the computer, I'm betting on it."

"And so am I. And Inspector, I think you should be sending those local cops to question Sharon Barnes of the Barnes Model Agency. I'll bet my good New Year it's her. And try Maha Mondragon. They worked together."

He closed his phone, stared down at it, as if hypnotized. His heart ached for the little gray waif, who at the end had only her cat for company in death. It wasn't grief he felt; he hadn't known her well enough or long enough for his heart to stop in that direction. It was simply pain for a lost soul.

"What's wrong?" Allie asked, reaching out her hand to him, concerned. "Is it Sunny?"

Mac looked sadly at her. "Not this time." They listened in silence as he told them the gypsy's story.

Then Allie said, "You know of course, it's not suicide. Just from what you've told us, I'm sure of that. She wasn't suicidal when you met her, and besides it's guys who put bullets in their heads, shoot their faces off. Women put on their mascara and take pills; after all they never know who'll be looking at them after they're dead."

"Vanity," Pru said, stunned.

Allie shrugged. "I'm not demeaning the act of death," she said. "Just explaining that this kind of woman would not shoot herself in the head."

"She didn't. There was no gun. Just a body."

"Ooh," Pru said, horrified.

"And what's more," Mac said, stroking Tesoro as though it would bring Sunny closer. "I believe I know who did it. And why."

Ron said, "Are you gonna tell us?"

Mac shook his head. "Not yet. I need proof, a witness, hard evidence. So far, it's only a theory. And so far I don't have all the story."

New Year's celebrations continued around them.

Mac said, "So, don't you think it's time you all told me where Sunny is?"

Allie and Pru looked at each other. "Yes," they said, together. "She's in Mumbai."

chapter 68

Cannes

Kitty Ratte paced the floor of her small apartment in her cut-price Louboutins, clacking back and forth on the wood, catching a heel in the rug and almost tumbling onto the sofa. The fatal sofa where Eddie had gotten seduced. She almost wished it had been real; that man had a wonderful body and was well-endowed enough to at least give a woman some sort of a game, though Kitty would have had to put the handcuffs on him, have him in her power for even a glimmer of excitement to creep through her own body. And then she would have had to use the vibrator, which anyway was failing in its claims, always failing to give her the high she sought and would never find.

Kitty had always used sex as a way to control and manipulate men, and by only ever faking her excitement, she had always retained that control. At the swingers' clubs, as well as the sexual encounters, in hotels, and the pickups for money, men thought they were giving her a really good time, what with all her moaning and yelping and the oooh-you're-so-wonderfuls, I've never come like this before . . . Poor fools. Sometimes, though, Kitty wanted it. She *really* wanted that elusive high, the thrill that would never be hers, no matter how many men took her body at the clubs, no matter how many masked men watched them while getting their thrills, Kitty's thrill was only vicarious, never real. She remembered the psychiatrist telling her she was a nymphomaniac, explaining the symptoms. Now she understood, and knew it was true.

Anyhow where was that bastard Johanssen? She had given him the blackmail note and the photos yesterday; she'd expected him to be filled with fear, back on the phone, setting up a meeting. Especially after she had called and let him know how sexually attractive and exciting she thought he was, and how he could never betray her. She knew a man like Eddie Johanssen would never allow his family to be put in jeopardy; he would pay up. She was certain of it. Nevertheless, she was nervous, pacing, eyeing the phone, waiting for it to ring.

Stumbling over the rug again, she banged her chin on the edge of the iron coffee table, stepped back, tripped, caught her shoe heel. Her ankle twisted and the heel snapped. It dangled by a thread of red leather.

Oh shit shit, shit! These were her "good" shoes. Like her "good" bag, they gave her entrée into real society. Wearing them, she could pretend she had a maid at home, taking care of a grand house where she entertained like a rich woman. Wearing a pair of seven-hundred-dollar Louboutins, bought for less than half that, had given her class.

Bristling with anger, Kitty grabbed the phone, called the hotel and asked to be put through to Mr. Johanssen. She was told he was not there, but yes, he was expected back, they did not know when.

Lying back on the rug, she threw the ruined shoe viciously at the ceiling. Ooh fuck! It hit the track light and thin shards of glass shattered down onto the table. *Shit, shit, shit!* She lay on the rug, her swollen ankle propped on the sofa, tears of anger streaming down her face. After a while, she got up and limped over to the kitchen where her laptop sat beneath the bank of cabinets. She summoned up Jimmy on Skype and sat there, red hair orange in the light, fringe stuck to her prominent forehead, buckteeth exposed in a snarl, ugly in her anger.

The picture came up. A woman was looking at her. "I know you," the woman said.

It was Jimmy's wife. "Listen, bitch," the woman was saying, glaring at her on the screen.

Kitty did not know what to do and by the time she realized *what* she must do, it was too late.

The woman was small, blond hair in a careful bob, beige twin-set buttoned at the neck. She even wore a string of pearls. Kitty noticed her teeth, small, white, even. No twin bad front-tooth veneers to haunt her in her mirror. The "wife," neat, perfect. And angry.

"Listen, bitch," the wife said again, staring deeply at her from the screen. "I've had it with this cheap bastard. You know what, don't bother to call him on Skype anymore because I'm cutting it off. And you know what else. I'm cutting *him* off too. I've thrown him out. He's all yours. And you know what he comes to you with? Nothing. He's out of here with zero in his bank account; no credit cards; no cash; no car. Did you really think I was just sitting around here letting him get away with spending my money on trips to France, on sex games and porn and cheap whores like yourself? Forget it. I'm much too smart for that. I have it all arranged legally. He has nothing, and now, he's all yours. You are welcome to him."

Kitty stared soundlessly at her, for once lost for words, lost for control . . . her life was spiraling downward . . . Jimmy had no money, nothing . . . now he offered her zero, except as her partner in the blackmail . . .

"Let me add something here," the wife's voice had a triumphant tone. "Looking at you, I'm telling you you're too old for this game. You are too old, too cheap-looking, too tired. What you are in is a young woman's game and you are way, way beyond it. Seduction is more than just opening your legs. Even we suburban housewives understand that."

Outraged, Kitty shut down the computer. How *dare* she? How dare that *bitch* talk to her like that? Where the fuck was *Jimmy*? Why hadn't he called? E-mailed? Skyped?

Her ankle was throbbing. Now it was swollen to twice its normal size, as fat as her calf, almost as fat as her fat thighs.

She got up, opened the cabinet, took a bottle of pills from the selection she kept there. Oxycontin. Shaking out three, she swallowed them without water. She could have powdered them, gotten a bigger hit, but she was in pain.

This blackmail had to work. She would not let Johanssen get away from her . . . she would accuse him of rape . . . she would destroy him . . .

Tears trickled down Kitty's face as she hauled herself back to the sofa, where she sat, staring into space, wondering what to do, until her eyes rolled up and her head fell back onto the cushions, and oblivion took over.

chapter 69

Mumbai

It was very late; the New Year had already taken over from the old; the jollifications and firecrackers had subsided and no bells were ringing as Rahm Singh walked down the driveway to the gate-house. The keeper was curled up on the floor, sleeping. Singh pressed the button to open the gates. The keeper woke, jumped to his feet and was struck down by a quick blow to the head. He gave a single cry, high pitched, like a seabird, then fell back, dead.

Singh pressed the button to open the tall iron gates, and the waiting car glided silently to the house. He followed on foot.

Sunny didn't know what it was that woke her. She lay on her back, still as the statue of Mahalakshmi who guarded the pool and who brought prosperity and wealth to this house. The lamp she had left on in a corner near the tall double doors leading into the vast room cast a comforting light, and a perfumed candle flickered in the slight breeze coming from the French doors that had been left slightly open. Sunny saw all this mistily, through sleep-glazed eyes, behind the gauze of looped muslin curtains that swirled around the high bed. The newly cold predawn air raised goose bumps on her arms. Or was that fear?

But why should she be afraid? She was safe, here at Maha's house. She had carried the jewels halfway across the world and tomorrow—no, it must be already today—she would complete her mission, then the following day she would be winging her way back to France, back to Mac . . .

A sound came from outside . . . a footfall, then a cry . . . It must be a bird calling? But her watch said three A.M. It was still dark. Surely even Indian birds slept in their nests and trees until dawn had them on the wing. *Then what was it?*

Real fear crept up Sunny's spine this time; freezing her in place. She knew no one here, had met only Rahm Singh and the silent maids, the gatekeeper who had waved the car in, the man who had served her supper. She was alone. Again. This time in India.

Numb, she strained her ears for any new sound. Nothing. Relieved, she exhaled. She had been listening so hard she had forgotten to breathe. Now the sound of her own gasp seemed to echo through the silence.

Mac flew into her thoughts, in her head, the image of him there, with her. He would be saying *come on, Sunny, baby, you're a strong woman, think about this, think what to do. Probably it's nothing, and all you have to do is get out of bed and take a look around . . .*

That's what Mac would say, and that's what Mac would do. It was no use her lying in bed, waiting for something to happen. If anything was wrong then she'd better be prepared.

Willing away the fear that had frozen her, Sunny told herself it was only because she was alone and in a strange house, in a foreign country. Of course everything was all right.

She sat up, swung her legs over the edge of the bed, bundled the muslin curtains to one side and stood for a few seconds on the small wooden steps.

She hurried to the open windows. She had on only a T-shirt and the jersey yoga pants she wore when traveling because they were lightweight and easy, and besides she hadn't wanted to be naked, alone in that big bed, in this strange house, in this strange country. She held back the sweeping heavy fuchsia silk curtains, covering herself with them as she peered out.

Stop it, she told herself, *stop this nonsense, Mac would want you to stop it.* Nevertheless, finally emerging onto the shadowy terrace she wished Tesoro was with her. The little dog could sniff out an intruder at fifty paces; be alert to any new sound, any thrill of danger.

Shadows swooped around the perimeter of the terrace and the little stream burbled over its rocks. Sunny permitted herself a little smile. You see, she told herself, relieved; that's all you heard, the water trickling over the rocks.

A sudden gust of wind rattled the jacarandas, sending clouds scudding over the half-moonlit black sky, bringing with it the marshy scent of the nearby sea, and causing the necklace of lights around Malabar Point and the Marine Drive to twinkle.

She stepped back into the room, letting the heavy curtains fall back into place, then stood uncertainly by the table where she had eaten her sandwich, so peacefully, only hours before. It had been cleared but someone had left a pitcher of juice and a glass, and a box of French cookies. Liu. The kind with chocolate on one side. They were a favorite but, nervous, she was not interested.

She couldn't stand this, being alone in the middle of the night. She should call for a servant, ask for tea; Lapsang souchong . . . No, maybe green tea . . . It was odd now she thought, remembering all the chai lattes she had drunk in those times in Malibu Starbucks when life was normal and she was not afraid; odd how Starbucks had appropriated the Indian word for tea . . . *chai* . . .

An old-fashioned tapestry bellpull was next to the bed. Another vestige of Raj antiquity, she guessed, giving it a hefty tug, though she did not hear an answering ring. Perched on the edge of the bed again, she ran her fingers through her tangled hair; she must look like hell. She took her BlackBerry from the night table and speed-dialed Mac's number. The call did not go through. She tried Allie's number, then Ron's. So much for high-tech India; her phone did not work.

She looked at the closed doors leading into her room. There was no sound of a servant's hurrying footsteps. Perhaps she'd been wrong to call in the middle of the night, but she was frightened. She needed help.

Getting up, she slipped her feet into her red Converse high-tops and strode to the door. She would go find someone, tell them she felt ill, that she needed help, she needed hot tea, needed to know she wasn't alone.

The brass door handles were long and narrow, horizontal against the pale wooden panels. Sunny pressed down on the one on the right. It didn't move. Okay, so it must be the other. She pressed the left. It did not move either. She jiggled first one then the other. The doors were locked.

Real fear hit her now, hot down her spine, burning like acid in her throat; sweat sprang from every pore, her hair was suddenly soaked with it. Panicked, she ran back to the safety of the bed, tripping over the rug. Groaning, she picked herself up, climbed back onto the safety of the great puffy bed. And felt an arm come from behind and snake around her neck.

chapter 70

"Do not utter," an Indian voice whispered so close to Sunny's ear she felt his warm breath. "Not one word must you utter, not one cry or a scream." She felt the thrust of a knife point against her ribs. "You will come now, make no sound, or other people will die too."

Die too . . . ? Other people . . . ? Sunny's brain was charged with the adrenaline of fear, the fight-or-flight mode humans inherited from their primal ancestors. Crying out would not help, she understood that . . . if she were to survive she must keep her wits.

A cloth was wrapped round her head, she could hardly breathe, could not see . . . There was a ripping sound, he must have torn the curtains from the bed, then she was being wrapped in them, spun round and round, a mummy in the muslin fabric. Her elbow was held in a tight grip.

"Walk," the man said, in his singsong Indian lilt. "Walk with me. Do not say anything or we are all dead."

We are all dead. What did he mean . . . *we . . . ? who else . . . ?* There was only Rahm Singh in the house, and the female servants she had met. Perhaps they did not live here, they must have their own quarters on the grounds, or in town. And none of them knew about the jewels, she was sure of that. Only Maha knew.

But anyway why would they want to steal the jewels? Why want to kidnap her? Maha was simply returning her precious necklaces and jewelry to Mumbai to be refashioned. They could steal stones like them from any jewelry bazaar, any dealer, right here. Why go to all this trouble?

She was slammed up against something hard, metal. The heat of an exhaust pipe seared her shin and she almost cried out in pain, stopping herself just in time. Suddenly she was lifted up, tossed helpless into what she realized must be a flatbed truck, she could feel the metal ridges underneath some cloths flung over the floor. He was standing over her. She smelled his garlicky breath and the spiciness of his skin as he wrapped duct tape over her already-covered mouth, over her eyes. Panic forced a soundless scream . . . *She could not breathe . . . She was going to die . . . Oh Mac, Mac I don't want to die, help me Mac . . .*

The muslin was loosened so he could bind her wrists; her ankles were tied. It wasn't rope he used, though; it had a strawlike texture and smelled the way it used to when her Mom baled hay for her horses back home, at the ranch near Santa Fe. He was a countryman, *oh God, oh God, don't let me die . . .*

The truck was thrust into creaking gear, bumped off down the road. Was it the driveway ? If so then surely the gatekeeper would be there? He would see her, he would help. But the truck did not stop at the gate, it must already have been open. Now they were curving down the long hill.

chapter 71

Ferdie and Giorgio waited until Rahm Singh had walked back to the house before getting out of the car. Silent, with a wave of an arm, Singh conducted them inside, via the kitchen entrance, separate from the guest quarters, and also separate from Maha's palatial sleeping rooms. He was unaware that from behind the fretted wooden screen dividing the kitchen the three silent women servants watched.

Singh went to the butler's pantry and took the bag from its hiding place. He walked back, put it on the white marble table, then stood, looking at the two men.

There was an air of richness about them that he envied, in the fineness of their custom-tailored tropical-weight suits, their Italian cotton shirts, their imported shoes. Rahm Singh did not look anything like them and he wanted to.

"Where is the woman who carried the jewels?" one of the men asked.

"She is taken care of." Rahm Singh had not yet dealt with her; he'd been caught off guard by the speed of their arrival.

Giorgio raised an eyebrow. "Who else knows about the diamonds?"

"Only the Mondragon."

"Not the woman?"

"I promise you, she will know nothing."

Rahm Singh unzipped the bag and took out a necklace, heavy gold, swirled and studded with large cabochon rubies.

Ferdie picked it up, turned it over, studying the smooth gold at the back. He took a metal tool from his pocket, inserted the tip beneath the largest ruby and prised it from the setting. The fake ruby had been hollowed out and came off like a shell from a nut, revealing the diamond hidden beneath. A diamond of such pure quality it glittered like Venus, the star of the heavens, under the single overhead lamp.

Ferdie grunted with pleasure, examining it. "Not that large, but of course excellent quality."

Rahm Singh zipped the bag back up. He sat at the table with the bag on the floor next to him. "The others are even finer, but first I need to see the money."

"Then there is nothing else to discuss," Giorgio said. But it was Ferdie, the ex–polo player known for his speed, who leapt at Rahm Singh. He stuck the metal tool into his neck with such force the Indian's chair fell backward and his yellow-and-red turban fell off. Blood spurted like a fountain from his aorta and Ferdie quickly jumped out of the way.

Giorgio got up and the two stood looking down at him. A gurgle came from Rahm Singh's throat as Ferdie leaned over and grabbed the tool. He tugged at it but it did not come out. He pulled again, but it was stuck deep in muscle and flesh and bone. Blood washed over his hands though it was no longer spurting because now Rahm Singh's heart had stopped pumping. He was dead. A great mass of the blood surrounded the Indian's head, congealing in his long, oiled black hair and on the marble floor.

Giorgio picked up the bag and thrust the necklace and the remains of the fake cabochon back in it. He put the diamond in his pocket, not noticing the trace of blood it left on his beautiful, tan, tropical-weight, custom-tailored suit that Rahm Singh had so envied. Then they left the kitchen, got back into the long black car and drove off.

The three silent women behind the fretted wooden screen could not cry out when they saw Rahm Singh murdered. Instead, terrified, they ran on bare silent feet out into the night. However, since Maha had taught them to read, they did have the presence of mind to note the car's number before they ran on, fast and terrified, the way they had when they were children of the slums.

chapter 72

Sunny rolled from side to side, smacking up against the metal at every curve, every swerve. The smell of the sea rushed at her again, that marshy odor tinged with salt and overlaid with the sweetness of the sugarcane sold at those seafront stalls. She heard the cries of children, the ones that never slept, the ones huddled in heaps like homeless puppies, thin and frightened and already aware of death . . . the way she was now.

The truck changed its course. Sunny lifted her head, gasping for breath; the hood over her face choked her, she rolled over onto her stomach, banged her head on the wheel hump, sobbed silently. Mac would expect her to get herself out of this but she did not know how. Would she ever see Mac again? *Oh yes, yes, please God, my God, Maha's goddess, any god in this country who loves mankind, who loves India, who loves us all . . . help me.*

There was noise all around now. The truck was weaving through a crowd; she heard voices chattering, shouting, raucous, heard the racket of metal shutters being raised, of heavy things being lifted from vehicles and thrown out onto the street; laughter; yelling; running feet. The truck swerved then cut quickly sideways, tossing her against the metal again. Sunny groaned.

With a great crashing of gears, it jolted to a stop. The backboard was unlatched, dropped down with a clang, someone jumped up. He stood over her, breathing hard, grabbed her arm, hauled her to her feet, jumped back down, dragging her with him. Her thighs scraped on the metal edge and she felt blood run down her legs. She told herself to ignore it; she must keep her head; must try to remember where she was being taken, what was happening . . .

He untied her ankles, told her to walk. The returning circulation was almost as painful as the scrapes on her thighs. Her feet sank into mud. There go the red Converse sneakers, she thought, and almost laughed at herself for behaving like a woman at a time like this when she might be going to die. *No. No. No.* She would *not* die. She would *not* let them kill her. She would *not* let them win. She wanted to go home, to Mac, she wanted to see Tesoro again, she wanted her life . . .

"Steps," the man's voice said in his stilted English. "To walk up them please."

He was saying *please*? Something had changed, she didn't know what, but there was a different feeling in the air.

"Now, in here." He thrust her forward into silence and suddenly Sunny knew she was alone.

She stood perfectly still, hardly daring to breathe, listening. Being alone was more frightening than being with her captor. She almost wanted him back again, at least maybe he would take the duct tape off her eyes and the hood covering her head and the fabric that wrapped her like a mummy.

chapter 73

"*There was no need* to be so rough with her," Maha said to the man, in the Hindu dialect they both understood.

"There were others in the house," he said. "What else was I to do? The gatekeeper was already dead."

Maha sighed. "I understand."

"I could not have the woman cry out, she would not have come willingly, and I knew there was evil going on."

"And you are not evil?" Maha looked at him, knowing he was but she'd had no one else to do this job.

He held out his hand, rubbing his fingers together. "The money," he said. "I did as you asked. She is here."

Maha handed him a drawstring cotton bag. He opened it, counted the money carefully, glanced once at her, nodded, then left. She heard the clash of gears as the rusty truck took off again, back down the alley, back into anonymity. No one would ever know. Except Maha.

She stood in the doorway for a moment, looking at the helpless woman, her hands bound, her body wrapped in bloodstained white muslin, a hood over her head, eyes blinded and mouth silenced with duct tape. Maha thought for a moment about Sharon Barnes; about the woman in Paris; about Yvonne Elman; about Rahm Singh.

Finally, she stepped toward her.

Sunny could smell her perfume, that gentle Indian oil she used. It was sweetly familiar, faintly spicy, of cedar and musk and amber as well as tuberoses and jasmine. It was the scent of a beautiful Indian woman. Maha's scent.

Maha unwound the muslin from her body, pulled the duct tape from her mouth, eased it gently from her eyes, took the hood from her head.

Sunny stood, eyes still closed, taking deep breaths.

"I could see that you recognized me, even with your eyes closed," Maha said.

"You are unforgettable," Sunny said.

"I hope not."

Maha cut the rope that bound Sunny's wrists and again Sunny smelled that sharply sweet scent of hay. "It was a man with horses that tied me up," she said, and heard Maha laugh.

"You are not the detective for nothing."

Sunny forced her eyes open and Maha stepped back, watching her as she took in the empty room, its ornate crumbling carved plaster cornices, its splintered teak floors, the arched windows with the broken panes and a glimpse of a withered plane tree outside; the door hanging off its hinges, the gust of wind bringing the smells of the bazaar into the derelict house.

Finally, Sunny looked at Maha. A different Maha from the one she knew. This one was dressed the way a village woman might, in a plain cotton sari worn over a round-necked top with no fancy jeweled pins holding it in place. She wore plastic flip-flops and her hair, her magical long shining black hair, was dragged back into a bun. Maha took the end of the sari and draped it over her head, hiding her face, so that only her eyes showed.

"So, my onetime friend, what do you think now of the 'chances life might offer'?"

"I wish I'd never heard of you," Sunny said.

Maha nodded. "I wish that also. But it's too late and we must move on." She clapped her hands and the three women servants from the house pattered in.

"Look at them," Maha said sadly. "I offered them safety, a new life, secure in my household. You will notice their scars, Sunny?"

They lifted their faces so Sunny might see.

"I knew the men who did this to them when they were little girls living in the slums like me, eating from the festering garbage dumps, running from men when we could, running, running, always running.

"You know they are mute?" Maha added. "Their tongues were cut out so they might make more pitiable beggars, cry for a few pennies more, with only pathetic choked sounds coming from their vacant mouths. Years later, after I had escaped, I went back and searched for my little friends. I took them with me, made them whole again, as far as any woman who had undergone such horror could be made whole, of course. Now, they will never leave me. Whatever course my life takes, they are with me."

Sunny struggled to take in the horror. She could not look at the women. She wanted to cry. Instead she glared at Maha. "And am I condemned to be with you forever too, Maha? Wherever you might go?"

Maha laughed. "I think I must explain something. What I asked you to do, bring my jewelry back to Mumbai, was *not* legal. Those beautiful big round cabochon stones were fakes, mere covers for the diamonds stolen from La Fontaine that night in Monte Carlo. Remember, Sunny? We were in the hotel bar and there was the sound of police sirens? It was at that moment I knew we had been successful, and then Sharon came hurrying in, and Ferdie and Giorgio. My accomplices in crime. And Rahm Singh, who betrayed me too, and would have killed you."

She moved closer to Sunny, put her hand on her arm. "You see, years ago I found how to beat my way out of the slums. Small-time at first of course, then I grew bolder and more clever. I was making my jewelry, selling well, but I wanted more. I wanted big. I wanted . . . *everything*. And that's how I became one of the best thieves the world has ever known."

Maha laughed, remembering, as she summoned the servants again. "Dress her," she said in their language. "Darken her skin, put kohl on her eyes, henna her hair. She must look like us."

To Sunny she said, "They will disguise you. You must allow them to do it if you wish to get out of here alive. When you are done they will escort you through the bazaar. They will take you to a man I know. A friend." She smiled ruefully. "I should probably say now, a once-upon-a-time friend, for after this he will no longer want to know me, maybe even deny ever knowing me." She shrugged. "It no longer matters. He has already received my message. He will take care of you. But you must not call the police, do not attempt to call Mac, not until my friend has time to work things out. Not until he is sure you are safe."

"And give you time to get away," Sunny said.

Maha smiled.

"You saved me," Sunny said.

Maha smiled again. "Corruption is everywhere, my dear Sunny. You can trust only this man. Your life is in this good man's hands."

"I won't say anything until he gives me permission," Sunny promised. Maha had saved her life; she knew that now. This was the least she could do.

The women were already rubbing a brown oil into Sunny's legs and her arms, putting henna in her hair. Sunny suddenly couldn't bear it.

"Maha," she cried. "This can't be true, this can't be happening. You only meant well, you only stole the diamonds . . ."

"I was wrong," Maha said, in a quiet voice. "I should have known that whenever money is involved, big money, anything might happen, and usually does. Men kill for money, it's as simple as that.

People you have trusted. But then, trust is often a misplaced emotion. Like love."

She stepped back, watching the women wrap a blue cotton sari around Sunny, tucking it in expertly, and because she would not understand how to wear it and manipulate its folds as she walked, they fastened it with a giant safety pin.

"My aquamarine would have been better," Maha said, with a little laugh. "And now my dear Sunny, with your dark eyes and the folds of blue cotton hiding your face, you look like my sister."

Maha clapped her hands again and the women went and stood beside her. She spoke to them, telling them what to do, handing them a piece of paper with an address written on it to give to the rickshaw boy. And another with the number of the killer's car to give to the man. Then she walked over to Sunny.

They looked at each other for a long moment. Maha put out her hand, touched Sunny's face. "I'm so sorry for the pain I have caused you," she said. And with that, she walked out of the room.

Sunny heard her footsteps on the wooden stairs, then she too was bustled down those stairs, and out through an alley, into a noisy bazaar thronged with men selling everything from CDs to old furniture; men chanting their wares; offering *chai* in tiny metal cups from the steaming hot water tanks slung around their necks; children selling mango juice and hot-pink sugar sweets; bicycle-rickshaws slamming their way through the stalls; a brown cow peacefully grazing off the green vegetables at another stall; the aroma of curries and fenugreek, coriander and cumin and the piles of yellow and red spices.

Two of the women servants walked in front, hurrying, heads down. Sunny trotted in back of them, sari held over her face, with the third woman tight behind her. She did not even notice the two men running past, dressed in the baggy Indian cotton pants and cheap shirts, dark glasses and Yankees baseball caps. Ferdie and Giorgio, wolves in sheep's clothing, on Maha's trail, the woman they needed dead so they would be safe.

The servants elbowed their way expertly through the crowd. They came to the end of the street and stood, searching until two bicycle-rickshaw boys squeaked to a stop. Sunny climbed in with one of the women, the other two followed. One of the boys was given the paper with the address and they both pedaled off, pulling their human loads as if they were nothing.

Soon they were leaving the crowds behind, entering a calmer, more residential area. Children in uniforms with backpacks full of books were heading for school; dogs were being walked by white-uniformed maids; cooks hurried to the bazaar to find what was fresh today; pastel-colored houses were set back behind hedges of bougainvillea, and shaded by tamarisk trees, pleasant, normal homes where real people lived.

The rickshaws stopped at a pale blue house, the color of Sunny's sari. The guard at the gate eyed them suspiciously until one of the women handed him a note for his employer. He picked up a phone and called the house. After a moment, he indicated that they were to go in, but the women shook their heads and backed away. They pointed at Sunny: only she was to go. They waited until the gate opened, then clanged behind her, before they left.

Sunny turned her head to watch them go. She hoped with all her heart they would find the kind of peace again that Maha had given them.

A man was waiting for her at the top of the short flight of marble steps that led into the house, both hands outstretched in welcome. He was shorter than Sunny, round with a pleasant face and a bristling mustache, and an air of quiet authority.

"Come in, my dear," he said. "I am Jai Lal and I will help you."

chapter 74

Mumbai

With Ron at the controls, the Citation hovered over Mumbai's aqua-green shore, leveling out, ready for landing. Garbage mountains lurked on the skyline amid the modern towers and streets choked with traffic, seething with humanity, cows and rickshaws, dogs and cats and roving bands of wild cockatiels escaped from the cages of smart households to find freedom nesting among the palms. Cricket was being played on green fields by boys in "cricket whites," and baseball was played in dusty alleys by different kinds of boys, using broken broom handles and a stolen ball. The racecourse was in full swing; glistening chestnut horses sweated in the paddock and hatted women drank champagne, while street-smart little kids stole anything they could get their scrawny hands on. Daily life in Mumbai went on as Ron landed the plane and taxied to the private hangars.

Two uniformed men lounged against a police car, waiting, and Mac was already on the phone to their chief. The news about the abduction of a young American woman had been held back while the chief's men searched the bazaars and all known hangouts. But now he had news.

Two bodies had been found in Maha Mondragon's house. A gatekeeper and Rahm Singh, Maha's assistant, the man who oversaw her life and her house on Malabar Hill. He told Mac that Singh had been stabbed in the neck. It looked as though the killer was unable to remove the weapon, which was still sticking out of the victim's throat when they found him, amid a torrent of blood. The weapon was a diamond cutter's tool.

No other people had been found in the house, though it was known Mondragon had ten servants.

"When trouble happens here everyone disappears," the chief said. "They go back to the streets, the bazaars, the countryside, to wherever it was they came from. Anywhere but where the trouble is." He paused, then added, "Miss Alvarez was not there, though there is evidence she was staying at the house, clothes still hanging in the guest-room closet, and the bed slept in. Unfortunately, Mr. Reilly, the room is in disarray, there may have been a fight."

The full force of Mac's energy got him across the tarmac and into the police car. Ron hobbled behind, as fast as he could on the crutches, and they were driven to Maha's house.

It was guarded by police but they were expected. They walked through its cool spaces with the rich furnishings in the bright colors of India that mimicked the blossoms outside in the garden.

Ron said admiringly, "Some place. Better than Bel Air . . . wonderful colors . . ."

"Shut up, Ron," Mac said through gritted teeth.

"Sorry." Ron shut up.

They were shown to the guest room. With a feeling of foreboding, Ron watched as Mac walked to the bed, touched the shallow imprint where Sunny's body had lain, looked at the little flight of wooden steps, fallen to one side, the torn muslin curtains and the blood staining the side of the bed, tracking across the silk rug to the open French windows.

Mac knew the police had already searched the room thoroughly, but he did it again now. He was looking for Sunny's cell phone. He did not find it. On an impulse he called her number, and, astonished, heard it ring. There was no reply.

He called the chief, asked him to try to locate the mobile phone reception area.

They walked back through the house to the kitchen.

"Wait." Ron had stopped and was looking at a fretted wooden screen, off to one side up a narrow stairway. "A good place to spy," he said.

Mac walked up the steps and stood behind the screen. He was looking down into a kitchen large enough to cater parties of at least a hundred. Banks of ovens, microwaves, walls of gas burners . . . Maha would have needed a dozen chefs, not merely a cook and a couple of assistants. The big doors were open to catch the breeze and also, Mac knew, to remove the odor of death. A slab of white marble was used as a table. Six chairs stood round it, one tumbled to the floor, two others pushed hastily back.

Young men in green scrubs were still working on the crime scene, examining the floor inch by inch, tweezering hairs, cloth fragments, fluff, dried blood, into small plastic bags.

Rahm Singh's body had been removed but pools of blood had congealed into blackish heaps, around which the everlasting flies buzzed. A half-unraveled turban lay where it had fallen when he tumbled backward off that chair, almost dead but not quite because his blood had still been gushing. And not, Mac suspected, before he saw his killers make off with what they had come for.

Standing behind the fretted wooden screen, he wondered who had been standing here last night? Who had witnessed the killing? Who knew the identity of the killers?

His phone vibrated; it was the chief telling him they had located the area where Sunny's phone had rung. It was in one of the bazaars, well-known for its criminal element.

When Mac and Ron arrived at the bazaar the police were already in full force, charging through the crowd that scattered before them; inspecting stalls, and behind stalls; searching alleys and old buildings because nothing here was too old or broken-down for the poorest who inhabited them. Only one house was ominously empty. They went inside and up the splintered wooden stairs to a room on the second floor.

They found the torn muslin bed curtains, the discarded duct tape, traces of blood. But no Sunny. The police photographers were already documenting the scene when Mac's phone rang.

"It's me," Sunny said. "Mac, *oooh Mac,* you have to come and get me . . ."

"Tell me where." He was already running down the stairs and out the door.

She gave him the address. "I'm okay, I'm safe now, a lovely man helped me . . . he's on the phone talking to the chief of police, I couldn't call you before, I'll tell you why when you get here, I'll tell the police, I know they'll want to question me . . ."

He pushed through the crowd to the police car where Ron was waiting, gave the driver the address, thought about calling the chief and decided to wait till he got to Sunny.

Soon they were driving through a respectable neighborhood; respectable houses; respectable children kicking respectable soccer balls. Life was normal here.

The guard at the pale blue house was expecting them and opened the gates. Mac saw Sunny on the steps. She was wearing a white cotton Nehru shirt that came just above her knees, and plastic flip-flops. Her legs were bandaged. With her silken newly hennaed hair streaming down her back and tears in her eyes, Mac thought she looked like an angel from heaven. An Indian angel. An Indian heaven.

She held out her arms and he walked into them.

"What took you so long?" she asked somewhere between laughter and tears, as she had once before, in Monte Carlo. They hugged tightly, as though tomorrow might never come. And this time it almost had not.

chapter 75

Their host, Mr. Jai Lal, stood discreetly back. Mac looked up and met his eyes, and the man gestured to a small room off the hallway. "You will be private in there," he said.

Mac swung Sunny up into his arms and carried her into the dim book-lined room, kissing her neck. The familiar scent of her skin was clean in his nostrils, her hair swung back in a glossy fall. The plastic flip-flops fell off as he set her down on the cushioned sofa. There were tears in his eyes.

She put up a finger, moving them away. "Strong men don't cry," she whispered.

"Oh yes they do when they find the love of their life is still alive, that she has not been murdered and her body thrown by the wayside, that I'm here with her and I'll never let her out of my sight again . . ."

"I'm sorry," she said. "Mac, I'm so sorry, it was so stupid, just stupid pride, showing off, showing you I could be independent."

"Sunny, Sunny, you are one of the most independent women I have ever met. There's nothing to prove except that you still love me."

She kissed him, long, lingeringly, her hands in his hair, holding his face to hers. "I'll always love you," she said, when they came out of the kiss. "I promise I'll never run away again."

"I need to know what happened."

His arm was still around her and Sunny rested her head on his shoulder and told him about Maha and taking the chances life had to offer, and about ferrying the jewels to India. She left nothing out and when she got to the end she said, "So you see, Maha knew that she was being betrayed by Rahm Singh, she knew the men would kill; and she sent that man to get me out of that house."

"Before they killed you too."

Sunny looked steadily at him. "Maha saved my life."

Mac thought about Danielle Soris and Yvonne Elman and the gypsy in the coffinlike Prague apartment, all done up so bravely in pink. He remembered the pools of Rahm Singh's congealed blood, blackish-brown on the pale marble kitchen floor; and the gate-keeper felled by a blow to the head. Who knew how many more had died in this trail of jewel heists and murder?

"She's guilty," he said, "even though I'm thanking her for protecting you. Maha is guilty."

"Have the police caught her?"

He shook his head. "Not yet."

She said, "Jai Lal called the police chief; he told him the whole story and gave him the number of the killer's car. They will be here soon. They will find them. I'll tell them what happened, answer their questions." Her eyes met Mac's. "I'll never betray Maha though, and she knew that. I don't know where she is, where she went . . . what will become of her. And that's the truth."

"I know." Mac understood, too, that Maha had been too smart to tell Sunny. Maha knew exactly what she had to do.

He kissed Sunny some more, then there was a discreet cough from outside.

"Mr. Reilly, Ms. Alvarez, I need to offer you some hospitality, please, before we are invaded by the police."

Smiling, they got up and walked hand in hand to the door. Mr. Jai Lal beamed up at them.

"Excellent," he said, turning and leading the way into his drawing room. "Excellent. All is well now. I can tell."

chapter 76

Mac shook Jai Lal's hand and thanked him, then their host escorted them to a lovely drawing room where Ron sat on a comfortable divan, his broken leg arranged on an ornate embroidered footstool. Outside, a spraying fountain sent cool drops into the air; goldfish darted in and out of mossy rocks and a gilded aviary held flocks of tiny jewel-colored finches and yellow canaries who sang nonstop. It was, Mac decided, like being in a Bollywood movie. Even his rotund, beaming host seemed like a movie character.

He was wrong. Jai Lal was no Bollywood movie actor. He was a man of education and integrity, who used his wealth to work with the downtrodden and displaced.

Sunny and Mac sat side by side on a gilded brocade sofa, holding hands, with Ron opposite on the green silk divan, and were served iced mango juice in tall cold glasses, and small sweet and spicy cakes while Mr. Lal, sensitive to their situation, filled in the awkward silence by talking to them about himself, while waiting for the police chief to arrive. But what Mac soon realized was that he was really talking about Maha.

"Like Maha," Lal said, "I lobbied to have the garbage mountains removed, to have the children taken care of; to get them homes and a glimmering of education, so they might at least read and write. And after that? We helped find them work. Even work as a gardener is good, it is creative, an expression of beauty instead of the degradation they knew. Or a cook. Food is a prideful thing to those who never had enough of it. Or a servant, because polishing floors in a calm cool safe house is better than huddling in alleys praying not to be molested."

Jai Lal went beyond that. He said that when he was able, he and Maha helped those special children who flourished in school, whose intellect and expectations were not blunted by their surroundings: the dreamers, the artists; the someday intellectuals whose curiosity took them to another realm, enabling them to get into universities on scholarships. It was obvious that Jai Lal was a wonderful man, but Mac needed to know how he knew Maha Mondragon.

"We worked for the same charitable causes," Lal said. "She's a dedicated woman. You may not know that Maha managed to drag herself up from just such a background. I admire her courage, her fortitude and her morality."

"But Maha is a jewelry designer," Mac said. "Where did she get the backing to begin that work?"

"Here, we do not ask those kinds of questions," Lal replied. "A woman's indiscretions are her own business. It was difficult for her, but when she showed me her first designs, I was able to find funds to help her pursue her work."

"And then she became successful internationally, and very rich."

Mr. Lal nodded. "I congratulated her."

And then the police chief arrived, with an entourage and a lot of questions.

chapter 77

It was very late when Maha finally came home. The stars were out, diamonds in an ink-blue night sky and far more beautiful, she knew, than any of La Fontaine's gems.

Two policemen stood guard at her front gate but Maha had her own secret entrance, slipping in from the top of the hill, following the narrow stream as it flickered silver over the mossy rocks, pausing in the stillness to savor the night-blooming jasmine that she herself had planted when she first made this place her home.

Where the hill leveled out, there was a small red Chinese-style bridge over the stream, where Maha had liked to stand and watch the tiny green frogs play at the edge of the water; and by the trees hung white wicker cages with their pots of seeds, inviting wild birds into her domain. Maha had no fear, walking softly through the beauty she had created. There were no more snakes in this Garden of Eden. All was peace, here. Now.

She walked around the side of her house, noticing open windows that should have been shut; a light still burning in a hallway, reflecting in the panes. She shrugged, permitting herself a smile. It was no longer her concern.

When she came to the front of the house she stopped to check the driveway. She knew she could not be seen from the gate where the policemen kept guard.

Her cotton sari rustled as she walked across the terrace to the long cobalt-blue pool where the bougainvillea blossoms floated and Mahalakshmi, goddess of wealth and prosperity kept vigil; tall, gilded and brightly painted. In the dead light of night, she almost looked alive.

Maha addressed the goddess.

"It was good, in the beginning," she said. "Knowing I was clever, cleverer even than the international police. You must remember that when I was a child the police were the enemy, scraping us off the streets and the muck heaps, out of sight, out of mind. But you already know all this. You have followed my every step."

She sank to the ground, looking at her reflection in the dark blue pool, remembering who she had been and no longer was: the mastermind behind the rash of high-level jewel robberies, the woman with the houses and money, on her way to a legitimate place in society. This was to have been the last robbery. She had decked out her female robbers in expensive furs, and their Marilyn masks. Sharon had recruited them, of course; lawless young women already on the run, eager to make money and then get out. Maha never used the same women twice and they never knew who she was. Sharon kept the chain of potential female thieves waiting to be summoned from Prague or Budapest.

She had met Sharon at a fashion show and Maha had recognized Sharon's craziness immediately. Sharon was unstable, dangerous and game for anything that would make money. And Maha had used her well. It would have been fine if Sharon had not finally lost it and in her rage and hatred attacked the woman in Paris, then killed the woman in Monte Carlo. And murdered the gypsy who had stolen her fur coat and found the diamond in the pocket, then fenced it on to the very man who they used to recut the stones. She had shot her with that Black Rose pistol. How very Sharon. Always stylish.

So many killings, Maha thought, remembering the slums she

had escaped from, where murder was an everyday event. She thought she had escaped that, and now she was back where she began.

She went and knelt in front of the goddess Mahalakshmi. She bowed her head to the ground three times. Then, with one push she toppled the statue into the pool.

There was a great splash, a torrent of water, a cracking sound like that of a cannon.

Maha heard the alarmed cries from the police guards. She looked into the cobalt pool where waves lapped the surface as though in a storm. The statue of the goddess lay, smashed into two pieces on the bottom. Bougainvillea blossoms, coral, fuchsia, orange and white floated over her.

Police sirens screamed once more in the night and Maha turned and made her way quietly back up the hill, slipping out as secretly as she had come.

She did not look back.

chapter 78

Pru and Eddie were with Allie, at the cottage in the Dordogne, sitting around the kitchen table with the poinsettia in its clay pot, drinking red wine, their latest vintage, and nibbling on pâte and cheeses. A log fire roared in the big old stone grate and the silly Lab, Lovely, sprawled belly up, eyes closed, in front of it. Outside, Christmas lights still twinkled and the January wind howled. Inside all was cozy. Except they were missing a few people.

The beep of the phone made them all jump. Allie leapt to answer it. "Is it them?" Pru asked.

Allie turned to look at her, nodding. She said, "Ron, what's happening? Is Sunny safe? Where are you?"

"Sunny's had a bit of what you might call 'an adventure,' but she's okay," Ron said. "She'll tell you the story when she sees you."

"And when is that?"

"Soon. We're on our way to Prague."

"*Prague?* What about your leg?"

"It hurts like hell but it's fine. What about yours?"

"I autographed my own cast . . . '*All good wishes, Allie Ray,*'" she said. "Then I added '*Perrin*' in brackets after it. In purple Sharpie."

"Glad I was included," Ron laughed, then he said, "Sweetheart?"

Allie beamed, she liked it when Ron called her "sweetheart."

"Promise me something."

"Anything."

"Well now, that's a bit rash, isn't it? You don't even know what I'm gonna ask."

"Oh yes I do." Allie knew her husband very well. "You're going to ask me to promise never to leave you and run off to India with a bagful of rubies and emeralds so I can prove myself to you."

Ron laughed. "Got it in one."

"When will you be back?"

"Tomorrow, day after. Mac has some unfinished business in Prague."

"Another murder I'm willing to bet." Allie was apprehensive.

"It's all connected," Ron said. "We'll meet you in Monte Carlo. As you know, there's also a bit of unfinished business to take care of there. Oh, and Mac says to tell Eddie he has things under control. I'll call you from Prague."

"Give my love to Sunny."

Allie replaced the phone and looked at the others, who stared anxiously back.

"Sunny's okay. That's the good news. They'll tell us all about it when they meet us in Monte Carlo. And Eddie, Mac says to tell you to stay cool, he has everything under control. I know that's true," she added, "because Lev Orenstein has been taking care of things. And Lev is the best. That woman doesn't stand a chance against him."

She could see Eddie was not convinced, but nevertheless, she fetched a bottle of champagne from the cellar and Eddie cracked it open and they drank a toast. "To Sunny and her safe return," Pru said, as they raised their glasses.

Alarmed by the pop of the champagne cork, Lovely lumbered to her feet and came and sat closer. She laid her head on Eddie's knee, eyes raised soulfully up at him. He stroked her smooth silly delightful head.

"I might just have to get myself a black Lab," he said. "Exactly like this one."

"Good idea." Pru beamed. It was the first time Eddie had spoken optimistically about the future since they had gotten to the cottage. Kitty Ratte loomed over him like the sword of Damocles, waiting for the thread to be severed and the blade to fall onto his head.

They looked at each other. "Exactly like Lovely," he said with a grin. "I want one just as daft." And they all laughed, relieved that Sunny's ordeal was over, and that she was safe.

chapter 79

Prague

Sharon was sitting behind her desk with the light behind her. Blue smoke from her Gauloise swirled around her elegantly cropped head. She glanced up as Mac Reilly walked into her office without so much as a knock. He took a seat and she stared at him across the table. Her face was expressionless.

Mac thought she was a cool customer. He didn't quite know how he was going to pull this off because he still did not have any direct evidence that tied her to the murders. He was betting though, that there was a Kahr Black Rose pistol in that big old iron safe. Along with some of Maha's blood money.

"It's over, Sharon," he said. "Maha has gone."

She shrugged. "It's not important to me."

"Of course, now it's not. You got what you wanted."

She gave him that mocking little half laugh. "If you will excuse me, I have clients coming. I must ask you to leave."

Mac's phone rang. He flipped it open. "Yes?" he said. A woman answered. "Mac Reilly, this is Danielle Soris. Do you remember me?"

"How could I ever forget," Mac said. He heard her laugh.

"I have something to tell you. Something I remembered, about the woman . . ." she hesitated again, obviously upset, then continued. "The woman who damaged my face."

There was a long pause while Mac thought she seemed to be trying to gather her emotions. He waited.

Then she said, "The robber was looking at me from behind that mask . . . I could only see her eyes. They were very beautiful, an unusual color. Dark green. She stared at me for that long moment, that *long, long* moment, before . . . before it happened."

Mac said, "Danielle, you have no idea how wonderful you are. I'll call you back later."

He sat back in his chair and looked into Sharon Barnes's dark green eyes. Very unusual. Very beautiful. He had his witness.

"Sharon," he said, "I think I'm going to have the police arrest you for the murder of Yvonne Elman and Valeria Vinskaya."

Sharon twisted her cigarette viciously in the porcelain ashtray. She gave a derisive snort "Of course you're not. I'm not involved with those women. I don't even know them."

"But one of them, the one you didn't manage to kill, knows you. She will identify you."

Shocked, Sharon pushed back her chair. It hit the window with a thunk that rattled the glass. "This is ridiculous. I'm calling my lawyer. All I can tell you is that I worked for Maha Mondragon, arranging models to show her work."

"You worked for Maha procuring women from the Balkans to act as rich fur-coated robbers in jewelry heists organized by Maha. How much did she pay you, Sharon, to act as her first lieutenant? Enough, I'm guessing, for you to retire from the procuring business, like right now."

He caught the sudden fear in her eyes, those big beautiful green eyes. He had his witness now. He was home free.

Sharon said, "Get out of my office. I'm going to see my attorney." She flounced to the door. Mac followed.

They stared hard at each other. She looked away first, turning to lock the office door, shrugging on her heavy coat. Not a fur but a good Hermès hooded cashmere, loose and flowing. Her boots came over her knees and had very high heels.

She clomped down the stairs, ignoring the elevator. Mac knew she was afraid to be trapped in there with him, waiting for the police to come.

Outside, he walked two paces behind her, speaking on the phone first to the Inspector in Monte Carlo telling him the Paris woman could identify Sharon, and that he was following Sharon now. The Inspector said he would contact the Prague police immediately.

Sharon strode down the cobbled street, stumbling every now and again in her heels. She knew Mac was right behind her. When she heard the wail of police sirens she began to run, clumsy in the high boots.

She made for the bridge, saw it was crowded, veered down a side street. Running, running . . . Chunks of ice bobbed in the river, heading toward the bridge in the opposite direction from her. She was heading away from it, away from them, out into the suburban wilds where she might be able to get lost, and where her money was stashed in a safe deposit box in a small bank, along with the diamonds she had stolen from Maha.

The path by the river became narrower. She could hear Mac running steadily behind her, the sirens coming closer. Desperate, she swung round to confront him.

Mac had been wrong. The Black Rose was not in the safe. It was in Sharon's hand and it was pointing at him.

"It's too late, Sharon," he called. "Besides, you're too far away to get me."

She knew he was right; the small pistol had a good range but he was a moving target and now he was moving away from her. She heard the police sirens wail to a stop, the slamming of car doors, the sound of running feet. She swung round again, slipped, lost her footing in the treacherous heels.

Mac saw her skid off the path and down the bank into the river. It was half-frozen and there was hardly a splash. He ran toward where she had disappeared. There was no sign of her.

The cops were there now, guns drawn. They stood, staring down into the black water. Suddenly her head popped up near the bridge. And then she was swept into the ice crushers that kept the arches holding up the ancient bridge safe. But not Sharon.

chapter 80

Monte Carlo

Lev Orenstein was more used to high-level security detail than playing the detective, but when he heard who the intended blackmail victim was, he agreed to do it. Rich powerful men like Eddie Johanssen, with families to protect, were exactly the type of client he was used to. Not that he had met Eddie, he had no need to. Mac had filled him in on the story and Lev had in his possession the manila envelope with Kitty Ratte's sex photos and the original blackmail note.

Tall, whippet-thin with the shoulders of a halfback and a full six-pack of abs, bald as a coot, black aviators propped on his chiseled nose, and wearing a Tommy Bahama flowered shirt, Lev was not easily overlooked. Trained in the Israeli army intelligence, he was the best at his job, as his clients would have testified had they not been required to keep their identities secret.

Now though, he had donned a disguise; a waiter's uniform; black pants, white jacket, white shirt, black bow tie. Lev had been following Kitty Ratte for a couple of days while Mac was in India. He had got her routine down pat. She would emerge from the small garden apartment around four in the afternoon, drive to her usual café in a Cannes backstreet where the food was cheap, take her time over the burger she seemed to always favor, clenching it in two hands the way the slobs in those TV ads did. Except this was a woman pretending to be a lady and she should have known better. Lev had come to the conclusion that whenever Kitty thought herself unobserved, she reverted to who she really was.

And who she was had not been that difficult to find out. Lev knew all about her past, and the identity of her "lover," though knowing their scene, Lev doubted Jimmy Franklyn was really her "lover." Jimmy was a voyeur; he got off on watching Kitty making out on the floor of swingers' clubs with other guys. Or other women. Kitty wasn't fussy.

Lev, however, had not enjoyed the brief glimpse he'd had of these activities, with men in leather masks with slits for eyes and mouths; with handcuffs and whips and dildos. Kitty and Jimmy belonged to that base world, each enjoying it in their own way, and though distasteful to Lev, it was not illegal. However, Kitty's other activities were.

He'd observed Kitty hanging out at bars along the coast, hitting the grander hotels where rich folk stayed, but with the young, attractive Russian hookers thronging the resort, she did not have much luck. Mostly, her clients came from the ads in the local newspaper . . . *Sexy Russian redhead ready to do your bidding* . . . That sort of thing.

Lev had followed her to various hotels, the big anonymous kind where middle-class businessmen on the loose at conventions stayed. Twice at one hotel on the same afternoon with different partners, and three times at another.

Kitty obviously did not realize that she was caught on camera every time she entered the lobby of one of those hotels carrying her little overnight bag. She did not realize that the camera caught her entering the elevator, nor did she know she was caught walking down the corridor, checking room numbers, stopping and knocking on a door, then entering. A hour or two later, she was caught again, coming out of the room, getting back into the elevator, with her little overnight bag, walking through the lobby and out to the car park. Kitty Ratte was caught on the hotels' cameras, but Lev needed more than that. He wanted evidence on his own camera. He already had room-service bills and waiters who reported seeing her shoes tossed next to the bed while she waited in the bathroom. Room-service waiters had quick eyes, they knew the scene, remembered things.

Tonight Lev had bribed the floor waiter and dressed in his white jacket, he waited for the usual summons for room service. He was in luck. The call came for a pastrami sandwich on rye, a Heineken and a Red Bull.

Ten minutes later, Lev was knocking on the door. The man who opened it was wearing shorts and a turquoise polo shirt. He was older, and Lev thought he looked tired.

"Put it down here," the man said, moving Kitty's open overnight bag from the coffee table. Inside it, Lev caught a glimpse of leopard-print underwear, a blue vibrator, bottles of oils and lubricants.

He put down the tray and offered the man his bill, then standing behind him he took out his tiny camera and clicked silently: the overnight bag, and its contents; the messed-up bed; the pair of Louboutins next to it where she had flung them off. He could hear her lurking in the bathroom, not wanting to be seen, and while the man tried to make sense of the deliberately wrong bill, Lev slid silently over there, and through the crack in the half-open door, caught her clearly as she changed back into her street clothes, looking at herself in the mirror. The picture would be a good one.

Lev was back before the guy even knew what had happened. "Sorry about the bill, sir," he said. "I will get it taken care of at once."

He closed the door behind him, pleased. Okay, it was a small thing, but now he had evidence that Kitty Ratte was also a prostitute. Lev wanted all the ammunition he could get in case it ever came up in court, in the blackmail cases. Not the one involving Eddie Johanssen. Lev had taken care of that, and the video cam and its photos. Eddie's name would never come into it. But more importantly, what he had traced were two other unfortunate men involved with Kitty.

Back on the floor, Lev thanked the waiter, handed over some money and made his way down the back stairs, avoiding the security cameras. He had all he needed. This would be an open-and-shut case.

chapter 81

Monte Carlo was pleasant in the late evening sunlight, trees dappling the sidewalks, lights beginning to go on in the cafés and boutiques, a pesky little wind ruffling hair and skirts, as Mac and Sunny walked hand in hand (as if, Sunny thought with a pang, she would ever let go of Mac's hand ever again) along the harbor, admiring the big yachts and the even bigger yachts moored out past the harbor and the cruise ships beyond them.

"Boats into infinity," she said, matching her stride to his long one.

"A city built on boats," he agreed. "A would-be Venice."

"I like it," Sunny said.

"Me too."

The wind whipped up and they turned and made their way back to the hotel where they had arranged to meet Ron in the bar. And Lev. And Allie and Pru and Eddie, who would arrive any minute now. Sunny was impatient to see them. And her Chihuahua.

"I miss Pirate too," she said.

Mac groaned. "Don't even talk about it." He loved that dog. His long-time assistant Roddy was dog-sitting at the Malibu house and Pirate was in safe hands.

The doorman knew them now and he smiled and saluted as they walked into the lobby and on into the bar.

Sunny remembered that first night, Christmas Day night, when she had been alone and had met Maha, and Kitty Ratte. She had been brought up to date on Kitty's activities and the blackmail plot, and her disgust and anger choked her as she thought about it. Poor sweet Eddie would never have met the woman if it had not been for her, and now look what a fix he was in. Maha had seen through Kitty immediately though; she had looked at Kitty and seen corruption, seen evil in her bland smiling face.

Ron was already there, sitting at a table, crutches propped against a chair. "Just checking out the competition," he said with a grin, indicating his glass of red wine. "And anyhow where the hell is my wife?"

"Flying commercial." Mac grinned back. "That's what happens, Ron. Flying commercial you're always late. You've just forgotten, that's all."

"Hah!" Ron knew it was true but he couldn't wait to get his arms around his woman. "There's Lev Orenstein," he said, as the unmistakable tall figure in a Hawaiian-print Tommy Bahama shirt and narrow jeans loped to the bar and took a seat. Ron glanced at Mac. "Aren't we speaking to him?"

"Let's wait and see." Mac sat down and ordered a Cosmo for Sunny, not too sweet, Grey Goose vodka and very cold. He also ordered a bottle of rosé, her favorite wine from last summer in St. Tropez. Their eyes were on Lev, who was propping up the bar, one elbow on the counter, the fingers of his right hand linked casually through his belt, one foot crossed over the other. Calm, cool.

"Here come our drinks," Mac said, moving Sunny's little faux-snakeskin handbag out of the way so the waiter could set the drinks down on the table.

"Well," Ron said, eyeing the two; so serene, so goddamn happy. "Well," he said again, "I have to confess there were moments when I thought I would never be lucky enough to see this again. The two of you together. First when you ran away, Sunny, and then when you nearly got yourself murdered."

She shuddered. "Don't remind me." The Cosmo was icy, delicious. She was a sucker for this girly pink drink.

"Lev was right," Mac said, his eyes on the entrance. "Here she comes."

Kitty Ratte in her blue-and-white wrap dress, skirt swinging open to show her thighs, trotted, knock-kneed, into the bar. Her eyes lighted on Lev, the first really attractive man she had seen in ages. *And* he was alone. *Perfect.* Without looking round, she climbed onto a stool near him.

"A glass of red wine," she said to the silver-haired barman, who never, ever looked at her. He poured the wine and pushed the glass across the counter.

She sighed and ventured a shy smile at Lev, chin down, eyes up, teeth agleam. "The service used to be so much better here," she said to him. "When a woman ordered a drink she was always offered a bowl of nuts or pretzels, or olives. Now—" She shrugged and looked appealingly at him, crossing her legs and allowing the split skirt to fall away from her thighs, "nothing."

Lev had been on his cell phone but now he closed it. He called the bartender and ordered olives. When they came he pushed the bowl toward Kitty. "Like the last supper," he said, unsmiling.

Puzzled, she bit into an olive, took a gulp of the wine. It was not her first of the day; she drank at least a bottle and a half, maybe two every night, plus what she drank at lunch.

"Last supper? Whatever can you mean? No, don't tell me, let me guess." She arched her brows, grinning at him. "You are wondering where to go for dinner, is that it? I can recommend some good places. Really good."

"You can? I thought maybe you'd be inviting me home, so you could cook for me. I heard you make pretty good meatballs."

Kitty frowned. What did he mean? Meatballs? What did he know? She glanced round, spotted Sunny and Mac at a table . . . *oh my God . . .*

"Sunny," she called, climbing off the barstool. "Oh Sunny *darling,* I'm so glad to see you. Where have you been?"

She was about to run over to her when there was a commotion at the door. She turned to look. Three armed policemen stood there, looking back at her. And behind them was Eddie Johanssen, with that woman Pru, and Allie Ray, who was holding Sunny's little dog.

"Allie, Pru," she called, ignoring the cops.

Allie turned her head. The woman Pru, who anyway Kitty hated, backed into the foyer. Eddie turned and followed her. "Eddie," she cried. But he was gone. She would get him later, go to his room, nail him this time. No threat would be beyond her.

She looked at Sunny, saw she was watching her with cold eyes, a cold face. She saw the cops striding toward her, turned to Lev. "What's going on?" she cried, clutching his arm.

"They're coming to arrest you, Kitty," he said calmly. "Better let them get it over with, after all we don't want a scene, now do we?"

The cops were all around her now; they had her trapped up against the bar; one put his hand on her arm. "Kitty Ratte," he said, in French, "you are under arrest for blackmail, attempted blackmail, prostitution, dealing in drugs, and administering drugs to unknowing persons, which, as you must know, is a federal offense."

The meatball was a federal offense? Kitty let out a yelp of laughter as she pushed his hand from her arm. She looked at him, looked at Sunny and Mac, turned and looked into Lev Orenstein's cool dark eyes. "Bastards," she yelled. "You bastards." And then she began to scream.

It was quite something, Sunny thought, horrified, watching Kitty being hauled away by the cops. The woman was to get what she deserved. Which, Mac said, would be a lot of years behind bars.

Shaken, Allie and Pru came back with Eddie. "Bitch," Allie said, shuddering.

Pru glanced at Eddie and smiled. They both knew she had a better word for Kitty.

They all kissed and hugged, and Tesoro sank into Sunny's lap, then leaned over and gave Mac a quick nip on the hand.

It was as though they had never been away. Life was normal again. Sitting in the bar in Monte Carlo where it had all begun, they drank the rosé wine, to celebrate.

There was a clatter of heels at the entrance, and expecting more conflict, Sunny turned to look.

A young woman stalked in. It was the bride, the one in the white silk-satin sheath dress, blond hair pinned up with a spray of jasmine and a crescent-shaped diamond brooch. She was carrying a tiny bouquet of lily of the valley.

The bride. Sunny's brows rose and she nudged Allie and Pru. Of course the men had already noticed her.

The bride stalked, heels clacking, to the bar, hitched herself onto a stool, flung down the lilies and said, "Martini, *s'il vous plaît, monsieur.*"

The silver-haired barman mixed, shook, poured, placed it in front of her. The bride downed it in one long gulp.

"Jesus," Pru said, awed.

The barman's eyes met Sunny's. Her brows raised in a question. He smiled. A first for him. "Second thoughts," he explained.

"Or even third or fourth," Sunny said.

Suddenly, trumpets sounded from the hall; the strumming of guitars; singing . . . getting louder as they approached.

It was a full-fledged Mexican mariachi band, the kind Sunny had grown up with because of her Mexican father and their ranch with the Latino cowboys.

Singing "Guadalajara," the musicians strolled over to the bride, who swiveled on her stool and sat, wide-eyed, staring at them. The trumpets blasted enough to lift the roof and the bride put her hands over her ears, laughing.

"She's *laughing*," Sunny said to Allie.

The mariachis parted. They turned to face the entrance, the

trumpeters blasted a fanfare as a young Mexican man appeared in the doorway, as golden-skinned and dark as his bride was fair. He stood for a moment, then stretched out his arms, looking at her across the room. Appealing.

Everyone held their breath as he began slowly to walk toward her. The mariachis parted as he drew close. Still the bride sat, eyes fixed on him. He stood in front of her now. Their eyes linked.

Then she slipped from her barstool, smoothed down her short white shift, picked up her lilies of the valley and looked at him. "I'm ready now," she said with a radiant smile.

The mariachis burst into song, and the young man took her hand and they walked laughing out into the night.

"*Oh my God,*" Allie said. "Did you just *see* that?"

"Of course we did." Pru had found a tissue and was dabbing away her tears. "Wasn't it just the most beautiful thing ever?"

"You should have seen her before," Sunny said, recalling the bride's previous solo visits to the bar.

Mac looked at her. He took her hand. "I vote we drink to the bride and happy endings," he said, squeezing the hand of the woman he loved. And that's exactly what they did.

chapter 82

It was a couple of days later, Eddie was still in Monte Carlo. He was working out his problems with his wife and was now to get equal custody of his children. His heart had lightened.

He drove to Nice, stopping on the Promenade des Anglais, leaning on the rail, looking out over the pebbly beach. It was empty. Its loneliness appealed to him and he walked down the steps, crunching his way to the sea. A couple of beach stands were still open, though most had closed for the season. He liked the emptiness. It cleared his head.

He stopped to watch a sleek, black young dog bounding in and out of the water, happy in that mindless way of just fun, enjoying the moment. It had no collar and Eddie guessed it probably belonged to no one and had no concept of where its next meal was coming from. Right then, though, the dog did not care.

It was a philosophy Eddie suddenly decided to adopt. He would change his ways. His work. His world. His life. Watching the dog's sheer antic pleasure, Eddie saw his own overcrowded, pushing, striving world exposed.

He whistled to the dog. It raised its head, looked at him. "Hey, boy," Eddie said, then saw it was a girl. Head down, she came at him in a fast joyous gallop, sliding to a crash against his legs. Eddie laughed out loud and bent to hug the dog. Its fur was wet and sand-filled and suddenly it broke away and shook itself furiously, sending sand and seawater all over him.

"Good dog," Eddie yelled, and the dog picked up its front paws and danced around him, barking. He could swear there was a smile on her face.

He took off his belt and the dog stood while he slipped it around her neck, then walked friskily beside him, back up the steps to the promenade. Eddie took her to the nearest vet.

"No microchip," the vet said, checking her ears. "No collar. Ribs too prominent, no food in that stomach, I can tell you. She's a stray all right."

"Not anymore," Eddie said.

With the dog bathed, vaccinated and fed, he returned to the hotel. The tired dog collapsed at the foot of the bed as he got on the phone.

At the cottage, Allie and Ron were stuck on the sofa, plastered legs up, playing gin rummy, so Pru answered. She was wearing her jeans and the brown sweater, as well as mascara and lip gloss. She felt she looked good. A new woman, in fact. If only she knew what she was going to do next, everything would be okay. Empty futures were scary things.

She picked up the phone on the fifth ring. "Perrin residence," she said.

"Pru?"

"Eddie?"

"I have something to tell you," he said.

"I hope it's good."

"It's good. It's wonderful. In fact I'm bringing it to meet you."

"It?"

"A silly black dog, just like Lovely. Not a perfect Lab but there's a bit of that in her somewhere. I found her on the beach and now she's asleep on my bed, here at the hotel. Can I bring her to meet you tomorrow?"

Heart jumping with joy like the dog's, Pru put her hand over the phone and called out, "Allie, can Eddie bring his new silly dog to meet us tomorrow?"

"Of course he can," Allie called back. "The more the merrier." Her eyes met Ron's. Brows raised, she said, "Could there be something in the wind?"

Ron grinned. "There could," he said. "I mean when a guy brings his dog to meet a woman . . . well, what else could it mean?"

chapter 83

Malibu

It had all begun in Monte Carlo. Or had it? Sunny wondered. Wasn't the truth more like it all began in Malibu, when she left her pink diamond heart-shaped engagement ring on Mac's pillow, with a goodbye note? When she had changed her life, and his?

Now, they were back, sitting on rickety old chairs on the deck of Mac's small house overlooking the Pacific. Pirate, beloved friend, was at Mac's feet and Mac had a glass of good red wine in his hand and a smile on his face. Tesoro crouched warningly at Sunny's side, ready to attack if necessary . . . which meant if Mac so much as laid a hand on her, which anyway Sunny was fervently hoping he would.

She remembered Maha telling her to take the chances life offered. Maybe she had not meant only the jewel-courier job. Maha had a sixth sense, she knew things, understood in a way ordinary mortals did not. Perhaps what she had really meant was for Sunny to take a chance on what life was offering her now. Take a chance on Mac, on their freedom, together. Sunny wished Maha luck. She knew she would need it.

The events of the past couple of weeks seemed far away from this peaceful spot; far away from her and Mac, whose hand snaked out now to grab hers. She smiled at Tesoro's warning growl. Mac was looking at her, those deep dark blue eyes that knew her so well . . . How could she ever have thought of being with another man, even one as sympathetic—and handsome—as Eddie? It had simply been one of those moments, one of those things; timing, sadness, loneliness . . . a feeling that she had lost her way . . .

Mac raised an eyebrow, still looking at her. She smiled. He put the glass of wine down on the chipped white metal table, got up and held both hands out to her. "Come with me," he said, pulling her up.

Lying naked on the bed, he held her close, body to body. She felt his heart beating. And then they were kissing, deep kisses that sent jolts of pleasure through her. With his hand in the small of her back, he pulled her even closer. Why did it feel so good when he did that? She felt so possessed, so part of him, so owned by him . . . so together . . .

Much later, they lay, bodies slick with the sweat of their lovemaking, high on serotonin and adrenaline, deep with passion spent, drowsy with love for one another's bodies, beautiful in their thoughts, in their heads, their eyes linked in that thousand-mile gaze as they slowly returned from their tumultuous joined journey.

A melody drifted through Sunny's head. What was that song? "All You Need Is Love"? She thought it was probably true.

epilogue

Ferdie and Giorgio were caught trying to smuggle the diamonds out of India, via Goa. They were arrested and charged with the murder of Rahm Singh and the gatekeeper. They were also charged with conspiracy in the string of jewel robberies, including La Fontaine, with theft and receiving stolen goods. They would face all charges in Mumbai.

Kitty Ratte faced her own charges, along with her coconspirator, Jimmy Franklyn. Kitty was a true psychopath, with absolutely no concern for the devastation she brought to other people's lives. For her, the next step, blackmail, had been easy. It wasn't hatred for men that drove Kitty; it was hatred for women; women who offered more than she did. More than she ever could. *Real* women.

She and Jimmy were found guilty of blackmail and six other counts of extortion, prostitution, selling drugs, and administering drugs to others, a federal offense. Kitty went away for a lot of years. Jimmy slightly less.

Maha Mondragon disappeared back into Mumbai's teeming slums, a clever woman who had played the wrong cards. There is always a price to be paid for what you want to be, and you have to be willing to pay the price. Maha was not a bad woman; she was a woman driven by circumstances and defeated by poverty.

Mac was certain that one day she would resurface, looking different, no doubt, and in a different business. But for now, she was lost to the world she had so longed to be part of.

Eddie and Pru bought a house in the hills of Provence, where Eddie now spends most of his time. The business could get along without him. He is enjoying life, enjoying his children's visits. And most of all he is enjoying the companionship of a woman who, by a strange quirk of fate, he was lucky enough to meet. They named their dog Goofy. She seems to like that name.

Allie's broken leg healed quicker than Ron's but he claimed that was because he'd been trekking round the globe while she was sitting on her butt drinking their red wine. Which, by the way, isn't half-bad now. Better next year, though, Allie says, still hoping for that *Appellation d'Origine Contrôlée* approval. Ron doesn't give a damn; he likes the wine anyway.

Sunny is wearing her pink diamond engagement ring again. She swears she never takes it off, except to wash her hands, which very nearly resulted in disaster when she removed it in the ladies' room at Nobu in Malibu and forgot all about it. She only remembered minutes later, back at their table, when Mac said, "Sunny, where's the ring?" She fled back into that restroom just in time to see a woman pick up the ring and admire it. "Mine," Sunny said, ramming it back on the third finger of her left hand. "Lucky you," the woman said, laughing at her.

Pirate is tolerating Tesoro, and so is Mac. Life in the small wooden house on the Malibu shore continues the way it always has, with Mac involved in his cases, his murders, his needy people, and Sunny taking care of her PR business. The furniture has not improved; the dog-hairy sofa is still there, and, Mac swears, it's still the most comfortable sofa ever. So does Pirate. Tesoro prefers laps.

The barbecue gets unfolded most weekends and the sea mist always comes in just as they are about to sit down and eat. Mac's old cashmere sweater comes in handy, and looking at Sunny wearing it and nothing else, Mac thinks she is the most beautiful woman in the world.

And maybe he is right.